LEGENDS

OF

LEMURIA

THE BRIDGE

ALLIE MICHELLE

THOUGHT
CATALOG
Books

THOUGHTCATALOG.COM

THOUGHT CATALOG Books

Copyright © 2024 Allie Michelle.

All rights reserved. No part of this book may be reproduced or transmitted in any form or any means, electronic or mechanical, without prior written consent and permission from Thought Catalog.

Published by Thought Catalog Books, an imprint of Thought Catalog, a digital magazine owned and operated by The Thought & Expression Co. Inc., an independent media organization founded in 2010 and based in the United States of America. For stocking inquiries, contact stockists@shopcatalog.com.

Produced by Chris Lavergne and Noelle Beams
Art direction and design by KJ Parish
Circulation management by Isidoros Karamitopoulos

thoughtcatalog.com | shopcatalog.com

First Edition, Limited Edition Pressing
Printed in the United States of America

ISBN 978-1-949759-82-2

For you, Dad.

Thank you for telling me fairytales every night and helping me believe I could one day create my own.

TABLE OF CONTENTS

PART I:

THE BRIDGE

Make me neither a hero nor a villain! Both live within all of us. Make me neither a leader nor a follower! Both are dependent upon each other. Make me neither a winner nor a loser! Both are blind to what is in front of them. Make me an honest sinner before you make me into a lying saint. Make me unafraid of treachery because I have faced the treachery within. Make me one willing to surrender my sword for love. Make me brave enough to face my own undoing with a wicked grin of honor. Make me honored to be crushed beneath the gods' dancing feet. Make me into whatever you need! Just don't strip away my humanity by making a hero out of me. Your life's journey is just that—a journey. And if you are to complete it, then you'll know the end was never the point!

—THE BOOK OF LEMURIA: PROVERB I

PROLOGUE

Long ago, in a land long since forgotten, an elder sat beneath the open skies. It was a night like many others—an ocean of stars swallowed the jagged mountain ridges, the great river flowed lethargically, and the trees swayed with the stubborn breeze.

The elder had spent thousands of years slumbering while her spirit traveled the cosmos. *A seer*, they called her. The past, present, and future all blurred together. Any moment that had happened or could happen appeared at will in the endless dark. At first, it was maddening. Yet, after nine thousand years of existence, her state of content passivity had gone undisturbed.

Until the vision.

Her withered hands shook as she felt the vision flood her body, rattling her to the bone. Out on the earth's surface, in a realm she had only heard whispers about, a little girl took her first breath in the world. All she saw was a pair of blue eyes, and the river of magic that ran in her veins—a power the likes of which she hadn't felt in nine thousand years.

The vision dissolved, and the elder raced to gather the bones and flowers she needed. A human child with *magic*. The prophecy had been clear, but after all this time, even the elder had believed it to be nothing but the senile ramblings of an ancient oracle.

The elder gasped, clutching her chest as she keeled over. She felt the blades of dewy grass beneath her fingertips and the soft breeze that swirled around her. It had been so long since she was awake, she had to remind herself how to take slow, shuddering breaths.

Finally, she rose to her feet. The elder knew every bump and hollow in the land she had been confined to for so long. Within minutes, she gathered the ingredients needed, feeling her way through the garden. She placed the bones in the shape of a pyramid, gathering helius and corellia flowers. They were rare to find and dangerous to grow, but it was worth the risk. Rubbing the petals between her withered fingertips, she crushed them into dust.

"Deus sermiya," the elder whispered in the ancient tongue, blowing the flowers from her palm and listening to the dust rain down on the bones.

Her breath shortened as the dust settled. A faint glow began to appear. The glittering powder rose from the point of the pyramid, swirling in two spirals up toward the sky. The earth quaked and rumbled beneath her. Cold sweat licked down her spine as the dust ripped open the veil between this world and the next.

The elder felt like her skull was splitting open as the full might of her magic was unleashed. She had sworn not to use it—that which she had been entrusted with long ago, but she needed to see the timelines. If this child could be the one they had whispered of for eons.

She peered into the future, and all possible outcomes, seeing flashes of the woman the girl could one day become.

The gathered bones turned to nothing but ash, swept away by the winter winds. The elder listened to the whistling breeze carry the dust up toward the stars and wondered if it may reach all the way to that little girl a world away.

A tear finally wriggled free, sliding down her cheek as she prayed for that baby, as she prayed for them all. And for the first time in a long, long time, the elder felt a fragile feeling bloom in her chest.

Hope.

CHAPTER 1

I'm awake in a world of sleepwalkers pretending that I'm still stumbling through a dream. What is more painful? To believe the beautiful lie and never live honestly? Or to wake up each day with a bent spine in an attempt to bear the weight of such an ugly world? Throughout all of the madness, I'll never forget those eyes. Green with flecks of gold like they swallowed sunshine. Those eyes that were both a comfort and a challenge for my still-beating heart. —Zia

Zia Alexander was once again flirting with death, and while it threatened to claim her many times in her life, she was not afraid of taking that final journey. She knew death was just a bridge between this world and the next, but she wasn't ready to walk it. Not yet. Every moment she had ever held back flashed before her eyes. But regret would not sink its claws into her. Not today. She had risked too much. Fought too hard. They all had.

And so, she ran. Not from death, but toward *life*, and all the possibilities that came with it. Her heart was pounding like a bone drum. Its unsteady rhythm roared in her ears despite the months of grueling training. Her legs barked in pain as she silently commanded her body to move *faster, faster, faster.*

Nothing had gone according to plan. Zia had been meticulous with every detail and tried to foresee every possible outcome, yet love had blinded her in more ways than she cared to admit. As always, the gods enjoyed making a mockery of her plans by flipping her world upside down until she was dangling by her toes. Sometimes, she wondered if this was all just for their entertainment. After all, what felt like life and death to *her* was really a way for them to pass the time of their boring, immortal lives.

The forest blurred green around her. She moved swiftly between every tree and rock. The mossy earth felt like a spongy springboard beneath her callused feet. Mud squished between her toes. The wind blew harshly in her direction, offering her its speed.

They were close.

Zia gulped down air and savored the sweet smell of the forest. A thick blanket of mist clung to its edge, offering her a semblance of cover from her pursuers. She strained her ears and heard the snapping of twigs. Six of them, by her count. She felt a little insulted that was all they thought it would take to capture her. They could have *at least* sent their finest warriors. Yet, even without her sensitive hearing, their footsteps were quiet as an elephant's.

Cold sweat trickled down her brow and burned her eyes. She blinked harshly as her vision blurred. Zia skidded to a halt just in time to see the roar of rushing water at the lip of the mountain. Whitewash tumbled into an abyss, landing amongst sharp black rocks. She hissed. Fear threatened to claim her as she wasted three seconds contemplating the drop. *Hesitation will get you killed faster than anything else.* That had been the first thing she was taught. Such good it did her now.

She heard laughter in the distance—the kind of horrific, triumphant laughter that turned her blood to ice. They almost had her now. There was no way out. She would be hunted until her final breath. Had it merely been the six sentries, she would have fought for her freedom and won, but there were more coming, and she had used all the tricks up her sleeve. It wasn't worth the gamble of losing what she had sworn her life to protect. Death was a far more appealing option than being captured, and she had her orders: protect the stone at all costs.

Zia clutched the raw stone in her palm until it dug into her skin. The emerald seemed to mock her as it shimmered in the fading light. She placed it in her pouch and sent a silent prayer that it wouldn't be lost to the river's unforgiving rapids. Her stomach churned when she realized what waters she stood above.

The Vasalisa River. They whispered stories of it in the castle. Named after a goddess from long ago. The love of Vasalisa's life was killed, and she went mad with grief as she wept for seven hundred years. Her tears flooded the dry land and became the vengeful waters that dragged any soul who dared submerge to the underworld, as payment for the lover that had once been claimed.

Zia laughed as she prepared to make the jump. At least her end wouldn't be a boring one.

"Zia!" a familiar voice shouted.

She froze on her first step. She would never forget that voice. Not in this lifetime or the next. Her heart twisted in pain. Zia dared a glance over her shoulder, looking at his face one last time. Bright green eyes with golden specks pierced through her. That strong, stubborn jaw tightened. He took a step toward her.

"Zia," he pleaded again.

Her name sounded like a prayer on his lips, and she cursed the gods that he had somehow found her. There was so much she ached to tell him, but none of it mattered now. He was the one person that could have delayed her, but it was too late. They were out of time.

"I'll see you again..." she whispered softly, swallowing the lump in her throat.

His face twisted in pain. Zia sprinted toward the edge without hesitation. Her final step came too quickly as she flung herself off the cliff. She vaguely heard him shouting in the distance, but she knew he wouldn't risk following her over the edge. Not into those waters. Not with so much banking on his survival.

Time seemed to halt as she was suspended in the air. Zia's breath caught as she gazed below. The drop was farther than she thought. Much farther. Maybe today would be the day. The jagged rocks looked like the mouth of Death grinning at her. She grinned back in challenge.

Any sense of control dissolved as gravity took over, bringing her closer to the ground. She always despised heights, so it felt like a cruel joke for her life to end in this way. Anything above ten feet and her limbs normally turned wobbly. This drop had to be one hundred feet.

The few seconds of the fall seemed to stretch on for an eternity. She crossed her arms over her chest and kept her body straight as she finally met the bottom. Water slammed into her bones like concrete, but she had triumphantly evaded the rocks.

The current held her under, and she couldn't tell up from down as her body tumbled. She kept fighting, trying to reach the surface, but the hungry rapids stole all sense of direction. Her lungs were on fire. She needed oxygen. Soon.

Zia opened her eyes in the murky water, and when she began to swim, a sharp pain shot through her collarbone. It was probably broken. Fantastic. Her stubborn protest of Death was her only tether to life. She just had to find land.

Zia slammed into a thick branch and barely grasped onto the end. Her palm stung as the bark cut into her skin. She managed to get her head above the surface and gasped for air. The current was too strong to stay above water for long. Her muscles desperately ached, but she tightened her grip on the branch.

A woman's scream shook her. Zia whipped her head around to the other side of the river to see a figure standing there with her hand outstretched. She looked familiar, somehow. Zia couldn't make out her face. The river was too wide, and she was using every ounce of energy to remain conscious.

She fumbled with her other arm for the pouch around her neck. She felt the stone inside and sighed in relief. Her collarbone was in agony, but she shoved the pain aside. She just needed to find a way across the river.

Then the branch began to break.

She fumbled for another handhold but there was nothing.

"*HELP!*" Zia shouted hopelessly to the woman. Terror ripped through her vocal cords with a scream until no more sound came out. She didn't fear for her own life, she feared that everything she worked for and fought to protect was about to be erased. The image of his face flashed in her mind again: those green eyes that had become home and a grand adventure all at once. At least she would die knowing he was safe.

"Zia, we're out of time. You have to wake up!" the woman shouted across the river.

The branch broke free, and a wave of whitewash pulled her under. The current was relentless. Vasalisa had no mercy. Exhaustion threatened to lull Zia into a permanent rest. She touched the stone around her neck, clutching it one last time as a comforting wave of darkness swept over her.

And then the world went black.

Zia woke up gasping for air. Her pajamas stuck to her skin, frozen with sweat. She kicked the thick duvet cover off her body and ran to the bathroom to splash cold water on her face. She scrubbed at her skin as though she could wipe the thoughts from her mind.

Zia gripped the edges of the sink and focused on her breath, counting in for four seconds and out for four seconds. Her heart no longer racing, she dared to look at herself in the mirror. Water droplets twinkled on her dark brown skin. Her eyes were always the first thing people noticed; they were so blue they nearly glowed, as though the ocean itself churned within them. Dark circles now lined them from the many nights of restless sleep.

"It was just a dream," she whispered to herself.

Zia rubbed at her temples in an attempt to ease her headache. The dreams had occurred since she was a baby, and they were always in the same strange forest. Oftentimes, they seemed more real than reality. When she woke up, she felt like a stranger in her own life.

A knock pounded at her door.

"Z! Are you still sleeping? There's a whole world outside your bed, you know!" A familiar voice shouted cheerfully.

Zia groaned. Her best and only friend, Hiro, often delighted in waking her up at the crack of dawn. They had been attached at the hip since they were children, though she still wanted to wallop him every time he barged into her place so early. She reluctantly stomped over to her bedroom door and flung it open.

As always, Hiro was dressed pristinely. He had on his favorite pair of light wash, ripped jeans, a simple white T-shirt, and the overcoat he found at a thrift shop a few blocks away. Hiro always wore a black top hat, slightly crooked so it dipped over his face, framing his thick, bushy eyebrows.

He leaned against the doorway, beaming with that wide smile of his, a toothpick resting in the corner of his mouth.

His dark brown eyes trailed up to her hair and widened.

"Hello, darling. Why do you look like you just stuck your finger in an electrical socket?" he asked, removing the toothpick from his mouth.

It was true. Her wild, thick black curly hair was sticking in fifty different directions. She had broken more brushes in her life than she could count.

Zia scowled.

"How about, 'Hello, Zia. My apologies for waking you up from your beauty sleep *every day.*'"

"'Beauty sleep' is a generous term," he chuckled, unphased by her mood.

She was about to snap back a rather unpleasant retort, but he seemed to sense it. Hiro immediately revealed a cup of coffee from her favorite hole in the wall café and circled it under her nose.

"*You're getting nicer...*" he said with his voice in a trance-like state.

Zia rolled her eyes and accepted the coffee. It smelled like home. Hiro often mocked her, saying that her drink of choice was more liquid cake than coffee, since she doused it in creamer and dumped a concerning amount of sugar in it.

His thick eyebrows drew together as he studied her. "You had another dream again, didn't you? How do you feel?" he asked quietly. Hiro had always been able to read her like a book.

"I'm fine," she lied. She avoided his eyes and gulped down the coffee too quickly. It burned her tongue and the back of her throat.

Hiro tilted his head to the side and smirked, "*Fine* is not a feeling, Z. Do you want to talk about it?"

She played with a rip in her oversized t-shirt as though there were something immensely fascinating in the fabric. A photo of her favorite band faded from too many brutal wash cycles, but she had never been good at letting go of things.

Stubborn to the point of recklessness. That's what her school shrink had called her when she did her involuntary counseling session after her mother's death. Zia had snorted at the absurdity of it all, then wired the shrink Somnium, the most popular cryptocurrency coin, to mark her off as healed and ready to resume a normal life.

She hadn't gotten much better at talking about her feelings since then. It felt like if she stopped holding herself together so tightly, she would fall apart. There was simply no time for that sort of chaos, so she sucked in a breath and forced her eyes to meet Hiro's.

"No," she replied simply.

He opened his mouth to say something, then closed it. Within a few seconds, the concern on his face was once again replaced with that comforting smile.

"Alright, my queen. Then shall we depart? We have to show those hooligans at The Trials who the real players are."

Hiro twirled his hat and pressed it to his chest, making a mock bow to her. Her heart squeezed at that. He always listened with a gentle ear when she needed him to and knew when to provide space when she wasn't ready.

Zia snatched the hat from him and placed it atop her frizzy, electrical-socket hair.

"Aye, aye, captain. There's pancake mix downstairs."

"Then you know where I'll be," he winked and nearly sprinted toward the kitchen.

Rain dribbled down her bedroom window. She stood in the doorway for a moment, listening to the pitter-patter sounds. Periculum had been in a drought for the last ten years, so she wasn't entirely sure what to think of the weather—not to mention the fact that it was the height of summer.

Zia sighed and climbed into the shower, cranking the knob until it felt scalding. There were only ever a few minutes of hot water, depending on how late they had been on bills that month, but she savored every second. She sat on the floor of the deep blue tiles, inhaling the scent of her cheap lavender shampoo and contemplating her dream. She couldn't shake the image of the man's green eyes, the familiar sound of his voice. She didn't know who he was, but it felt like she *knew* him. It wasn't the first time he had appeared in her dreams, but it was all fragmented in her memory.

The dream melted from her mind with the hiss of the steam. She had to focus. The cops were closing in on the game, and if she stood a chance at winning, it would have to be soon. *Legends of Lemuria* was a mythological virtual reality world created eighteen years ago, and it had captured the attention of every nation. People could either find an escape in the fantasy world or participate in The Trials.

The Trials were the different volatile levels a player had to pass through within the world. Despite the game looking like a fantasy, the prizes were *very* real. Buried in the game was a map that led to three priceless stones.

People were more desperate than ever since the economic collapse, but with every passing year, fewer believed the stones even existed. It was rumored they could power entire countries, like a battery that never died. Regardless of what they actually did, the winner would be wealthy beyond measure.

The government knew it was losing control since The Trials were decentralized, meaning no one world power could lay claim to it. In a desperate attempt to maintain a sliver of control, they used the same age-old tactics: terrify the people until they handed over their freedom in exchange for "safety."

Zia brushed her teeth, carefully paying attention to each stroke to try and get out of her head. She shut off the water and wrapped a black towel around her body, feeling the cold hardwood floors beneath her bare feet as she made her way to her closet.

She selected her usual outfit for The Trials: black jeans, knee-high leather boots, and her mother's cloak that she had sewn herself. Zia only had a few things left of her mother—little clues to the woman she had been. The fabric of the cloak felt soft, with markings on the back embroidered in a language she didn't recognize. The wide hood covered Zia's face, concealing her age when she entered the underground pit where The Trials took place.

Zia slipped on the cloak and tossed her wet hair behind her back, tucking it behind her ears. Guilt gnawed at her gut, threatening to eat her alive. She wondered what her mother would make of The Trials— what she would think of the years Zia spent ditching school to illegally participate in such a dangerous game.

She sat on her bed for a moment and bent over her knees, cupping her face in her hands. The scent of pancakes wafted up to her room. Hiro was probably in a cooking frenzy, making an unnecessarily large stack dribbled in his homemade berry sauce. Since he had a photographic memory, he refused to ever write the recipe down. In fact, he refused to ever write anything down, claiming that forgetfulness was a lack of focus, and everyone gave themselves digital dementia by lazily outsourcing information.

"Z! Hurry up, or I'm gonna eat your breakfast!" Hiro threatened from below.

She went to unplug the lamp and glanced at the old film photo of her mom on her nightstand. Her dad's arms wrapped around her, a rare smile on his face. She was laughing, her crinkled nose dotted with freckles, and her wildly curly hair as unruly as she had been. A light blue crystal necklace hung around her neck. The same necklace that Zia had worn her entire life, refusing to ever take it off. She ran a thumb along its sharp edges.

"You're taking so long I'm fossilizing," Hiro taunted from below.

She snorted and made her way downstairs to find him sitting on the marble counter, smug as a cat with his cheeks full. Syrup dribbled from his chin, which he seemed to have no intention of wiping.

The kitchen was immaculate as always. Her father kept it so clean that surgery could have been performed in there. It was so at odds with Zia's nature that he threatened to throw an explosive device into her room just to wipe it clean. *The human tornado.* That's what he called her.

The house never felt like home. There was a single grey couch in the living room with a small wooden coffee table that he had built. No plants, no photos, no personal effects that would have remotely warmed up the place. It felt like living in a museum without any art.

Zia tossed Hiro's hat at him and piled several pancakes onto her plate, dousing them in peanut butter, strawberries, and his secret sauce. She joined him on the counter and sliced off a big bite with her fork, plopping it into her mouth. Her taste buds exploded with mouth-watering sweetness. Hiro licked the rest of his plate clean, a triumphant smile on his face.

"How was your date with Austin?" she asked him through a mouthful of pancake.

"He has the emotional depth of a pebble. Probably not a soulmate. Some people are just perfect on paper. I have more chemistry with this pancake." He rolled his eyes and told her of their painfully boring date.

Zia winced. Hiro didn't have the best of luck when it came to romance. Boys always tried to use him to level up in The Trials. His mother, Mei, owned the largest underground Virtual Reality Library in the country. Since the game was illegal, it was the only place they could play. The cops never touched it—so long as they continued receiving a cut of the profits, of course.

Once Hiro gave them access, and they got what they wanted, his heart got steam-rolled over and over again. Periculum wasn't the ideal place to find "happily ever after." She couldn't help but admire his hope though. For most, any relationship was either a distraction or an attempt to guarantee a better life for themselves.

"A rarity has to be with a rarity, Hiro. No exceptions," she pointed her fork at him for emphasis.

He pinched the bridge of his nose and sighed.

"And what about you, Z? I don't see you putting yourself out there."

She cut him a glare.

"I don't exactly have a line of suitors out my door, Hiro. Besides, I don't believe in *soulmates.*"

Zia had never been like Hiro—capable of giving love freely and to all who crossed his path whether they deserved it or not. The blunter she was, the more uncomfortable men became in her presence. She didn't understand why people preferred small talk. She found it to be exhausting.

Besides, she didn't dream of a prince on a white horse whisking her away. She dreamt of feeling the wind on her face as she drove far away from this place. The possibility of freedom made her get out of bed in the morning.

Hiro squeezed her shoulder, interrupting her thoughts.

"I believe we have many soulmates, Z. Some of them are found in friendships, others in romantic relationships. Soulmates carry keys that unlock hidden doors inside of us we otherwise wouldn't have found. And sometimes, when you're lucky, you find a match. Someone to evolve with for a lifetime. Maybe even after that."

Hope shone in his sherry-colored eyes. Zia knew how dangerous hope could be when it was crushed—that oftentimes, hope was merely despair dressed up. Yet she couldn't bring herself to tell him that she doubted a true match was anything other than a fairytale to keep the loneliness at bay.

"When did you get so wise?" She stuck out her tongue at him.

"Wisdom is at odds with knowledge. You have to be brazen enough to make mistakes to earn wisdom. Until the knowledge lives in your bones, it is merely a recycled ideology!" he winked back at her.

Zia made a gagging noise in response. Hiro spoke in bumper sticker. It was often difficult to get a straight answer from him. He was one year older than her, and somehow thought that gave him the right to spout monologues about the mysteries of the universe.

She playfully elbowed him in the ribs, grabbing the rest of the pots and pans and washing them in the sink. She shivered—the apartment didn't have heat or air conditioning, so they were always subject to the elements.

"We have to find that map soon, you know. It's our only way out of here," Zia said as casually as she could.

"We'll find it."

"But what if—"

"We'll *find* it, Z." He winked.

She flicked water at him, and he held up his hands innocently.

"You know Mei and I would take you in if he kicked you out," Hiro said quietly.

"And be another mouth for her to feed? No, she's already training me. I won't add to her burden," She avoided his gaze and hung the dishes to dry, then wiped her palms with a rag.

"You are not, and have never been a burden," Hiro replied softly.

She swallowed the lump in her throat.

"It's not an option."

"You're such an easy-going, flexible person."

She glared daggers at him in response.

His mother started training her at nine years old. Since they would play the game anyway, Mei decided it may as well be under her roof. There was one caveat: Zia would need to attend evening training sessions. Knowing how to defend herself in the real world was more than a skill; it was a necessity.

The players in The Trials weren't just brilliant nerds like herself. Gangsters, thieves, corrupt cops, and all the other wicked creatures got their fix of violence in the virtual world. If only they knew that Zia, an eighteen-year-old girl, was the player they were all striving to catch up with. It was rare enough to see a woman play, let alone one with such a high score.

Players would do anything to get their hands on the stones, including robbing and murdering each other. The government had snitches in every city who watched a player's skill, then sold the information to the cops. Shortly after, the cops would find a reason to arrest the player, and they were never seen again. Anyone caught playing was sentenced to life in prison. The more skillful prisoners were detained in underground training facilities, sentenced to a life of searching for the map in service to the government as a "champion."

A key turned the six locks of the front door, and the sound of boots stomping echoed on creaky wooden floors. Her spine stiffened as she braced herself for her father's cranky mood after the night shift. Hiro plastered a lazy grin on his face, ready to defuse any tension.

Her father stalked into the kitchen. His shoulders slumped over, and his salt-and-pepper brows knit together in a permanent frown. He grunted as he chucked his coat off and onto the rack, then untied his boots. His muddy brown eyes looked sunken and weary.

"There's breakfast," Zia said flatly.

Her father nearly jumped out of his skin. He had somehow been unaware of their presence.

"Are you trying to give me a heart attack?" he snapped.

She rolled her eyes, "Yes, I thought I would *feed* you to death."

He chose not to hear her comment, his eyes narrowing when he saw Hiro.

"What are you doing here?" he said coldly.

"Is there even a here? Or is reality merely your brain's best interpretation of the sensory information we perceive? Prove to me I'm real, David!" Mischief twinkled in Hiro's eyes.

Her father waved Hiro off, slumping over to the kitchen.

Zia cleared her throat.

"Alright, well we're off—"

"To school?" her father interrupted.

Zia clutched her keys in her palms with white knuckles, her mouth tightening into a thin line.

"It's Saturday, Dad."

He ignored her, muttering to himself as he shuffled food onto his plate. Work and school were his answers to everything. *Get an education. Get a job. Get married. Start a family. Find a nice, white picket fence and question nothing.* Yet, the system had long since been broken, and what was once a promise of opportunity became a breeding factory for obedience.

The map was her ticket out.

"If you gave me more time, maybe I could—"

"Could what? Waste your life playing games?" He looked up at her with cold, glaring eyes.

"I don't know what you're talking about," She folded her arms across her chest.

He huffed, then walked over to the old wooden dresser next to the couch. He slid open a drawer and pulled out a bag. *Her* bag. All of her crypto cards that she had been stashing from her wins. He unzipped the bag and dumped the cards onto the couch. Hiro winced.

"I know what I'm doing—" She started.

"You *don't*. The cops could kick down our door at any moment and drag you into a cell, or worse, force you to play as one of their champions!" Her father rose from his chair, and his eyes lifted to hers, empty and dark.

"It's time to grow up. You want to keep playing? Then move out, and pay for the roof over your own head," his lips pressed into a thin line, "Or, you can swear to me you will never play again. That you'll start taking life seriously and get a government job."

"And what? Work construction like you?"

His nostrils flared, and he closed his eyes.

"I have a friend, Sean. He works in accounting. I can get you an internship there—"

"I'm not going to be an accountant."

"Then you're not going to be able to take care of yourself! You *need* security," His eyes flickered to the crypto cards. "Winning won't bring her back."

Zia felt like he had punched her in the gut. She stopped breathing. Her father had always blamed her for her mother's death. She died giving birth to Zia, and the loss had fractured something in him. He had no trouble reminding Zia that if she didn't exist, he would still have his wife.

"You have one week," He rose from his stool and stalked up the stairs.

She felt his rage and contempt toward her. Ever since she was a baby it had been that way. She could feel everyone's emotions like they were her own. It was part of why she found people so difficult to deal with. Especially when what they said didn't match up with how they felt.

She had never told anyone about it. Not even Hiro. Being different was a death warrant.

Hiro gently grabbed her elbow, tugging her out of the room. He knew the longer she spent around her dad, the more in danger she was of exploding.

Zia shoved the thought away, refusing to open up that door in her mind. Her jaw locked up with all the hateful words she wanted to hurl at him, but she let Hiro lead her outside. One more week. If she aggravated him, then she would have even less time.

They stepped out of the front door, Zia locking the six bolts behind her. The rain pounded down relentlessly, washing away the muck and grime from the streets. The yellow streetlamps winked out one by one at the first light of dawn. Zia heaved a great sigh, letting her emotions wash over her like a wave.

After all, she now had nothing to lose, and that made her a formidable player.

"Your chariot awaits," Hiro said cheerfully, gesturing toward the scrap of metal he named Betty. Despite his smile, she could see the wariness there as he watched her. She schooled her face into neutrality.

Zia smiled fondly as she faced the vehicle. Hiro named his van after his grandmother. It was their adventure mobile, but the thing was ancient. No matter how many times it broke down on them, Hiro insisted that she had spunk other cars lacked. He regularly droned on about how new cars had no personality. The van had been imported from Japan, so the wheel was on the right side of the car. They were lucky that they had never been pulled over for it. Every time he started the ignition it would yell at him in Japanese saying, "Don't forget your toll money!"

Though Zia did have a soft spot for the van, she was tired of it overheating every time they sat in traffic. They spent many afternoons on the side of the road, waiting for Jack, the tow truck guy, to come save Betty whilst praying not to get jumped. Having a tow truck guy's personal number was always a red flag.

They climbed into the van, and Hiro twisted the key. The engine roared to life and was so loud she could barely hear him talk. A eucalyptus air freshener hung from the rearview mirror, twisting and turning from the broken vent that blew hot air.

"Must you always drive at a glacial pace?" She asked.

"Must you *always* be a gremlin in the mornings?" He replied sweetly.

She chuckled and playfully whacked his shoulder.

"No hitting the driver! Save all your suppressed rage for the game," He pointed a finger in the air.

She rolled her eyes.

"I'm breaking past the forest boundary."

"That is the worst idea you've ever had, which is saying something," He stopped at a yellow light. A *yellow* light.

"It really is, isn't it?" She grinned wickedly.

Not a single player made it through the forest boundary, because it required going through the castle. Elymentals guarded it—Lemurian magic-wielders capable of harnessing a single element. She figured the map had to be passed the boundary, since it was the one level that no one had braved. The forest was always pixelated, which meant she would either be obliterated or find the map. If she was wrong, she would lose all of her Somnium coin, and go straight back to level one—but what was a dream without risk?

The dark, gloomy clouds hung above them. Zia had never been one to believe in signs, but it sent shivers down her spine. She leaned her head against the cold window, gazing out at the only world she had never known. Periculum was a sea of concrete and strangers. Rotting apartments stacked on top of each other. Some of the buildings crumbled, and many of the cell towers tilted with wires that dangerously sparked in the rain. Much of the world had fallen to such conditions. Zia had never seen the mountains or the ocean before. Her only experience with nature was from The Trials or her dreams.

The wheels screeched as he maneuvered through the tiny streets of Periculum. The city lights twinkled in the reflection of the puddles that stuck to the pavement. Trash blew down the roads in the wind. Camps of homeless people huddled together at the corners of the road. For the most part, the cops left them alone. They had created their own underground city.

After the financial collapse of 2039, the government stopped taking care of its people. They fended for themselves, yet still had to pay taxes. Taxes that only increased every year.

Periculum was the bleakest part of Fallen Angels—a larger crumbling city of slums that occupied an enormous chunk of Southern California. Though it had been segregated between The Electi and the rest of the people long before the collapse, things were far more drastic now. No one bothered to pretend anymore. Periculum stretched for nine miles, with compact housing. The Electi neighborhoods were sectioned off with electronic gates guarded by the military.

The only time they crossed paths with The Electi was in Mei's VR library. The rich were addicted to betting on players. Mei's was curated perfectly. There were no windows or clocks, so time became irrelevant. She pumped extra oxygen into the place, so players and gamblers always felt awake. A moment at Mei's was an eternity. Being there felt like sinking into quicksand.

"Hiro, I have a strange feeling about today," she finally admitted, chewing her nails. A habit she tried to quit many times, but her anxiety was an ever-present companion that left her with nubs.

"That 'feeling' you're talking about is your intuition. I've been telling you to listen to it for years," he fiddled with the knob of the air conditioner to try and turn it down.

"Maybe if you stopped speaking in bumper sticker, I would listen to you more."

"You wound me." He clutched a fist over his chest. She rolled her eyes.

Hiro abruptly stopped in front of a restaurant on the street corner. The rubber on his tires nearly burned with his old brakes. Zia wrinkled her nose at the smell of the place. She would never eat there to save her life, mostly because they had found a myriad of disgusting things that *weren't* food in the dishes. Unfortunately, Mei's VR library existed in the back of it.

Hiro shut off the car and put a new toothpick in his mouth, smiling. "Together?" he asked.

It was their pact from the beginning. Whatever life threw at them, they would figure it out together. With Hiro, there were no problems, only puzzle pieces.

"Together," she agreed.

They leaped out of the car and ran toward the dry haven of the restaurant entrance. She tucked her mother's necklace into her shirt and pulled her hood over her head, concealing as much of her face as she could.

The pungent smell of curry filled her nose. The restaurant was already busy. Waiters hustled and swirled about. The paint on the red walls was peeling, and many of the booths had bullet holes in them. It was a miracle the place did so well.

They snuck into the kitchen, gliding through the two large metal doors. A bouncer stood in front of the large refrigerator, which was really the entrance to Mei's. He was an enormously muscled man who had a large assortment of weapons hidden on his body, though the two pistols on his hips made enough of a statement.

The bouncer, whose name was Sam, had a blue dragon tattoo snaking down the left side of his face, and a large silver nose ring. He wore bright gold contacts. Usually, only The Electi changed their appearance to match the Lemurians from The Trials. However, there were a few players in Periculum, like Sam, who had acquired enough wealth from playing to spend coin on their appearance. It was a way to show off that they were at a higher level. Zia thought it was completely self-indulgent, bordering on idiotic, since a high score put a target on his back. Though Zia supposed if *she* looked like her muscles were made of granite and she had swallowed three full-grown people, she wouldn't mind either.

He took one look at Zia, recognizing her, and his mouth pressed into a tight line.

"No," He growled.

Hiro held out his hands.

"Come on, Sam! Didn't you miss me?"

Sam folded his arms across his chest.

"No."

Zia raised a brow, "Quite the vocabulary you've got there, friend."

Hiro stomped on her foot in warning, still smiling at Sam. She winced at the pain radiating from her toes.

"You know she's the best player you've got. How much money has your boss made betting on her?"

Hiro didn't mention that Sam's *boss* was his mother.

Bets were the only way VR libraries made their money, since no one took a cut of the game. There were players and watchers. The Electi were the only ones who could afford to buy a gambling table, and they didn't want to get their hands dirty playing. Instead, they used headsets to view the players in-house, betting on who would level up first. Since it was the most volatile library with the clashing of classes, people became addicted to the high winnings and terrible losses.

Sam's eyes flickered to Zia. He pursed his lips, debating.

"Last time she was here, she caused a fight with one of our best clients."

Zia suppressed a smile. The fight had been with one of the nastier gamblers, Atticus Ashwood. He was a spoiled, pompous pretty boy who lost a large sum of his father's money betting on a mage who was naïve enough to go up against her. His mistake.

From behind his back, Hiro took out a box of doughnuts from the same café he had gotten Zia's coffee. "I brought you these. Your favorite—strawberry glaze with sprinkles. I promise we won't cause a ruckus." He charmingly handed the box of pink doughnuts to the bouncer.

Sam pursed his lips, "Are you bribing me, boy?"

Hiro raised his hands innocently, "No."

Sam's eyes twinkled with amusement at the word. He glared at Zia one last time in warning, then opened the large refrigerator door, revealing the blazing music below, and invited them in. Zia stepped in first, then Hiro followed her.

"Thank you, my fri—" Hiro began to say, but he was cut off by Sam slamming the refrigerator door behind them.

Despite the rough conditions of the restaurant, no expense was spared in the VR Library. Mei wanted to remind The Electi of their homes, and the players of what they could win if they kept playing. The golden, spiraling staircase led them down into the heart of The Trials. The ceilings were nearly ten stories high, with a rendition of the Lemurian night sky at the top. Their constellation was different than the human realms—a thousand twinkling stars swirled and eddied in geometric patterns.

Thirty VR pods lined the middle of the room, all with players of different ages and backgrounds. The one thing they had in common: they were all in search of the map.

The pods were made of an iridescent, sleek material shaped like a closed pyramid to provide privacy. The newer models didn't even require a headset or bodysuit—the moment a player stepped inside of the pyramid, their consciousness was transported into the game.

In the front of the library lay a stage that featured different live music throughout the day, usually as a tribute to a different decade in history. Today was jazz themed, specifically as an ode to the 1920's. It flooded the library with a buzzing energy. The sound of the saxophone and piano blaring drowned out all of the conversations.

The gambling tables were sectioned off by the bar. The Electi dressed in their most glamorous attire: women in silk, sparkling dresses with jewels that would be stolen off them by the end of the night, men in suits with suspenders, their feet kicked up on the tables. Some of them changed their eye color and bore tattoos like the Lemurians, others dressed as flapper girls with cropped hair as an ode to the theme of the night.

They all puffed cigars and wore headsets, swiping their crypto cards to place bets on their favorite players. The drinks flowed generously, and since it was so early in the day, a sense of comradery hung in the air. Yet, Zia knew after the first bet was lost, Sam would have to carry a gambler out by the neck before someone was killed.

Zia had never been bet on, save for Hiro's mother who owned the club—she was something between a mafia leader and a fussing grandmother. No one dared mess with her, yet she made everyone feel at home and taken care of. She was the type of woman who could cook a meal that fed the whole city, then stab a man with the same spatula.

Zia heard Mei before she saw her.

"Listen, Benny, if you don't pay your tab this time, I'll kick your balls into your throat! You know I love you, Benny baby, but I'm not putting up with this garbage!" Her voice boomed across the library.

Mei was a rotund woman in a purple suit who had no trouble speaking her mind. Her jet-black hair was cropped at her shoulders, and she had the same beaming smile as Hiro. She was puffing on a cigar when she spotted the two of them.

"Zia! Welcome home, honey." Mei clapped her shoulders, then pulled her into a bone-crushing hug.

"Back for more trouble, Hiro?" She squished his cheeks, pride filling her eyes. Hiro hugged his mom warmly. Zia felt a pang of jealousy at the ease of their relationship.

"Always, Mama," he smiled crookedly.

One of the waiters called Mei over to deal with a rowdy gambler.

She snorted, "The work never stops. Alright, listen you two, I've got your pods ready for you and a huge pot of coffee brewing. You let me know if you need anything else!" She squeezed Zia's shoulder again and sauntered off toward the tables.

Hiro whistled, looking at the vast expanse of the library. The stacks and stacks of shelves weren't filled with books, but games dating back to the very first video games ever made. Yet the only VR world anyone bothered to enter was Lemuria, so it was more for show. The government had attempted to create its own game, even, but the people were sick of feeling bound. They played in The Trials because *no one* could lay claim to it.

Zia strutted over to her pod of choice. The smell of booze, cigarettes, and coffee permeated the air. She kept the hood of her cloak over her head and walked with the swagger of a scrappy older woman, her clothes thwarting any suspicion.

Hiro was protected because of Mei, but if anyone guessed how young Zia was, they would immediately report her to the cops. It was rare enough that she was a woman so high up in the game. The last thing she needed was for them to find out her age, too. Despite her high score, she could never liquidate the Somnium she won, or the government would immediately trace it to her. Her crypto cards only contained enough coin for her to get by.

"Let The Trials begin, Z!" Hiro said quietly before climbing into his enclosed pod.

She nodded at him and then stepped inside of the pyramid. It opened and shut within seconds. The floor beneath her glowed, and then the pod did a toe to head body scan, ending at her eyes with facial recognition.

Within seconds, the anti-gravity suspension lifted her body from the ground. She hovered several feet in the air, relaxing into the dream state they were all trained to be able to drop into at will.

"*Welcome back, Zia,*" said a robotic female voice.

She felt the familiar jolt of her consciousness transferring, and then her mind went blank.

Let The Trials begin.

CHAPTER 2

Fear shows us what we love. Greed shows us what we value. —Zia

The sounds of crickets and tumbling waves filled Zia's ears as the city of Lemuria was revealed to her. A pyramid-shaped castle floated between two enormous, twisting Albizia trees. The structure was made of opaque Lemurian crystal and could be spotted from miles away. The city below was hugged by black sand, with the surrounding sea stubbornly trying to kiss the shore.

Red fire birds with flamed tails swooped in front of the castle, guarding its entrance. They left trails of smoke in their wake. Their yellow beaks and sharp barbed talons were enough to deter most players from attempting to break in. A great river ran through the heart of the city, twisting and winding around the different quarters. No one dared swim in it—those currents belonged to the sirens, deadly water creatures believed to be half demon, half woman.

Zia sighed in relief at her return to this place. She rolled her shoulders out to loosen her neck, adjusting to her avatar's body. Though her face looked completely different for anonymity's sake, she tried to keep her Lemurian character somewhat true to her. In an age of mass exposure, privacy quickly became the greatest currency. Keeping her identity secret was vital to her survival. She had glowing, blue tattoos that snaked up her arms with ancient symbols. Her hair, no longer frizzy, was sleek and braided down her back.

She was a foot taller than her usual height, nearing seven feet, and dressed in Lemurian fashion. High wasted, flowy turquoise pants embroidered in gold hugged her curves. A bandeau top that tied around her neck left her toned arms bare. Twin blades with glittering sapphire jewels rested at her back. Several hoops pierced her ear, and she had an anklet of solid gold she bought with her coins. A superfluous purchase, but she had long since learned the power of appearances in the game. She needed to look like a girl more concerned with her clothes than finding the map. Besides, the goldsmith was an artist, and it was rare for an artist to be properly compensated for their devotion to their craft.

In many ways, Zia's avatar felt like who she wanted to be—strong, confident, sure of herself. Yet, she knew it was all a fantasy. The only thing that mattered was the map. She glanced at her surroundings, scanning the perimeter. The climate was hot and sticky, the air so humid it was nearly drinkable.

It was dusk, and the sky was painted in pastel colors as the sun dipped beneath the horizon. The full moon rose just above the castle point, a sprinkle of stars speckled around it. A firebird *cawed* in the distance, its silhouette swooping and gliding before the pregnant moon.

She gazed over her shoulder at the forest that beckoned just beyond the city. Thin swirls of mist cloaked it, but the winding trees were so tall they nearly met the sky. Her lips twitched into a smile as she stared at the blurred forest. Today was the day.

A player could level up in many ways: through acquiring artifacts, solving riddles, sparring with high-level creatures, or unlocking new areas within the game. The identity of The Architect remained a mystery. People had spent years trying to figure out who created the world, but all rumors had proven false. Each theory was more absurd than the next—that it was the president, a celebrity, one of The Electi, or even a lowly gamer hiding out in Periculum. The most ludicrous theory was that Lemuria was based on an ancient civilization that still existed, hiding in plain sight. Of course, there was no proof.

Plenty of zealots went in search of Lemuria, convinced they'd be the chosen ones. It was a delusional form of escape from the harsh world they lived in. The number of times she and Hiro had made fun of crowds of people wearing white, dripping in crystals, and praying to the gods that they would be allowed in was comical.

If the gods had ever existed, they left this place a long time ago.

Zia walked along a mossy tree trunk. It was one of the ways to travel throughout the city, moving from quarter to quarter. Some players had enough coins to buy a Zhulu—great white birds with the head of a lion that traveled swifter than the wind. Others purchased horses or hovercrafts, but they were often stolen and attracted unnecessary attention. Zia preferred the natural tree highways above. They kept her hidden and able to see the mischief happening below.

Though Lemuria was designed as an ancient civilization, it had far more advanced technology than the real world. Teleportation, mind-to-mind communication, telekinesis, advanced weapons…it was endless, really. She wouldn't be surprised if the government attempted to fashion its own arsenal after the game.

Zia carefully avoided the red-braided vines that wrapped around the trunks of the trees. Some of them had tiny thorns that had once left poison in her bare feet, costing her several coins at the apothecary. A patch of sky-blue grass with blades nearly as tall as Zia beckoned below. Children rolled around and played in it. A young Lemurian sniffed one of the orchids, and violet pollen exploded all over her face. The child howled, laughing with infectious freedom. She could not remember the last time she laughed like that. Or at all, really.

The city was split into four regions: The Ghost Market, Artists Square, Ace's Quarter, and the Stone Quarter. The Ghost Market offered the quickest way to level up, and was naturally the most dangerous part of the city. Gatekeepers of Death, also known as ghouls, guarded the entrance and demanded a life sacrifice to enter. Most players brought them the bones of animals, which allowed them to enter the lowest levels of the market that sold basic weapons, opiates, or maps of the sewage system.

The bones of other players, however, gave people access to the most volatile goods and hidden gates within the market. The more a player was worth, the more access granted. Hiro would be furious if he knew her plan, but she needed an invisibility charm if she was going to make it through the castle and breach the forest boundary.

There was only one place to find it.

She gracefully hopped over to the next trunk, wondering where Hiro went as she made her way toward the gushing sound of the river. Night came quickly, revealing the thousands of stars that took Zia's breath away. She preferred the dark night in Lemuria. Emerald and topaz-colored lights lit up the sky above as a thick, shooting star raced across the universe.

She swung off the trunk of the tree and landed on her haunches, her feet hitting the cobblestone street. Black, obsidian gates glittered before her. Two ghouls carrying swords swayed on their feet. Their loosely held flesh barely concealed shards of white bone. She did her best not to breathe through her nose. The smell of rot and death made her want to vomit.

Zia strutted toward them, plastering a lazy smile on her face as she chucked two shards of bone at them. The taller one on the left growled as he looked at the bone at his feet, but the shorter one sniffed and picked it up.

"Who did you kill for this?" It said in a whispery breath.

"No one who didn't deserve it," She placed a hand on her hip. "Come on boys, that should be at least enough to gain access to the third level."

They grunted in unison, sniffing the bones one last time. Then the shorter ghoul waved a hand, and the door furthest to the right yawned opened.

"Pleasure doing business with you."

She pulled out her twin swords and walked through the cave. It was wet and sticky. Turquoise moss coated the walls, and she could hear voices in the distance. She picked up her pace, wanting to spend as little time in the Ghost Market as possible.

She swiped the bones from the Boneyard yesterday, just for this. Grave robbing wasn't her finest moment, but she would do whatever it took to find that gods-damned map.

The maw of the dewy cave opened up into a mass market. Rare animals were sold in cages, along with an endless row of poisons, and a whole host of other stomach-churning contraband she chose to ignore. She kept her head down as she made her way to the potions master.

He was a stout old man with round glasses, a large nose, and a permanent pout that had likely been there since the day he was born.

She cleared her throat.

"Yes?" He said, not looking up from the black, bubbling liquid he was brewing.

Chills snaked down her spine as she looked further at his shop. She could see jars of blood-mist, an explosive powder capable of devastating whole cities, casually up for sale as though they were bottles of wine.

"I'm looking for an invisibility charm, and I hear you're the best there is." She batted her lashes, trying to muster up whatever ounce of feminine charm she had.

"My services are expensive," He looked down at her from his nose.

"I'm sure you're worth it," She tried to keep the sarcasm from her tone.

He hobbled over to his station, and she could hear glasses clanking together in the back. Within seconds, he had returned with a small vile that had a clear liquid in it.

"It will last no more than an hour," He dangled it in front of the light so she could see properly.

She pulled out her crypto card and swiped it against his screen. Somnium had shot up in value, so it pained her to spend so much on a tiny vile, but it was necessary. She pocketed the vile, and he returned to stirring the liquid in his pot.

"Enjoy, it tastes like feet."

Zia gave him a mock bow, then turned on her heel to walk out. A deafening growl rattled the skies before she could take another step.

"WHO DARE ROB ONE OF MY GRAVES?" A lethal voice snarled.

She looked over her shoulder to see a black wolf the size of a car, baring his yellowing teeth like he would rip out a throat at the slightest annoyance. His name was Thanatos, and he was the ruler of the Ghost Market.

Before she could take a step, he sniffed the air, and his coal-black eyes narrowed on her.

"You," He growled.

She backed toward the potion master's shop, who had already disappeared.

"I don't know what you're talking about," She held her chin high.

He struck a massive paw into the stony ground, then prowled toward her.

"It is against my rules to rob a grave to gain access to the highest levels of the Ghost Market instead of dueling for them fairly. You think you're the first player who has thought of this?"

"It seems I'm the first one to have pulled it off," Zia muttered.

The wolf snarled.

"Check your arrogance, girl. People who think so highly of themselves have a long way to fall." Then he sank back on his haunches, "I think I'll enjoy ripping out your throat. Perhaps going back to level one will remind you of how things work here."

Just as he lunged for her, she threw the blood-mist at his face and *ran.* Seconds stretched before the glass shattered on the ground and exploded, sending her tumbling on the ground. She scrambled to her feet as people shouted and took cover. She didn't bother to turn around and see if Thanatos was still there. She knew she couldn't kill the undead, but she could certainly delay him.

Zia ran faster than she ever had in her life. The market blurred as she cleared the cave entrance and sprinted out of Thanatos's territory. The two ghouls waited for her, but she easily sliced through them with her blades, leaving a bony arm on the ground in her wake.

Zia gripped the tree branch and climbed up, up, and up until she made it to the tallest trunk. She did not stop running until she made her way through the other quarters, all the way to the royal castle.

An ear-splitting howl rang through the sky, and she couldn't help but smile to herself a bit. She had gone toe to toe with death and won. For now.

A firebird flew so closely above her that she could feel the heat of its flames. Before climbing off the trunk and into the castle territory, she screwed off the cork and downed the vial of clear liquid. Then clutched her stomach, and nearly keeled over vomiting. She took slow, shuddering breaths to keep the liquid down.

"It does taste like feet," She grumbled to herself, but when she looked down, her body was gone. Completely disappeared. Zia smiled brightly as she examined her new non-form. Yes, this would be perfect. The map was so close, she could feel it.

She swung off the branch, freezing at the battle cry of a firebird. Yet, when her feet touched the ground, they didn't notice her. With a satisfied smile, she walked right up to the pyramid-shaped castle. It was carved from thick, opaque crystals that glimmered in the moonlight. Vines grew over the crystal, covered in red roses.

When the guards at the front didn't notice her, she began to trust more in the potion. She walked over a high, curved bridge built between two cliffs, with a deadly drop below that ended in a gushing river. Perfectly trimmed roses and vines grew over every archway, and torches burned brightly. She could hear the crackle and pop of their embers as she walked.

Zia made her way through a fragrant spiraling garden. She cleared an ogee-shaped archway that led to an outdoor stone corridor. Careful not to step inside the castle, where there were undoubtedly more guards, she kept her footsteps soundless as she walked toward the forest. A gust of wind blew through the corridor, and her teeth chattered as she walked.

The grounds were built like a labyrinth, and she kept looking up at the stars to make sure she was moving north toward the forest. They twinkled as if in encouragement. Just as she turned around a corner, she saw two guards walking toward her. Men covered head to toe in armor, with bejeweled swords hanging from their belts.

"Did you hear about the Ghost Market?" One of them asked.

"What about it?" The other replied, a hand on his sword.

"Someone blew up half the market with blood-mist powder."

They looked at each other and chuckled.

"My gold is on those mages."

Zia pressed into the wall and held her breath, waiting for them to walk past. They turned a corner, and she could hear their laughs echo on the stone as they passed. She hurried her pace.

Finally, the corridor opened up into a massive stone wall covered in more vines. Treetops swayed gently above it, some of them curling over the wall. Leaves fell and swirled in the icy wind as a breeze picked up. It would be a rough climb, but she could make it. She clamped her teeth together and dug her fingernails into the stone, hauling her body up.

Sweat dribbled down her brow, burning her eyes as she climbed. Her arms shook and ached in protest, and she regretted skipping training yesterday. She swung her leg up toward a stone that was jutting out, but her foot slipped.

"Stop!" She heard someone shout.

Zia looked over her shoulder to see one of the guards from the hall standing there, his sword raised. She blinked, gazing down at her body. The potions master had cheated her. Regardless, there was no way that guard could catch her with a sword.

"An hour my ass," she muttered.

Zia's heart raced as she hauled herself higher, climbing as quickly as she could. She would make it to the top. There would be no other option. It had to work. She could hear the scuffing of boots on stone as she grabbed onto the edge of the wall, hauling her body onto the top.

Right as she rolled onto the edge, she saw three archers had appeared, and two more guards. They aimed their arrows at her.

"*Stop!*" The first guard called again.

Zia gulped down air, her chest shuddering from the climb. Her eyes slid to the forest. It was still pixelated, and there was no telling what would happen. An arrow whistled past her ear, skimming the top of her flesh. She didn't give them the chance to strike true as she leaped off the edge, and the wall shattered. The ground shook and quaked. It felt like her skull was splitting open as darkness swallowed her whole.

"*What* were you thinking?" Mei snarled in a hushed whisper as she gripped Zia from under her armpits and hauled her up. They were both inside of the pyramid-shaped pod. Zia blinked, her blurry vision coming into focus. Her forehead was cold with sweat.

"I...the wall..."

"I saw everything. You're lucky I hid your player from viewing after your little stunt with Thanatos. Everyone's wondering who was stupid enough to blow up half the Ghost Market."

Zia's ears rang.

"My player. Did I—"

"You died. You will go back to level one. You will not be able to look in higher levels for the map. You are restricted to the Ace's Quarter and Stone Quarter."

She blinked back tears, fighting the wave of emotions that threatened to drown her.

"No, p-please. Mei, I only have one week until my dad kicks me out!" She sank to her knees.

"Get up," Mei snapped.

Zia stood, her head hung.

"You are not the first one to have tried breaking passed the boundary, but it is *unbreakable*. Your arrogance cost you any leverage you had in this game," She huffed. Then she lifted Zia's chin so that she would look her in the eyes. "But you still have six days. And we aren't going to waste a single minute of it."

Zia threw her arms around Mei and squeezed her tightly.

"Thank you," She whispered.

Mei cleared her throat.

"Don't thank me. You'll be training double time with me for the next week. Drills on the roof. *Now.*"

Zia shook her head.

"I feel sick. And Hiro—"

"Hiro started blocking footage of you after your little stunt at the Ghost Market. He told me your plan to go for the boundary and was in the control room hacking the signal." She sighed. "Your recklessness draws attention to yourself as a player and could expose me for protecting you." She grabbed Zia's shoulders, "I know you want the world to see your talent, but every time you try to prove yourself, you risk our lives."

Zia felt like someone had poured a pile of sand down her throat. She swallowed several times but nodded.

"Now put your cloak over your head and try not to draw attention to yourself. I'll meet you up there."

Zia shrugged the cloak on. She stepped out of the pod casually, like she was going home for the day. Then she made her way through the crowd, walking at a fairly normal pace, and climbed into the elevator that was passed the gambling table.

The Electi at the tables laughed, pointing out the different players they watched. They spoke in hushed tones about which one of their men likely blew up the Ghost Market. Her blood boiled, but she kept walking until those elevator doors shut.

It felt like the walls narrowed in on her. The horrible silence of the elevator left her with nothing but her own thoughts. She had been such a fool, jeopardizing everything not just for her, but Hiro and Mei too. If Mei was seen helping her, favoring her over the players, it could jeopardize the integrity of the gambling tables.

The ding of the elevator bell interrupted Zia as she stepped onto the icy roof. Luckily the rain had stopped, but harsh winds blew. Mei converted the roof into a training ring. There was a rack of weapons—a bow and arrow, swords, daggers, axes. Zia hadn't been allowed to touch one for her first five years of training, until she could master the basics of breathwork and strength training.

There was also a balance course with beams so thin she could tumble to her death. It seemed like the perfect place to start. Balance had always come easily to her, but her hand-to-hand combat could certainly use work.

She climbed on top of a beam that was hardly wider than her foot and focused narrowly on the path in front of her. All of her thoughts melted away with the need to balance. The icy wind blew harshly, threatening to sway her weight one way, but she kept her limbs loose and focused on taking slow breaths. For a moment, there was nothing but the roaring stillness within her. No games, no maps, no fathers or disappointed friends. Nothing. Peaceful, blissful, *nothing*.

Until the beam shook beneath her, and she tumbled backward onto the concrete roof. Her tailbone rang out in agony, and she lay there for a moment, stunned.

"Serves you right for blowing up the Ghost Market and getting yourself killed, Z." Hiro leaned against the beam with his arms folded over his chest. She had been so consumed by her failure that she hadn't even heard him climb onto the roof.

"Thanatos….and I….had a *teensy* disagreement." Zia panted, trying to muster the strength to get back up. She could already feel the bruise in her lower back.

"A *teensy disagreement?* Z, talk to me. What's going on?"

She shrugged.

"I…I don't know. I thought I could get the map on my own."

"Why?" Hurt flashed across Hiro's eyes.

"Because you have done *enough*! You, and Mei. I thought if I could do it on my own without risking you losing it all, then I could pay you guys back for everything you've done for me…"

He looked up at the sky and sighed.

"What is the point of our pact then, Z? Mei and I see you as family. You don't owe us for that." He took a step toward her, "You're my best friend, and a raging pain in the ass. I wouldn't have it any other way."

She tucked a strand of hair behind her ear, searching for the right words.

"I think the words you're looking for are, 'I'm sorry.'" He grinned.

Zia fought a smile.

"I….am sorry." She said through grit teeth.

He cupped a hand behind his ear.

"Sorry, what was that?"

"I am *sorry!*" She shouted.

"Ah, perhaps a bit louder. I don't think they could hear you in Canada," He chuckled.

Zia lunged for him, but he easily side-stepped her. He whirled around her like mist, faster than she had ever seen him move, and the heel of his palm met her chest with a harsh blow. She went skidding backward on the ground again.

"That's twice now, I have knocked you on your ass."

"When did you start fighting like this?" She blinked slowly, like she had never seen him before.

He just shrugged and grinned in a way he knew would make her see red.

She was on her feet within seconds, circling him. Zia waited for him to strike this time. She knew most of his maneuvers, so when he went for her right side, she flipped over him and dug her elbow into his spine.

He fell face-first to the ground.

They fought for the better part of an hour, until her nose was bloody, and he was limping. Eventually, they stopped counting who won what, and just fell into a dance. That's how Mei had taught them to see fighting—a brutal dance with your partner.

They lay on the ground with their heads side by side, looking up at the cloud-covered sky. It began to drizzle on them, but Zia hardly noticed that her body shivered. Eventually, the elevator doorbell rang out, and Mei stepped onto the roof.

"I see training is going well," She placed a hand on her hip.

Zia was instantly on her feet, her mouth open to give a list of excuses, but she shut it when she saw the look on Mei's face. She could feel the blood crusted dry under her nose.

"You," She pointed at her, "Are on drills. And you," She pointed to her son lying on the ground like a starfish, "Are with me. We're sparring."

Hiro mumbled something about how none of the other kids had to spar with their mother, until Mei gave him a withering stare that would have made a lion cower. He scrambled to his feet, preparing for their first round.

Zia began her drills. Core workouts, thighs, weights, and sprints back and forth on the rooftop. After two hours, when her limbs shook, Mei had them switch. Zia couldn't help but feel awe when she fought Mei. She moved like water, as though she had been dancing through battlefields since she was born. Her breaths were slow and controlled. It had been her first lesson to Zia: movement without breath was just useless circus tricks.

Neither Zia nor Hiro had ever won against Mei, but they improved each round.

They trained on that roof until dawn, when Mei seemed satisfied enough that Zia had learned her lesson. Her eyes burned with exhaustion, and she felt like she could sleep for three days. Hiro had fallen asleep on the ground. He was snoring loudly, with a pile of drool dripping from his chin.

"You can wake him up if you need a ride." Mei huffed.

Zia shook her head.

"It's okay. He needs to rest."

Amusement twinkled in Mei's brown eyes.

"Mei, I really am sorry. I don't deserve all that you guys have done for me. I feel like I haven't...earned your love," She choked on the last words.

Mei gripped both of her shoulders, her eyes softening.

"You don't earn love, honey. It's a gift."

Zia didn't have the words to respond, but she was saved from trying when Mei pulled her in for another one of her bone-crushing hugs and then walked back toward the elevator.

"Are you taking the streets or the roofs?" She asked.

Zia grinned, "The roofs."

"That's my girl," Mei saluted her, and the elevator doors shut.

Zia shrugged her mother's cloak back on and looked at the first light of dawn. The cotton candy sky was lit up in hues of orange and pink. She breathed in the crisp air, despite the smog that coated it. Then she sprinted several steps with all the speed she could muster.

And leaped off the roof.

CHAPTER 3

There are some people you meet, and you just know you've found a once-in-a-lifetime friend. You only really need one true friend. A dance partner to laugh and swirl through this circus of illusions with. That was her for me. I would have followed her anywhere, but I never expected we'd end up here. —Hiro

The rooftops connected in varying levels of height. She climbed and leaped from each one. A preferred method of travel, since walking the streets alone as a woman came with the risk of being snatched or robbed.

The ceramic and asphalt roofs were all falling apart. It took all of her focus not to twist an ankle. Most of the apartments didn't even have windows, just holes in the wall. She heard music and laughter and shouting as she ran on top of each home—so much life happening all at once.

The sun rose with her as she sprinted, offering a bit of warmth and encouragement as she made her way. Zia pushed her body, drowning out every emotion and thought. She had gloriously failed, but she knew in her bones that she would find it in time.

The full morning light covered the entire crumbling city. Plumes of smoke rose from buildings as factory workers began their shifts. The sounds of saws and cranes rang out as construction began—her father had probably already started his shift.

When she finally leaped onto her own roof, her ankles rang out in pain at the impact. She swayed on her feet, fighting to stay awake.

Zia shimmied down the fire escape and through her bedroom window. She didn't even take off her shoes before she stumbled face down in her bed and tumbled into a world of dreams.

Zia was surrounded by black, icy water. Her limbs went numb. She flailed her arms and legs, desperately looking for the surface. There was nothing. No light. No air. She calmed her mind, knowing she only had a few minutes of oxygen.

She swam slowly, using as little energy as possible. It was an empty abyss for as far as she could see. She pressed harder, treading water as she swam up further. She was at the bottom of a deep chasm.

Zia squinted and could barely make out a figure in the distance. At first, it looked like a shark. She fought the urge to gasp for air and swallow a mouth full of water. Then, as the fish grew closer, she realized it was a siren.

The siren had flowing gold hair and a long, coral tale that glowed from bioluminescence. Moss coated the tail, and she wore a top woven from shells and seaweed. She circled around Zia, eyeing her curiously. Zia pointed up toward the surface, asking if there was a way out.

The siren swam inches from her face and smiled sweetly, revealing pearly white teeth. Zia pointed up to the surface again, but the siren cocked her head to the side, eyeing her curiously. There was an unmistakable warmth to her gaze. She held out a slender hand that gripped a piece of parchment.

Zia instantly knew what that parchment was. She went to take the map from the siren when an icy dagger pierced the siren's chest, and she shrieked in pain. Her eyes turned empty, and she sank down below into the darkness, taking the map with her.

Zia screamed and water flooded her lungs just as she saw a redheaded Elymental throw a flaming dagger clean through her heart.

Zia woke up clutching her chest with a phantom pain. She looked down and realized she was still in her knee-high leather boots, covered in sweat and dirt from roof-running. She groaned, rubbing her temples.

"Just *one* night without a dream where I plunge to my death, *please*," She muttered to herself.

Zia eyed the clock. 8:12 PM. If she didn't reach the library by 9 pm, it would be past curfew. She had slept all day. She scrambled for her phone, only to see a whirlwind of text messages from Hiro, Mei, and her father.

Mei: Where are you? You didn't play all day, and you're late for training.
Hiro: Z!!!! I want breakfast. Let's go to the waffle house?
Hiro: WHERE ARE YOU? If I find out you're still asleep...
Hiro: I tried to come in and wake you up, but your dad wouldn't let me.

She clamped her teeth together, suppressing the urge to call her father and shout at him. There were more messages.

Hiro: I'm at Mei's. Get your ass over here, or I'll break a window!
Dad: You have 6 days. Did you pick a job yet?
Dad: I came home and you were asleep in the middle of the day. This kind of lazy behavior will get you nowhere in life.
Dad: Hiro stopped by. I told him he is banned from the house. I knew he and Mei were horrible influences on you. If I find out you've been playing again, you will no longer be welcome here.

Zia growled and threw her phone on the floor, then slumped back into her bed. She focused on her breathing, letting the rage go from a wildfire in her chest to a small candle flame. Her phone buzzed from the floor. It was Hiro.

"I'm sorry, I just woke up," She yawned.

"Two apologies from you in one week! Is it my birthday?" He chuckled.

"So clever. I'll be there in thirty," She grumbled.

"Do you need a ride?" He asked.

It would be safer, but she felt a pang of guilt for what she put him through yesterday.

"No, that's alright. I've got it," She replied.

"See you soon, darling!" He hung up.

Zia raced to get ready, though the five minutes of hot water she got before it turned icy cold was delicious. She braided her hair back and slipped on a pair of black baggy pants, an oversized shirt, her mother's cloak, a larger jacket, men's boots, her cloak, and a few silver daggers Mei had gifted her for a birthday a few years ago. When she walked on the streets, she always dressed like a boy. She pulled her hood over her head and wrapped a scarf around her face so only her eyes would be seen.

Zia opened her window and climbed out of the fire escape, landing on the street pavement. She kept her head down but her focus sharp as she listened to every sound in the street as she walked several blocks.

The air was now hot and humid, like a tropical storm brewing. She could feel the dirt cling to her skin, and the streets smelled like piss and unwashed bodies. She walked with the swagger of a man confident enough to brave the streets at night untouched.

Though she passed a few people, they walked quickly passed her when they saw her daggers on plain display.

She turned a corner and saw Hiro's favorite hole-in-the-wall café, The Magic Bean. The small brick building was dimly lit, but there was always a crowd inside. She adored Mei, but the woman couldn't brew a decent pot to save her life, so the two of them often snuck in their own drinks of choice.

Zia shouldered her way through the rickety glass doors and ordered two cups of coffee and a box of pink, sprinkled donuts for Sam. Since she wouldn't have Hiro with her to charm him into letting her through the entrance, the donuts were her best bet.

Zia kept toward the lights as she walked. She walked in the middle of the road, since getting too close to an alley or blind corner put her in a vulnerable position.

Twenty minutes later, she approached the restaurant and could see the dim yellow lights in the distance. She was covered in grime and sweat—her shower felt completely pointless. But she wasn't dead, so there was that. Zia was about to cross the threshold when she heard marching. All of the waiters at the restaurant scrambled away, and customers hid under tables. Only a scrawny boy who couldn't be more than fifteen remained at the host desk.

Zia raced back toward the dark alley she had marked on her way in. She pressed her body into the brick wall and waited, panting. The police always traveled in packs and didn't bother being the least bit covert. Why would they, when they were worse than any of the gangs in Periculum?

She craned her neck around the corner and saw rows and rows of cops marching. Some of them wore navy blue, others were in camouflaged military uniforms. She frowned. They didn't usually have military policing Periculum, just the borders of the Electi neighborhoods.

Their faces were stony; Empty eyes scanned the street, waiting for someone to dare step out of line. Men and women, each carrying rifles, with tranquilizer darts, pistols and tasers strapped to their hips. A few motorcyclists lead the pack at the front and back. Even from the alley, Zia could see the restaurant host shaking in his boots.

One of the military men shouted for them to stand down and hopped off his motorcycle. They all paused in front of the restaurant. He walked up slowly, with a swagger and a lazy smile plastered to his face.

"You know it's almost past curfew, boy."

Zia could only see the back of the boy's raven-black hair. Both of his hands raised as he shook his head. She glanced at the time. 8:50 pm. They still had ten minutes to shut the restaurant down.

"Are you mute, boy?" He asked, tapping the tip of his rifle on the table. His silver hair gleamed under the dimly lit street.

Zia's palm went toward the dagger at her side and hesitated. It took every ounce of self-restraint not to let her dagger fly.

The man held up his rifle and shot into the sky, grinning all the while. The host screamed and ducked under the table, curling into a ball. The cop bent down into a squat, tilting his head as he looked at him and chuckled.

"Is this how they raise men in Periculum? Highest crime rate, they say. Look at you," The man poked the boy's knee with the tip of his rifle, and the boy curled up further into a ball. "You tell your *boss*, your real boss, that the next time she's late on a payment, we'll shut her down. For good. You hear?"

The boy nodded.

"Good lad," the man said.

He rose to his feet and jerked his chin for the squad to continue marching. Then he straddled his motorbike and whistled, pointing down the street. Zia kept her body pressed toward the wall and held her breath, waiting until they had passed around the corner. She strained her ears, listening for any more footsteps. All she heard was the underground sewage system.

Zia darted toward the restaurant table and found the boy still hiding under the table. All of the other waiters and customers had cleared the restaurant, leaving him alone. He immediately scrambled backward when he saw Zia. She realized what she looked like—a man armed to the teeth.

"It's alright, you're okay," She said gently, pulling the bandana off her face. Recognition flashed across his dark eyes as he sighed in relief. Zia took off her oversized jacket, only wearing her mother's cloak now. She wrapped it around the boy's shoulders, then pulled out one of her knives and pressed the handle into his palm.

"Do you know how to use this?" She asked.

He shook his head, unable to speak.

"Alright. Don't stick yourself with the sharp end."

That earned a small smile from him.

"Let's see if Sam can take you home, you shouldn't walk alone."

The boy shook his head, staring at the ground. He looked so young.

"What's your name?" Zia asked. He was new to the job, but likely only worked there for access to Mei's.

"S-shazi," his lip quivered. "H-he said that Mei…was late on a payment."

Zia pulled the jacket tighter around the boy.

"Don't worry about that. You're okay, come here." She gripped Shazi's elbows and helped him out from under the table, then grabbed the coffee and donuts. The two walked under the dimly lit restaurant, back toward the kitchen.

Sam leaned against the door with his arms folded over his chest. His eyes widened when he saw her, and he brought his hand to his pistol, not recognizing her.

"It's me!" She shouted, holding her hands up.

"Oh joy, she's back," He shook his head, taking his hand off his pistol. Then he noticed Shazi cowering behind her.

"What happened?" He asked.

"Did you not hear the gunshot?" Zia snapped.

"I was dealing with one of the gamblers," He examined the room, looking ready to smash skulls together.

"Relax. No one got hurt, the cops just reminded us of their position, as if we could forget," She laughed bitterly, then squeezed both of Shazi's shoulders, "Can you take him home? They were rough on him," Zia asked. Despite their…less than friendly relationship, she trusted him to protect the boy. Sam blew out a breath.

"Of course. After my shift. I'll escort you myself. You'll be safe, I promise," His golden eyes flicked toward Shazi.

Shazi swallowed, nodding silently as his dark eyebrows knit together. Zia held out the box of doughnuts she had gotten for Sam. He opened it, examining the contents of the box, then looked up at her.

"Just like you like it," She winked, trying to shake off the moment.

His lips twitched into a smile.

"Heard you died yesterday."

She cut him a glare.

"Open the door, would you?"

He chuckled but opened the refrigerator door. Zia brought a hand to Shazi's back as they walked inside. They descended the winding gold staircase. Shazi's shoulders still shook as he walked, and Zia kept that steadying hand at his back.

The theme of the day was the seventies. The band on stage did a cover of a Fleetwood Mac song. Everyone dressed in flair pants, neon-colored glasses, beaded shawls, and funky hats. They smoked cigarettes and laughed with ease like all they had to do was listen to the music, and everything would be alright. It felt like a mockery of what had just happened.

Zia spotted Mei smoking a cigar with one of the gamblers. She blew smoke out of her nose like a dragon, telling the story of how she started the VR library. She smiled when she saw Zia, but when her eyes fell on Shazi, the smile fell instantly.

Mei excused herself and hopped down from the table, leaving the Electi to their bets. She gripped Shazi's shoulders.

"Sweetheart, what's wrong? Talk to me."

The boy explained what happened in hushed tones, his head hung as he spoke. To Mei's credit, if she felt afraid, she didn't show it.

"Don't you worry about them, my friend. I'll take care of it. We'll make sure you have an escort home. In the meantime, go hang out in my office. There's some dessert in there I've been hiding from everyone," She winked.

Shazi nodded and gave Zia a grateful smile. Zia nodded at him.

"You'll be alright."

The boy disappeared in the crowd, scurrying as quickly as he could to her office. Mei turned toward Zia, her face stony.

"Don't mention this to Hiro."

"If you need money—"

"I don't. Everything's fine. Just focus on the map. Look! There he is—" Mei held out both arms for Hiro, pulling him into a tight hug. Hiro winced as his mother crushed his ribs. He was wearing bell bottoms, his top hat, and a button-down shirt. He looked more like a theme park cowboy than a Woodstock hippy with his toothpick, but Zia wouldn't tell him that.

"I come bearing gifts." She bowed in greeting, handing him the latte.

"Did you risk your life to bring me coffee that doesn't taste like stale bean water?"

Zia winked.

"Of course."

"My coffee doesn't taste like stale bean water!" Mei quipped.

Hiro rolled his eyes.

"Mom."

"I birthed you, you know." She arched a brow.

"You can't say that to end every argument."

Mei chuckled and waved him off, giving Zia a warning look as she walked back toward the gambling tables. Zia shoved down the guilt brewing in her stomach as she forced a smile at Hiro. If the gamblers weren't paying their debts, and Mei was late in giving the cops their cut… it wasn't just a matter of the library getting shut down. They could be taken to prison, Mei killed for the data she held. Zia balled her hands into fists. She *would* find the map and give Mei the profits she won to keep the place running.

Hiro looped his arm through hers and led her toward the pods, sipping on his coffee.

"You are the best friend a guy can ask for," He said cheerfully.

She snorted.

"I'll try and be worthy of that statement."

"Meet me at the Ace's Quarter. No detours," He wiggled his eyebrows.

"No detours," She promised.

They took two pods next to each other, and Zia took a deep breath before stepping into hers. She flexed and clenched her palms. She could do this. It was all a game—even if her life depended on it.

Besides—now she *really* had nothing to lose.

Zia stepped into the pod and winced as it scanned her body, knowing she was about to respawn at the beginning. She closed her eyes and felt an electric jolt.

She opened her eyes to the familiar empty ruins. Every player began in the Stone Quarter. The first thing she saw was the riddle written in Old Lemurian. No one had deciphered what it meant over the years, but everyone assumed they were just introductory rules to the game.

Her avatar wore black cargo pants and a simple white shirt. No money. No charms. No weapons. Her heart ached a bit as she thought of her twin blades, but she shoved the thought away. She waded through the loose gravel, making her way to the tree highways.

The Stone Quarter was a ghost town built on crumbling ruins. It also resided next to the local cemetery, The Boneyard. She blinked slowly, remembering Hiro's instructions to meet him at the Ace's Quarter. She made her way to the tree highways, wrapped her arms around a mighty trunk, and hauled herself up. She walked along the highways as an ocean of stars swallowed the sky. She moved swiftly, avoiding the poisoned barb on the moss until she saw the Ace's Quarter in the distance.

The Ace's Quarter was especially busy that day. The market buzzed. The wealthier players took animal forms: phantom panthers, dragons, and Zhulus.

She hopped off the trunk of the tree and landed on the cobblestone street. No one noticed her arrival, luckily, since she didn't have the money to disguise her features yet.

Zia walked along the river. Will-o'-the-wisps bobbed, hovering above the misty waters and lighting her way. The entire city came alive at night. The trunks of the Albizia trees turned translucent and glowed. She could see the energy traveling from their roots up toward the branches. Bright orange fireflies swirled about like burning stars. Turquoise and lilac moss coated the streets, leaving glowing footprints in her wake.

The first person she spotted was Alita. Lemuria's finest blacksmith and a force of nature. A muscled Lemurian woman with dark skin and bright gold eyes—Alita scared the living wits out of absolutely everyone, but she had earned the respect of the realm through her craftsmanship. Part of her head was shaved, and she wore two thick dagger earrings in her ears. Bright blue tattoos covered every inch of her body—she claimed they told the story of every weapon she ever made.

Alita gave Zia a curt nod, not recognizing her avatar. Zia nodded and gave her a half smile back. They weren't exactly friends, but Alita had always been fair to her. She gave her discounts on weapons and told her who to avoid in the markets, claiming that women had to look out for each other, especially in The Trials.

Zia disappeared into the crowd, keeping a low profile as best she could until she could find Hiro. Music floated toward her, beckoning her. Someone played a flute. Her heart twisted at every note—the song was one of terrible sorrow. It sounded like loss.

"STEP RIGHT UP, FOLKS! Get a good look at the wonderfully magnificent siren!" A voice boomed.

She made her way to the center of the quarter square and froze in place.

The siren was crammed in a small tank with a tight lid on it. The water in it was murky, as if they had captured her weeks ago and didn't bother to give her fresh water. Her eyelids drooped as she kept her head in the small air pocket, playing the flute and letting her fractured soul pour out.

Everything about the siren was alluring, and it reminded Zia of a rule Mei had taught her when she first started playing: the most beautiful flowers in the jungle are poisonous. Her red hair flowed below her waist, sticking to her shimmering pink tail. Coral flowers were woven into her small braids. Her large, round eyes were a bright honey color, and her full mouth bore an ironic smile that would have sent most people running. There was something familiar about her that nagged at Zia, like a memory she couldn't quite locate.

Zia could feel her sorrow—she understood it like an echo in her own heart. Sometimes her empathy felt crippling. She either had to shut off her emotions completely, building a wall between her and everyone else, or the floodgates opened.

The siren's eyes flickered toward Zia and she held her gaze. Zia looked away, not wanting to attract attention in case one of the mages spotted her. Yet she could still feel those eyes burning into the back of her neck.

"If you're going to stand there and gawk, folks, cough up some coins!" The mage's voice pierced the crowd. He folded his muscled arms over his chest and smirked at the siren.

Zia recognized him. His name was Dex. He had tried to steal her blades last week, and she had pummeled him back to the first level, making one of the richest gamblers lose their bet. At least he wouldn't recognize her with her true face. There was a power in being invisible, she realized.

She had heard whispers about the other mage, Stefan, who was clearly the brains of their operation. The two of them stole from unassuming players rather than risk their lives by dueling or acquiring artifacts. Men who played not to lose, instead of to win.

Stefan chuckled as he shuffled cards behind his back, promising to fulfill any wish or desire—for the right price, of course. His black nail polish was chipped, and a brutal scar ran along his forearm. A lanky man whose limbs looked like they could be snapped like a twig, but his cunning mind was greater than any brute strength. He had two different colored eyes, one brown and one blue, and his pale skin looked as though it had never seen the sun.

It was hard for her to tell if they were NPC's meant to make the game more difficult or just terrible human beings hiding behind their avatars. Likely the latter.

The siren's tail swished in the small tank. She must have been cramped in that same position for weeks. Zia felt like she had been struck when their eyes met.

It was the same siren from her dream who had given her the map.

Zia knew what she was about to do could just be another impulsive move that earned her more drills from Mei and a one-way ticket back to the Stone Quarter.

But she trusted her dreams.

Zia looked up at the night sky and loosened a breath, reminding herself that she had nothing to lose. Hiro was going to kill her if she survived.

Zia inched her way through the crowd until she stood behind a mercenary that had a saber resting at his back. It was a brutal weapon. The light glinted off the silver, and the curved, sharp blade was carved for hacking off heads.

She grinned wickedly. It would do.

Within seconds, she lifted the weapon off the mercenary and sprinted for the tank. Gasps broke through the crowd as she ran. She raised her arms in the air to bring the saber down on the glass, freeing the siren, but Stefan laughed darkly.

"I wouldn't do that if I were you." Zia paused, turning on her heel to see the mage circling her. He wriggled a finger, "She would last about ten seconds before drying up. Not enough time for you to fight us, make your way through the crowd, and dump her in the river."

Within seconds, a blade was at her throat, and she could feel Dex's hot breath at her ear.

"What's a level one brat doing freeing a monster?"

"The only *monster* here is currently making my eyes water with his stench."

He nicked her throat, tightening his grip with his meaty hands.

"Clever girl. You won't be so clever when I cut off your head."

Then a silver arrow sailed right passed her head, whistling by her ear, and straight into Dex's forehead. He slumped to the floor, his character convulsing and then disappearing. Only one archer in Lemuria had that aim. Zia coughed, gasping for air as she spotted Hiro in the crowd with a silver arrow at the ready for anyone who dared harm her.

Stefan scurried off like a little mouse retreating into the night.

Hiro looked exactly the same as he did in real life, save for the grey robes he wore. He was likely the only player in Lemuria that didn't pay to change his appearance. The only purchases he ever made were for his robes, and his bow and arrows. It had taken him years to gather enough coins for one of Alita's finest creations. Every player was allowed to bring one personal effect with them into The Trials, so naturally, Hiro had brought his top hat. Zia had brought her mother's necklace.

The crowd began closing in on them. A captured siren was worth enough coins to bring any player up ten levels if they sold her. Zia knew it was a matter of seconds before they broke out into a mob. The hunger in their eyes and the violence in the air was palpable.

Zia wrapped her arms around one side of the tank, cutting a desperate glance toward Hiro. He shouldered passed the crowd and quickly grabbed the other side.

Hiro rolled his eyes.

"You just *had* to go saving one of the deadliest creatures in The Trials, didn't you?"

Zia grit her teeth. "I know, I know," she half panted.

Hiro sighed, but didn't question her further. They lifted the glass case. It was immensely heavy, but their heightened Lemurian strength made it possible to move her. The crowd blocked their path. Many of them had weapons at the ready. Zia and Hiro were skilled fighters, thanks to Mei, but they were entirely outnumbered.

A sharp cracking sound filled the square. Black smoke exploded, obliterating a third of the crowd as their players glitched and disappeared. Zia nearly dropped the tank as she coughed at the smoke. A strong hand gripped her arm, and she whirled to see Alita standing there.

"*Move*, you two. I'll watch your back," She whispered harshly.

"How did you know it was me?" Zia whispered back.

"The necklace you always wear," Alita grunted, "Now *move*."

Alita had used the blood-mist powder from the Ghost Market. The fact that she wasted such a precious powder on helping them made little sense, but Zia was grateful for the window of escape.

Hiro grunted at the weight of the tank as they moved swiftly, with Alita escorting them to the river. The market was still in a frenzy, with everyone lost in the blinding smoke. Zia wasn't sure how much time it would give them, but she doubted it would last beyond a few minutes.

They finally made it to the water's edge. A few Lemurians stopped to gawk at them, then saw the burning look in Alita's eyes, the machete strapped to her back, and her pointed teeth. All of them fled.

They set the glass case down sideways so the siren could easily slither into the river waters. Zia looked at the siren, who pressed her webbed hands against the glass.

"I'm going to free you," she said in warning.

"Yes, and please don't eat us," Hiro added.

Zia arched a brow, and he held his hands up innocently.

She took the saber from behind her back and wedged the top of the glass case open. The siren instantly slithered out of the murky waters and made her way into the river. Zia assumed she was gone, but then the siren poked her head above the river's surface, her tail swishing in the twinkling rapids.

"Why?" the siren asked hesitantly. Her voice was magnetic, and Zia easily understood how so many players became enthralled in their magic. Zia crouched by the river's edge, all too aware that she could be dragged beneath the surface of those icy waters within seconds.

"I don't know. I just felt you, like there was a thread between us..." Zia replied quietly.

It was the only honest answer she could offer. The siren nodded in understanding, her features softening. She examined Zia, and then her eyes widened when she caught sight of Zia's necklace. The whole game froze in time, the siren's face momentarily glitching. Not once in Lemuria's entire history had there been a glitch. The coding was flawless. Which meant they had somehow stumbled upon something they weren't supposed to.

The siren began to sing a song in Old Lemurian. The hair on the back of Zia's neck stood up as she felt a faint whisper of recognition.

Hiro cleared his throat and said gently, "Can we get that in English?"

Amusement danced in the siren's golden eyes, and she sang in English that time. A part of Zia knew what the song was before she spoke it in their tongue. The sirens were the oldest creatures in Lemuria. They still spoke the ancient language. She translated the riddle that no one had been able to decipher in the Stone Quarter.

"True power is held
by humble hands.
The bridge will restore
balance across the lands.
To wield the stones,
one needs the key
passed down through
blood of the royal ancestry.
Where better to hide a lock
than with those who will never talk?"

"Do you have any idea what she's saying?" Hiro muttered, scratching his nose.

Zia had gone completely still, puzzling over every line.

"The key..." She frowned, looking at the siren in question.

The siren looked pointedly at her mother's necklace. It glowed in the faint light of the will-o-the-wisps. Understanding settled into Zia as some of the pieces of her fractured life clicked into place.

"Remember, daughter of Sahara. Destiny is a path that is open to everyone but walked by few," The siren said with a formal authority that made Zia's skin crawl. Time resumed, and then the siren disappeared beneath the rapid waters.

Zia's eyes widened at the sound of her mother's name, and Hiro's breath hitched.

Zia glanced toward Alita, who smiled at her knowingly.

"You knew," Zia whispered.

Alita shrugged, resting a hand on her hip.

"I knew you had the key the first time you walked into my shop."

Zia swallowed, her heart racing.

"Why didn't you rip it from my neck?" She kept her voice low.

Alita glanced around the quarter, making sure no one watched them.

"There is far more at stake in The Trials than finding the map, girl."

The voices from the crowd grew closer. The black smoke had cleared, and they would be furious at losing the chance to earn so many coins. Zia dug her nails into Hiro's forearm and hauled him up off the ground.

"We have to go. *Now*," she urged.

He opened his mouth to demand an explanation, but Alita hushed him.

"Wait until you get to the Stone Quarter. Even the trees are listening here."

He dipped his chin in acknowledgment and was about to walk away when Alita flung her machete out in front of him. He nearly lost his balance.

"An uncomfortable truth is better than a comfortable falsehood, Hiro Sato. Tell her soon."

Hiro's cheeks reddened and he avoided Zia's gaze. She didn't have time to unravel what Alita meant. Zia turned to her, a thousand questions thundering through her at once. The fierce woman that had looked out for her, and now saved her life more than once.

"Thank you," Zia said, sheathing the saber behind her back.

"*Go*," was Alita's only response as she jerked her chin toward the tree highways.

They broke into a run, keeping their footsteps as silent as they could. Her breath hitched as question after question tore at her. They remained silent, not daring to reveal anything in case someone listened.

Zia hauled herself onto the massive tree trunk and bent down to give Hiro a hand up. He muttered his thanks, and they pressed on. Her lungs burned as she pushed her body beyond its limits, hopping from tree to tree and running with all the speed she could muster. Her ankle contracted in pain as she nearly twisted it, but she kept going.

They made it to the Stone Quarter. As per usual, there was not a single player in sight. Silence enveloped the empty square. Dimly lit torches sputtered under the dark night, causing shadows to dance on the wall. The riddle carved on the stone wall now seemed like a joke. Zia couldn't believe it took her so long to figure out that the sirens would be the only ones capable of translating it. How perfect, to hide the answer within a creature everyone would overlook.

"Why are we here, Z?" Hiro whispered.

She shimmied down the tree, and dust kicked up at her landing. No one bothered to clean the crumbling ruins. Zia waltzed over to the edge of the square, looking out at the Boneyard. Hiro made a *plunk* sound as he landed, and his footsteps hurried behind her.

"*Where better to hide a lock than with those who will never talk?*" She repeated the line from the riddle. Only the dead could keep such a secret. The map was hidden somewhere in the Boneyard. Everyone had assumed it dwelled within the castle, including her, but the answers were always hidden in the most unlikely places.

"Why do you always manage to get us into the worst possible situations?" Hiro whined.

"Scared of the dead, Hiro?" Zia grinned crookedly.

He hopped over the Stone Quarter wall and stepped onto the grass of the Boneyard.

"Yes, darling. And you should be, too. They don't like to be disturbed."

She knew he was right. The ghouls she encountered the other day had nearly dragged her into the underworld, seeking to drain her of every last drop of life. It didn't matter now. Not when they had a shot at freedom.

Zia walked ahead of Hiro, carrying her stolen weapon. Hiro drew an arrow and kept a close pace behind her. There was no one else she would trust to watch her back. Her mother's necklace felt warm against her chest.

The silence of the Boneyard felt eerie. Even the crickets didn't dare go near it. Many graves existed there for Lemuria's forgotten. A small sliver of land ended just near the forest's edge with tall headstones and mausoleums speckled throughout. The gates were made of sharp bone, with Lemurian words engraved on them—a warning not to enter.

Zia felt a strange thread again, pulling her toward the edge of the forest. She was careful as she neared the edge, sensing the electric wall. The wilting grass poked her bare feet. Hiro let out a yelp as he stepped on something sharp, and she immediately hushed him.

The thread that had drawn her to this spot seemed to go taut. Zia stopped at a grave that had been carved into the ground, covered by thick vines and mold. Her breath hitched as she saw the markings on top.

It was the symbol of the stones. The three of them joined together, with a small hole in the middle with a familiar shape. An animal screeched in the distance, and Hiro nearly jumped ten feet in the air.

"Relax," she said gently.

"Relax, Hiro. We're not surrounded by dead people and about to be hunted by every player in the game or anything," he muttered to himself.

Zia fought a smile as she turned her attention back to the carvings. She sheathed the saber and took off her mother's necklace for the first time in her life. It glowed brightly in the dark void of the Boneyard.

"Z, wait—" Hiro held out a hand. He opened his virtual wallet and pulled out an item. It expanded, and then he held her blades, the glittering sapphires shining in the moonlight.

"I bought them back for you," He handed them to her.

"I—that must have cost you everything you have!" She gaped.

He rubbed his neck.

"I know what they mean to you."

Zia's eyes lined with silver. She threw her arms around his neck, reigning in her half sob. He hugged her back. "Hiro—I think this is really it."

"You did it," He smiled.

"*We* did it," she corrected.

With a shuddering breath, Zia placed her mother's necklace in the small hole of the tomb, unsurprised when it fit perfectly. It felt like it had always belonged there. The moment stretched on for what felt like an eternity, and then the grave hissed open, revealing a dark box that was empty save for a single piece of paper that rested within.

Magic left the ancient scroll perfectly preserved. Zia's hands shook as she carefully took it out, unbinding the string around it. The page looked like it had been torn from something, its edges jagged.

It wasn't just a map to the stones. It was a map of all of Lemuria. Every secret passageway or territory that existed. Almost as though it was a real place.

"Hiro," Zia's face turned ashen.

She forced herself to meet his eyes.

"I need you to read this carefully before I destroy it," her voice trembled, as though the words wouldn't come out fast enough.

"*What?*" He nearly shouted.

"You have a photographic memory, Hiro. We have to destroy this map before it falls into the wrong hands. This isn't a game anymore."

He shook his head and took the map from her clammy hands, studying it for a minute before handing it to her and nodding. He handed her a flaming lotus flower from his virtual pocket, and she lit the map on fire, not noticing the ashes float away on the wind.

As the paper finally burned into nothing, Hiro's gaze shifted back to Zia and he blinked rapidly, trying to comprehend the sight before him. Following his gaze, she looked down at their bodies. Light shone from them, transforming their avatars as they reached level after level. Within minutes, she and Hiro reached the highest level possible.

And then, as though someone had simply flipped a switch, a sharp pain shot through Zia's head and the world went dark. When she opened her eyes, she was face down on the ground in her pod. She rose to her feet and had to manually force the doors open.

Zia slowly stepped out of her pod and turned to see Hiro stumble out of his. They scanned the room, only to find every single person in the library staring at them. All of the monitors had shut off. Every player had deserted their pod.

By finding the map, Zia and Hiro had ended The Trials.

And standing there, leaning against the nearest pod, was a man whose face she would never forget. His familiar, twinkling green eyes locked on hers, his lips slightly parted in disbelief. Her heart leaped from her chest in recognition.

It was the man from her dream.

CHAPTER 4

I loved her; you know? Not the kind of casual love we toss around like we're noting the weather. I loved her like she was my own. She had a hellish grin across her face. Teeth that sank into the marrow of life. She laughed when people tried to tell her who she could or couldn't be. And that's because she was no stranger to herself. She knew security was too steep a price to trade for her wildness. She was worth fighting for, because she represented one of the most dangerously powerful things on earth: something worth living for. —Mei

The man stared at Zia with a gleam in his eyes, like she was a mystery he could spend his whole life unraveling. He leaned against the pod with such ease, completely unconcerned by the fact that a room full of people was watching them.

The music halted. The jazz band had disappeared from the stage and was nowhere to be seen. Only the gamblers remained at the edge of their seats. Every cell phone, TV, and VR monitor had shut off like someone cut the power to everything but the lights.

Zia steadied herself. She couldn't reveal how unnerved she was. She looked the stranger up and down, sizing him up like he was an opponent. He looked to be around twenty years old, but there was a level of confidence in him that made him seem far older. As though everything he had lived through was written across that handsome, rugged face.

He was at least a foot taller than her—around the same height her avatar had been. He was wearing a leather jacket, gloves, and black pants. The only skin that showed was his sun-kissed face. He had a strong jaw, curly dark hair, and a full mouth that was now smirking at her. Even beneath his clothes, his broad shoulders and packed muscles were noticeable. It was obvious he had spent much of his life training. Whether his head was filled with sawdust or he had a cleverness to match the brute strength was the question.

He took a few steps toward her with an unnatural level of grace, and she spent a split-second debating whether to run or whack him upside the head. A playful grin spread across his face, like he knew the silent debate she was having. He had the kind of charm that, had her mother been alive, she would have warned her about.

He extended a gloved hand, "I'm Jace."

His silken voice sounded exactly as it had in Zia's dreams, when he shouted at her just before she had leaped over that waterfall. She didn't know what to make of it. Had he dreamed of her before, too?

Zia stared at his hand blankly but did not take it.

"What's your name?" Jace asked, bringing his hand back to his side.

"Why should I tell you?" Zia narrowed her eyes. She did her best to ignore that he was the most attractive person she had ever come across, mainly because he seemed to be all too aware of it.

"Because Jace is the first person to ever have bet on you, Zia Alexander," a familiar booming voice answered for him.

Mei was strutting through the aisles of the pods in her purple suit, the *click-clack* of her heels echoing through the library. A broad smile was plastered to her face that didn't touch her eyes. Zia could feel her terror.

Jace tilted his head to the side.

"Yes, you've just made me a very wealthy man."

Zia did the math in her head. If he had bet on her just before she won The Trials, then he won the coin of every gambler in Mei's VR Library. Which made him, Zia, and Hiro the richest people on the continent, and put them straight to the top of the government's WANTED list. Zia ran her thumb over the crypto card in her pocket, checking to make sure it was still there.

Mei's hands were suddenly behind both of their backs, ushering them up toward the stage with a strength that said it was not optional. The top of Mei's head barely went up to Jace's broad chest, but he didn't dare question her as she nudged him onwards.

Zia looked over her shoulder, desperately searching for Hiro, but he was nowhere to be found. Her legs felt wobbly as she reluctantly stepped onto the marble stage with Jace. Harsh, white lights blinded her as she looked around at the library.

The silence was eerie, and it suddenly felt like she was in a tomb. Gamblers remained in their seats, waiting to see what would happen next. She spotted Atticus Ashwood, his nostrils flaring as he bared his unnaturally white teeth at her—all of his father's coin that he had gambled now belonged to them.

Her identity being revealed was the least of her concerns. Zia needed to know if the gamblers had been watching her when she found the map. If they knew that she had burned it, and that Hiro was the only person alive who knew the coordinates of the stones, they would go after him. She had to protect him. Where the hell *was* he?

Mei tapped the rose gold microphone and it made a screeching sound. Her forehead was covered in a sheen of sweat, and all the color had leached from her face.

"*Congratulations, Zia Alexander!* You've reached the highest level of The Trials," she said with a cheerfulness that was followed by a terrible pause. Not a single person in the library clapped. Mei swallowed.

"My associate here will escort you and Jace out to collect your prize winnings. I thank you all for playing and apologize for any technical difficulties here in the library. We'll get everything up and running shortly!"

Mei shook Zia's hand gruffly, and she felt the paper inside of her palm. She quickly pocketed it into her cloak. Before Zia could respond, Sam was already grabbing her by the neck with a grip that would surely bruise, forcing her out of the library as quickly as possible with Jace trailing behind them. Before she knew it, they had been hauled up the golden staircase and shoved out the refrigerator door.

Jace stood protectively close to her in the kitchen, towering over Sam. Zia was about to ask why he was acting like a territorial ape, but Sam interrupted her by passing Jace a new crypto card that would be filled with more money than any sane person could ever need. Jace gave him a swift nod of thanks.

"Sam, what's going on?" Zia's voice trembled as she spoke.

Sam took both pistols out of their holsters and stepped back into the VR library. He paused just before he shut the door, those golden eyes filled with sorrow.

"Hurry now, Zia, you don't have much time."

He was gone before she could say anything else.

Sam had made it seem like he never cared about her, let alone bothered to learn her name. Perhaps he knew more than he had let on, and Mei had given him instructions for if The Map was ever found.

Jace stood in a wide stance with his arms folded over his chest. It was difficult *not* to notice those powerful legs or the sheer dominance that radiated from him. She was about to tell him to piss off, but decided her energy was better spent finding Hiro.

Jace seemed completely unruffled by the chaos of the past few minutes. He never took his eyes off her. Did he ever stop *staring*? She grunted, ignoring him as she pulled the crinkled note out of her cloak pocket, frantically reading Mei's messy handwriting.

I cut the power just before you found The Map, but everyone will have been notified of your score by now. You have twenty minutes at most before they come for you. Go to your dad's room and remove the photo of your mother from the wall. There's a safe there. The passcode is her birthday. Jace will know what to do with what's inside. Hiro's waiting for you in the van around the corner. DO NOT LEAVE EITHER OF THEIR SIDES. They're your only hope of survival, and with them, you have a shot at finding treasures far more valuable than the stones.

I love you,
Mei

The world started spinning. Zia felt nauseous and nearly collapsed on the floor when strong, sturdy arms wrapped around her waist and hauled her up. The comforting scent of sandalwood flooded her nose. She could feel the warmth of his breath as he whispered in the shell of her ear.

"You won't get very far if you faint," He grunted.

She tried to elbow him in the ribs, and he released her. He tilted his head to the side, assessing her like a soldier.

"If you want the answers that you've sought your entire life, you need to come with me now." His voice softened, and she tried to hide her surprise at the tone.

Zia blinked, weighing the truth of his words. Mei didn't trust anyone outside of family, so if she told Zia to stay with him, it was for a good reason. Besides, he was the first person to ever bet on her. That counted for something. She would pry the answers about who he was and why he was in her dream from him later.

The sound of a pistol firing made her jump out of his arms. She moved to yank open the refrigerator door as screams rose, but Sam had locked it from the inside. Jace grabbed her from behind and dragged her out of the restaurant.

"We have to help them!" She shrieked, trying to fight her way out of his grip.

More gun fires went off. It sounded like a rifle. Even just one bullet could melt a person's face off, let alone several rounds like she just heard. Only the military and select Elite had them. Zia was horrified to think that Mei could have been on the receiving end of that blast.

A half sob broke from her as she yanked at the door handle desperately. All of the waiters and customers in the restaurant had vanished, as though Mei had warned them to run. Zia nearly choked on her horror. What would happen to her?

She stomped on Jace's foot and elbowed him in the ribs, then bit down hard on his forearm. Most men would have crumbled at the maneuver, at least enough to release her, but he held her with unnatural strength.

"It's too late. Hiro's waiting for us. His life is in danger too. Mei may have cut the power, but the rest of the world was watching. How long do you think it will be until they find you two?" He growled.

"Who gives a damn? The government can have the money back! *Mei* is in there!" She shrieked.

"Mei knew what she was doing when she sealed those doors. She is one of our best, so she has a chance, but she is sacrificing herself to give you a shot at surviving!" He barked.

Zia was hyperventilating. Her breathing exercises felt like a joke. He squeezed her tighter, and she could feel her heart rate slowing down.

He lowered his voice.

"It's not about the money, Zia. You saw that map. Don't you get it? This was never just a game."

She relaxed in his grip—a silent concession. He was right. When Jace was certain she wasn't going to throttle him again, he let her go. They faced each other for a moment. His breath shortened under her stare. The rain was pouring mercilessly, and his silky dark hair now stuck to his forehead. The gold specks in his green eyes glowed brightly. It wasn't just Mei giving her a sign, it was her dreams, too. She had to trust him—at least temporarily.

They spotted Hiro's van right where Mei said it would be. Betty was parked on the street corner, the engine already running. Zia sprinted toward the van, and Jace kept pace right beside her. She squinted her eyes in the rain, ignoring the large drops that felt like icy daggers, blinding her. They made it to Betty, and Zia yanked the door open. Her face crumpled with relief as she saw Hiro in the driver's seat.

He spotted Jace and gave him a nod of recognition. They *knew* each other.

Jace pulled the sliding door open and hauled himself to the back seat. Before the door even clicked shut, Hiro slammed on the gas pedal, driving at a speed Zia didn't think was possible for the car. Everything about him seemed different. His usual mocking grin was gone. His knuckles were white as he gripped the steering wheel, skirting around traffic to get to her dad's apartment.

"Someone tell me what the *hell* is going on!" she barked.

Zia looked like a seething wet rat. Her clothes were soaked through, and she couldn't tell if she was shaking from shock or the cold. She turned her full torso toward Hiro, waiting for an explanation.

"We never thought you'd find the map this early," Hiro said quietly. He avoided her gaze, keeping his eyes fixed on the road as he ran red light after red light.

An uncomfortable truth is better than a comfortable falsehood, Hiro Sato. Tell her soon.

Alita had said those words just after Zia figured out where the map was.

"What are you not telling me, Hiro? Why did The Trials end as soon as we found it?" She was nearly shouting. They never kept things from each other. Zia felt like she was talking to a completely different person.

Jace cleared his throat. He was casually slouched in his seat like they were on the way to the park and not outrunning every cop and assassin in the country.

"The map ended The Trials because it leads to the *real* realm of Lemuria, where I am from, and where the stones are hidden. The map doesn't show *where* the stones are, it shows how to get into our world," He leaned forward until his face was inches from hers. "It is the lost page of a book that was stolen from a tyrant king and contains a prophecy that tells us *how* to wield the stones. By hiding the stones in Lemuria and the book in the human world, neither species could gain too much power," Jace explained bluntly, as though he was giving her a battle report. She had to admit, it was nice to meet someone as direct as she was.

Zia's head roared. She pulled her knees into her chest, trying to discern the truth.

"And you knew this?" She asked Hiro.

"Z…. I'm kind of Lemurian," he replied, his ears turning red.

"You're kind of *what?*" Her nails dug into her palms, leaving little crescent-shaped moon marks on her skin.

Jace chuckled, "This is going to be fun."

Hiro slammed on his brakes with unnecessary force at a red light and Jace nearly went flying into the windshield. Zia knew he had done it on purpose. Jace whacked Hiro on the back of the head and scowled, then leaned back in the seat and clasped his hands behind his head.

"Look, we don't have much time—"

"Then *make* time," Zia snapped.

Hiro sighed, "I was born in Lemuria. Mei and your mom were best friends. Your mom saved her life, which is a story for another time. Eighteen years ago, The Architect stole the *Book of Lemuria* from a healer and ripped the map out of it. They created the game and hid the map within, thinking the human realm was the safest place to keep it— especially in a game that so openly exposed our realm without anyone realizing that it's a real place," He loosened a shuddering breath, "It kept the Lemurians from going after it. The king ordered your mom to the human realm alone, with the task of finding the map, but she deliberately chose not to play in The Trials. The last thing she wanted was for him to find the stones." Hiro nearly hit a dumpster as he made a sharp turn down her street. They were a few blocks away from her dad's.

"Your mom met your dad and fell in love. She never meant to get pregnant. It's forbidden for us to mate with humans. We're sworn to keep our true existence secret. She knew the king would kill you both if he knew, and so she left when you were born, returning to Lemuria and telling him she failed her task in finding the map." His eyes darkened at that.

"She begged Mei to help her. She didn't know how much of her Lemurian blood would show up in you—if you would have magic or look like one of us. The government has long since known of our existence. Ever since The Trials started, the decentralization has weakened their control. If they knew one of us existed amongst them and could lead them to the map...they would have done unspeakable things to you, Z." He slammed his hand on the car horn, running another red light.

Hiro glanced over at her, making sure she was still breathing.

"I was sent here with Mei to protect you. We promised your mom. It's why Mei started her VR library. It's why she trained you in our fighting techniques. It's why I got you into The Trials in the first place, though I never dreamed we'd find the map. We made sure that one day, you would be prepared for the truth, and you would be ready." He parked in front of her house and cut off the engine. Thunder crackled above.

Jace leaped out of the car and ran ahead to make sure the apartment was clear. Zia looked back at Hiro, her eyes burned with hot tears.

"Is she alive?" she whispered.

He didn't answer.

"IS SHE ALIVE?" Zia shouted, not caring how feral she looked.

Hiro took her hand in both of his, blowing warmth onto her icy fingers.

"Yes, Z. She's alive, but I don't know for how long. The only way to free her and keep the stones from falling into the wrong hands is to find them first. If you can wield them, you'll be able to overthrow him. I know you have a million questions, and I'm so sorry I didn't tell you the truth. Sorrier than you can know, but it was to protect you. Please believe me."

Zia was feeling too much at once. She despised that everyone had lied to her like she was some fragile thing that couldn't handle the truth. *It was to protect you.* Well, anytime someone tried to protect her, they automatically ended up hurting her.

It wasn't just Hiro who had lied to her, it was her dad. He let her believe that her mother had died—that it had been her fault. She couldn't sort out one betrayal from another. Yet this wasn't the time to figure it all out. If it was true that Lemuria was a real place, and her mother was there, then Hiro and Jace were her best chance at finding her.

She had burned the map, which made Hiro and his memory her only hope. Mei was right: there were treasures far more valuable to find than the stones. Zia slowed her breathing, using her exercises to still her mind. The tumbling waves of her emotions ebbed, and a calm settled into her.

Hiro waited silently, aching for her to say something—to yell or cry or forgive him. She stared out through the windshield, watching the rain stream down the glass. Her best friend was Lemurian, and so was Mei, and so was her mother. Which made her...half-Lemurian?

Jace opened her door, interrupting the rabbit hole she had fallen down in her mind. He offered his hand, not saying a word about the tears that still clung to her cheeks. She couldn't stand the flicker of sympathy in his gaze, it made her want to elbow him in the ribs again.

"The perimeter is clear. We have to move now," He said gruffly.

Zia hesitated, looking into the eyes that had haunted her dreams. Her gaze flickered to his outstretched hand that she had refused to take before.

"You might be more stubborn than me," He winked.

Stubborn to the point of recklessness. Zia shrugged, tossing her damp hair over her shoulder.

"I'll take that as a compliment."

She took Jace's hand and ignored the guilt written all across Hiro's face as he circled around the car. The two of them flanked her as she ran right up to the front door. Zia quickly fished for her keys in her coat pocket and unlocked the six bolts. She sighed in relief that her dad wasn't home.

They raced upstairs to her dad's bedroom. She had only been in it a few times as a child, before he had threatened to ground her with no visits from Hiro. Her chest squeezed in pain. How had they lied to her for so long?

Her dad's bedroom reflected the rest of the house. He had a small bed pressed against the corner of the window and a single wooden dresser that he made himself. The only decorative thing in the room was the photograph that hung on the wall of him and her mother—the same one that she had on her nightstand.

Zia took the photo off the wall, carefully placing it on the floor. A round metal safe was revealed, right where Mei said it would be. She swallowed and punched in the combination of her mother's birthday. She was born on the summer solstice, the brightest day of the year.

The safe hissed and clicked open. The old, musty book was in the front, but a shiny gleam of silver caught her eye toward the back. She took out the book, blowing on the dusty cover, and handed it to Jace. He studied it, and his eyebrows nearly raised to his hairline.

"All my life, I've heard stories about this thing. It's exactly as the king described..." he trailed off. Zia barely heard him.

She reached in and grabbed the silver that caught her eye. She pulled out two familiar blades that shimmered even in the dull light. They were the exact same ones that Alita had crafted for her in The Trials. Even Hiro's jaw dropped at the sapphire jewels glittering at the hilt.

"They were Sahara's," Her dad said, his voice hoarse. They nearly all jumped at the sound. No one had heard him come in.

He blinked back tears as he looked at Zia for what felt like the first time. Zia's knees nearly buckled at the sight of him. He was in the same outfit he always wore: old blue jeans, a rock band t-shirt, and his wedding ring which was a silver band with a small, indigo crystal in its center.

Alita had known her mother's name. She had known her well enough to give Zia little clues, teaching her to use the blades that she would one day need to wield in real life. This meant that her mother must have played in The Trials before. There were too many pieces to the puzzle.

Hot tears streamed down Zia's face.

"She's alive. She's alive, and you let me think her death was my *fault!*" Zia shouted at him. Red spots clouded her vision.

Her dad took a step toward her, but she raised the blades. He froze.

"I'm sorry, honey. It was the only way they would never come looking for you, and you would never go looking for her. Your very existence would be a death sentence for you both."

He never called her honey in her life. Not once. He wiped his nose with his sleeve and nodded toward the blades.

"Take them. They were always meant to be yours, when it was time. I never wanted you playing in The Trials. I was protecting you from all of this."

"You were *protecting* me from the truth." she snapped.

"I was protecting you from pain," he choked on a sob.

She shook her head.

"Pain is a part of life, and by trying to shield me from it you only caused more of it."

Jace gently squeezed her shoulder, "Zia, we have to go."

Hiro looked out the window and nodded his head in confirmation. A black car had pulled up. It was already too late. Her dad walked over to his closet and pulled a rifle out from behind his hanging clothes. Zia's eyes widened. It should have been impossible for him to own one unless Mei had it smuggled in. He unclicked the safety and jerked his chin toward the door.

"Go out the fire escape. I'll buy you time. When you see Sahara again… tell her I—" his voice cracked.

"Tell her that I never stopped loving her. Not for a single moment. That she was the north star that always guided me back home, and I will see her again someday. In this world or the next."

He didn't wipe the tears that flowed from his eyes. Zia had never once seen him cry, yet behind the tears was that formidable strength, that stubborn will that he had passed onto her. He may not have been the father she needed, but he would go down swinging so she had a fighting chance at survival and seeing her mom again. She felt like she was going to break apart when Hiro put a warm, steadying hand on her back.

Zia nodded at her dad, looking at him for what could very well be the last time.

"I'll tell her."

Zia couldn't find the words to say goodbye. She tore her eyes away from him and ran out the door toward the window in her bedroom. She slid it open and stepped out onto the fire escape, Jace and Hiro trailing behind her. The rain drowned out the noise of their footsteps as they moved as quietly as possible down the winding metal stairs. When they reached the bottom, they hid behind the brick wall of the apartment. They were fifteen feet from Betty, but the black car sat between them and freedom.

Jace took off his jacket, revealing the tattoos that were inked onto his golden-tanned skin. They were written in Lemurian, she recognized the language from The Trials. He still wore the thick, black leather gloves. She knew better than to ask him why, despite it making no sense for him to wear gloves in the midst of August. He bore several knives, all hidden along his body. She spotted four of them but knew there were more.

"Are we going to—" she started, but Jace interrupted her.

"I can hear the heartbeats of two men in the black car. They most likely have guns. The odds aren't looking great."

Zia could barely process the fact that he said he could *hear* their heartbeats. Lemurian senses were far sharper than those of a human.

"Z and I thrive with terrible odds. It keeps life interesting," Hiro tried at humor, but it was half-hearted. Zia took her blades out from behind her back. Hiro was right—her whole life had been a gamble, but never once had she hesitated to keep going. She certainly wasn't going to start now.

Zia sprinted out into the rain and heard Jace curse behind her. Shots immediately rang out. She ducked and rolled. The bullet narrowly missed her by a few inches, but shattered part of the sidewalk. Her shoulder groaned at the impact of the cement.

Jace immediately followed her and hurled his knives through the window, directly into the chests of the two men. He then sent two more flying at the tires, they flattened within seconds. Zia winced as he went to grab the weapons, moving faster than anyone she had ever seen.

They made it into Betty, nearly ripping the door off its hinges as they climbed inside. The engine roared to life, the chipper Japanese greeting making a mockery of their situation. Hiro slammed on the gas, driving twice as fast as he had before. Zia didn't dare look back at the apartment. She silently prayed her dad was able to make it out in time. That Mei was alright.

They drove several miles in silence and didn't dare speak until they reached the city limits. They made it onto the highway without anyone following them. Wherever they were going, they would need an Electi pass to make it onto the toll road. It was the only path out of Periculum. Luckily, they all now happened to be one of The Electi since their winnings from The Trials were monumental and transcended any class lines. They just had to hope luck was on their side, and that their faces hadn't been plastered all over the system's wanted list.

Jace broke the tense silence first. He was cleaning the blood of the two men from his blades when he loosened a breathy laugh. His whole body shook. Zia was startled by the sound, whirling her head around to glare at him. It only made him laugh harder, until he was howling and nearly falling onto the floor of the car.

"*What is so funny?*" she demanded.

He steadied his breath, doing his best not to lose it again.

"I have been the commander of Lemuria's deadliest legion for a century, and in all of my battles, in all of my training, I have *never* come across someone so prone to getting killed, who somehow manages to clumsily escape a situation so unscathed."

"She's the lucky cricket," Hiro muttered, his lips twitching into a smile. He looked at Zia as if to say, *Do you know how hard it's been to keep you alive the past 18 years?*

"Good, because she'll need luck to get through the entrance to Lemuria," Jace replied, wiping the tears from his face. It was true. Both the stones and her mother were there. Making it through the entrance was not optional.

Zia didn't know what to make of either of them. She was in a car with her best friend - who turned out to be a creature from a mythical realm - and an ancient warrior who was a complete stranger who had somehow haunted her dreams. As always, her life was a perfect mess.

"And where is the entrance?" she asked between her teeth.

Hiro turned toward her and gave her that crooked grin she had seen so many times in her life, placing a toothpick in his mouth.

"There are several around the world, of course. The closest one to us is in Mount Shasta."

She had heard of the mountain before, it was in Northern California. Mount Shasta was in a neutral territory, not belonging to any class line. No one was allowed to live on the mountain but the wild animals, though it was rumored there were some squatters who were brave enough to camp on the deadly, snow-covered peaks.

It would be at least an eight-hour drive. That was if Betty didn't break down, or they weren't killed by assassins.

The sun was beginning to set, its golden rays giving Zia one last chance to see Periculum. Fallen Angels was the only place she had ever known. The lights in the crumbling buildings winking out into nothing. There was a city-wide blackout.

Her father and Mei might have died to give them a shot at finding the stones. The thought nearly tore her apart. She couldn't think about that now—she couldn't let herself feel the hollowness in her chest, or the sliver of hope that they might have made it.

Hiro had lied to her, but he was still her family, and had sacrificed a life growing up in his home to protect her. Zia wondered who he would have become, had he grown up there.

She knew it would take time for her to forgive his dishonesty, but if they were to have a shot at survival, they would have to honor the pact they had always sworn by.

"Together?" she asked.

Hiro's eyes shone brightly with hope.

"Together."

They stared out into the open road, watching as the last of the pastel colors faded from the sky. In two miles, they would officially be out of Periculum, and on their way to Lemuria. On the way to the stones. On the way to her mother. And if she dared, on the way to discovering who she *really* was.

CHAPTER 5

We've lost touch with the two harshest realities of life: birth and death. Because of this, we don't know where we've come from and we don't know where we're going. It's a world riddled with anxiety. A world of apathy. It keeps us indecisive. Unable to boldly step forward. We're more easily controlled that way because it stops us from going all the way. And isn't that the point here? To go all the way. That horrible question of, "What if?" will keep you from a life of going over the edge. A love that is both your awakening and ultimately, your undoing. A destiny that asks you to let go of everything in search of what could turn out to be nothing. A world that will try to break you, only to reveal your spirit can never be broken. "What if?" will keep you safe. Lock your heart away in a box where love and life cannot touch you. That is why we tell stories. So, one day, you will remember. And you will go all the way, wherever your way may be. —Aaliyah

"You're telling me that you can teleport yourself anywhere, and we've been driving a car that's older than dirt?" Zia whacked Hiro on the shoulder.

They had just made it passed the toll road, showing the guard their crypto cards that had been automatically upgraded to Electi status. He let them go without a second glance. Mei had saved them by unplugging the power, but it wouldn't be long before the bounty on their heads was advertised everywhere.

Zia sat in the front seat, resting her clunky black boots on the dashboard. She was pestering Hiro and Jace with incessant questions about Lemuria to figure out how accurate it was to The Trials. The two of them whined that they couldn't stand another eight hours of her interrogation.

"We're called *Folders*, Z. Think of it like this: you have a piece of paper with two holes in it. One hole is where you are now, the other is where you desire to be. My magic simply folds the paper in half." Hiro explained. He caressed the steering wheel and added in a hushed tone.

"She didn't mean it, Betty."

Zia most certainly did mean it.

"That still doesn't answer my question," she said.

Jace, who had been pouring over *The Book of Lemuria* in the back seat, interrupted their conversation. "Magic doesn't work in the human realm. The technology The Electi built keeps the earth at a lower frequency. We don't know how, only that we stopped being able to use our powers here in 1984. It's why we need to go to Shasta. Hiro can't Fold us into Lemuria, and it is one of the few places with an entrance into our world."

Zia didn't miss the way he said *our world,* like it was inevitable she would wind up in a van with him on her way to a mythical realm. She twisted her torso back to face him. Jace ran his fingers through his curled, shoulder-length hair. When he noticed her stare, he gave her a wolfish grin. She swallowed.

"And how has a whole realm been kept secret this entire time?"

Jace leaned toward her, eyeing her up and down. A muscle feathered in his jaw, and for the first time she felt the deadly edge that lurked beneath the handsome exterior.

"Fear isn't the best way to control people, Zia. It's distraction. Why bother to look for the truth when you're so entertained by the rabbits being pulled out of a hat? Until you've sat there for so long, enjoying the show, that you've lost the ability to think for yourself."

His haunting words echoed in the silence, settling into her with an icy feeling in her gut. Neither of them said anything for a moment. Zia looked away first, unable to stand getting lost in his piercing sea foam eyes—they nearly glowed like the lights in the Lemurian sky. The glimmer of amusement in his gaze made her bristle, like he knew he had gotten under her skin.

She *certainly* wasn't going to give him the satisfaction of telling him that he had been in her dream.

There were no other cars on the highway, since only The Electi could travel, and their homes were so nice there wasn't much of a point to them going anywhere other than Mei's library. Zia wished it was daytime just so she could see what the world looked like outside of Periculum.

"So, if Hiro's a Folder, what are you?" Zia asked, breaking the silence.

A half smile played on Jace's lips.

"What would you like me to be?"

"Hiro, didn't you install an eject button into Betty?" Zia asked sweetly. She turned to Hiro for backup, but he had a hand pressed to his mouth to keep from laughing. Clearly, he was enjoying himself at her expense. He had never seen her so unnerved by someone and was enjoying every minute of it. She glared at him as if to say, *traitor*.

"Moving on swiftly," she said sharply, slumping into her seat.

The highway was completely unlit, save for Betty's dull headlights. Zia was grateful the moon was nearly full, flooding the road in silver light. They had several hours until morning and would only stop at a store once to get enough supplies for the climb up the mountain. Zia was careful not to hit Hiro's silver arrow resting by her feet. Though he didn't have his own set in real life, Mei had given him an engraved one for his eighteenth birthday that he took everywhere.

"The Trials were very accurate to the real Lemuria but did leave out a few key pieces. There are *Healers*, who can work with the earth and the ancestors to heal not just the body, but the soul as well—the closest thing to them in the human realm is a shaman. There are *Shifters*, faeries with strong enough magic that can take any form. There are *Folders*, like me. And the most powerful of the magic-wielders—*Elymentals*. The Crown Prince of Lemuria is one. He's able to bend fire—" Hiro cut himself off as his eyes flickered to Jace in the rearview mirror.

Jace's nostrils flared, and he shook his head. A loose curl fell over his brow.

"Wait, there's a prince?" Zia asked, crossing her arms. There hadn't been a royal family of NPC's in The Trials—not even when she entered the castle.

"There are two princes," Jace answered curtly. His whole body tensed at the subject, but she wasn't about to give up so easily. Hiro seemed disinclined to share any more information. He was waiting on Jace, too.

Zia's stubbornness outlasted Jace's patience. He sighed in concession.

"Long ago, when the continent of Lemuria first rose to the surface, the original queen, Katya ruled the realm. She was beloved by all creatures and was said to wield a rare magic that hasn't been seen since her death."

He was staring out the window into the dark void of the night as he spoke.

"The Lemurians were a peaceful people and believed themselves to be equal to even the smallest grain of sand. Their role was to protect the balance of life, and in return, they were gifted immortality and magic that was powered by three stones."

Zia held her breath as she listened, digging her nails into the leather of the seat.

"On the other side of the world, existed another continent called Atlantis. They possessed no magic but created technology advanced enough to conquer their side of the world. But it began to poison the earth, angering the gods. Their once abundant and flourishing land dried up into an empty wasteland, which you now call the Sahara Desert."

His eyes darkened as they finally looked into hers.

"Hungry for power, the king heard a rumor of the three stones. He traveled across the world with his court, seeking to steal them, but did not expect to find the beautiful Queen Katya. He immediately offered her an alliance through marriage, claiming he loved her, but he really wanted to use her for her lands and to infuse his bloodline with magic."

Hiro snorted at that, shaking his head. It seemed even thousands of years later the king's brutality was still a scar amongst their people.

"The queen refused. She saw into his dark heart. That night, she received a vision of a wave taller than the mountains that would wipe out both of their peoples forever. She split the stones apart and gave them to the first Elymental to ever exist, Aaliyah. Aaliyah hid the stones, so the king could never abuse them. That night, he launched an attack on Lemuria and seized the land. He ordered Katya to bow to him, but she said she bowed to no one but her heart. So, he ran his sword through her heart and dumped her into the sea. No one ever found her body."

Zia felt an eerie sense of familiarity at the story. It was as though she heard it before in a dream. If Hiro could Fold across time and space, then maybe it was possible to relive the same moment of life, like an endless circle where the clues to her future lay in the past and she was meeting herself back where she started.

"What happened then?" she asked quietly, not quite wanting to know the ending.

Jace whistled, tapping his knuckles on the cover of the book.

"The legend says that the gods loved Katya dearly. They were so enraged by the king's bloodshed, that they sent what your history books call the Great Flood to erase the realm entirely. Katya had warned the Healers in time of her vision, though. They all came together and sealed the realm in another dimension, protecting Lemuria from complete ruin. It now resides in Middle Earth. A third of our population died that day, but the king survived, and still rules over Lemuria to this day."

He spoke as though it had happened yesterday, and Zia couldn't quite read the emotion on his face. Usually, she could feel what someone else was feeling, but with Jace it was impossible. She wondered if that was true for all Lemurians, but she was always able to understand how Hiro and Mei felt. Perhaps it was because Jace grew up in the realm. She frowned, turning back toward the open road. She was about to ask what happened to the princes when Hiro interrupted her.

"Alright, alright. That's enough history for today. You both make a sport out of brooding and I did not sign up to come experience earth so I could be trapped in a car with your dramatic monologues." Hiro cranked up the music and began belting one of their favorite Bob Marley songs in ear-splitting tones.

Zia narrowed her gaze at him, but he just shrugged.

"What? I'm just here to use humor to deflect my emotions and get us safely to Lemuria so we can save the world."

He continued singing, and Zia couldn't help but laugh. Hiro had a theory he called *majestic absurdity*: a way of living life as though it were a game or a quest. He said that life was meant to be lived *sincerely*, but not seriously, otherwise one gets stuck on an endless loop in their minds. He was a master at it.

Zia sank into her seat, fiddling with the fabric of her mother's cloak. She stole a glance at Jace in the rearview mirror. He was still staring out the window with that unreadable expression on his face.

Zia mulled over the story in her mind and couldn't help but feel as though their lives were being woven in a web of fate by some invisible hand. Sometimes, she believed life was one long thread of random occurrences; that purpose and meaning were something people came up with to feel better about not knowing why they existed in the first place. Then there were other times, where she felt as though even the way she sipped her coffee affected the delicate balance of the universe. That some otherworldly force was nudging every step along her path.

She still wasn't certain how her mother fit into all of this. Her necklace was the key that ended The Trials, and Alita had somehow known precisely what the twin blades looked like in real life when she crafted them for Zia. It had always felt like The Trials were rigged in her favor, like someone *wanted* her to find The Map.

"How did my mother know where *The Book of Lemuria* was when she came to the human realm?" she asked.

Hiro ran over a piece of debris on the highway and her teeth rattled in her skull as Betty attempted to recover. The last thing they needed was a flat tire.

Jace passed the book to her. It was heavier than she thought it would be. She ran her fingers along the leather cover. He had cleaned most of the dust off, but there was still something fragile about the binding. She handled it delicately, afraid it might fall apart in her hands.

"How do you think?" he asked.

She ignored his question as she tried to open it, but the book was practically glued shut. There was ancient writing on the cover, with the same symbol of the three stones carved into it with a hole at the center. It looked like the seed of a flower.

Hiro bit into an apple, and juice nearly sprayed all over the book. She hissed at him, and he gave her a sheepish grin. She turned toward Jace, and he raised one of his thick, arched brows as if to say *figure it out yet?* Yet no matter how hard she tried the book would not open.

"What does the writing say?" She ran her fingers along the carvings.

"*To wield the stones, one needs the key passed down through blood of the royal ancestry*," he quoted. The Lemurian language sounded like a song rolling off his tongue as he translated it.

Those were the exact words in the riddle the siren had given her. She tapped her chin, puzzling the pieces together in her mind. Hiro rolled down the window and chucked his apple core out of it. The cold, gushing wind thundered through the van and sent shivers through Zia's body.

She unclicked her seatbelt and hurled herself toward the backseat, carrying the book. She sat a few inches from Jace. Light danced in his eyes at their closeness. He rested an ankle on his thigh and waited.

"My mother's necklace ended The Trials. It was the key the whole time, and the one object I was allowed to bring. Did a royal descendent give it to her?" she asked impatiently.

Jace leaned in, and the scent of sandalwood flooded her nose again. She could tell he enjoyed his secrets, taking pleasure in grand reveals. It made her want to smack him in the head with the book, just to wipe that arrogant look off his face.

"No Zia. Katya had a child she kept hidden away. Right after the birth, she gave the child to Aaliyah to pass off as her own for protection. That child then mated with one of the realm's most skilled healers. Their great, great grandchild was your mother, who is now the most powerful healer in Lemuria. It is why the king keeps her enslaved in his inner circle."

Zia's blood roared in her ears. Her mouth was dry as she tried to speak. Jace hooked a finger beneath her chin and lifted her head up to look at him. There was nothing but the truth swirling in his glimmering eyes.

"You are a direct descendant of the original queen, Zia. Your blood is the key to unlocking this book."

Her eyes darted from him to the book. She stared at the small little hole carved in between the three stones. Could it really be, that just a few drops of her blood would open it, and perhaps give her the answers she sought? Yet it had to be a mistake. She was only human. She was from *Periculum* after all. This was idiotic. And morbid.

Hiro slammed on the brakes in the middle of the highway.

"You're telling me my best friend has been *royalty* this entire time? Z, why have we been living off pancakes!"

Zia glowered at him, "*Maybe* if you had bothered to tell me the truth, we could have figured it out sooner."

"Everything happens at the right time, and not a moment sooner or later!" Hiro said, sticking his pointer finger in the air defensively.

Jace rolled his eyes.

"You're practically a walking fortune cookie, you know that?"

Zia pressed her lips together to hide her laughter. She was glad someone else shared the sentiment about Hiro being one of the corniest people alive.

Hiro twisted toward the backseat to look at the book himself. He whistled, "Well, Z? Are you going to unlock the book or what?"

The weight of both their stares settled into her. She could feel that she was at a crossroads. If she opened the book, the answers she craved may be ones she wasn't ready to hear, but if she didn't, they would remain unanswered forever. Then again, they had already ended The Trials and were at the top of every watchlist regardless. The only way out of her fear was through. She looked back at them both. They were giving her a choice, she realized. Despite the fact that all of their lives depended on it, they respected that her destiny was her own to claim.

"Give me one of your knives, Jace," she said softly.

Pride glimmered in Hiro's eyes as he turned back toward the road, slamming his foot on the gas pedal again. They hadn't seen a single car the entire time. All she could see were silhouettes of endless wheat fields and empty plains beneath the moonlight.

Jace took out one of his smaller knives and gently took her hand in his. She was grateful for the way his presence steadied her. They sat there, knee to knee, with the book on her lap. The sound of his slow, deep breathing calmed her.

"Ready?" he asked, holding out the blade.

It would only be a few drops of blood, but it wasn't the cut she was concerned about. It was everything that might happen after her blood met the cover.

She shrugged, brushing off his question.

"Is anyone ever ready for anything?"

He tilted his head to the side, studying her for a moment, until his lips spread into that crooked grin of his. He lowered his voice so Hiro couldn't hear.

"No, but that's part of the beauty of it all, isn't it?" he squeezed her hand.

She loosened a breath, taking in his words. The chance of finding her mom was the first time that she felt like her life meant something—that she wasn't just doomed to spend her years barely surviving. All people really want is a sense of belonging, she realized—to feel like they are part of something bigger than themselves.

"Then let's keep going," Zia replied, holding his gaze.

Jace pricked her finger gently and turned it over the hole of the book. Several drops of blood slowly dripped into the center carving. For a few moments, nothing happened.

"Well? What's the deal?" Hiro called from the front.

The book seemed to sigh in relief, like it was exhausted from carrying so much knowledge for so long. It hissed open, and the pages within were pristinely preserved. All of the ink was handwritten in the ancient language. Then Zia felt it. There was a pulse, a ripple of power that echoed out from the book. When she met Jace's eyes, she knew he felt it too.

"I thought magic didn't work here," she nearly whispered.

He shook his head in confusion.

"It doesn't, but this object has a far older magic that binds it. It must work like a loophole."

She handed him the book, feeling lighter as he took it in his gloved hands.

There were a few drawings of each of the stones, and then she saw a rendition of Katya, the first queen. Zia knew it was her before Jace even told her. Everything in Zia seemed to shout *I remember you, I remember you, I remember you.*

He scanned the page over and over again. His thick brows knit together as he reread it until he was nearly blue in the face. She elbowed him in the ribs.

"You might spontaneously combust if you keep being so damn intense."

His shoulders loosened as he passed the book to her.

"I'm trying to find anything that might tell us what the stones do. Or how to wield them. Hiro, do you remember the lines on the map?"

Hiro twirled the toothpick in his mouth, squinting to remember.

"*Long ago in the land of Mū lived a mighty people whose power ran true. The gods gifted them life eternal as the sun, through three stones that were joined as one. True power is held with humble hands, the bridge will restore balance across the lands. To wield the stones, one needs the key, passed down through blood of the royal ancestry. Nobody can master the first stone, most lose their minds to time, and never return home. The second stone is the heart of the gods, give up your own and you'll forever be lost. The third stone is wielded in Death after you have given your final breath. The original queen will once again rise, and unite with the true king, a union of the bloodlines.*"

Zia grunted, "In what universe is that supposed to be helpful? Even the rhymes are trash."

Hiro chuckled, "You'd think they'd be a little less cryptic. Why is it always a riddle? If I were writing a prophecy, I'd put it plain and simple in a nice manual. Step 1: The stones are here. Step 2: Use them like this or you'll probably die. Step 3: Congratulations, you've saved the world. Here's a cookie."

Zia rolled her eyes and didn't bother to tell him that there was a good reason why the truth was often buried. It was a rare person who could handle it. It seemed the more answers they found the more questions sprouted. Where was the bridge located in the riddle? Perhaps the stones were hidden there.

She was about to ask Hiro if he remembered anything about a bridge in the map he memorized when Jace took the book from her and placed it into his pack. He folded his jacket into a pillow.

"You should get some rest, Zia. We'll be close to Mount Shasta by morning, and you'll need your strength for the brutal climb. We have to try to make it to the entrance by sundown. It's not safe to travel the mountain at night."

Zia had no idea how she was supposed to sleep with the incessant chatter in her mind, but he was right—both Jace and Hiro had Lemurian strength. She couldn't be the one to slow them down. She curled up in the backseat, resting her head on the pillow he had made for her with his jacket. Before she knew it, her eyelids felt heavy as though she was melting into the car seat like honey. Thoughts of her mother, the king, and the stones swirled in her mind until they all dissolved into a peaceful emptiness. She could have sworn she felt a warm hand brush her hair from her face just as darkness tugged her under.

CHAPTER 6

I had spent too many years surrounded by sycophants. Tiptoe around enough egos, and suddenly you make no sound in life. It's easy to serve a king or worship a perfect god. What's difficult is to embrace our fellow people for all of their flaws. I was never afraid of being seen for those flaws until her—of being too much or not enough. Love is like that. It tests all that we are. Exposes the parts of us we have kept tucked away. Yet a warrior knows that sometimes strength is not in wielding a sword with brute force but in knowing when to gently surrender. She was a catastrophe to who I have been. The walking, breathing manifestation of my own undoing. —Jace

Zia was walking through a garden that was shaped like a labyrinth. She felt small as she looked up at the gnarled, twisting trees that hugged the pathway. Icy stone nipped at her bare feet as she wandered aimlessly through the garden, unable to find her way. She ducked just in time as a large black owl swooped overhead, sending a gust of wind passed her ears from its flapping wings.

There was no doubt in her mind that she was in Lemuria. Bright orange fireflies that looked like little suns swirled around her, lighting the way forward. She followed the direction of the owl as she pressed on through the winding labyrinth. When she found herself at a crossroads, she noticed a silky black feather had fallen on the path to the right.

The faint sound of humming shook her. At first, she thought she hallucinated it. Yet the further Zia walked, the clearer the voice became. She halted just around the corner, hiding behind one of the gnarled trees.

The center of the labyrinth was a storybook come to life. Silver ferns and violet orchids spiraled all the way to the middle, where a small moon pool rested. There had been one moon pool in The Trials, but it cost too many coins for Zia to justify swimming in it. Rumor had it that whoever swam in it would become drunk on infinity, forever lost in a blissful stupor.

In the corner of the garden was the woman the voice belonged to. She was an elder with long, silver hair that draped onto the floor. Her back was turned to Zia, but her withered hands gave away her age. She was trimming the vines of one of the trees, entirely unaware of Zia's presence as she sang into the night.

"Have you heard the story
of the two little princes?
Born and bred to fight
one was born of fire
the other born of night"

Zia shuddered at the way the elder sang the lullaby with such cheerfulness. She tucked her curls behind her ears and strained to listen. Something about the song gave her a queasy feeling. The elder continued without a care in the world.

"The golden prince delighted
in setting the kingdom aflame,
he terrorized his subjects
to prove his power
would make him king"

Zia took a step forward to hear better. The elder's back stiffened and she stopped singing. Her ears twitched as she listened. Zia held her breath, doing her best to remain invisible. She thought the elder had discovered her, but then the woman continued singing as though nothing had happened.

"The dark prince was banished
for defying the Crown Prince.
As punishment his skin was burned,
And nothing was the same since."

The elder fell silent and gazed up at the ocean of stars. They gleefully twinkled, as though mocking the insignificance below them.

"If you keep hiding behind that tree forever, you'll soon be as old as me!" the elder chuckled.

Zia nearly fell face-first into a rosebush, throwing her arms out in front of her. She stumbled into the clearing and looked up to find the elder only a few feet away from her. Zia was surprised to discover that she was blind. Her silver eyes had a filmy haze over them as she stared off into the distance. She stepped lightly toward the moon pool, her arms swinging as she walked.

"What am I doing here?" Zia asked, prying several sharp thorns from her elbows, ignoring the way her arms stung.

"If you stopped asking so many questions, you'd live your way into the answers!" The elder smiled, her crooked teeth too big for her face.

Zia glared at the elder, knowing full well she wouldn't be able to see it. The last thing she needed was yet another person talking to her in riddles. The elder sat by the moon pool and dipped her feet in the waters. The water ebbed and flowed in gentle ripples.

"Sit," she said in a way that made it clear Zia had no choice in the matter.

Zia looked around, debating whether or not to run, but decided to join her. She dipped her feet in the moon pool and was surprised at how warm the water was. It felt like silk wrapping around her ankles. The elder lifted a hand, and with it, a stream of water arose from the pool. Zia looked in awe as the elder made lovely shapes with the water, bending and dancing with it.

"Do you know who I am?" the elder asked.

Zia put the pieces together. Lemurians lived incredibly long lives without showing age. If the elder was an Elymental, then there was only one person she could be.

"You're Aaliyah. The first Elymental of Lemuria," she breathed.

Aaliyah grinned and nodded, never taking her eyes off the water. The drop shifted into leaves, then wind, then flame, then back to water again. Zia let out a sharp exhale. Aaliyah had mastered every element. She gently let every last drop fall back into the moon pool.

Aaliyah reached for the pouch around her neck and took out a small object. When she opened her palm toward Zia, a small emerald stone rested in it.

"Do you know what this is?" Aaliyah asked.

Zia blinked. It was the same one from her dream.

"It's one of the lost stones."

Aaliyah threw her head back and laughed until her eyes watered. She wiped a tear before it slid down her cheek.

"My dear, nothing real can ever be lost!"

Zia raised a brow. Clearly, the woman had lost her mind after nine thousand years.

"Right. Well, we have the map already. We just need to find the stones to bargain for my mother's life from the king. So, if you could point us in the right direction, that would be fantastic."

Aaliyah grasped Zia's shoulder with a surprisingly strong grip.

"Aren't you curious why your blood was the key to unlocking the book?"

Zia stared at the ground.

"Because I'm the descendant of the queen. So what? I'm going to Lemuria to find my mother. That's it. After that, all I want is my freedom."

Aaliyah chuckled, "Is that so? You never wondered why you've dreamed of our world your whole life? Or why The Trials came so easily to you?"

Zia grit her teeth.

"You really enjoy hearing yourself talk, don't you?"

Aaliyah slapped her thigh, "When you get to be as old as me, you realize you are your own best company! Why, I find talking to myself to be the only thing that keeps me sane!"

Zia groaned and went to stand up, but Aaliyah grabbed her shoulder and sat her back down.

"When you make it through the entrance, follow the river upstream and come find me in the Redrock Mountains."

"I'm going to the castle to get my mom," she said sharply.

"All of our fates are woven together like a tapestry, and not one string can be cut. If you want to succeed in finding your mother, you need to first find all of the stones," Aaliyah replied cheerfully.

Zia wanted to pull her hair out. She felt like everywhere she turned, someone was handing her a cryptic prophecy with a list of demands that she had no desire to carry out.

"Why?" she asked, knowing Aaliyah would understand what she meant. *Why me,* was her true thought. Aaliyah gave her a knowing smile.

"I may be blind, but you are the one who must learn to see, Zia." She turned toward Zia and pressed two fingers on her forehead. Zia's forehead burned and ached at the touch. A white light flashed, and Aaliyah was gone.

Zia jolted awake. Her skin was sticky with icy sweat. The morning light was peeking through the car window. Hiro was snoring loudly in the driver's seat—he had parked just outside of a supplies store. They were in Mount Shasta's town.

She touched the frozen glass of the car window. It was snowing outside. Little flurries were spiraling with the wind, but it hadn't yet stuck to the ground. Zia had never seen snow before.

"Morning, sunshine," Jace's voice jolted her.

Zia whirled toward him. When his eyes flickered to her forehead, his face paled.

"Where did you go in your dreams?"

She shook her head, "What do you mean? I've been in this car the whole time."

"No. Your soul traveled somewhere. Dreams are just a different layer of reality. Who'd you speak with?" he demanded.

Zia turned toward the window to see her own reflection. Three tiny vertical dots were tattooed in the center of her forehead, right where Aaliyah had touched her skin. Three dots for the three stones. Her eyes widened.

"*Who* did you speak with?" he asked again harshly.

"The first Elymental, Aaliyah. The one who hid the stones. She told me to go to the Redrock Mountains and find her when we got through the entrance."

Zia rubbed at her forehead, but the marking was permanent.

Jace frowned, "That's impossible. The Redrock mountains are uninhabited, crawling with the realm's deadliest creatures. Aaliyah's been dead for thousands of years."

"Well apparently not, if she has time to go tattooing people's foreheads without permission," Zia snapped.

Jace's lips twitched into a smile.

"We don't choose our tattoos in Lemuria. Think of it like every time you level up in a video game, you gain a new marking. They form based on our path, like little clues."

Zia rubbed at her temples. It was the most absurd thing she had ever heard.

"Well, your *little clues* are obnoxious."

He smirked and opened the sliding van door. His bag fell off the seat as he jumped out, and a sketchbook tumbled onto the floor. It opened to a drawing of a waterfall that looked just like the one from the dream she had of him. The Vasalisa River. Her jaw dropped as she stared at it.

"I didn't know you were an artist," she said.

Jace's head snapped up as he realized the sketchbook had fallen out. He shoved it into his bag hastily and slung it over his shoulder.

"I'm not," he said coldly.

"There's no need to be embarrassed. You're actually really good..." she trailed off.

"Drop it, Zia," he said with a harshness that surprised her.

She pretended his tone didn't sting and looked away.

"Fine," she muttered.

Zia braided her hair down her back, trying her best to tame the wild curls that had gone completely rogue as usual. She snuck up to the front seat, moving as quietly as she could. It was her golden opportunity to pay Hiro back for the years of being woken up at the crack of dawn. He was still sprawled out like a cat, snoring so loud it could have woken the entire town.

She grinned wickedly and slammed on Betty's horn.

"RISE AND SHINE!"

Zia hadn't seen the coffee cup Hiro had been holding in his right hand. When the horn sounded, his whole body flailed, and he chucked the remnants of the stale coffee at her. He turned toward her, panting as reality settled into him. When he realized that her prank had backfired, he threw his head back and cackled.

Steam was nearly blowing out of her ears as she sat there, her shirt completely soaked. Hiro couldn't stop laughing until he was snorting and keeling over. Anytime he looked up at her he'd double over again. She wiped the coffee from her face.

Jace opened the front door.

"*What* is going on in here?"

She glared at him as his eyes roamed over her body, taking in the scent of stale coffee that she was now covered in. He was doing his best not to smile as he saw Hiro holding the empty coffee cup and pieced it together.

Jace cleared his throat, "Right. Well, they have breakfast here."

Hiro leaped out of the car and wrapped a scarf around his neck.

"You don't have to tell me twice!" He beamed as he simpered off toward the shop.

Zia looked at both of them incredulously. What had she gotten herself into?

She looked down at her soaking shirt and sighed. At least it was black, and she would be able to purchase new clothes in the store. She grabbed her mother's cloak and slipped it on. It certainly wasn't enough to protect her from the unforgivingly cold weather, but it was the warmest thing she owned.

She stepped out of the van and welcomed the icy wind that bit into her skin, clearing her mind of her dreams. Jace waited until she began walking toward the shop and trailed silently behind her. She wanted to demand what his problem was. Why did he feel the need to hide his sketchbook? Especially if he was such a good artist. She wouldn't have thought a warrior would make time for such things, yet it was clearly important to him if he carried the sketchbook with him everywhere.

She grabbed the cool handle of the shop door and yanked it open, nearly groaning at the warmth that enveloped her as she stepped inside. It was a strange shop with maroon walls that had various paintings of spaceships hanging. They sold everything from snow boots to crystals.

Attached to the shop was a restaurant called *Nightshade*. According to the shop manager, the restaurant was a major tourist attraction because it was supposedly haunted. The manager refused to give any other information, other than that the place had burned down twice in the past fifty years. Zia wondered why they kept rebuilding it.

She looked over to find Hiro seated in one of the booths. His face was practically glued to the menu as he was no doubt getting ready to order three meals for himself. The sound of pots and pans clanking in the kitchen flooded the shop.

Zia sauntered over to the clothing rack and grabbed a pair of snow boots that were her size, along with a cream-colored sweater, leggings, and a thick snow jacket. She needed to get out of her baggy men's clothes—they were hardly suitable for trekking up a mountain. For once in her life, she didn't bother to look at the price when she swiped her card. She ignored the twinge of guilt she felt. Having money was a strange feeling she wasn't yet used to.

Zia changed in the cramped unisex bathroom that had graffiti all over the walls and flickering fluorescent lights. The only thing she still wore was her mother's cloak. She sighed in relief to finally be wrapped in layers—it felt like she had been freezing for a week straight. Then she stuffed her dirty clothes back in the shopping bag and walked back out.

Jace was leaning against the counter with his arms folded over his chest. His eyes burned into her when she walked out, and despite the three layers of puffy clothes she wore, she felt stripped bare. He was holding a few of the new knives he purchased—as if he didn't have enough already. She rolled her eyes, though they *were* rather nice. He also bought extra supplies: toe warmers, wool socks, beanies, and various lighters. They would only be hiking for one day, but it didn't hurt to be overprepared.

They made their way to the café and slid into the black booth, sitting across from Hiro. The restaurant was empty. It looked like it was frozen in time. There were brick walls with red velvet curtains that had gold embroidery, several old jukeboxes that lined up the corners of the place, and old wax candles that illuminated it all, dripping slowly. There was a small magic shop in the corner with tarot cards, wands, and a black hat that Hiro couldn't take his eyes off of. Zia noted a photograph of two magicians in white masks breathing fire out of their mouths. She gawked at it—they reminded her of Stefan and Dex.

Zia tried to swallow the fact that there was an entire civilized town no one knew about. She thought the continent was separated between The Electi and the lower class, and had no idea there were occupied rogue territories. It felt silly but, the world was so much bigger than she thought.

"Think of it like a port town," Hiro interrupted her thoughts. He always seemed freakishly aware of what was going through her mind.

"After the economic collapse, there were certain remote areas that made deals with the government. The population was low enough that it wasn't worth controlling, so long as they paid their taxes and allowed them to smuggle weapons, missiles, and whatever else they needed through the town. It's rumored that they even test certain...weapons under the mountain."

She frowned as she stared at the menu. It felt wrong to use a town like this for testing and smuggling. Especially since it was so rural.

Zia sighed, re-reading the menu. There were far too many options, so she settled on French toast and a large mug of coffee. Jace decided on oatmeal and an omelet, claiming that they were fools to eat sugar before a hike and would burn through the fuel in an hour. He lectured them on the importance of protein until Hiro flung a packet of sweetener at him and clocked him in the eyeball. He was silent after that.

"Do you know what you want?" A waitress appeared out of thin air. Zia nearly jumped in her seat. She needed to get better at noticing her surroundings. The girl had bright red hair and deep blue eyes. She couldn't have been older than fourteen. She was the type of girl who didn't say much but noticed everything, and every thought was written across her very expressive eyebrows.

"Yes, one of everything on the menu please," Hiro said cheerfully. The girl did a double take, unable to tell if he was serious.

"We're not wheeling you out of the restaurant when you're so stuffed you can no longer walk," Zia arched a brow.

"Kill joy. I'll take a large stack of waffles, toast with jam, and scrambled eggs," Hiro beamed at her, handing over the menu.

When the girl took Jace's order, she blushed sheepishly and stuttered as she read his order back to him. Jace gave her a charming smile in return, and she stared down at her notepad intensely, a blush creeping into her cheeks that matched her hair. Zia decided to spare her from further embarrassment.

"Hey- why do they say this place is haunted?"

The girl opened her mouth, then closed it when she saw the tattoo on Zia's forehead.

"I drew on her forehead in her sleep," Hiro smirked, stretching out his arms.

Zia doubted that the girl believed him, since the tattoo was *glowing*, but she didn't press further. She glanced over her shoulder to make sure no one could hear her and spoke softly.

"This place has been passed down through my family for a hundred years. Every time it passes through a new generation, something happens. It burns down or the owner goes missing. My dad and brother owned this place together until they disappeared. When we come of age here, we have to survive living on the mountain for thirty days and thirty nights. Shasta is different. It tests you in ways you cannot imagine..." she swallowed, meeting Zia's eyes now. There was a strength there she did not expect to see.

"My brother was eager for dad's approval, so he went to brave the mountain early and untrained. He died on the mountain, and dad disappeared after. Some say he's still alive, wandering like a wild man. I've looked for him hundreds of times..." she trailed off. She had this far-off look about her, like she had fallen into the black hole of a memory that was unpleasant to relive. The girl shook her head and blinked several times, coming back into reality.

Jace leaned in close to her, with that wild, protective look in his eyes. He tapped his knuckles on the table.

"What's your name?" He asked gently.

The girl's eyes widened, "Cara."

"You're running this place by yourself, aren't you Cara?"

That certainly explained her age, Zia thought. The girl tucked a loose strand of her shiny hair behind her ear. She looked at Zia instead of Jace, and there was a curious recognition there. Two girls who grew up too fast, carrying responsibilities that would crush the spines of most adults.

"I'll get your coffee right away," Cara replied meekly, ignoring Jace's question. She practically ran into the kitchen.

They relaxed into the booth, patiently waiting for their food. Zia mulled over the girl's story. Mount Shasta was a strange place, she thought. Though it was lovelier than Fallen Angels, there was something about the town that made her skin crawl. It gave her the same feeling that the Boneyard had.

The waitress brought out the coffee first, which Zia shamelessly chugged, much to Jace's horror. She wiped her mouth with the back of her wrist and gave him a feral grin. He just shook his head and stared out at the window. The morning light poured through the glass, brightening up the darkness of the restaurant. An old soul singer played on one of the jukeboxes, filling the awkward silence.

Zia kept rubbing at her forehead, hoping the ink of her tattoo would come off. Hiro grinned like a monkey that had swallowed a plate as he noticed her attempts. His legs were sprawled out across the entire booth.

"Hiro, why don't you look Lemurian?" Zia asked.

If he was born in Lemuria, it didn't make much sense. He wasn't tall or built like Jace, nor did he have any tattoos. She had always been the fighter between the two of them, but it occurred to her that he might have played down his skills to keep his cover, like when they had fought on the roof two nights ago.

Hiro took his hat off and placed it on the seat.

"I was four years old when Mei told me that we were leaving home for a very special mission. I had already begun training in archery. I wanted to be the best sharpshooter in the realm, like my dad. He was too valuable to the king, so he couldn't come with us," he shrugged, as though abandoning his father and his home was as casual as the breakfast he just ordered.

"Before I left, your mom found a faerie to transform me. Full-powered faeries have the ability to slightly alter the appearances of others, since their magic works on a cellular level. She made me look human, and a bit younger so I'd blend in. She did the same for Mei—" he stopped talking as the waitress brought out their food. The French toast and waffles made Zia's mouth water.

None of them touched their food as he spoke.

"I promised your mom I would protect you. Mei educated me on all of our customs, legends, and how to speak the language so I would grow up knowing my roots. I barely remember what Lemuria was like, honestly. The Trials were strange for me, like living in a doll house that looks exactly like your home."

He drizzled syrup over his waffles and then stabbed a fork into it. He took a bite and said through a mouthful of food, "And that is how you were blessed with the ravishing creature sitting before you."

Zia scoffed and shook her head, diving into her own plate of food. Her heart twisted at the story. He had given up everything to protect her. Zia wouldn't have survived Periculum without Hiro and Mei. When she met his warm, brown eyes, his face softened like he knew every thought that had just gone through her mind.

"Together, Z," he raised his fork in a salute, then took another bite of his waffle.

Her rage at him for not telling her the truth melted away. Hiro once told her the greatest gift in life was a true friend. One true friend. Zia didn't have the words to respond, hearing what he had given up for her. She ate her food in silence.

This wasn't just about her, or The Trials. Hiro was going to go home for the first time, and maybe even see his dad again. She had been so absorbed with her own grief that she hadn't considered the cost of their friendship.

They finished their food, Hiro licking his plate unabashedly. Zia brought a hand to her belly and sighed. It had been a while since she felt so full. The waitress brought them their bill, and they scanned their crypto cards. Jace overpaid her, tipping her enough to buy the entire restaurant ten times over. She would be set for life with that sort of coin. Zia looked at him incredulously when the girl left, not yet noticing the sum.

Jace noticed Zia's stare and shrugged.

"What? I have no use for it."

"You're just…not what I expected," she replied, unable to think of anything else to say. It was true. When they first met at the VR library, she thought he was an overconfident, self-centered bastard. Now she found him to be an immeasurably kind, overconfident, self-centered bastard.

He gave her a roguish wink.

"Well *you* have nearly given me at least ten heart attacks since we've met, so I'd say we're even."

Zia smirked. It took all of her self-control not to stick out her tongue at him.

The front doorbell jingled as albino twins walked into the restaurant, sliding into a booth three tables away. They were impossible not to notice—both had platinum blonde hair and eyes that were nearly white. The man had thick gages on his ears and a black lip tattoo that ran down the center. The woman's hair was slicked back into two tight braids, her blood-red nails sharp and pointed. They looked at Zia with an icy cold expression, not blinking. She ignored the way her stomach dropped at the sight of them.

"So how do you two know each other?" she asked Jace specifically, doing her best to shrug off the weight of the stranger's gaze.

Mei had trusted Jace enough to tell Zia to stay with him. She wanted to know their history. Hiro hesitated, placing a toothpick in his mouth and waiting for Jace's response. It was the second time Hiro had looked to him for approval. Did Jace outrank him, somehow?

Jace's eyes flicked toward the twins a few booths away.

"Hiro's father trained us both," Jace replied curtly, in a tone that made it clear he wasn't going to provide further explanation. His whole body went rigid as he strained his ears to listen to something. Or someone.

Jace brought his hand on top of hers and swiftly handed her a dagger, then brought his mouth to the shell of her ear. His breath tickled the skin on her neck, sending shivers down her spine.

"Don't look behind you. Get up and say you're going to the bathroom, then sneak through the kitchen and we'll meet you around the back. *Don't* react. Smile and laugh at me like I just told you something funny," he nuzzled his nose in her neck. She ignored the panic that was starting to rise, despite the thrill that shot through her at his touch.

She opened herself to feel the twin's emotions behind her—hatred that felt like ice. It took everything in her not to turn around. Zia looked at Jace and did her best to laugh, though she had never been good at faking anything. When she glanced at Hiro, she noticed he was holding several knives under the table.

Zia stood up and announced she was going to the bathroom, then began walking toward the door. She stole a glance toward the assassins. They were armed to the teeth and watched her every movement like a hawk, not bothering to pretend they weren't there for her.

One step, and she could feel their eyes burning into her back. Two steps, and she could hear them stand up. Three steps, and she heard a big *crashing* sound. She whirled around to see that Jace had flung a plate at the man's head like a frisbee. He fell to the ground and crimson blood trickled down his face.

The woman looked at Zia and snarled. She pulled out a gun with a silencer on it and aimed. The bullet barely missed Zia as she tumbled to the ground. The waitress opened the kitchen door to see what was going on, and the woman raised the gun toward her. Zia jumped in front of Cara and tackled her to the floor behind the counter. Her arm sang in pain as the bullet ran clean through her shoulder. She hissed in agony.

Cara's eyes went wide as she saw Zia's arm. Warm blood was already gushing out of the wound.

"*Run!* Tell no one what you saw here." Zia shouted at her.

Cara girl brought a shaking hand to her mouth.

"But your arm—"

"I said *run!*" Zia barked at the girl threateningly.

The girl's eyes watered.

"I won't forget this," She whispered.

"*GO!*" Zia snapped.

Cara scrambled up to her feet, sprinting out the kitchen door toward the back. Though Zia was only a few years older than the girl, Cara still had an innocence about her. As though life had not touched her yet.

Zia winced as she pressed her hand to the wound in her arm—at least the bullet had gone straight through. She stumbled to her feet in time to see the female assassin throw Hiro through the plate glass window, as the male knocked Jace hard in the back of the head with the handle of his gun.

"*You*," the twins said in unison as they stalked toward her.

The man smiled horrifically. His teeth were red from the blood that dribbled into his mouth. He didn't bother to wipe it.

"Your magic called to us when you opened the book. It called to all of us, like a beacon. It's too bad you'll never see Lemuria, really. Oh, the glory you could have won for yourself there..."

"Never had much interest in glory," Zia replied, doing her best to keep them talking.

The girl with the braids sneered.

"There's a bounty worth 50 million on your head, you know. There are more of us coming."

Zia frowned.

"50 million? That's *it*?"

The man snickered and raised a gun toward Zia, but Zia didn't move. She looked into his eyes and saw there was no strength there. It was like looking into an empty void. The assassin smirked at her mockingly as he twisted the gun to the side.

It was a strangely intimate experience to feel her life in someone else's hands. Such a precious, fragile thing, she realized.

A knife ran cleanly through his rib cage as Jace twisted it for good measure. The assassin's eyes went wide with shock as his knees sank to the floor. He coughed up blood as he lay there, dying slowly. Before his sister could react, Hiro hurled his body back through the empty window, kicking her straight in the chest. He then delivered a blow to the back of her head with the hilt of his knife, and she fell to the ground, passing out instantly.

Zia had never seen someone die before in real life. It was common to see dead bodies in Periculum, but she had never seen the life leave someone's eyes. It was paralyzing, to feel that dark angel hover so closely. She opened her mouth to speak, but Jace had already grabbed her arm with painful strength to examine her shoulder wound.

He was already shouting.

"Are you *insane*? What the hell were you thinking jumping in front of a goddamn gun?"

Zia jerked her arm away from him and nearly whimpered in pain.

"I was thinking that the girl was going to *die*, you prick."

Jace got within inches of her face. She could feel the heat of his breath.

"Can't you see? This is bigger than you and your selfish impulses! You might be our only hope at having a *future*, Zia."

"Don't give me that prophecy bullshit. Was I supposed to just let her get shot?"

"You were supposed to let us protect you!"

"I don't *need* your protection. Go find some other damsel to save," she huffed.

"Accepting help doesn't make you a damsel, you stubborn, self-centered, *reckless*—"

Hiro stepped between them.

"*Hey*! If you haven't noticed, we have bigger problems than your constant bickering. Zia set off a beacon when she dropped her blood on the book, which means every assassin and bounty hunter knows where we are. Our only hope of survival is making it to the entrance before sundown, where they can't reach us."

Zia nodded at Hiro in agreement. She glanced at the dead assassin, the blood that was now pooling onto the floor, and felt sick. She raced over toward the woman who was passed out and hauled her body away from him, bringing her toward the booth.

"What the hell are you doing *now*?" Jace grunted.

Zia released the girl and stood up.

"She doesn't deserve to wake up in a pool of her brother's blood," her voice cracked. She was feeling too much at once. Her emotions were more heightened than normal, and she wondered if being closer to the entrance was somehow enhancing her sensitivity. Every word was an effort. She slipped off her snow coat and covered his body with it, closing his eyes with her two fingers. She wasn't the religious sort, but she prayed that his soul made it to wherever it was meant to go.

Zia swiftly walked toward the exit of the cafe, shoving Jace hard with her good shoulder as she passed, ignoring the puzzled expression on his face.

They all left the restaurant out the back. Hiro and Jace raced toward the van. Betty's engine roared to life. Zia breathed in the cool air as she tried to fight her nausea. She took one look at her arm, and at the male assassin's blood on her hands, and ran straight for a bush to hurl up her guts. She heaved and heaved, until her limbs felt wobbly and her whole body was shaking. The world was spinning as she fell to her knees. It was too much. A warm hand lightly pressed on her back.

"Breathe through your nose and out your mouth," Jace's voice said gently, steadying her. He pulled her braid back from her face and held her steady. She kept throwing up until there was nothing left. Warm blood trickled down her arm, and she felt unbelievably lightheaded.

He handed her a cloth and she wiped her mouth, then threw it in the garbage. He hauled her up by her uninjured arm, studying her face with an expression she couldn't read.

"Does it ever get easier?" she asked him, her voice shaky.

His eyes softened as he brushed her cheek.

"No, Zia. Death will never be easy, unless you've lost your heart."

Betty's tinny horn sounded, jolting them both back into reality. They ran into the backseat of the van and barely closed the doors before Hiro took off, racing out of the town and toward the highway. She barely noticed the lovely red fir trees or the burnished fall leaves that swirled through the streets. Her head was roaring as she tried to calm herself down.

Jace reached into his pack and pulled out a tonic, a clump of lilac-colored moss, and several bandages. He wiped the wound clean with the tonic, and it bubbled and stung as he disinfected it. She had to bite down on her lip to keep from screaming.

He took off his gloves and rolled up his sleeves to properly wrap the bandage around her upper arm, and she suppressed a gasp as she noticed the horrific scars on his hands and arms. They were covered in tattoos, but still visible. He had the rough calluses of a true warrior, which meant he likely only recently started wearing the gloves.

Jace placed the bit of healing moss on her wound. He probably brought it from Lemuria, since it looked similar to what the healers had used in The Trials. He wrapped the bandage tight, tying it perfectly around her shoulder. Aaliyah's song floated into her mind, replaying on a loop.

> *"Have you heard the story*
> *of the two little princes?*
> *Born and bred to fight*
> *one was born of fire*
> *the other born of night"*

Zia stared at Jace's dark features. The way his curly hair was black as night, and his eyes reminded her of the lights in Lemuria's twilight sky.

When Hiro brought up the Elymental prince who could bend fire, Jace immediately changed the subject.

"The dark prince was banished
for defying the Crown Prince.
As punishment his skin was burned,
And nothing has been the same since."

She studied his hands as he continued examining her wound. Even with the healing capabilities of a Lemurian, his arms and hands were still scarred. Judging by the level of burn marks, they shouldn't even be functional. It must have taken a powerful healer to work on them. Jace noticed her stare and abruptly released her arms. His nostrils flared and his eyes looked like saucers as he realized what she had somehow pieced together.

"How did you—" he started. She gazed at him unflinchingly as she said the words that he so desperately had never wanted to hear from her.

"You're the banished prince of Lemuria."

CHAPTER 7

It was a difficult time to be alive. Everyone was terrified of each other. They kept us cut off from everything that made us feel connected. We were isolated from nature. We were isolated from each other. They stuffed so much entertainment and information down our throats we forgot what our own voices sounded like. It bred fear like wildfire. They tried to convince us they were protecting us. But it was for control. Suddenly, thinking for yourself became an act of rebellion. I felt alone even in a crowded room. But I knew then, that I would rather be rejected for me than loved for someone else's idea of me. And so, no matter how terrible things got, I held on. I embraced what they made fun of. I refused to let my light go out, no matter how dark it became. —**Hiro**

The drive up the mountain had been brutal. The higher up they got, the thicker the snow became. Zia nearly threw up again from the winding road and Hiro's maniacal driving. They drove as close as they could to the mountain base until Hiro nearly skidded off the cliff racing over black ice. Between the lack of snow chains and the heavy snowfall, they had to walk the rest of it on foot.

Yarrow and Azalea flowers peaked out from the spots where the icy snow melted. Hiro had paused to sniff them several times, until Jace swiped his top hat and threatened to chuck it off the cliff if he slowed them down again. He hadn't spoken to Zia since she figured out that he was the lost prince, and Hiro claimed it wasn't his story to tell. They all settled on bitter silence, which was better for conserving their energy anyway. If he wasn't going to be honest with her, then she would find her answers some other way.

The air thinned as they made their ascent. Every breath was an effort for Zia. Her shoulder ached terribly, but the wound was healing at a miraculous rate thanks to the moss. She pressed on without complaint—the last thing she needed was for either of them to make some comment about her being human. She put in twice the effort of both of them just to keep pace. Hiro still wore his top hat, refusing to don it for a beanie or earmuffs. The silver arrow stuck out of his side. *Hope is never a fool's errand.* That's what the engraving said. It felt like a mockery now.

Jace led the way, though Zia wasn't convinced he knew where he was going. They were barreling through the snow. Some of it had gotten into her boots, melting and turning her ankles to ice. She was grateful for the toe warmers she had purchased at the shop.

There was no pathway or markers of any kind. Jace's ears and nose were red from the icy wind, yet his breath remained steady, as though the hike was barely any effort for him. Zia's sore legs ached to rest, but she forced herself to continue putting one foot in front of the other as her mother's cloak snapped in the icy wind. Perhaps giving her coat to a dead guy wasn't her brightest idea.

She felt a warm embrace at her back and realized Jace was wrapping his coat around her. Zia nearly groaned at the warmth but didn't want to let him off the hook so easily. She eyed him skeptically.

"Don't read into it. Your teeth were chattering loud enough to wake up every creature on the mountain. It's for our survival," he said as he walked past her.

It was around noon. The mountain was too quiet. The only sounds were the snow crunching beneath their boots and Zia's heavy panting. The silent lull they were enduring felt like a mockery of the chaos they would soon face. A few hours of peace, and then they would be at the entrance to another world.

They came across animal tracks and a clump of black hair at one point. Jace sniffed it and declared it was from a bear. Zia did her best not to think of all the creatures that could shred her to ribbons on the mountain. Street smarts did her absolutely no good in the wilderness. Her Lemurian ancestors were probably rolling in their graves seeing her ineptitude on the mountain.

The sun hung directly above them, its strong rays harsh and unforgiving as it burned through the cloud cover. Eventually, they found their way to one of the main trails called Panther Meadows. Zia was convinced Jace had been lost, but too proud to say it. Regardless, she was just relieved to find semi-flat ground for a moment.

The sound of a flute made them all pause. It sounded just like the one the siren had played in The Trials. When she glanced at Hiro, she knew he was thinking the same thing. They looked up to find a man standing at the top of a hill. He was dressed in thick white robes with black goggles over his eyes and a giant staff.

Jace looked over his shoulder at her, "Don't worry. There are plenty of new-age zealots who come here thinking they can find our realm. Most of them are just high from eating the mountain's mushrooms."

Zia didn't bother responding as she kept her eyes fixed on the man. They approached him, and he indeed looked like he had lost his marbles. He had a brassy bun tied on top of his head with a silver and orange beard that went down to his stomach. Several crystals hung on his chest. He raised his staff and smiled.

"Hello there! I'm Brad from the Pleiades. It's a blessing to meet you on the sacred temple of Shasta!"

"From the what?" Hiro muttered.

The man chuckled, revealing his yellow teeth. He grabbed Hiro by the shoulder and threw his hand up toward the sky like he could see his alien planet through the cloud cover.

"The Pleiades constellation, my boy! I was sent here on a spaceship to raise the vibration of the planet with love and light!"

Jace looked like it was taking everything in him not to hurl a knife at the man, but Zia could feel Brad's emotions. Mei had always told her the brighter someone tried to appear, the greater the shadow they cast. She could feel the rage and contempt brewing like a storm beneath his skin—everything about his presence made her want to run. She tugged at Hiro's sleeve in warning.

Completely unphased by the absurd explanation, Hiro shrugged.

"Sounds cool. I like your stick," he nodded at Brad. It was impossible to read Brad with those thick, black goggles, but he looked down at Hiro and slammed his staff into the snow.

"It is not a stick. It is an ancient talisman from the first Telosians who guard the entrance to Lemuria, which I bet you're in search of. I can take you there if you'd like."

Zia wanted to ask who the Telosians were, but that would require talking to Jace or Brad, neither of which she had the slightest inkling of doing. Brad's eyes fell on her, and even beneath the goggles, she knew he was staring at her necklace, the mark on her forehead. She promptly tucked the crystal into her shirt.

"What did you say your name was, dear?" He gave her an oily grin.

"I didn't," Zia snapped.

"Thanks for the offer, but we're not in search of anything. Just enjoying the hike." Jace said in an icy tone.

Brad looked like he was debating letting them pass. He noted the daggers Jace left plainly displayed beneath his jacket and the way Hiro stood protectively close to Zia.

Brad finally bowed with his staff, gesturing for them to continue onwards.

"Many blessings for a safe journey. This is Mount Shasta, after all. You never know what kind of tests She'll bring you."

Zia balled her hands into fists. She wanted to knock his rotting teeth in for the subtle threat there. Jace grabbed her hand, pulling her onwards. When they were about to turn the corner of the mountain, she glanced back at Brad from the Pleiades one last time. He was standing there, staring at her beneath those black goggles. Just before they disappeared out of site, Brad gave her a horrific smile and nodded his head once. A silent promise that she would see him again.

When they were a safe distance away, Hiro and Jace went back and forth debating if he had been a threat. Zia didn't need to debate. She felt what it was like to *be* Brad. For whatever reason, being on the mountain made her even more sensitive than usual. She didn't know how to explain that to either of them without sounding crazy, so she silently kept focusing on the steep climb.

Zia had never seen anything like Shasta in her life. It was her first taste of freedom. The full moon still hung above the mountain even in the daylight, with disk-like clouds hovering atop its peak. *Lenticular clouds,* Jace had called them. He said that most of the New Agers mistook them for UFOs. They were a phenomenon that occurred when the winds and the moisture in the air mixed at a certain temperature level.

They were frugal with their supplies, only drinking water when they needed to. Zia's hands were so frozen they were practically rendered immobile. Luckily, the intensity of the hike made it difficult to think, and she rarely got a break from her overactive mind. Instead, she lost herself marveling at the mountain.

They pressed on for several more hours, until they came across a cluster of enormous trees blanketed in frozen droplets. The scent of bark and snow hung in the air, filling Zia's lungs. How had she gone her entire life without being in wild nature?

Hiro unceremoniously dropped his pack and fell backward into the snow like a starfish, letting out a loud groan. Despite his Lemurian strength, he had never done a climb so brutal before, so neither of them had Jace's endurance. Zia plopped down beside him, preferring to sit on the trunk of a fallen tree than lay in the wet snow.

Zia didn't bother to hide her exhaustion as she released her pack off her aching shoulders. She began kneading at the tight muscles with her knuckles, doing her best not to complain that Jace was running them both ragged.

Jace climbed one of the trees effortlessly, scouting the perimeter from the top branches. Zia had half a mind to tell him to stay up there so she and Hiro could have a moment of peace without him barking orders at them. Snow fell as he shook the tree, sliding back down its mighty trunk.

Zia sighed as she looked around at the density of the forest. Had her insides not been frozen, she wouldn't have believed it was real. Never in her life had she been somewhere so still, yet so full of *life*. She ran her hand along the rough bark of the trunk and noted the mushrooms and moss that grew off the side. Despite the harsh conditions of the mountain, life still prevailed. She could be content to spend the rest of her days with the trees, she decided. They understood what it was to silently endure.

Hiro interrupted her dramatic thoughts by chucking a snowball at the back of her head. The icy powder instantly melted into her braid. She whirled around to see him doubling over laughing. She did her best to bunch a pile of snow in her palms and aimed it right at his face. He rolled to the side just in time.

"Are you two *trying* to announce to every creature on the mountain where we are? Brad from the Pleiades isn't the only thing out here," Jace grunted.

Zia and Hiro stared at him with innocent smiles. When he turned around, they looked at each other the way they always had when they were children plotting a scheme that would land them in trouble. The two of them bunched up a few snowballs behind their back, and as Jace walked away, they rapid-fired the balls at the back of his head.

He just stood there and took it, his hands balling into fists. Zia wondered if he was going to decide that he didn't need her for the stones after all and leave her to die. He turned around slowly, his eyes lifting to hers with a sensual lethality.

"You better run," each word slowly rolled off his tongue.

The two of them didn't need to be told again. Especially since Zia wasn't sure if he was still pissed at her for seeing his sketchbook, discovering his true identity, or the long list of rude remarks she had made since they met. Zia's overactive mind started spiraling.

He probably should have killed her a hundred times by now. Especially since he's the son of the man who had her mother enslaved. But then again...that very king also banished his own son. Why?

Hiro and Zia began to race through the trees, doing their best to move quickly despite the knee-deep snow they occasionally stumbled into. Zia knew Jace was giving her a head start since he was far faster than she. It felt good to *run*. The wind blew past her ears, singing its secrets to her. She was never going back to Periculum again. The reality shook her to her core. She let a loud *howl* rip free from her vocal cords as she felt her thundering heart celebrate her new freedom. Fate and prophecies be damned, her path was her own to paint—if she dared.

She saw Hiro's silhouette racing alongside her. There was still no sign of Jace. Zia pressed on, running faster than she ever had. She looked over her shoulder, but there was no longer any sign of Hiro. Or Jace. She stopped running and did her best to slow her breathing. The eerie silence of the mountain enveloped her. She looked up and noticed the birds had stopped singing. One of the only facts she remembered about the wilderness was that when birds fell silent, it usually meant a predator was near.

Faster than she could blink, a knife was at her throat and her arms were bound. Her heart nearly stopped until she breathed in the comforting scent of sandalwood. She hadn't even heard him drop from one of the trees.

"Your greatest skill in combat is what, Zia?" His voice was low as his breath tickled her ear.

"My dazzling personality," She panted, still gulping down air.

"Funny, but this isn't a video game anymore. If you die it's for real," Jace growled as he released her.

"Really? I hadn't the faintest idea," She placed a hand on her hip.

He pinched the bridge of his nose.

"Your greatest skill is your *awareness.* You didn't notice the men outside of your father's, or the danger the twins posed in the restaurant, or the fact that I was right above you the entire time. You're brave as hell, but impulsive. You get tunnel vision. That sort of thing will get you killed before you even make it through the entrance."

Zia backed away several steps, sinking into a defensive position. She jerked her chin at his knives, "Show me then."

A muscle feathered in his jaw. He surveyed their surroundings, then focused his attention on her stance.

"First of all, you fight and run on your toes, which makes you more prone to breaking an ankle," He circled her, "If you aren't rooted, you'll waste your energy. You also favor your right side, which has become a crutch. Oh, and you don't kick from your core. You're sort of just swinging your limbs about," He folded his arms over his chest.

"How do you *know* all of that?" She scowled.

"Because I was watching you that night on the rooftop. Mei invited me so that I could see where you were at in your training. You'd keep yourself from dying in the human realm, but Lemuria..." Amusement danced in his eyes.

"Well you're older than dirt, why don't you demonstrate for me?" She tossed her braid over a shoulder, preparing herself to punch that smirk right off his face.

He arched a brow, giving her a look that seemed to say *you really don't want me to do this.* She just took out her twin blades, waiting to bury them in his spine. Faster than she could comprehend, he threw a knife passed her head. It was barely a few inches from her head.

"I said *demonstrate how to fight.* Not throw a knife at my head!" She shouted.

"If I really wanted to hit you, I would have. Do not think for one moment even the smallest bug in our realm will show you mercy, Zia. No human has ever made it through the entrance to Lemuria. The fate of both our worlds may rest in *your* hands," He said.

"And throwing a knife at my head is supposed to prepare me for my grand destiny? You're right. My apologies, your majesty." She gave him a mock bow.

His eyes narrowed at her contempt. Zia had a knack for knowing where to hit a chord in people. He was poised to strike like a snake, but she ducked out of the way. He moved on her again. Once. Twice. Three times. She was mist, evading his every attempt to grasp her. Jace may have been a warrior, but by no means was she a defenseless human. Mei had trained her well, and she had been the top player in The Trials for a reason.

"Much better," he said with a look of approval. Color bloomed in his cheeks from the cold. She did her best not to notice how handsome it made him look. He jerked his chin toward her feet.

"Stay rooted," he warned.

She snorted at Prince Jace of Lemuria, His Royal Pain in Her Ass. Until he swiped a leg out, knocking her knees from behind and she tumbled backward into the snow.

He held out a hand and winked, "I warned you. Didn't I?"

Jace expected her to stay down, but Zia flipped onto her feet and delivered three swift strikes: solar plexus, groin, and shins. Mei had taught her to always use the strongest points of her body against her opponent's weakest ones. He keeled over in the snow, holding himself with both arms, and looked like he might vomit.

"Cheap...shot...but...not...bad," he panted. His face paled.

She grinned and offered him a hand.

"Thanks, prince."

Jace looked her up and down with a mix of awe and disbelief, then clasped her hand firmly and stood up.

"Remind me not to get on your bad side," he gave her a half-smile.

"Too late," she winked.

The smile fell from his face. He ran his fingers through his hair and took a step toward her. She wanted to step away so he wouldn't hear the way her traitorous heart skipped a beat.

"Zia, I—"

An ear-splitting scream interrupted him, echoing through the mountain. Her whole body went rigid at the sound and the realization that her friend had disappeared. She silently cursed herself for being so focused on Jace.

"*Hiro*," Zia's voice was barely a whisper.

They both broke into a sprint, racing toward the origin of the scream. Jace became a blur as he barreled ahead of her, daggers in hand. What if the birds hadn't stopped singing because of Jace? What if they were silenced by a far more dangerous predator? The questions nearly paralyzed her as she ran. *Please be alive, please be alive,* she thought to herself. The trees were a blur around her as she sped toward her best friend.

She made it to a clearing and skidded to a halt, taking in the horrific scene before her.

Hiro was lying in the snow, his leg covered in blood. Two long, thick gashes ran along his thigh. A chunk of his flesh was missing—it looked like a bite mark. The snow was turning crimson around him. His eyes flashed to her in a panic and he silently mouthed one word with his white, colorless lips.

Run.

Zia raced toward him and sank to the ground. She ripped a piece of her t-shirt off, tying it around his leg to stop the bleeding. All the color had left his face.

"What did this to you?" Zia's dark curls fell around her face as she worked to tighten the makeshift bandage. She desperately looked for Jace, but he was nowhere to be seen.

Hiro gripped her arm with a bloodied hand.

"Run," he said again, panting. This time it was not a plea, it was a command. She had never heard him use that tone before.

An otherworldly growl shook the mountain. She turned around just in time to see Jace's body being flung across the clearing. He slammed into the trunk of a tree and fell to the ground. It would have broken a normal human's spine.

His eyes bulged when he saw Zia. He dragged himself off the ground and pulled several knives out of his boots. Jace hurled his knife with precision toward what appeared to be nothing. The knives bounced off something invisible and hit snow.

She would never forget the feeling of the creature's presence as long as she lived. She had felt it once before in The Trials, though it was a muted version of what stood across from her now. It was a real-life *Hantu*, a phantom panther. The creature's pelt was camouflaged, allowing it to take down any enemy without warning as it blended into the snow.

The Hantu revealed itself. It was enormous, perhaps four times the size of a regular panther. Its horrific eyes looked like twin blood rubies, though the most concerning part was its fangs. They looked sharper than Zia's blades, with a green saliva that was no doubt poisonous. Hiro was lucky to still have a leg.

The Hantu locked its hungry eyes on Zia and began stalking toward her slowly, savoring each step. She stood in front of Hiro, sinking into a defensive position. Jace threw every knife he had at the panther, trying to keep its attention off her. Blade after blade merely bounced off of the Hantu's pelt like sticks—its armor was far too thick.

"*Come on!*" he snarled in challenge, daring the beast to face him. Zia knew he wanted her to run, but carrying Hiro was a risk. He was bleeding out too quickly, and she was unsure of how long he had left with the poison seeping into his body.

The Hantu dug into the snow with its sharp, beastly talons, leaving a scar on the earth. Jace climbed up a tree soundlessly, trying to attack it from above, but the Hantu was prepared for him and smacked him with its talon when he attempted to drop in on it. Jace hit the ground hard and was knocked out cold. Zia had to cover her mouth to keep from screaming.

She stood over Hiro's body, blades at the ready as the creature slowly stalked her. Zia couldn't tear her gaze away from those horrifying eyes. There was an intelligence in its stare that told her the animal wasn't a mere beast. It felt ancient.

The Hantu opened its massive jaws, a growl building in its throat. Then, its eyes flickered to her forehead, and it tilted its head to the side in a way that looked human. She should have taken the hesitation as an opportunity to bury her blades in its side, but all she seemed able to do was stand there as they stared, motionless at each other.

Zia felt like she had fallen into a trance. Several images flashed in her mind: a black box at the bottom of a faraway sea, an elder's withered hands weaving a pouch, a tarot card of the queen of hearts, a forgotten graveyard overtaken by thorns.

It took her a moment to realize the panther was communicating with her, sending those images. She felt like the two of them were linked, somehow. Zia took a step toward the creature when it cried in pain. The wind was knocked out of Zia's lungs as she felt something sharp plunge into her ribs, but when she inspected her body there was nothing there.

Someone had shot an arrow into the Hantu's side. When their minds had linked, so had their bodies.

The Hantu attempted to remove the arrow with its teeth, but it was stuck in the flesh between two bones. It was no ordinary arrow to be able to pierce through armor like that. She scanned the clearing, looking for the owner of the arrow, but no one was there.

Zia immediately ran over, only to have the animal snarl at her in warning.

"Hold still, please. I'm trying to help you," she said gently. The pain of the wound was excruciating. She was barely able to breathe as she felt it in her own body. The Hantu's eyes flickered to her hesitantly, but it hung its head in concession.

She carefully moved to its side. It took all of her strength to rip out the arrow as quickly as possible. Her arm fell as she felt the surprising weight of the arrow and a sharp shooting pain at her own rib cage. The panther made a horrible, ear-splitting cry at the arrow's removal.

The wound had already begun to heal. It was so deep she could see the bone of the panther's rib cage. The flesh was closing around it before her very eyes. Zia knew then, that no matter how long she spent in Lemuria, she would never get used to magic.

The Hantu looked at her through heavily lidded eyes, and she could have sworn gratitude flickered there briefly. Before she could try to communicate with it again, the creature turned invisible before her. Zia could no longer feel its presence and knew it was gone. The pain in her side had disappeared. The link had been severed.

Zia ran toward Jace, who was still on the ground, and turned him over. He wasn't breathing. She pressed two fingers onto his neck and felt for his pulse. His heart had stopped. Mei taught her how to resuscitate someone. She didn't know if it would work on a Lemurian, but she was willing to try.

She clasped one hand over another and pumped hard at his chest, then brought her mouth to his and blew air into Jace. Zia repeated the movement for several minutes until his chest heaved and he sat up, coughing. Relief washed over her.

He blinked, his eyes coming into focus.

"Did you just kiss me?" His voice was hoarse.

"What? No! I gave you CPR. It's a life-saving procedure," she replied defensively.

He gave her that wolfish grin of his, and she suddenly wished to be anywhere but there.

"Is it now?" he said slowly.

She glowered at him and scrambled to her feet. The smug expression on his face was wiped away when he saw Hiro, who appeared to be hanging on by a thread. Jace immediately took his healing supplies out of his pack and began cleaning Hiro's wound. Hiro's eyes rolled to the back of his head at the pain, and he was mumbling nonsense. The poison made him delirious.

Zia scanned the perimeter, looking for who may have shot the arrow again. She picked it up from the snow and gasped. It looked exactly like the arrow Alita had made for Hiro in The Trials. The material was the same silver and steel, with the ancient language engraved at its tip.

"Jace," she said quietly.

He looked up from the work he had been doing on Hiro and paused when he saw the arrow.

"Where did you get that?" he asked wearily.

"It's mine," a familiar voice sounded.

Brad from the Pleiades stepped out from behind a tree. He no longer appeared the belligerent hippy from earlier. Every move he made was calculated. His beady, black eyes darted from the three of them. The goggles were gone. He drew another arrow and pointed it right at Hiro. Zia immediately stepped in front of him.

Brad laughed, revealing his crooked yellow teeth.

"You're welcome, for saving your life. No one has survived the Hantu before. Except me, of course."

Jace moved swiftly in front of Zia. He looked like he was plotting about fifty different ways to dismember the man.

"Who are you?" Jace asked, his voice echoing through the trees.

Brad held up his pointer finger.

"That's not the question. The question is, what do I *want*? You see, venom from a phantom panther is lethal. The only thing that can save your friend now is The Guardians."

Zia looked back at Jace in question.

"They protect the entrance," Jace muttered under his breath.

Brad made a *tsk-tsk* noise and waved his finger.

"You really haven't told the girl much, have you, Prince?"

Jace's palms twitched at his side.

"How do you know who I am?"

Brad laughed.

"It's no matter, really. I told you this mountain tests you. Now back to what I want. I want the necklace the girl wears. Give it to me, and I'll let you continue on your journey in peace."

Zia brought her hand to her mother's necklace and shook her head. There was no way he was getting his grimy hands on it. She would sooner snuggle up to the Hantu. There was something familiar about Brad, a piece of the puzzle that nearly clicked into place in her mind.

Brad raised the arrow, pointing it directly at Zia now.

"That necklace is my ticket into Lemuria. And so is your friend. Do you know how rare a Folder even *is*?" he chuckled silently and shook his head.

"I have lived on this wretched mountain for five years. Five years, since it took my son from me. He found the entrance, you know. But The Guardians killed him on site. He wasn't worthy to enter, they claimed. Such arrogant creatures. They'll pay for that soon."

Jace's eyes darted between the two of them. It was a risk to do anything. If he wasn't fast enough, Brad would either kill Zia or Hiro. They had to keep the man talking, if only to stall him until Jace could disarm him.

"Why do you need my necklace?" Zia asked.

Brad seemed to debate telling her the truth but shrugged.

"Folders are rare, but heart stones are even more rare. A folder can walk between worlds. Navigate time travel. Without one, it is impossible to get to Lemuria. Unless of course, you have the key..."

She looked at Jace for confirmation, but he seemed just as clueless as her. She had never heard of her mother's necklace being referred to as a heart stone. It was a key to unlock many, many things it seemed.

Suddenly, the puzzle pieces in Zia's mind snapped together. She took a careful step toward Brad, holding her palms up in the air.

"You're Cara's father," she said gently.

Brad hesitated, lowering the bow and arrow slightly. There was a clarity that sparked in his eyes, and she saw a glimpse of the man he had once been before the mountain claimed him.

"How do you know my daughter's name?" he asked, unable to keep the desperation out of his voice. Zia took another step toward him and spoke as softly as she could.

"Cara told me about you. She's been running your entire café herself for the past few years. She said she looked for you on the mountain hundreds of times..."

Brad looked at the ground, his guilt all too apparent. He nearly choked on his words.

"She shouldn't look for me. It's better she thinks I'm dead."

Zia shook her head.

"Trust me, Brad. No child is better off thinking that. She loves you. Please, don't abandon her," Zia pleaded, knowing the weight of those words all too well.

A single tear fell from Brad's eyes, and he sniffled, still staring at the ground. For a moment Zia thought he would do the right thing—that he would go home to his daughter and let them pass.

He looked up at her, and she again felt that darkness curl around his heart. There was nothing more dangerous than the greed of a desperate man with something to prove.

"It's too late for me. I *need* to get to Lemuria."

He lunged for Zia and tried to grab her necklace, but Jace was far swifter. He disarmed him and slammed him in the back of the head. Brad hit the ground face-first into the snow. Jace grabbed Zia by the shoulders, examining her. She hissed as he touched the spot where the bullet had gone through her arm. He released her apologetically.

"Are you hurt?" he asked, his eyes darting all over her body.

"I'm fine," she said.

He sighed in relief and shook his head as he stared at Brad. He rolled the man over so he wouldn't suffocate in the snow, then made a sour face.

"I never liked that guy."

Zia nodded in agreement. She bent down and grabbed his bow and arrows, slinging them around her shoulder. When Jace looked at her in question, she shrugged.

"Hiro will love these when he survives. They're just like the engraved one he always carries."

"What does the engraving say?" Jace asked.

Zia smiled.

"Hope is never a fool's errand."

Jace again looked like he was about to say something, then decided against it. She knew he was withholding information from her, but now was not the time to pry it out of him.

Jace bent down and carefully picked up Hiro in his arms. It normally wouldn't have taxed him, but the panther had hit him hard. He grunted and looked out toward the open mountain.

"Let's go meet The Guardians."

CHAPTER 8

It takes courage to dream in a world that is barely surviving. It's far easier to think of all the worst-case scenarios so that you will be prepared for loss and suffering. You will be right about the world being cruel and unforgiving. Perhaps it will ease the pain if you're prepared. This is a fallacy. It is a risk to love. It is a risk to dream. Hope is never a fool's errand. —Hiro

They were on high alert for the rest of the hike, moving as quickly as possible. The moss Jace placed in Hiro's leg slowed the poison from spreading, but he only had a few hours to live at most. He was lucky he was Lemurian—a human would have been dead within minutes from the Hantu's bite. They made it through the forest and were walking across the exposed, open land of the mountain's ridge. Their only prayer of survival was making it to the entrance.

Zia wrapped her arms around herself, trying not to let the bitter cold chill her insides. She moved quickly, keeping her body warm and focusing on the sound of snow crunching as they walked. The air was thin, and her breath was shallow. A sense of dread crept in as she thought about The Guardians and how they had killed Brad's son. She shook her head. They *would* save Hiro—she would not accept any other outcome.

The light turned golden as the sun moved closer to the horizon. The snow was sparkling in a honey color. It would have been lovely, but each passing moment filled her with dread. Time was draining for Hiro. Jace carried him in his arms without complaint. They had done their best to make the bleeding stop, but Hiro's veins were starting to turn black like little spider webs. He seemed to go in and out of consciousness, occasionally mumbling nonsense they couldn't understand.

"Not too long now, Zia," Jace said. His green eyes glowed in the setting sun, and the tip of his nose was red. "The Guardians will be able to heal Hiro." He was trying his best to comfort her. His throat bobbed as he stole a glance at her. Was he *nervous*?

"Are they Lemurian?" she asked curiously.

Jace grunted as he adjusted Hiro in his arms lightly, bringing him over his right shoulder. Hiro didn't make so much as a sound at the movement.

"There is always one representative from our realm at the entrance. Lemurian, faerie, siren…it goes in rotation. The other Guardians are Telosian, they don't belong to either world. They are from an underground city that dwells within the mountain called Telos. Their sole purpose is to protect the balance of the realms."

Zia balled her fists in her coat pocket, doing her best to trap any semblance of warmth in her hands. She focused on the sound of Jace's long, deep breaths.

"How many realms are there?"

He shrugged, "No one knows, Zia. There is an infinite number of dimensions just within earth's plane. Imagine the rest of the galaxy."

"That gives me a headache just thinking about it."

He chuckled, and his laugh softened something in her. Zia debated telling him about the Hantu and the way that she was able to communicate with the animal, but she wasn't ready to explain. She had never told anyone about her abilities before and was afraid he would start with *the chosen one* nonsense again.

"Why didn't you tell me you were the prince?" Zia asked, feeling like a hypocrite.

His jaw locked at the question. She thought he wasn't going to answer, but the words finally tumbled out.

"My father and I always had a very difficult relationship. I never possessed any magic, so he favored my brother, Leo. Leo loved to terrorize people with his flames. Sometimes, he would chase the servants through the castle as if it were a game, " Jace sighed, "As for my mother…I have no memory of her. I don't even know her name. Neither does Leo. The king said she was killed by rebels shortly after birthing us, but I don't believe him. No one in the castle remembers her. Not even the wet nurses. It's like someone erased her from all our memories. We've tried to look, but it turns up empty every time."

Zia's chest felt heavy. She had at least known her mother's name, had seen her face in a photograph, heard a few stories from her father. He continued on.

"One day, Leo burned someone from the kitchen staff alive. I fought him, but he threw out a dagger of flame. I blocked it with my arms but… well you can see what happened." He blew out a breath, "For my weakness, my father exiled me to the Redrock Mountains for a decade without healing my burns. I was twelve. The mountains are home to some of the worst creatures in Lemuria, but I found a way to make a friend out of the darkness there. My wounds healed enough to be functional, but the scars will always remain," Jace flexed his hands at the memory.

He looked up at her face, reading the sympathy there, and smiled softly.

"It wasn't all sad. After leaving the royal court, I spent some time traveling, having my adventures. I rode sea serpents, stole from sirens, and was trained by faeries. I realized then how poorly my father treated anyone who wasn't in his inner circle. When I returned, it was as a warrior trained by the realm. I promised myself I would make a difference when I went back. I faced my brother in battle and won, despite his magic. My father made me commander of his deadliest legion, after that. The Shadow Warriors. Nicknamed because you'll be dead before you see one. They are a different breed of Lemurian that originally hailed from the other side of the continent in the desert. I led them for over a century."

Guilt shone in his eyes.

"Then my father began hunting the stones. I don't know why he waited so long. He sent many Lemurians out to search for them, and then would publicly execute them when they failed. His heart darkened even more over the years, and my brothers with it. I stopped one of his executions of a young Lemurian warrior who had been in my charge. He wasn't even fourteen yet. As punishment, my father found a faerie woman I had fallen in love with during the time I spent in the court. We were young, but she was like sunshine to me. She showed me there was another way."

His voice cracked.

"He chained me up and made me watch Leo incinerate her. I tried to kill them. Both of them. So, the king imprisoned me for treason. I was meant to be executed."

He turned to Zia and studied her, as if debating telling her the rest of the story. She waited patiently, giving him the space to decide what he needed. She could have sworn gratitude shown on his handsome face.

"I was in the palace cell the night before my execution when I heard light footsteps. A woman with dark skin and eyes blue as the sea was staring back at me. She told me she would free me, on one condition: that I find and protect her daughter, who lived in the human realm in secret. She told me I would know you by your eyes. That you would need my help finding the stones, and that I had to stop at nothing to find the bridge that will restore balance."

Zia stopped walking. Her heart was pounding too loudly like thunder cracking in her chest. She knew he could hear it. Jace smiled brightly at her.

"Sahara healed me, then freed me. She told me if any harm came to you, she would drag me to hell herself," he laughed. She could've sworn his eyes were watering.

Zia couldn't stop the sobs that broke from her. Her chest heaved as she nearly fell to the ground, bawling her eyes out. All the tension she had held onto, the hope she kept tucked away in the back corner of her heart finally released. Her mother really was *alive*. Jace lifted her chin up to look at him.

"You and Sahara are more alike than you know, Zia." His hand was warm. He wiped the tears from her cheek. She grasped his hand with her own. His eyes flickered to hers.

"Why are you telling me all of this?" She asked.

He squeezed her hand.

"Because letting people in can destroy you, but without it, life is empty. We have nothing without trust."

Zia nodded, considering the words. He was right.

"What was her name?" she asked quietly.

Jace closed his eyes, and she could tell it had been a long time since he had spoken the faerie's name. The first girl he ever loved.

"Meaghan," his voice was heavy. Zia knew he carried that name like an albatross for many years. It became clear to her that Jace felt responsible for protecting as many lives as possible. For him to think he failed the girl he loved...she knew that was an invisible wound that may never leave him.

For the first time since they met, she could *feel* him. She wasn't sure if it was because he was letting his guard down or if being close to the entrance was amplifying her abilities. Still, she felt the weight and responsibility he carried. There was nothing she could say to fix it, so she just gave space for him to feel it.

Zia nodded and squeezed his hand, "Thank you, Jace."

His brows knit together, "For what?"

She looked him square in the eyes.

"For finding me. For telling me nothing but the bare truth whenever I ask. For going against even your family for what you believe in. For being my friend," her voice cracked at the last word.

His eyes were still lined with silver, like he was stubbornly keeping his tears from falling. She knew he didn't take those words lightly.

"She wasn't supposed to die," he whispered.

She felt like she had been punched in the gut hearing those words. Zia took his palm in both of her own and lightly kissed his knuckles, where the worst of the burn marks were. She looked him in the eye with every ounce of strength.

"Never again," she promised. She felt a bond form between them—that they would have each other's backs through whatever lay ahead.

As he looked at her, the moment cracked open and a wave of silence rushed in. The rest of the world melted away for a split second. For that moment, there were no kings, prophecies, or stones. They felt as though they had somehow become infinite within finite time. There was only them, and the unspoken language that existed beneath their words.

"Never again," he agreed, breaking the spell.

They hiked the rest of the way in silence. Zia's thighs burned, but there was hope in her heart. Somehow, despite centuries of cruelty, there was a warrior who remained kind when he had a reason to be anything but. Though he was a thorn in her side at times, he hadn't let the world harden him. It softened something in her, too. And for the first time in a long time, she thought that maybe, if she stopped holding herself together so tightly, she wouldn't fall apart.

Her mother's necklace felt warm at her chest, and she knew they were getting close to the peak. An enormous eagle swooped overhead, circling them for a moment before moving on. Zia watched the silhouette of its wings glide in the setting sun.

Zia practiced her awareness as they walked, wanting to prove Jace wrong the next time he attempted to spar with her. She isolated various sounds—the creaking of the trees, the crunch of the snow, the whistling wind, the sound of Jace's long, deep breaths. An unshakeable calm settled into her.

They were about to come around a bend in the mountain when Jace held his arm out and stopped her. It felt like walking into a concrete wall. There were piles of enormous, black rocks all stacked on top of each other in the middle of the pathway. They were far too heavy for a mere human to place them there, and she knew stones were significant to Lemurians. They were never supposed to move rocks unless they were in a river, in which case one would be helping the stones fulfill their destiny downstream. She had learned that the hard way when she moved one of them in The Trials and a Lemurian NPC had crushed every bone in her hand with that same rock.

Zia started shivering. Snow had gotten into her boots, soaking her socks and freezing the tips of her toes. She eyed the rocks curiously and noticed several markings were carved into them with a single sentence at the bottom in Lemurian.

"What does it say?" Zia asked.

Jace swallowed, "It's a warning that promises a very unpleasant death to all who enter."

Zia gave him a lazy smile, "Sounds like my kind of place."

Jace snorted. He ran his free hand along the stone wall, studying its every edge, still balancing Hiro on his broad shoulder.

"Didn't you see this when you left Lemuria?" Zia asked.

His brows knitted together in confusion, "No. I paid through the teeth for a rogue Folder to take me through. I was planning on getting back with Hiro, but his magic is drained..."

"Can't we just climb it?" she asked.

He smirked. "This wall was made by magic older than humans. Don't you think they *might* have anticipated that?"

The last rays of light trickled in. Nightfall was coming quicker than they hoped. A gust of wind whisked passed them. Zia hugged her arms close to her chest, savoring the last bits of warmth.

Zia walked over to the stone wall and placed her palms on the carving. She closed her eyes and cleared her mind. There was something off about the wall. It wasn't like the redwood trees, where she could feel the pulse of life thrumming through the trunk. Or like the panther, where she could feel its body as though it were her own. The wall felt lifeless.

Almost as though it weren't real.

Her eyes flew open and she looked over her shoulder at him.

"It's a veil," she said.

"That's impossible. If it were magic, I would be able to see through it," he said haughtily.

She arched a brow.

"Well, your highness, I'm telling you it's a veil. I can feel it."

Zia was surprised by her own words. She had never felt so confident in her sensitivity before, nor did she think it would ever be useful. Zia was familiar with veils from The Trials. It was a magic that only faeries could perform in Lemuria. They could spin any illusion, whether it be through their own appearance or a place.

"What do you mean, you can *feel* it?" His tone had an edge to it.

Zia ignored him as she thought of Brad. He had viciously attempted to steal her mother's necklace to make it through the entrance, which meant he must have known about the wall.

She closed her eyes and kept feeling into the wall until she felt a tiny pulse of life. She followed that pulse, trailing her hands along the rock until they found their mark. It was a small hole.

She took off her mother's necklace. Her hands were shaking from the cold. She looked over her shoulder at Hiro, who was wheezing with each breath. She placed the crystal in the keyhole and waited, standing next to Jace.

The veil dissolved before her eyes. She had not expected what lay beyond it. It looked to be around morning time, the golden rays of the sun streaming in thick beams. Canopies of trees hugged the dome of a lush mountain. A mighty waterfall tumbled into an abyss. The center of the dome seemed to fall into a bottomless void.

Her breath caught as she saw two twin fire birds dive and glide in front of the waterfall, their flaming tails flashing bright beneath the clear sky. She knew the entrance to Lemuria must be behind it, then. Fire birds were only stationed where there was something incredibly important to guard.

Zia looked over to find Jace staring not at the entrance, but at her. He was looking at her like he had never seen her before. His mouth parted slightly as he tried for words and failed. She knew she would have to tell him about her gifts soon, but not now.

"How did you—" he started.

"Was it supposed to be difficult?" Zia asked. She stepped through the veil, which felt like walking through silk.

Harsh wind from the waterfall immediately blew in her face, nearly knocking her over. Darkness beckoned below them, and she wondered if she would fall right out of the earth itself. Her palms were sweaty as she realized how high they were.

The only place to walk was a crumbling limestone pathway along the mountain's ridges. It was very thin, and one wrong step would lead to their end. Zia tilted her head to the side, eyeing the fire birds curiously. Their flames intertwined as they swirled around each other, never moving more than a few feet away from the waterfall. Behind it, Zia could see a black void. A cave.

There was a large gap where the pathway ended, and the mouth of the cave opened. A very old wooden bridge tied with rope hung between the two points, though it looked like it could barely carry the weight of one person, let alone three.

Hiro let out a groan, and Jace set him on the ground for a moment, assessing his injury. His face was pale and sheened with sweat, his lips were colorless. The black, spidery veins were spreading up to his neck.

Zia pressed a hand to his forehead. It was boiling.

"Don't worry, Hiro. We're almost there. We've got you," she whispered. She stroked his hair back from his face. He weakly grabbed her forearm and mumbled something she couldn't hear. She brought her face closer to him, and it seemed to take all the effort he had to say.

"My.... hat...."

A deep laugh escaped Zia. Her whole body was shaking as she began cackling loud enough to rattle the fire birds. Of all the things for him to worry about, of course it was his hat. She had stuffed it in her pack as they left, knowing that he loved it so much it may as well have been glued to his head.

"I have your hat, Hiro," she said soothingly, wiping the tears from her eyes.

"Everything ends where it begins, Z!" he said again with a chuckle that turned into a horrible cough. His eyes rolled to the back of his head, and black blood sprayed from his mouth. Jace took out a vile from his pack and dropped a clear liquid into his mouth. Hiro immediately passed out.

She looked at Jace incredulously, ready to yell at him for knocking out her friend with a sleeping potion. He held up a hand.

"Don't start. He was in pain and would've been a liability. He'll wake up after The Guardians heal him."

Zia stripped down a few layers, adjusting to the humidity. She stripped down into her cropped tank and leggings, placing her mother's cloak in her pack. The snow boots were making her feet sweat. She hadn't anticipated such a change in weather. She chucked them off, opting for bare feet so she'd have a better grip. Jace raised his eyebrows nearly to his hairline, but she ignored him.

Jace scooped Hiro up in his arms, and they immediately began shimmying the side of the mountain, sticking as close to the wall as they could on the crumbling pathway. The limestone was slippery, and it took every ounce of Zia's concentration not to slip. She gripped her toes as best she could, but little pieces of rock broke away with each step.

"What is this place?"

Jace gracefully placed his feet around all the loose rocks, balancing Hiro's weight so it wouldn't tumble them both off the edge.

"It's a waiting room. An 'in between' for our two worlds. Only those who know it exists can find it …" he trailed off.

"How many people have these necklaces?" she asked, touching the crystal around her neck.

He frowned as he squinted at it.

"A heart stone is somewhat rare. They are earned amongst our people. Usually only healers or elders have them. The markings tell the story of their greatest vulnerability, so it may be worn openly as their greatest strength."

Hiro had once said something similar to her when they first became friends. Zia stubbed her toe on a rock and sucked in a sharp breath.

"Are they all keys?" she said through her teeth, doing her best to ignore the pain radiating from her big toe.

"Only to move in and out of Lemuria, as Brad said. But it shouldn't have unlocked the tomb to the map. I can feel it. There's a different kind of magic within yours. Sahara must have had a faerie spell it."

Zia felt a ray of hope at the sound of her mother's name again. She fell silent. The path was thinning even further, and she needed Jace to focus since he was carrying Hiro.

They reached the edge of the mountain ridge, and she could see glimpses of the cave through the harsh mist that blew toward them. The wind whipped Zia's hair back and forth, and she had to claw the side of the mountain to keep from stumbling backward.

She squinted at the creaky, wooden bridge that swayed in the wind, bridging the gap between the crumbling path and the mouth of the cave. "Impossible. It's too easy," she said. Zia's gut was screaming at her, and she felt the same *tug* she had felt in The Trials. *Look,* a voice seemed to say. It felt like an invisible hand gripped her shoulder, guiding her.

"Everything is figure-out-able, darling." Jace walked past her and winked. Had he not had her best friend's life literally in his hands, she would have walloped him for calling her darling.

He carefully took a step onto the wooden bridge, testing it with his weight. He decided to go first, measuring its stability. She remained on the edge of the ridge, doing her best not to focus on the empty void below. He carried Hiro across after deeming it safe.

Look! the voice whispered again with great urgency.

"Jace, wait!" she called.

He kept walking and called over his shoulder, "While you're waiting, Hiro's dying."

He was almost to the end of the wooden bridge when Zia felt a presence behind her. She heard the running of footsteps and turned around just in time to see platinum-white hair flash before her eyes. It was the female assassin from the café. She howled as she nearly plunged the dagger into Zia's heart, but Zia blocked it with the blades that she instinctively withdrew from her belt. The assassin backflipped as Zia lunged for her and skidded along the path, dust kicking up behind her.

"You *killed* him!" she shrieked. Her face was completely feral as she ran toward Zia, her white hair illuminated in the morning light. Zia maintained her focus, paying attention to the way the assassin moved. How had she followed them without Jace sensing her?

"Zia!" Jace called for her. She could hear the horror in his voice. She drowned out the sound and yelled through her teeth.

"Just get Hiro to The Guardians!" she pleaded.

They came to blows, and the woman got a solid punch into Zia's left cheek. Her teeth rattled at the impact and she tasted blood in her mouth. She twisted the assassin's arm around, disarming her as the dagger fell into the endless void. The assassin knocked Zia to the ground and got on top of her, attempting to claw at her with her with her sharp, red nails.

"You little *brat,* thinking you're so special because you unlocked the book," her face twisted into an awful grin. "Was my brother's life worth it to you? To get through the entrance to your precious realm?"

Zia could feel the assassin's rage boiling. She knew that anger caused blind spots in a person, creating the tunnel vision Jace had warned her about. Zia reached her hand to the side and grabbed onto a limestone rock, then clocked the assassin in the face as hard as she could.

The assassin lost her balance and fell to the side, blood spraying everywhere. Zia got up and sprinted toward the wobbly bridge, when the woman tackled her to the ground. Her only relief was when she saw Jace clear the other side of the bridge with Hiro, disappearing behind the waterfall.

The assassin leaped up and ran in front of Zia, removing a hidden dagger from her tall boots. She cackled, throwing her head back with the kind of laugh that only occurred when one went mad with grief.

"They're coming for you. They'll hunt you until the day that you die. You'll never so much as touch the stones. How does it feel? To fail everyone you love..." Zia saw the pain flicker in her eyes. She knew the assassin was thinking of her own brother, but her words landed a blow to Zia's heart all the same.

"This is for Gavyn."

The assassin brought the dagger down on the ropes that held up the bridge, and it immediately fell into the endless abyss. She could hear Jace call out for her behind the waterfall, but it was too late.

It hadn't occurred to either of them that the bridge was woven by magic, and if it fell, so would the path to the entrance. The fire birds immediately let out a godly battle cry and sailed toward both of them. The ground began to rumble beneath them. Closer and closer the birds came as they dove for them, taunting them. One of them narrowly missed Zia's face by a few inches, and she could feel the heat of their flames.

The limestone path was disappearing from underneath them. Zia dug her two blades into the mountain and gripped on for her life. She saw the assassin's eyes widen with panic. Zia groaned, knowing full well Jace would be infuriated by what she was about to do.

"Hold onto me!" Zia called.

The assassin turned to her. There was nothing but pure, deadly rage on her face.

"How noble of you," she laughed darkly. Blood was smeared on her forehead.

Zia winced as she struggled to maintain her grip. The fire birds were circling them, and she wasn't sure what would kill them first—the path crumbling, or their deadly flames.

"Don't be an idiot! Revenge isn't worth your life. Hold onto me!" Zia pleaded. The path fell out from beneath her feet entirely. It was seconds away from swallowing the assassin into the void.

The woman locked eyes with her, and Zia recognized the stubbornness there. She would rather fall into the void than be helped by an enemy.

"Death's an old friend, Zia."

The assassin tilted her head up toward the canopy of trees, as though she could see into another world there. Zia could have sworn she saw a smile on the woman's face as the ground disappeared from underneath her, and she fell into the darkness, laughing her way into death.

Jace was still yelling Zia's name, but there was no way for him to help her. The bridge was gone. Her palms were sweating as she tightened her grip on the handles, her bare feet dangling in the air as she tried to dig them into the mountainside.

But the fire birds were still coming for her.

There was no way she would be able to clear the gap between her and the cave's entrance. She knew there was a very thin line between insanity and genius. Jace warned her of her rash actions, but what if that was her strength?

Zia heard the ear-splitting screech of the firebird as it lunged toward her. She wasn't sure how her abilities worked, exactly, but her life depended on it. Zia locked eyes with the firebird, linking her consciousness with it.

"Zia, *don't*—" Jace shouted. It was the last thing she heard before the link snapped into place, and she was suddenly looking through the bird's eyes, then back through her own. Without having to speak, they understood each other.

The firebird banked within a few feet of her and she leaped on top of its back, gripping hard to the feathers of its neck. Her flesh burned at the impact, but she held on. The bird was in far too much shock to shake her off, and if it harmed her, it harmed itself. The link was strong.

She couldn't hold on for much longer with the pain of the fire. The bird nose-dived toward the entrance, crash-landing at the mouth of the cave. Water pounded onto her body for a few brief seconds as she cleared the waterfall. It felt like a hundred liquid daggers falling onto her at once, but it was better than the white-hot flames of the bird.

Her body met hard ground as she rolled, keeping her arms and legs tucked in. She made it. Her eyes were squeezed shut, but she knew by the absence of light and warmth that she was in the cave. She could hear feathered wings flapping as the firebird left the cave, and the sigh of relief from Jace that she had joined them. When she was certain that she wasn't dead and no bones were broken, she slowly opened her eyes.

And standing there were The Guardians.

CHAPTER 9

I had been bored for a century. Always drunk on summer wine, dancing into the long nights. I felt that I had read every book, explored every edge of the continent, acquired more wealth and stature than anyone could need. I had seen things I wished to forget. Forgotten things I longed to remember. The mortals kept dying, and the immortals stopped truly living. Meeting her was like meeting a part of myself again. I wasted so much time strutting around, acting untouchable to avoid revealing how tenderly life touched me. I never knew sensitivity could be a strength, not a weakness. That it was a gift to feel so deeply. She showed me that. I felt fiercely protective of her from the moment we locked eyes. I knew I had found the other side of my wild, brilliant coin. —Ren

There were only three Guardians. Zia immediately saw why that was more than enough to protect the entrance. She remained on the cold, hard ground for a moment, unable to do anything other than stare at them. Two of them were nearly as tall as the cave. A power that was palpable seemed to suck all the air out of the room. It felt like standing before a black hole.

Zia stifled a scream when she saw they each had one large, violet eye in the center of their foreheads. Despite the wrinkles that gave away their immeasurably long lives, they seemed no less strong or spry than Jace. She felt a pang of sympathy for Brad's son, who lost his life trying to survive these creatures.

One of the Guardians held a long, pointed staff made from some kind of bone, and the other carried a drum made from an iridescent material that shimmered in the blue light of the cave. Their heads were shaved on both sides with a tight braid that went all the way to the stone floor. Various symbols were tattooed on either side of their heads.

Perhaps the most surprising of the three Guardians was a faerie who stood in the center of the other two. She looked no more than a few years older than Zia. Her shimmering golden hair was tied in a bun with two chopsticks on either side. Pointed ears poked out, and her full lips were in an unconcealable pout. Her magnificent wings were tucked in, but Zia could see gold whorls shimmering in the dim light of the cave. She wore knee-high leather boots and a black and gold silk corset dress with a slit down the front of her thigh. Her skin was barely visible beneath the decadent jewelry she wore. She was the type of woman who either sent men running or dropping onto one knee.

Zia was surprised they chose such a young faerie who clearly seemed more obsessed with her appearance than protecting the entrance. She could tell that Jace was thinking along those lines when he eyed the faerie up and down, looking away with obvious dismissal. Yet, when her amber eyes bore into Zia's, she saw that the faerie had turned beauty itself into a weapon—there was a hint of violence written across her stunning face. The faerie winked at her, then flashed her sharp teeth at Jace. Zia instantly liked her.

Zia examined the cave. It was not very wide, nor did it go very far back. Hundreds of little Lemurian crystals grew along the wall, each one with its own markings similar to the necklace Zia bore. It felt like being inside of a geode. Water dripped from the ceiling, interrupting the haunting silence as droplets fell to the ground. Through the Guardian's magic, they remained in a sonic cocoon that blocked out the harsh waterfall.

Zia squinted her eyes and saw there were turquoise-colored lights on the wall of the cave behind the guardians. They looked like little stars. A cluster of glowing lights were concealed within several lanterns along the wall. She prayed this cold, wet, dark place was not where her life would end. Her eyes watered as she felt the pain that stung her arms and legs from the burn marks of the fire bird. She did her best to ignore her blistering skin.

Jace gently set Hiro on the ground and then got to his knees and bowed. His eyes slid toward Zia to do the same, but the words of Katya floated into her mind.

Bow to no one but your heart.

After several seconds, Jace gave her an exasperated look. Zia hesitantly rose and dared a step toward the guardians, much to Jace's horror. She didn't have time for pleasantries when Hiro's life hung in the balance. Besides, she had never been one to kneel.

Jace cleared his throat before she could speak.

"I am Jace, Prince of Lemuria. I bring with me Hiro Sato, son of Mei Sato and the great assassin Zayne. He is greatly injured by the bite of a Hantu and needs immediate assistance."

Zia frowned at the formal way he spoke. His usual flirtatious, snarky tone was gone. She realized this was how the Prince of Lemuria usually appeared. One of the guardians slammed their staff onto the ground, and a terrible power rippled throughout the cave.

"You dare bring a human girl to the entrance of our world, traitor?"

Zia nearly screamed when the voice sliced through her mind. It felt like it echoed in the chamber of her skull. Her whole body shivered in response. This was nothing like The Trials. Jace kept his forehead low to the ground, not daring to look them in the eyes.

"She is The Bridge," he stated. His voice echoed along the walls of the cave. Zia frowned as the prophecy itched at the back of her mind. What was he talking about? *True power is held with humble hands. The Bridge will restore balance across the lands.* It couldn't be possible. The bridge was a place, not a person. She had assumed it was where one of the stones was hidden. Jace had to be lying so that the guardians would allow her to pass through. She examined the cave, looking for any way out, but there was nothing but hard rock.

"That's not possible," the horrific voice replied, violating their minds. Zia felt a knot unwind inside of her. It was a relief to hear their doubts echoed her own, instead of everyone telling her two worlds rested on her shoulders.

"She is the daughter of the healer Sahara, and a direct descendant of Queen Katya. Her father is human. Look at her necklace. Look at her eyes. She is The Bridge. With a foot in both worlds, she can restore what was lost," he said in an exasperated voice.

The faerie's gaze fell on Zia's forehead, and then her eyes bulged. She instantly sank to one knee before Zia, bowing her head. Zia flinched at the site of someone kneeling before her. She looked at Jace in desperation, but he was focused on The Guardians.

"*Get up, Ren. Do not bow before this mortal!*"

The faerie, Ren, looked up at Zia and gave her a warning look. Though she appeared to be in her early twenties, the confidence with which she carried herself made her seem far older.

Ren kept her voice low, but there was an edge to it that made even Jace pause.

"You know the prophecy, Yetiri. Are you so blind that you would deny what is right in front of you? She could be the one to save us."

Yetiri, the guardian with the staff, grabbed Ren's shoulder and hauled her up. Ren snarled at his touch. The faerie was not a fan of the other Guardians it seemed. Zia's palms twitched at her sides. She wanted to knock Yetiri's teeth in for the way he looked at her like she was nothing but a speck of dust floating amongst the stretch of his long, eternal life.

He glared at Ren with that creepy, violet eyeball.

"*The world has suffered enough in the hands of heroes.*"

Jace's head snapped up at that and he rose, the hilt of his silver knives gleaming in the blue light. Even those deadly sharpened blades couldn't have cut through the tension in the air. Ren's eyes darted between him and Zia. Her spine stiffened as she braced herself for the violence that was stirring, praying he wouldn't do anything stupid.

"I am the Prince of Lemuria, and you will—" Jace took a step toward them, and Yetiri slammed his staff into the ground twice. A gust of wind knocked Jace to the stone floor.

"*You were banished and stripped of your title. We do not answer to you.*"

Jace hauled both feet out before him and jumped up, going for his knives. Zia brought a hand to his chest, stopping him. His gaze flickered to her, a mix of wrath and curiosity. She silently pleaded for him to leash his temper. When his shoulders dropped from his ears, and she was certain he wasn't going to filet The Guardians, she turned toward them.

"I agree with you," she said, keeping her chin held high. Yetiri blinked, and Zia wondered how often he was surprised in his horribly long life.

"I don't believe in fate, heroes, or prophecies. I don't believe that I am the one to save your people." She pulled her mother's necklace off her neck and held it out before them. It was warm in her palms, the markings clearer than before. She did her best to keep her hands from shaking.

"This is all I have left of her. If you truly cared about Lemuria, you wouldn't let a tyrant sit on the throne. I have no desire to rule or conquer anyone, but my best friend lays before you, dying. He is one of you. He looked out for me when no one else would—" she choked on the words and paused for a few breaths to steady herself.

Yetiri slightly tilted his head, watching her with his violet eye.

"Very well. We will heal Hiro Sato. He has broken no laws and belongs to our realm. Despite your claimed inheritance, you are an ordinary human and will not be allowed to pass. Neither will your fallen prince."

Zia's cheeks warmed at the way Yetiri sneered "your fallen prince." She didn't dare look at Jace to see what his reaction was. Her heartbeat raced. They couldn't have come this far to be turned away. Ren was staring at the ground blankly with her head hung, her body unnaturally still.

Zia's chest tightened as Yetiri walked over to Hiro. All of the color had drained from his face, and his breaths were short. He was her best friend. Her family. Even in the past few days, he had risked his life countless times. She knew it was rare to have such a friendship.

Yetiri slammed the staff on the ground three times while the other guardian began to play the drum. She chewed on her nails, never taking her eyes off Hiro.

The guardian placed its strong, wrinkled hands on Hiro. The cave was silent for a moment, and then Hiro instantly woke from the slumber the potion had placed him in, screaming. It was the horrible scream of a person in excruciating pain. Yetiri's eye rolled to the back of his head, and as he lifted his hands, black liquid came out of Hiro's body.

Zia cupped a hand over her mouth to keep from gasping. Even Jace and Ren looked like they might be sick. When the last drop of liquid came out, color returned to Hiro's cheeks and he began to breathe normally. Yetiri sent the black liquid into the ground of the cave, returning it to the earth. Hiro sank into a deep sleep again and was snoring louder than a bear within a few moments. Zia let out a half sob of relief, unsure whether to cry or laugh.

"Leave him here. He will need time to heal before he can make it through our entrance. Now, go."

Zia was panting, debating what to do next. They couldn't send her back. The government would kill her, and she would never see her mother again. She tightened her grip around the necklace. It vibrated in her hands. A memory flashed before her eyes as she remained standing, frozen in time.

She was in her crib. Her mother was looking down at her with proud blue eyes. Her warm smile felt like home. "Zia, I love you," she whispered. She stroked Zia's cheek with her soft hand, gazing at her like she was the most precious thing in the world. There was a buzzing, a hum inside of Zia's veins. She could feel the magic inside of her, flowing as its own force.

"Bow to no one but your heart, Zia. Even when all feels lost, follow that beating compass in your chest..."

Tears slid down her mother's cheeks. She placed her necklace around Zia.

"This necklace is very special. It will protect you. Do not take it off until it is time." she whispered. The magic inside of Zia slumbered, recoiling as the necklace was placed around her. That buzzing permanently silenced. There was nothing but a dull whisper of it.

Her mother kissed her forehead with wet lips.

"Sahara, you have to go now." Her father's voice.

She could sense the fear in his tone, she could feel it in her own body. Her mother took one last look at her and smiled with such sadness it broke Zia's heart.

"I've left behind a map for you, so you may know our world someday. Follow the clues and you'll find your way home, my little bridge." She kissed Zia's forehead.

"When you unleash the power that sleeps inside of you, hold nothing back."

Only a few seconds had passed, but it may as well have been a lifetime. Her heartbeat raced. She opened her palm, looking at the one piece of her mother she had left. Sahara had stifled her magic, keeping it hidden so she could live safely in the human realm, unnoticed. She slowly turned her head toward The Guardians and knew there was only one way she was gaining access to Lemuria.

Zia threw the necklace on the ground and smashed it with the back of one of her blades. The crystal shattered into pieces, the glowing light from it fading. There was a sharp pain in her gut at the release of the bind her mother had placed. She nearly fell to the ground, bringing a hand to her stomach. Jace immediately grabbed her by the waist, keeping her steady.

Ren's breath caught at the site of the broken necklace and the magic she felt permeating from Zia. Yetiri's face showed nothing but a promise of death. She pushed Jace's grip away as she walked right up to Yetiri, standing inches away from him. She could feel his every thought and emotion as though it were her own. His mind was an open book, a labyrinth she could easily become lost in. Warm blood trickled down her nose as she felt her power coursing through her veins.

"You're not protecting the entrance. You're the king's spy. That's why you won't let me in. You've served him all this time out of fear, not honor."

Yetiri bared his teeth at her.

"I am a Guardian. Fear is not in my vocabulary."

Zia smiled slightly.

"No, but it's in your eyes."

Yetiri brought his hand to her throat and lifted her into the air. Her feet dangled as blood rushed to her head. Red spots clouded her vision. She reached for her blades, but he punched her in the gut with his other fist. She could vaguely hear Jace shouting her name and the sound of a great *thud*.

There was a flash of gold as Ren took out the chopsticks from her hair and they turned into fighting knives with the flick of her wrist. She dug one of them into Yetiri's side, and he immediately dropped Zia. The bones of her knees groaned at the impact of the cave floor. She coughed, gasping to get air back into her lungs.

Jace instantly moved to attack, but the other Guardian threw out his hand and a gust of wind slammed Ren and Jace into the wall of the cave. The Guardian let out the snarl of an animal as he pounced toward them with vengeance in his eyes. Jace darted out of the way just as the Guardian was about to strike. He hurled one of his knives clean through the guardian's back and into his heart.

Ren didn't waste any time as she unleashed herself on Yetiri, who lunged for Zia. Ren locked her legs around his head and flipped him onto the floor of the stone cave. She dug her nails into his shoulder, blood trickling down.

"Unfortunately, I have to leave you alive, or the realm will be unguarded."

Yetiri's eyes widened as his airways collapsed.

"But when this *ordinary* human decides she is capable of extraordinary things and saves your miserable ass, I want you to remember this moment." Ren placed her palms over him.

"Sleep," she commanded, her magic pouring into him.

His eyes instantly closed. She brought her hands to the wound where she stabbed him, healing him in his slumber. Then she stood up, dusting off her skirts and frowning when she saw a spot of blood on her corset. She stepped over Yetiri's body to inspect the other guardian. When she found him to be dead, she shook her head.

"You shouldn't have killed him."

Jace glared at her. "He decided his fate the minute he attacked Zia."

Zia fought the way her heart skipped a beat at the protective tone in his voice.

Ren sighed, "Yes, but his death will alert the king now. You could have slipped through undetected, but you had to go acting like a heroic prince."

"I saved her," Jace snapped.

Ren rolled her eyes as she looked at Zia, who was watching both of them, speechless. She eyed her up and down, as though examining every inch of her. Then she clapped Jace on the shoulder.

"That girl does not need saving."

Zia's heart warmed at that, even if she had needed help. Ren walked over to Zia and pulled her into a bone-crushing hug. Zia winced as she hit the burn marks. Ren laughed, and when she pulled away, bowed with a mock courtesy.

"Ren Hayes at your service," she winked at Zia.

"You are a Guardian, aren't you? Why risk yourself to help us?" Zia frowned.

Ren shrugged.

"Technically I'm a faerie, but my queen sentenced me to guard duty for mouthing off. She's a miserable old fossil." Ren raised her eyebrows which framed her face in pristine symmetry. She was unbearably beautiful. It was like looking at a living, breathing work of art.

Ren grabbed both of Zia's arms, inspecting the burn marks and the still-healing bullet wound. She ran her manicured hands over where the injuries were. Zia's skin prickled like a thousand pins and needles. When she looked down, she saw the burn marks fading, replaced by smooth brown skin.

"And to answer your other question, you're The Bridge. That's why I helped you."

Ren took a step back, examining the rest of Zia to make sure there were no other wounds to heal. Zia would have protested the statement, if not for the memory in her mother's dream. Her shoulders drooped at the pressure of what it could mean.

Ren's mouth quirked to the side, like she could read Zia's thoughts.

"It's not about you, Zia. It's about the hope that you represent. The world that Katya once tried to create."

"It's not worth dying for," Zia said with an edge to her voice. She glanced toward the remaining pieces of crystal on the ground and the dead Guardian whose blood stained the cave floor. Her mother had given up her freedom to protect her. Hiro had given up his home for her. She couldn't even think about the fate her father and Mei most likely met.

"Perhaps not. But it is worth living for."

Ren's smile was more of a challenge than anything. She seemed to stare *into* Zia, as though she saw all that Zia might one day become and was demanding she rise to the occasion.

"Got a way out of here, or are we going to just stand here all day while you do your makeup?" Jace chided, examining the walls of the cave. Zia knew he was goading the faerie to stop her from continuing their conversation. The walls were shallow, and there was no doorway or marker of any kind. She had expected enormous, grand gates with dragons guarding the front—not a dreary, wet cave that felt little better than a coffin.

Ren, however, took the opportunity to bite back.

"Missing your luxurious suite in the palace, prince? Shall I fetch you some summer wine, exotic spices, or perhaps golden toilet paper for you to wipe your—"

"*Alright.*" Zia snapped, throwing her arm between them. She silently prayed Hiro would wake up soon. Three different creatures with varying levels of miserable tempers didn't bode well for travel.

Jace's nostrils flared and his chest rose and fell in shallow breaths. She could tell it was taking everything in him not to slice off Ren's pointed ears with his knives. The faerie triumphantly smirked at him.

"I am exhausted. And hungry. And my best friend is currently comatose after getting bit by an overgrown housecat. So, if we could *move on...*" Zia gestured toward the wall of the cave. Ren examined her nails, then rolled her eyes and strutted over to where Yetiri still lay on the floor, unconscious.

"Fine, but if he keeps taking himself so seriously, I'm going to feed him to my Zhulu. He could use a hearty breakfast."

Zia blinked. Zhulu's were magnificent animals in The Trials. They possessed the head of a lion and mighty wings that carried them for hundreds of miles each day without tiring. The fact that Ren had one meant she was either royalty within the faerie queen's court or somehow collected a fortune by other means.

"They're real?" Zia whispered, her mouth slightly parted.

"Oh, yes. Named after the queen's consort, Zhu. He hailed from the dunes of the Ordos desert. He was our finest warrior, and the first Lemurian to ride the mighty birds." She raised her chin in the air with pride.

"The queen didn't have a consort," Jace said harshly. There was an unreadable expression on his face, but Zia noticed him shifting his weight uncomfortably. Ren brought a hand to her hip.

"I suppose you wouldn't know that, since it technically is *our* history, not Atlantis's. Though you should know it, since he was also the first Shadow Warrior. All Shadow Warriors hail from Ordos."

"Yes, I know—" Jace interrupted, but Ren talked over him, pacing around the cave.

"No one ever mentions Zhu, which is surprising since the queen obviously mated with *someone* to have descendants, and it sure as hell wasn't your father. I only found out when I was spying in the castle, rummaging through the gated section of the Lost Library. The king burned nearly every book in our world before he arrived. All but one: *The Book of Lemuria*. But I'm getting ahead of myself. After all, why would you remember anything that happened before you pillaged and plundered our lands?"

"That wasn't me, it was—"

"Your father, yes. And we're all still paying the price for our ancestor's choices, aren't we?" Ren took a step toward him. There was a murderous look in her eyes.

Zia stepped between them again.

"*Enough*, both of you. This isn't helpful."

Jace let out a bitter laugh. He gruffly rummaged through his pack, pulling out the book. Ren's breath hitched.

"But it was lost—"

"Nineteen years ago. Sahara stole it and hid it in the human realm so he couldn't destroy it."

Ren went to grab the book, but Jace held it out of reach.

"Get us out of here and I'll let you read it."

Ren's wings twitched in agitation, but she conceded. She rolled over Yetiri's body with the toe of her boot, like he was a piece of garbage on the floor. Then, she grabbed his staff and sauntered over to the cave wall.

Jace kept his mouth shut as he begrudgingly slung Hiro back over his shoulder, then stood next to Zia. He brushed her hand with his callused thumb for half a second. She glanced over at him and saw the wariness in his eyes. They had kept so many things from each other. Trust was not something she gave easily, but she could no longer ignore the part of her that ached to let him in.

Ren wriggled the staff into a small hole in the ground and twisted it like a lever. She took out a flute made from white bone, and her eyes rolled to the back of her head as she played. The song echoed across the cave walls. As the melody seeped into every nook and corner, hidden carvings in the rocks began to glow. The entire wall was illuminated in a blue light creating hundreds of little markings and symbols. Had Hiro been awake, he could have memorized them so they could later de- code what they meant. Like a curtain being pulled back, the wall simply opened and parted, revealing the darkness of a tunnel. Jace sighed in relief that there was nothing waiting on the other side.

"Got a flashlight handy?" Zia asked, knowing the odds of a Lemurian prince or a faerie carrying such a simple human object.

Amusement twinkled in Ren's eyes. She took out a pouch that had blue powder inside. She shook some into the palm of her hand, faced the tunnel, and blew the dust into the cave with one long breath. The dust seemed to travel much farther than a single breath.

The entire cave began to glow in a thousand blue twinkling stars. Not stars, Zia realized. Glow worms. Zia was rendered speechless, her eyes wide with wonder.

"Much better than a flashlight," Ren grinned, stepping through the cave. Her steps were somehow silent, despite the boots she wore. Zia had an endless list of questions to ask about faerie magic, but exhaustion hit her. The adrenaline from leaping on the firebird had at last drained, and it took everything in her to keep her eyes open.

Hiro was snoring loudly. He was completely unaware they were about to enter another realm. Jace's eyes darted back and forth skeptically, but he stepped through the cave entrance. He looked over his shoulder at Zia, waiting. She took a deep breath, glancing at the fallen Guardians one last time. The world she might never see again. Zia stepped inside the cave. Ren played the flute again, and within a few seconds, the walls of the cave sealed them in like a curtain closing shut.

There was no going back.

PART II:

LEMURIA

Your path will be found as you walk blindly in the dark, stumbling until you learn to see through the eyes of your heart.

—LEMURIAN PROVERB II

CHAPTER 10

People came from all around the world to lose themselves in The Trials. Most of them found an escape from the mundane when they played. It was a golden ticket to evade their misery. The real Lemuria wasn't a numbing escape or cheap entertainment. The land was not just alive... it was a teacher. Not the kind of stuffy, elitist teacher who pretends to know something you don't. Lemuria was like an earthquake that shook awake the knowledge already slumbering within you. It heightened everything. Tested you in ways you never thought possible. I knew she had to go there eventually. Lemuria was the part of herself she felt was missing all along. —Mei

"**Y**ou jumped on top of a *firebird*. What is wrong with you?" Jace stood a mere few inches away from Zia. He looked like he wanted to knock her to the ground. Apparently, his gratitude for her survival was short-lived.

"I improvised." Zia barked back.

"I thought it was badass," Ren cut in. She was leaning against the wall of the cave with her arms crossed over her chest, smirking. Her wings fluttered slightly behind her.

"No one asked you," Jace glowered at her. Ren's eyes danced with mischief. She looked at the prince like a cat with a yarn ball, as though she was debating testing just how many threads she could pull from his sanity.

Zia poked at his chest with her finger, like she could pop his inflated ego like a balloon.

"Do you plan on getting over yourself at any point? Those are *my* choices to make—"

"Not when you *burned* yourself in the process! You have no idea what your life means to people," he seethed.

"You mean what it means to you," Ren's mouth quirked to the side. She walked over to the two of them with such grace, Zia suddenly felt as feminine as a pile of bricks. Jace pressed his mouth into a tight line. He didn't like the faerie one bit. Zia, however, was liking her more and more with each passing second.

"I suggest you keep your voices down. There are ancient creatures in these caves which are best left undisturbed. Especially now that Zia's magic is no longer hidden," she added cautiously.

Jace examined Zia closely, making sure not a hair on her head was harmed.

"When were you going to tell me you had magic?" he asked.

Zia suddenly felt a pang of guilt in her stomach. Her cheeks heated.

He had been honest with her from the beginning, but she had never told anyone. Not even Hiro. She didn't even understand that it was magic until the phantom panther. He nodded once in disappointment, then walked away, stomping into the darkness of the tunnels. She wanted to yell at him. It seemed that no matter what she did, she got under his skin. She was about to walk after him when Ren gently grabbed her by the shoulder.

"Give him the space to sort out how he feels," she said wisely.

Zia was about to retort that it was none of Ren's business, but she admired the faerie. She knew her mother would have liked Ren. She also had never had a female friend before. Women were competitive with each other in Periculum. Perhaps a friendship could rewrite the story of those wounds.

"Walk with me," Ren said in gentle understanding. She grasped Zia's hand and pulled her along, trailing after Jace in the dim light of the caves.

The humidity was unbearable. Every breath felt like Zia was drinking the air. She wiped a bead of sweat from her brow. The twinkling glow worms looked like fallen stars lighting their way. Zia would never forget watching Ren make them come to life with that dust.

Every sound was amplified, echoing along the wet walls. Hiro's snoring was a steady symphony, which Zia found oddly comforting. Drool oozed off his chin, and Jace kept switching him from shoulder to shoulder to even out the weight.

"Are you a healer?" Zia asked, ignoring the way her swords shifted uncomfortably at her back. Sweat streamed down her spine and she could feel her skin becoming irritated.

"No, I'm a shifter. One of few faeries left with undiluted magic. It was why I was the queen's spymaster for so long. My powers give me the ability to tend to shallow wounds, but anything beyond cuts and bruises requires a healer." She gestured a hand across her face and her hair shifted from blonde to blue. Her eyes turned yellow, and her teeth grew fangs. Jace paused at the magic, turning to see what happened. Ren hissed at him, smiling with those terrifying fangs before changing herself back. Jace grumbled and kept walking.

Zia couldn't help but smile, but Ren's eyes grew serious.

"Our real magic comes in the bond of our word. We deal in unbreakable bargains, and they usually aren't favorable. Death is often a better option than cutting a deal with a faerie," her voice was grave.

Zia swallowed, "Thanks for the warning."

Ren saluted her and kept walking. She pried the *Book of Lemuria* from Jace's bag. He tried to stop her, but her head turned into a snake with a forked tongue. He resigned, giving her the book but kept a hawk's eye on her the remainder of the time. Ren then shifted to have glowing eyes that worked as a reading light. She never looked up from the pages once but still walked with feline grace.

They fell into silence after that, trudging through the caves for what felt like hours. It was impossible to tell time without the passing light of day. Zia's feet ached without her shoes. It would take time for her to develop calluses, she supposed. She could feel the pads of her feet getting cut up, but she said nothing, doing her best to keep pace.

The further they walked, the more Zia pondered her magic. Ren could change her appearance, Hiro could fold between spaces, the other prince could bend fire. She rolled her eyes. Of course, her magic was feeling other people's feelings for them. That couldn't be the extent of her abilities. If she was able to link with the Hantu and the firebird...she wondered what else she could do if she dared to find her edge.

She was so lost in her thoughts she didn't realize the other two had stopped walking and slammed straight into Jace's back. He huffed.

"Good to know your awareness is improving."

She stuck her tongue out at him. They stood there silently for a moment. Ren's pointed ears twitched as she listened further. She brought her hand to Zia's back.

"You're half Lemurian. Your senses should sharpen as you move into the heart of our world. Tell me what you can hear."

Zia strained her ears to listen. It was subtle, but Zia heard it. There was running water in the caves. A lot of running water. That must mean they were close to the exit. Relief washed over her. She couldn't escape the wet, claustrophobic caves fast enough.

The walls of the caves opened up, growing wider with each step they took. Zia could breathe easier, knowing she had more than a few feet of space. They walked around a corner and finally found the water source. It was a wide river. The water was black and uninviting. Zia had no interest in finding out what lurked beneath the surface.

Jace's tattoos glowed in the darkness of the cave. He scanned every inch of the walls, making sure nothing lurked in the shadows. There was a small wooden boat by the river's edge. It seemed to be waiting for them. There was the carving of a serpent at the bow. Luckily, it was big enough to fit the four of them somewhat comfortably.

Ren leaped in first, not making so much as a sound as she settled into the stern of the boat. She smoothed out her silk skirt and rested her back against the wooden side. Zia followed next, her legs wobbling slightly. She had never been in a boat and wasn't used to the shaky movements. She gripped the edge tightly as she finally sat down.

Jace climbed in, gently setting Hiro down. He folded his jacket beneath Hiro's head and sat at the bow of the boat. Before they understood what was happening, there was a strong tug as the boat launched forward, moving downstream. It felt peaceful to float along the gentle rapids. Though the black water looked less than friendly, Zia felt safe within the boat. She sat there with her knees curled into her chest, looking up at the ceiling of the cave in wonder. She wished she could understand the prophecy. It kept tugging at the back of her brain, like a memory she couldn't quite place her finger on.

Jace leaned back, resting an elbow over his knee. Despite his relaxed posture, Zia could see the tension in his shoulders. The way his eyes constantly darted around the cave, looking for any possible danger. She wondered if he had ever let go of control in his life.

Ren, on the other hand, leaned over the edge with her whole torso staring out at the black waters. She had a huge smile on her face, her eyes wide as she gazed at what was beneath. Zia got a glimpse of what she must have looked like when she was a child with that girlish grin. It was like a kid on Christmas morning. When she caught Zia staring at her, she pointed toward the water.

Zia scooted over next to her, and when she peered over the edge, her breath caught. Little twinkling stars surrounded the boat, guiding them along the river. It looked exactly as it had in The Trials, only better. They had called it bioluminescence. It looked like a liquid galaxy.

She gripped the wooden edge tightly with her hands and peered closer to the water. Something moved beneath the water and Zia yelped, immediately jumping back. There was a splashing noise, and then a flying fish leaped over them, landing in the water on the other side. It wasn't like any fish she had ever seen. When she looked back over the edge, there were more of them. Their vibrant scales were made of every color, and their fins looked like butterfly wings.

"They are *Antiqua*, the oldest of spirits. After we finish our final lifetime, we come back as one of them, making one last journey home through the Great River," Ren said softly.

Zia watched the fish race down the stream in awe. The patterns on their wings were so intricate and vibrant. It almost looked like a language.

"The stories of all the lifetimes they have lived are etched onto their fins," Ren said gleefully.

Zia couldn't help it as a broad smile took over her face. When she glanced over at Jace, his eyes burned into hers with such an intensity that she had to look away. She tucked a strand of hair behind her ear and brought her attention back to the butterfly fish.

To lose a sense of wonder is to die before death, Zia thought to herself. This tiny, perfect moment made whatever they would face going forward worth it. Her thoughts were interrupted when a butterfly fish leaped out of the river and landed directly on Hiro's face, smacking him with its slimy tail. Zia scooped the fish up, and it squirmed in her palms. She was careful not to touch its delicate fins as she carefully placed it back in the water.

Hiro moaned, stirring from his slumber. He sat up and scratched his head, yawning loudly. He blinked several times, coming back to reality. His mouth parted as he looked around at the cave walls.

Zia yelped in happiness and threw her arms around his neck. Hot tears of joy streamed down her face. Jace assessed Hiro to ensure he was truly healed from the poison. Zia couldn't stop smiling.

It was Ren who spoke first.

"You have slobber on your chin."

They all burst out in laughter. It was the kind of laughter that felt like a release, as though all the hurdles from the past few days were melting away. Zia's ribs hurt as her whole body shook uncontrollably.

Hiro scratched his head and wiped the water from his face with his dirty T-shirt.

"So…I'm guessing we got through the entrance?"

It only made them laugh harder. Even Jace couldn't help it. When they finally calmed down, they caught Hiro up on everything that had happened since he had been bit by Hantu. He listened with wide eyes, and when they finished telling him the tale, he grinned.

"So…you're saying I got to sleep through all the hard parts while you guys carried me?" he said with a smug expression.

Zia playfully smacked him. Jace looked inclined to toss him into the freezing waters. They continued to answer his questions about what The Guardians were like and how they managed to escape them, thanks to Ren. Zia took his hat out of her pack. He caught it, twirling it in the air before placing on his head.

They moved gently downstream, and the river only grew wider and deeper as they floated along. Zia tested the temperature with a finger and shuddered. It was the coldest water she had ever felt. She wondered when they would see sunlight again. She missed feeling its warmth kiss her skin. There was so much about Lemuria she wished to know. It felt like her whole life had been a distant dream, and she was finally waking up.

They took turns keeping watch. Hiro went first, since he had been asleep for the day. It was odd to not be able to tell whether it was day or night. Time had become an irrelevant concept altogether. Zia curled up on her side and used her jacket as a pillow. Dirt was stuck under her fingernails, and she noticed bloodied scratches and bruises all over. The journey was wearing on her body. The sound of the rushing water eased her thoughts as they floated from her mind. Her exhaustion tugged her into a dreamless sleep.

A few hours or a few days could have passed. The only sounds were the gentle water lapping against the wood and the occasional butterfly fish leaping in the air. Jace barely slept. He couldn't help but look after Zia, at the rare softness in her face as she slept. When he glimpsed her joy from watching the Antiqua, it had sparked something in him that he hadn't felt since Meaghan. It was the same feeling he got when Zia had marveled at the forest on Mount Shasta—like she couldn't help but fall in love with the world again and again. It made him feel awake after centuries of a slumbering heart.

Zia stirred, shifting from side to side. She slowly blinked her bright, blue eyes open and sat up. Ren and Hiro were fast asleep. Her gaze fell to Jace and she frowned at him.

"Why are you on watch?" she asked.

Jace shrugged.

"Couldn't sleep."

Zia eyed him hesitantly, debating whether or not to close the gap between them. She never took the first step, especially when it came to apologizing, but as she looked at him, she couldn't help it.

Zia carefully scooted over, settling next to him at the bow. The cuts in her feet ached with each step, but she ignored it. Their shoulders barely touched, but she could feel his warmth. She waited a few moments, gathering her words.

"I'm sorry I didn't tell you. About the magic."

He sighed and looked up at the ceiling of the cave.

"I know why you didn't. I understand. It's just—"

"You need to trust that I can take care of myself," she retorted, interrupting him.

He looked at her incredulously.

"Apologies aren't your thing, are they?"

They stared at each other stubbornly for a few moments. He chuckled and shook his head.

"I am well aware you can take care of yourself. An eighteen-year-old girl who not only survived Periculum but had the highest score of any player in the most volatile game the world has known. It's just that—" he ran his fingers through his dark, silky hair in frustration. "You run into the danger most people cower from. It's like nothing scares you. And that scares me, because I don't know if you'll lose yourself to that one day." Relief flooded his chest as the words finally tumbled out.

Zia turned toward him, tilting her head to the side thoughtfully.

"Why do you care?"

He slowly turned toward her, the ghost of a sensual smile playing on his lips. Yet there was raw emotion in his face. Beneath all his flirtation and teasing, there was something deeper there that she didn't dare name.

"You know why," his voice was hoarse.

Those words cut through every shield she had. Every time she threw up a wall, he found a way to create a window with his words. She cleared her throat, looking away from him.

"Some things scare me, you know."

He arched a brow.

"What scares you?"

Zia's stomach did backflips, but she forced herself to look at him.

"You know what."

He couldn't hide his surprise and hope at her words. She had the sensation of the ground slipping out from under her.

"Why did you bet on me? At The Trials. You were the only one."

He didn't hesitate.

"Because you saved someone you believed could do nothing for you."

Zia wasn't expecting that to be his answer and was unaware he had been watching when she rescued the siren in The Trials. She had felt the same feeling with the assassin before the woman tumbled to her death—the thread of her life connected to another.

A stream of light peaked through, nearly blinding them. They were nearing the end of the cave. Before Zia could ask any more questions, he moved over to wake Ren and Hiro. They sat up and sighed in relief at the exit of the cave. It had felt like a short eternity being stuck beneath the mountains.

The boat cleared the exit, and the harsh rays of the sun had all of them covering their eyes, blinking until they adjusted. They came to an abrupt stop next to a wide meadow with rolling hills at the edge of a forest. It wasn't the forest from The Trials, but it was still familiar. Zia again had the strange sensation of the past and future overlapping on itself.

They all climbed out of the boat, helping each other up onto the soft, vibrant grass. Ren stumbled, her boots getting soaked in the water. She pouted but said nothing, knowing that Jace would ridicule her for it.

"Did anyone notice the boat wasn't pulling itself?" Hiro asked, pointing toward the emerald serpent that was now tugging the boat back in toward the cave. Zia's stomach dropped. She had assumed the boat moved due to magic, not because there was a river serpent pulling them the entire time.

"Thank you!" Hiro called after it.

The serpent's tail slithered, as though in farewell, before it disappeared into the cave. Ren, who was sitting on the ground shaking out her boots, squinted at the creature.

"Those serpents go for your weight in gold at the Ghost Market. Just one of them can pull up to a hundred tons. Invaluable to smugglers."

She shook out the other boot, then shrugged both of them onto her feet.

Zia slowly looked around, taking in the light of day. Her heart ached, having gone a lifetime without knowing such a place. Exotic flowers of every hue hugged the riverbed. Silver rocks were covered in violet moss. Lush vines wrapped around the trees that were so tall she couldn't see the tops of them. Beams of sunlight stubbornly peaked through the canopy.

That familiarity nagged at her again. Understanding dawned on her. It *was* familiar.

"This is the forest from my dreams," she breathed.

"Sure is, Z." Hiro grinned, tossing an arm around her. He would know, since she had described her dreams to him since they were kids, trying to make sense of her fragmented world. Little did she know he had the answers the whole time. Her eyes watered.

This was the forest she had dreamed of her entire life. She had run barefoot on the red dirt and bright green grass. She had touched the soft moss on the mighty trees. She had climbed the ridges of the haunting mountains. In disoriented snippets, she had seen Lemuria. Half of her life was spent here, except now she could smell the bark and taste the fruit. Now this land was *real*, and all her senses were alive waiting to experience it.

Ever since Mei first taught Zia how to play in The Trials, she had been walking toward this. A part of her had always been holding back hope that Lemuria was real. Now, here she stood, having stumbled right along a destiny that she wouldn't have thought possible in a thousand years.

And somewhere, in the dense forest, or the proud mountains, or the empty meadows, was her mother. Alive. Zia remembered her voice and every detail of her face. She remembered the kindness in her mother's eyes, but she did not know what it felt like to hug her. To *talk* to her. Despite the exhaustion, she suddenly found herself very impatient. Her heart leaped. What would the first words they exchange be?

"Not bad for a *Psukhē*, is it?" Jace stepped beside her.

Hiro stumbled a bit.

"A Psukhē?"

Jace nodded.

"I only realized when I saw her with the firebird. I suppose you can think of it like she is a voyager of the psyche. She can link her consciousness with others—read their thoughts, emotions, and memories. She can absorb their powers if she trains. Even travel to their subconscious. But it is very dangerous without training. She can lose herself and become trapped in the mind of another." He emphasized the last part in warning.

The two of them discussed her powers—the potential benefits and dangers. Zia curled her toes up in the grass, grateful not to be in a cramped cave anymore. She looked around. The forest was quiet. Too quiet. Where were the crickets or birds? She had expected to be ambushed by Lemurians, or another legendary creature. *Some* sort of life. The stillness was more unnerving than anything else.

Beyond the forest were enormous mountains of varying hues. Their sharp ridges looked like the spine of a dragon. Though they were lovely, there was something daunting about them. She prayed Aaliyah didn't live there.

"Are there others like me?" She asked, half paying attention to their conversation. Her skin was covered in goosebumps.

"The Guardians have the gift, in their own way. It is why you could communicate mind-to-mind with them. But there hasn't been a Lemurian Psukhē for nine thousand years," Jace replied quietly.

"Let me guess: the last one was Queen Katya," Zia pursed her lips.

Jace nodded, deep in thought. Zia wasn't sure what her connection to the queen was, but she was finding more and more tethers between them. *The original queen will once again rise...* the riddle echoed in her mind.

Could Katya be brought back from death after all this time? Zia knew the stones were powerful, but there were some natural laws that seemed unbreakable. She felt a twinge in her heart as she thought of her father, and silently prayed he escaped.

"We shouldn't discuss this here. Even the trees are listening," Jace muttered. Ren strutted right past him, toward the forest ahead.

"I know of a safe place we can rest a few miles from here."

He immediately protested.

"We have very different definitions of *safe*."

The two of them were insufferable. Jace eyed the forest skeptically like it might swallow him whole at any second. They didn't have much of a choice. There wasn't exactly a hotel lying around. Ren was a faerie—she would know the forest better than any of them.

Zia looked at her new friend.

"What happens when night falls?"

Ren's lips spread into a slow, mischievous smile.

"Don't worry, Zia. Our days are lovely, but our nights are what have inspired your human fairytales. There is no place in any realm as beautiful."

Sunlight peaked through the trees, creating golden beams that illuminated the path ahead. It didn't look very menacing, but Zia knew better than to let her sight betray her. Ren gestured a hand toward the forest, which seemed to whisper in invitation.

"Welcome home, Zia," she said with a grin.

Zia took a step toward the world she had dreamed of her whole life.

CHAPTER 11

When they came to see me, I tried to tell them to stop searching so hard for the answers. They were in a rush to complete their mission, and it was causing them to miss what was right in front of them. I've been alive for over nine thousand years. I have loved and lost more than anyone. It is only now that I realize the mistakes we make become our greatest stories. In my youth, ambition was the fire that fueled me. I, too, wanted to know everything. Now, I realize what a gift it is to not know. To marry the mystery. To wonder. —Aaliyah

Despite her aching, tired bones, Zia had never felt more alive. They trekked through the forest and stuck close to the river so that they wouldn't leave any tracks. The rocks were slimy and slick with moss. After Hiro nearly face-planted in the stream, they all decided to go barefoot.

Jace kept growling at Zia for moving at a snail's pace while they were in search of shelter, but she couldn't help it—there was so much to take in. She felt that as she watched the forest, the forest watched her back.

Smokey mist curled around her feet, blanketing the forest floor. The river was filled with Antiqua and glittering stones at the bottom. Ren explained that when a soul first incarnates into Lemuria, they choose to be a stone to observe and listen. It made Zia feel strange about stepping on them, but leaving footprints was not an option.

The forest was far too quiet. It felt like they were still in the cave. There should have been birds or crickets or *something*. Zia practically held her breath the entire hike, waiting for someone to attack them. Ren assured her that it was always this way—most Lemurians outside of the royal city preferred to sleep during the day, which made traveling that much safer for them. Besides, they were in the southern part of the continent. It was sparsely populated.

Ren ensured that at moonrise, even the smallest spec of dirt would come alive.

Zia barely looked where she was going, her eyes darting all around the forest. She wanted to pause and study every plant and insect they passed. Hiro kept pace alongside her, pointing out different parts of the forest and comparing the experience to The Trials. She didn't realize that Lemuria was, in some ways, as new to him as it was to her.

Zia saw a large yellow flower the size of her head that drooped down toward the forest floor. Ren told her it was known as *Helius*, the flower of death. Lemurians drank its nectar as a bridge to the underworld to be able to talk to the other side. The soul became trapped in purgatory until the flower was out of the body's system. Zia went to touch it when Ren smacked her hand away. Hiro renamed it the zombie flower, and Zia wisely backed far away. She had danced with death enough for one day. Hiro wrinkled his nose as he walked past the cluster of flowers. They smelled like rotting flesh.

Everything in the forest had a purpose, Ren explained. The roots of the trees were tied together in a network, like a brain. The king often tapped into that network to spy, but Ren said there were parts of the forest that were still loyal to the old ways. No matter how much the king had caged Lemuria, the people still found a way.

Art was seen as sacred to the Lemurians. It was a way of transforming their pain and saying, "I am still here. Throughout it all, I am still here." They whispered old legends by the firelight, sang forbidden songs of their past, wove tapestries with the stories of their fallen, or practiced magic in hopes there would one day be a world they didn't have to hide in. Ren looked pointedly at Zia as she said that, but Zia refused to let the weight of that hope settle into her.

Find her mother. Learn to control her magic. That was all she was there for.

Zia tested her senses as they sharpened with each passing step. Sound was the most jarring. She could hear the heartbeats of the group. Ren's sounded like a hummingbird. Faeries had completely different anatomy than Lemurians. Jace's was so slow that Zia at first wondered if he was alive.

The smell was overwhelming. Whether her nose was filled with diverse flower species or the pungent scent of four unbathed travelers, she wished she could tone it down. *That* would certainly take some getting used to. As she walked, she ran her fingers over various rocks and trees. It felt like several layers of skin were missing. She could feel even the individual beads of moss so clearly.

The hike was a rare reprieve from the stressful few days they had. Nothing tried to kill them, much to Hiro's discontent—he even had the nerve to say he was bored at one point, which earned him a smack in the back of the head and a glare from Jace.

The sun dipped beneath the mountains. The last of the light peeked through the trees. The hour before sunset had always been Zia's favorite. The world seemed to pause for that speck of time as honey-colored light flooded every corner of the forest. Little moths wove in and out of the trees, their small wings backlit by the light.

Ren told Zia legends of Lemuria along the way—mostly of the wicked faeries and their unbreakable blood bargains.

"The faerie court was sheltered from the king's reign of terror," she exclaimed, delicately stepping around the rocks, "He agreed not to touch their territory in exchange for Morganna's alliance."

"What does that alliance entail, exactly?" Zia asked.

Ren raised her brows.

"I would give a whole summer's worth of wine to go back in time and find out."

"Have you two met before, since Jace spent his ban—" Zia stopped herself, "Since he spent some time in the faerie court."

"It's alright, sweetheart. Everyone knows I was banished," Jace winked as he fell into stride with her.

Ren's eyes danced with amusement.

"While I have heard harrowing tales about our most magnanimous prince—"

Jace cut her a glare.

"—we haven't met. As the queen's spy, I spent little time in her court. Few faeries still exist with the ability to fully shift their appearance," Ren waved a hand over her face, and her eyes turned bright red. "That is, until she tired of my presence and sentenced me to guard duty."

Though Ren had attempted to say the last bit in humor, there was a heaviness to her tone. Zia could feel her sorrow, but she didn't push the faerie further.

Ren continued chatting about the faerie court. Their lands had unparalleled beauty, but everything came with a price. The more power they were given, the tighter their leash to their queen. She grew quiet when she spoke of Queen Morganna, looking over her shoulder to make sure no one was listening. From the fear that crept into Ren's voice, Morganna sounded little better than the king.

The sunset was filled with hues of orange and pink, backing the silhouette of the Albizias. It looked like a god had spilled their heart across the sky. The sun offered one last performance before the moon took its reign.

They finally arrived at the spot where they would set up camp. It was a little nook surrounded by a grove of trees, providing them cover. Spring water flowed generously from the mountain, and Hiro folded a leaf at the end of the stream, creating a natural fountain. They all took turns drinking their fair share. The cool water sang to Zia's taste buds as she drank. She wiped the water from her chin and sighed in relief.

They unloaded the little supplies they had left. Zia gave Hiro the bow and arrows she stole off Brad. His face lit up with joy as he held the silver arrows in his callused hands. Aside from weapons, they were completely out of food. Jace announced he was going hunting. He glanced over his shoulder and looked pointedly at Hiro and Zia.

"Don't do anything life-threatening while I'm gone."

Zia glared at him, swallowing the string of insults she wanted to throw back. Hiro merely smiled in response. It was impossible to get under his skin. A quality Zia had always admired about him, since she had the tendency to take *everything* personally.

Hiro sprawled out on the soft grass, heaving a loud sigh. They had gathered enough wood for a fire but waited to light it until Jace came back for dinner. No need to announce to the realm where they were with a cloud of smoke when the most capable warrior among them was missing.

Ren came and sat down next to Zia, tossing her golden hair behind her shoulder. Her pointed ears twitched as she listened for any potential threats. Yet somehow, she maintained a complete sense of ease, like she was so comfortable in her skin that nothing could throw her off balance. Zia couldn't help but admire her like she would a painting. The golden hoops that pierced her pointed ears. The string of delicate, jeweled necklaces at her throat. Her cheekbones that could have cut glass. They sat there for a few minutes, taking in the setting sun.

Ren smiled softly, turning toward Zia.

"I can help you, you know."

Zia knew what she meant.

"For what reason? I don't have anyone to dress for."

Hiro interrupted them with a cackle, "Not even a prince?"

Zia threw her empty pack at Hiro's face. He caught it before it could hit its mark, still chuckling. He was cleaning his bow and arrows carefully, gazing at them fondly like a newborn. It was perhaps the only material item he had ever given a damn about.

Ren eyed Zia up and down. Her thick lashes fluttered, framing the way her amber-colored eyes glowed in the setting sun.

"You don't dress up for men. You dress for *you*. You choose how you want to express yourself. What makes you feel good in your own skin. Most people use beauty to cover up who they are. You can use it to *express* who you are."

Zia couldn't help but wince at that. The only time she felt close to pretty was in The Trials, when she was able to become someone else. Ren shook her head, like she understood that too.

"Turn around," she said gently.

Zia reluctantly turned around, with her back facing toward Ren. She swallowed nervously. The only woman that had ever been in her life was Mei, who had never been feminine or soft in the way Ren was. All the girls she knew who bothered with such things scared Zia, making her feel like they spoke a language she would never learn.

Ren took a rose gold brush out of her backpack and began to brush Zia's hair. No one had brushed her hair before.

"Why don't you just magic the knots away?" Zia asked, staring ahead at one of the fluttering moths.

Ren kept brushing her hair out in gentle strokes.

"My mom always brushed my hair when I was younger to comfort me. She told me grand stories while she did, and then would teach me how to style it. Every day she was like a new character, expressing a different side of herself."

"She sounds amazing," Zia replied.

Ren sighed, finishing the last of the knots.

"She was, until the king stormed our lands and found he enjoyed her beauty. He killed my father and took her away, leaving my sisters and me without parents. I never saw her again, until years later when I was spying for Morganna in the court. I was disguised as one of his guards and found her name etched into the list of the people he had executed."

Ren's voice cracked at the last bit. She heaved a heavy sigh, like she could breathe out some of the pain that still lived within her. She began weaving Zia's hair into a bunch of little braids.

"I'm sorry for your loss," was all Zia could say.

Ren smiled sadly.

"You know my loss well. The thing is, when the ones we love shed their bodies, their spirit remains with us—their legacy and strength live through us. And nothing, Zia, is more powerful than a woman who decides she is only bound only by the limitations she acknowledges."

Ren let go of her hair, handing Zia a small mirror. Zia's mouth parted as she looked herself over, seeing that Ren had placed little flowers in her braids. She smiled, twirling one of the braids around her finger, feeling like she had never seen herself before. Ren grabbed onto both her shoulders and squeezed gently.

"Like I said, you're beautiful."

Zia swallowed the lump in her throat and grinned from ear to ear, turning to her new friend.

"Thank you," she said, meaning for more than just the braids.

Ren winked at her.

"We ladies must look out for one another."

"Do I count as a lady then?" Hiro called again. He was once again sprawled out on the grass like a starfish, his top hat covering his eyes and his bow and arrows clutched in his arms like a stuffed animal.

"Maybe if you didn't pick your nose," Zia replied. Hiro grinned in response.

Zia looked down at herself, horrified aside from her new braids. The dirt caked under her nails. The sweat that still clung to her back. Her face paled when she saw the dried blood from the assassin that was on her pant legs. She groaned as she stood up.

"I need to bathe."

"Why? I think your smell is an excellent weapon. We can make our enemies' eyes water without even lifting a finger," Hiro chuckled.

"Remind me again *why* I saved you."

Hiro was twirling a violet flower between his fingertips, playing with its petals.

"Because you would be so bored without me, dear."

She rolled her eyes and walked off. Ren reached into her small bag and pulled out a fresh pair of clothes—the magic woven into the threading made the bag have an infinite capacity. She insisted Zia surrender her mother's cloak for her to wash. Zia took one look at Ren's corset and felt nervous at the thought of what Ren would have her wear. It didn't matter. She needed to get out of the disgusting clothes. She shrugged off the ragged cloak, gave it to Ren, and decided to burn the rest.

"Make sure you do something life-threatening while you're gone!" Ren called, mocking Jace's last words to them. She wriggled her fingers in farewell, her red nails matching the sunset.

Zia gave her a salute and disappeared into the forest. She took her blades with her to clean them off. Her feet felt tender against the earth as she stumbled over various rocks. Many of them glittered with a thousand tiny quartz crystals that were embedded into the stone.

Zia sighed. She *really* needed to build up her calluses. There was something liberating about being barefoot, though. It reminded her of being a little kid running around in Mei's yard with Hiro, building forts and reenacting The Trials.

If only she had known, those fantasies would one day become a reality.

Zia made it to the edge of the river. Its gentle waters beckoned to her. She dipped her ankles in and found that it was far warmer than the icy rapids of the cave. She stripped down and submerged up to her shoulders, scrubbing away the dirt and blood. The riverbed was shallow enough that she had to remain on her knees to fully bathe. Zia groaned. She would have to ask Ren how she was supposed to handle her menstrual cycle when it came. If faeries even dealt with that sort of thing. Living off the land was something she would need to adapt to. She kneaded at the tight muscles in her neck, feeling like she would be content to disappear within the river.

Zia hugged her knees into her chest and closed her eyes, listening to the silence. It felt comforting instead of eerie. She thought of her dad's apartment in Periculum. She had once merely wished to leave the crumbling ruins of the city. It wasn't a dream so much as a wish to survive. She hadn't dared hope for anything beyond that.

Psukhē. The word echoed in her mind. She cupped water in her palms, watching every last drop drain, thinking of the journey ahead. It was easy enough to link her mind with another's. The trouble was getting out. Every time she had done it, she had been fortunately kicked out. If Yetiri or the Hantu had wanted to trap her, they could have easily.

Zia didn't even know where to begin when it came to the stones. All she had was a dream from a crazy elder and a cryptic prophecy. There wasn't much to go on. Zia let out a bitter laugh and splashed more cool water on her face. She lay on her back, feeling weightless and enjoying the sound of silence as the water filled her ears.

When she opened her eyes, she realized night had fallen. What felt like a few minutes could have been a few hours. Time worked differently in Lemuria. Sapphire blue painted the sky as the moon began to rise. It was nearly full. There was something comforting about the fact that the moon looked the same as it had in Periculum—a small tether to normalcy. The constellations, however, were completely different. She hadn't been able to see more than a cluster back home.

Ren was right. The forest came alive with music. It was unlike any bird or cricket she heard before. She closed her eyes and isolated the sounds, trying to decipher what creatures they were coming from, but it all swirled together in one symphony.

Leaves rustled behind her. Zia snapped her head back and immediately stood up, waiting for whatever it was to reveal itself. She tried to steady her breath as her stomach did several summersaults.

Nothing. She sighed and rolled her shoulders back, releasing the tension in her neck. The whole journey was making her paranoid. Forests made noises. It was nothing to be scared about. A good night's rest would ease her mind.

The hair on Zia's neck stood up. She couldn't shake the feeling of eyes on her. Years spent in The Trials had given her a deep reliance on those instincts. She whirled around, trying to see if anyone was there, but it appeared to be just her and the gnarled trees.

Zia stepped out of the river and hastily slipped on the clothes Ren had left for her. The sand-colored pants were flowy, with slits on the outside of the upper thigh, revealing straps beneath that she could house daggers in. The top was little more than a band that covered her breasts, wrapping around her neck and revealing her collarbones. There was a silk hood that was attached. The clothes no doubt cost as much as her blades. They were easy to move in and far more fit for the humid climate than her jeans. If she was being honest, she did feel different wearing them.

She was about to head back to the camp when she heard a twig snap again. Zia shot a look behind her and saw a pathway of fireflies swirling about the trees. Their little wings emitted a bright, burning light in the darkness of the forest. She took a few steps toward the pathway to the camp, but the fireflies swarmed her. She swatted a few away, but they swirled around her, beckoning her to move deeper into the forest.

Zia knew she should go back to the camp or at least have someone to accompany her, but she doubted the fireflies would still be there if she left. They had led her to Aaliyah in her dream. Perhaps they would lead her somewhere vital now.

"Alright, my friends. Lead the way," she said tentatively, doing her best to calm her thundering heart.

The fireflies swarmed, creating a lit pathway as they guided her through the forest. She kept her wits about her, remembering Jace's incessant warnings about awareness. The trunks of the trees were translucent, as they had been in The Trials. She could see the energy drawing up from the roots.

The fireflies stopped at the wall of an enormous, twisting Banyan tree that was covered by silver ferns. She slowly peeled back the ferns and gasped as she discovered the tree was hollow. There was a small archway. A few of the fireflies flew inside, lighting the way. It revealed a spiraling wooden staircase that descended into the earth.

Zia swallowed. She was sick of confined spaces and knew how ridiculous it would be to follow a bunch of bugs. Yet there was that feeling in her gut again, tugging her forward. There was something she needed to find.

Zia ducked her head as she stepped inside of the tree, the ferns closing in behind her. She inhaled the scent of wood and bark, carefully descending down the spiraling staircase.

She finally met the bottom, looking around her. There were underground tunnels with multiple passageways that probably ran throughout the entire realm. She wondered if Jace knew these existed. They most likely went directly to the kingdom.

There were lanterns all along the walls of the tunnels with fireflies inside of them, dimly illuminating the tree tunnels. She squinted at the various tunnels, trying to determine which path to take.

The fireflies lead down the narrowest passage, much to her dismay. She grunted. Clearly the gods wanted her to get over her fear of confined spaces. She went to grab her mother's crystal necklace in comfort, only to remember that she smashed it. She felt naked without it. She sighed, following the fireflies down the tunnel.

As they went deeper and deeper, Zia noticed carvings along the walls with similar symbols to the entrance of Lemuria. She wished she could read the Old Language or had a way of remembering the symbols. They had to be important if someone had bothered to carve them in secret underground tunnels.

The tunnel opened up into a cavern. Her eyes adjusted to the low light. As she looked around, her blood turned to ice. Someone lived down here. She could see the makeshift bed and personal trinkets strewn about the room.

She walked deeper into the cavern, spotting a pile of something in the corner. Upon approach, she realized they were bones. Judging by the skeletons, they were of every creature. Sirens, faeries, and Lemurians alike. As though someone brought them down here, where no one would be able to find them, collecting the bones like a treasure trove.

Zia brought her hand to her mouth to keep from vomiting at the smell. She was about to turn on her heel and run when she saw a small red light. Nestled in the nook of the wall was an altar of sorts. There were crystals, flowers, and what looked to be owl feathers. Right in the center was a glowing necklace. There was a glittering black stone in the middle, surrounded by a pyramid shape made of gold.

The fireflies swarmed her as she stared at the necklace.

"This is what you wanted me to find, isn't it?" she whispered. Zia knew the answer before asking. She had seen the necklace before, but she couldn't place where. She picked it up, and her body jolted as her fingers touched the stone.

Zia was racing through the crystal castle. Only this wasn't her body. Her thighs burned as she descended the winding staircase. Her silk, beaded skirts trailed behind her as she tightly gripped the fabric so as not to trip. The whole palace was in chaos. They were out of time. He had come for them. The warriors held the gate for as long as they could. That was more than she could ask of them.

She made it to the bottom of the stairwell and raced to the library, where she knew she would find Aaliyah waiting with her daughter. She had to keep the knowledge of her child hidden, distracting the king with the stones. There were two sculptures against the crystal wall carved after the heads of the Zhulu birds. She grabbed the top of one of their heads and yanked the sculpture down like a lever. The crystal wall pushed back and opened. She had to make it to the entrance at the bottom of the library that led to the tree tunnels. She raced through the many stacks of books, descending down deeper into the heart of the library. The walls shuddered like an earthquake. If he didn't kill them all, The Great Wave would.

She gulped down air as she ran faster than her legs had ever carried her before. She passed shelf after shelf of priceless information. Records of their magic and technology, all about to be wiped out forever. She ignored the sorrow in her heart, knowing what she had to do. When she made it to the bottom of the library, there were two torches lit next to the shelves of their most ancient books and an enormous portrait of a dragon with black scales and white tips at the wings. Her daughter, Kehlani, and Aaliyah were waiting. Aaliyah looked barely over nineteen. She was not yet blind, her silver eyes darting to the hands of what she carried. Her hair was black as night.

Zia knew then whose memory she had fallen into. Queen Katya's.

She placed the stones into Aaliyah's grasp with shaking hands.

"Promise me that you'll separate them. You have to hide them. We can't destroy them without destroying ourselves. Promise me you won't let him have them."

Aaliyah grasped Katya's hand with both of her own.

"I promise."

Katya shoved down the sobs that threatened to erupt from her. She couldn't fall apart. Not yet. She bent onto her knees, placing both hands on her daughter's shoulders.

"Be brave, little one."

"Don't leave," Kehlani begged, wrapping her small hands around Katya's finger. She nearly broke, wanting nothing more than to run away with the two of them. Yet if her daughter was to have a chance at surviving, the king could not learn of her existence. She wiped the tears from Kehlani's cheeks.

"I will be with you every step of the way, just not in body."

She gave her one last hug and kissed her forehead. The walls of the library shook again, and dust fell from the ceiling above them.

"I'm scared," Kehlani whimpered.

"I know, baby. I am too, but we must go on. Our fear is a map to our freedom, if we are willing to face it."

"My queen, he's close," Aaliyah said, nudging Kehlani toward the entrance of the tree tunnels.

Katya nodded and took off the necklace she wore. The same black stone glimmered in the torchlight.

"This necklace contains all of my memories, Aaliyah. Along with my knowledge of the stones. Give it to her when it is time. No one but my bloodline may unlock the memories. I had to leave her a map..." she trailed off, looking over her shoulder at the sound of books falling.

'I left you a map, little one," she said softly to her daughter.

Aaliyah raced through the tree tunnel, looking at Katya one last time.

"Protect her." The queen gave the final command that she would ever make.

Aaliyah nodded.

"I will raise her as my own."

The entrance shut, sealing Katya on the other side. She wiped the tears that finally fell, jutting her chin upwards in defiance as she looked up toward the spiraling labyrinth of the library. She would make sure the king paid for this one day. When the time was right.

Zia snapped out of the memory, gasping for air as she clutched the necklace tightly in her palms. She placed a hand on the wall to steady herself, panting in disbelief.

Zia paused. It wasn't dark when she had touched the necklace, but now, every single firefly was gone, as though someone had snuffed out their light. She felt like she was going to be sick as she took in the scent of the cave. It smelled like the Helius flowers, like rotting flesh. *Run*, her instincts screamed at her. But she did not run. She couldn't move.

Zia focused on her breath, clearing her mind. Fear would paralyze her. Fear would get her killed. She had spent a life making friends with her fear—she would not allow it to claim her now.

Suddenly she felt hot breath on the right side of her neck. It felt like the kiss of death. She squeezed her eyes shut, not wanting to know what stood behind her.

"What a delightful day it is…I haven't had food wander into my home in *ages*," said the voice into her ear. It was nothing more than a slimy whisper that echoed throughout the cavern.

Cold, bony fingers moved her braids from behind her neck and breathed in her scent. Still, she couldn't move.

"Not just any food…you are human. No—wait. You are half human. After all this time, the esteemed Bridge has wandered into my humble home."

She yelped as the creature plucked a strand of hair from her head. She whirled around and couldn't make out his full form, only his fingers that were made of strictly bone. Everything about him seemed to be rotting.

"What a tragic existence you've had, human," the creature chuckled as he examined the strand.

"Not as tragic as yours," Zia bit back, finding the ability to speak again. Her anger was a steady anchor amongst the chaos of her fear. She took a few steps backward and slammed into the wall.

The creature cackled.

"Did you know that hair holds memory? I can see not just this lifetime, but all your other lifetimes." He took the strand and wrapped it around a necklace that was made of black bone. She saw thousands of other strands wrapped around it and nearly threw up. He collected memories and kept an essence of the lives he devoured. She had to get out of the cave before she joined that pile of bones.

Zia slowly started to back away.

"A very old soul you have, ancient really, you must be exhausted…"

He kept talking as she backed toward the edge of the cavern, toward the tunnel. Yet he continued to walk toward her. She still grasped the necklace in her palm. He tilted his head to the side like she was every bit his prey.

"That necklace is my prized possession. I enjoyed sipping on the sweet nectar of life from the queen's daughter. What was her name? Kehlani…" Every syllable rolled off his tongue.

"They had lost it, outrunning the king in these very halls, you know. She came back for the necklace years later, not realizing these tunnels belong to *me*."

Zia grabbed one of her blades, pointing it toward the shadows. The creature laughed darkly. She shone the light of the stone in front of her, illuminating the face of her pursuer.

His eyes were mere slits of darkness. She stifled a scream as she realized he wore the face of her father. Then it shifted and became her mother's. Then Hiro's. Then Mei's. He was wearing the different skins from her memories, still holding the strand of her hair.

Zia tripped over a rock and fell to the ground. A sharp pain shot through her tailbone at the impact. She crawled away from him.

"Your memories will be so sweet to feast on. It's a shame you didn't get the chance to see her again..." His taunts sent shivers down her spine.

This was *not* how she was going to die.

She waited until he brought his face inches away from hers, the smell of blood and rot on his breath. He was about to bring his bony fingers to her forehead, to steal and feed on her memories, when she smiled defiantly.

"Feast on *this.*"

Zia whirled her blades and sliced the threads of his talisman from his neck, catching it in her palms, and drove the other blade through his rib cage. He screeched in surprise as she pulled the blade out. She stumbled to her feet and attempted to run, but the creature had magic. The shadows of the cave started snaking toward her, and they bound her wrists and her hands, pinning her to the ground.

The creature recovered from her blow and stalked toward her.

"You have fight in you, little human. A woman of true spirit. But you were too slow to find the stones. Hidden in plain sight, really. It's a shame it took you so long to realize the map your mother made you," he chuckled.

She tried to wrangle free of the shadows but couldn't.

"What do you mean the map she made for me?"

The creature advanced on her, towering over her. He was nearly ten feet tall.

"Didn't you know that your mother was The Architect? The king enslaved her for revealing the secrets of our world in a human *game.* Clever woman," he chuckled again.

The creature wrapped his bony fingers around her throat, hauling her to her feet. The information he revealed barely registered. Her mother had built The Trials. She hid the map inside of them, hoping Zia would find it before it was too late.

"What does it feel like, to know the entire world will perish because you weren't smart enough to figure it out sooner? How does it feel, to have failed the ones you love, again and again…it's no wonder they all leave, really."

Zia didn't reveal just how deeply the creature's words cut her, so similar to the assassin's final words to her. She knew he could taste her fear and was voicing the darkness she had yet to face in herself. He tightened his grip on her throat. She could barely see straight. She gasped for air as she tried to wriggle free, but the shadows restrained her. Tears streamed down her face as the darkness beckoned.

All of her memories began to surface. Her mother holding her just after her birth, singing Lemurian songs so she may one day remember. Hiro bringing her food and playing The Trials with her for days on end. The countless nights he slept on the floor of her room so she wouldn't feel alone.

She couldn't lose those memories. He couldn't take them from her. She wouldn't let him. Her vision blurred as the remaining air was nearly choked out of her. Zia closed her eyes, feeling an unfamiliar power rise up inside her like it was its own force.

Zia linked herself with the creature and reached into the well of his consciousness with invisible hands. She ripped free his magic, taking all that she could. He let go of her in shock and she fell to her knees, coughing on the ground.

"What have you *done*?"

Zia rose to her feet, shadows curling around her as she advanced on him with her blades. The darkness answered to her now. She had absorbed his power. She threw him against the wall with a blast of the shadow and heard the crunching of bone.

She stalked right up to him and held a blade inches away from his bony, hollow face.

"Thank you for the helpful information."

The creature tried to wrangle free, but his own shadows held him pinned.

"You have yet to learn the cost of your magic, little human…" he taunted, his voice rasped beneath the weight of the shadows. "Do you have any idea of the ancient power I wield?"

Zia put a hand to her chin, pretending to think about it.

"Perhaps. But I'm willing to bet you're nothing without this talisman."

His black, soulless eyes widened. She slammed his chin upwards with the hilt of her blade, and his bony head rolled backward as he fell to the ground. Zia clutched the memory necklace, and the creature's bone talisman and ran as fast as she could. She raced through the tunnels, up and up the winding wooden staircase until she made it back out into the forest. The fresh air felt like a triumphant celebration in her lungs.

Zia didn't stop running until she made it back to the camp. It was the middle of the night. She stumbled into the clearing, emerging to find Jace pacing in circles looking like he was about to rip his own hair out. He paused at the sight of her, taking her in. The hair that was out of place. The marks around her throat.

Ren stood up from the fire and whistled.

"You've been gone for hours. We tried to track you, but your scent just disappeared. What happened?"

Zia walked over slowly to three of them, sitting down to finally rest her bones. She was panting as she pulled out the talisman that was little more than black bone wrapped in hair, dangling it before them.

The three of them gasped.

"I made a new friend," she said flatly, trying to shake off the slimy phantom touch she still felt.

Jace was immediately at her side, his eyes darting from her to the talisman.

"Where did you get that?"

She didn't answer.

"You found The Mortemys."

All she could do was silently nod. Ren was instantly at her side, healing her. She ran a hand over Zia's throat, and the marks disappeared. Zia gulped down the fresh, humid air. She gazed up at the stars as they twinkled and eddied, trying to calm herself down.

"I honestly thought The Mortemys was a myth. Every mage in the realm tried to hunt him for the knowledge he possessed. After sucking out so many memories from his victims, he contained more information than the Lost Library. No one ever returned from the hunt," Ren explained.

"What happened?" Jace demanded. His thick brows were furrowed as he seemed to be wrestling with the decision to yell at her or embrace her.

Zia slumped her shoulders, exhaustion finally hitting her. She pulled out the other necklace she carried. It was Hiro's turn to be shocked.

"That belonged to Katya. I remember the symbol from The Map."

"My mother was The Architect," she said quietly.

The toothpick fell out of Hiro's mouth.

Jace shook his head, "And after giving you this information, The Mortemys just let you go on your merry way?"

Zia turned toward him, watching the firelight dance in his green eyes. She didn't fail to note the way his jaw locked up.

"Not exactly. I touched the stone and saw one of Katya's memories." She explained to them what happened. The details of Aaliyah, Kehlani, and the Lost Library. The tree tunnel passageways. The memories stored in the stone.

"It is called black serpentine. A rare gemstone that has only been found in the siren court. It has the ability to store knowledge and memories. Their queen's palace is made of it, so that each ruler may inherit the wisdom of those who came before them." Ren explained.

Zia stared blankly at the ground.

"The Mortemys almost killed me, but I absorbed his powers somehow and ended him...if you can kill an undead creature. He warned me there would be a cost."

She closed her eyes and noticed that her body was shaking involuntarily. Jace began to pluck the wilting flowers from her hair. They had shriveled up in the presence of the Mortemys.

"The king's finest warriors couldn't survive The Mortemys. Yet you did. A human girl."

He was looking at her with awe on his face. She shook her head in doubt.

"What is the cost? Of this power."

Jace turned her palm over and stared at the serpentine necklace. His warm touch steadied her, like her body finally knew it was safe. She stopped shaking.

"If the queen had the same power, and her memories are stored within the necklace, I'm sure this can tell us. Especially once we find Aaliyah. She would know." His gaze darted to the talisman.

"We need to keep that hidden. It is full of dark magic that will most likely call many unwanted, curious eyes to us."

Ren plucked the talisman from Zia's hands and spun it around three times until it was magically sealed in a cocoon. Zia could no longer feel the energy radiating from it. Jace dipped his chin in approval, and then took the talisman from her, placing it in his pack.

"Tell me everything he told you," Jace demanded.

"Can we eat first and *then* dissect the creepy old monster?" Hiro whined.

Ren nodded in agreement, and Zia's grumbling stomach answered. Jace was outvoted. He began to cook the fish he caught over the fire. They weren't the Antiqua, as those were sacred, but rather a different fish with pink scales. They ate in silence, entranced by their food. Zia chewed slowly, savoring each bite and avoiding the tiny bones. It brought the life back into her.

When they finished eating, Zia lay back in the soft grass, resting her head on her pack. She had a hand on her belly, savoring its fullness. It was the first time she felt like she had eaten enough since the diner in Mount Shasta. Despite only being a mere few days ago, it felt like lifetimes away.

She told Jace every detail she could remember, and he listened intently as he lay next to her. His whole body went rigid when she told him of the Mortemys attacking her. Hiro clapped at the part where she knocked him out.

Words failed her as a yawn escaped her, and they all fell silent. Hiro decided to take watch for the night. Ren shrunk herself to be the size of Zia's thumb and nestled into the petal of a flower to sleep, her little golden wings fluttering beneath the starlight. She smoked from a pipe made from vine, puffing minuscule little O's into the air.

Zia and Jace lay shoulder to shoulder. She savored his steadying presence, doing her best not to think of their conversation in the caves. He was far too observant to not notice the way it made her blush or sped up her heart rate when she thought of him. Her tired bones felt heavy. Her eyelids slowly closed and the last thing she saw was the silhouette of an owl swooping in front of the moon.

When she woke in the middle of the night, she found herself curled up by Jace's side, his strong arms wrapped around her. She dared glance at him, and all the tension on his handsome face was gone. He squeezed her a bit tighter, like his subconscious was answering her silent question. She closed her eyes, squeezing him back. For the first time in a long time, there was nowhere else in any world she would rather be, and no one else she'd rather be with.

CHAPTER 12

I always thought our world was the envy of the gods—the way we feel and experience so much all at once. They live in black and white. Heaven and hell. Yet to have a heart that beats rebelliously against time is to live in the gray area. Nothing is so easily definable where love exists. It blurs all boundaries. That's why, when faced with what path to take, all I could tell Zia was to keep going, despite there being nowhere to arrive. —Sahara

The world was burning. Flame snaked up every tree until each one crashed and tumbled. The smoke made her eyes water. She could barely breathe. Zia stumbled, racing through the forest to find any way out. An enormous black owl swooped and glided above her, as though guiding the way. She followed it, dashing around the scorching branches. Her muscles ached. She ignored her blistering skin as she leaped through a wall of fire, following those feathers into the night.

Zia fell to the ground and cool grass met her body. Her lungs wheezed as she coughed, every breath burning. When she opened her eyes, the fire was gone. She was in complete darkness. The owl circled overhead and landed on the shoulder of a figure. She nearly broke into sobs as she realized who stood there.

Her mother. Her long, dark hair fell below her waist and was tied up in a half knot atop her head. She wore a light blue shimmering gown that pooled onto the forest floor, a gold sash tied around her waist. Zia's eyes froze on the collar around her mother's neck.

"Mom—," Zia's voice cracked as she took a step forward.

Her mother held a hand up before she could get any closer.

"He knows you're here. He's hunting you."

Zia knew who she meant.

"I came to find you."

Her mother shook her head. Her throat bobbed as she glanced up toward the sky, reading the stars.

"A part of me prayed you would never have to know our world. To know him. But it is too late. Your only hope now is to make it to Aaliyah."

Zia's lip quivered.

"You're The Architect. Why did you design The Trials if you didn't want me to discover all of this?"

Her mother smiled sadly, clasping her hands delicately behind her back.

"Because destiny is not something you're forced into, Zia. It's something you choose. I wanted you to have a choice."

Zia balled her hands into fists.

"What if I choose this? To go against the king. To help free you, and all of Lemuria?"

Even as she said it, those words were a heavy weight that settled into her. Sahara walked toward her, her silken dress swishing with each step, until they were a mere few feet from each other. Her face was heart-shaped, like Zia's, and she had a speckling of freckles all over her nose.

"This isn't you versus the king, honey. We want things to be understandable. Heroes and villains. Good versus evil, but the only person you need to overcome is yourself. If you want your destiny, then take it. Don't place your faith in some prophecy. Place it in yourself."

She grasped Zia's hand in her own and squeezed. Her palms were soft and warm. A healer's hands.

There was still one question that had been nagging the back of her mind.

"Mom, why do Katya and I have the same magic?"

Her mother opened her mouth to speak when there was a great roar behind them. Zia turned around to see the enormous silhouette of a dragon circling the moonlight. Sahara brought a hand to her lips in awe.

"The dragons will return with the rise of the queen..." she trailed off, quoting part of the prophecy.

Zia frowned.

"Mom—"

The dragon nose-dived straight for them, and the last thing Zia remembered was great big yellow eyes piercing her soul before it blew icy fire onto them.

"Do you have to have a nightmare *every* night, Z? Some of us need beauty sleep," Hiro's voice shook her awake. He was curled up on his side with his eyes closed, still half-asleep.

Zia shot up straight, panting. She was shivering with a kind of cold she had never felt before. She blinked several times, taking in the forest. Dawn was just breaking, the trees still a silhouette against the orange sky. She rubbed her temples, trying to discern reality from dream.

She sat up to find Jace already standing over her, staring at her.

"A nightmare, huh? Here I was, thinking you were dreaming of me."

He winked at her, trying to distract her with humor. A dark curl of hair had fallen over his face. He was tanner than before from the days they spent traveling.

She glowered at him, not quite able to speak.

His eyebrows drew together.

"Are you alright? What did you dream about?"

"Nothing," Zia shook her head.

Jace sank into a crouch and knelt down until he was at eye level with her.

"You and I both know it's not nothing. You're The Bridge. Your dreams carry messages from the other side. Messages that could be the difference between life and death for us."

Zia moaned, not ready for the *holier-than-thou* nonsense so early in the morning. She begrudgingly relayed the dream to him and Ren. Hiro was still curled up on his side, clinging to any semblance of sleep. Jace pursed his lips at the mention of fire. She knew he would understand more than anyone the symbolism of that flame.

"Do you think it's true? That he knows we're here?" Zia swallowed.

"If that is true, then we're already dead," Jace answered.

"Not necessarily," replied Ren.

Jace arched a brow at her in question.

"That's not his style. I know he's your father, but I spied on him for many years. He's not a brute. He would bide his time, studying Zia's limitations and power. He'd want to know if she had magic. How her magic works. He'd want to see if she leads him to the stones. And even then, I still don't think he'd kill her. Her blood is too useful."

She was filing her nails with one of her chopstick daggers, sharpening them into fine points that may as well have been tiny machetes. Jace cringed at the site.

"She would be better off ending it before he could capture her."

Zia shuddered, thinking of the dream she had of Jace. The way she had leaped off that cliff into certain death, willing to do anything to keep the stone safe. She didn't dare mull it over any further.

"It doesn't matter. We keep going. We'll be safe with Aaliyah for the time being. Hiro, where did the map say the first stone is located?"

Hiro groaned in response, still attempting to sleep.

Jace frowned at him.

"Hiro," he said impatiently.

Ren rolled her eyes, "God, do the women have to get *everything* done around here?"

She grabbed her tin of water and chucked it at Hiro's face. He leaped several feet in the air, landing in a fighting stance. Ren snapped her fingers in his face.

"Wake up, slowpoke. *Where* are the damn stones?" she hissed.

Hiro's eyes blazed with fury. He took a deep breath in, bringing his palms together. One minute he was there, the next he disappeared entirely. Until he appeared right behind Ren a few seconds later and knocked her legs out from under her until she fell face-first into the mud, her perfectly done hair ruined.

Zia had never seen anything like it before. Hiro had described it as being able to fold across space like a piece of paper, but she didn't think he would vanish like that. Of all the crazy things they had seen, watching her best friend evaporate shocked her the most. After all, this was the same Hiro who wet his pants the first time they played in The Trials when a Zhulu nearly ate him.

Ren didn't bother to wipe the mud off as she was instantly upon him, her stunning face shifting to have fangs and red eyes. She lunged for him, but he vanished again. They waited for him to appear, but he was nowhere to be found.

Just then, they heard a chuckle echo across the clearing. Zia looked up to see Hiro standing on a tree branch, leaning against the trunk. He was at least twenty feet off the ground.

"Who were you calling slow?"

Ren's eyebrows nearly raised to her hairline.

"I didn't know you were a folder. There aren't many of your kind left. That's quite useful for us, actually...."

Hiro grinned crookedly and pulled his hat over his eyes.

"Yes, I'm quite rare. Unfortunately, since I spent my life not being able to use the magic, I can only use it for short distances. You should've seen my father. He can fold from the Ordos Desert to the royal city."

Jace clapped his palms together.

"Are you two going to waste precious daylight hours brawling or do you plan on being helpful?"

Hiro rolled his eyes, disappearing and reappearing right in front of Jace. The warrior nearly jumped out of his own skin, then warned Hiro that the next time he did that he'd start swinging. Zia tried her best to suppress a smile when Jace glared at her.

Ren snapped her fingers and was instantly free of mud. She had swapped the skirt and corset for high-wasted, flowy black pants and strappy sandals. She wore an off-shoulder black top and her signature golden chopsticks at either side of two buns. Her eyes were framed with dark, winged eyeliner, making the amber color pop like the sun at dawn.

Hiro looked at her appreciatively.

"Nicely done. Though I thought eating dirt looked good on you."

Ren gave him a look that made it seem like she was about to make *him* eat dirt just as Jace cleared his throat. Ren sighed in defeat.

"The stones, Folder."

Hiro put a toothpick in his mouth and closed his eyes, recalling the details.

"Whoever made that map was drunk on faerie wine. The map didn't say the location of where the stones were, only a riddle on how to use them. It did have the missing prophecy, which was more of a poorly written poem than anything else."

Ren shook her head.

"I've read the *Book of Lemuria* three times since Jace gave it to me. It mentioned symbols that encoded clues to where they were. Were there symbols?"

Hiro shrugged.

"Yeah. There was an owl, and a black pearl..."

Zia rubbed her neck. Cold sweat still clung to her skin from the dream. She knew that owl.

"Aaliyah has it."

Hiro's eyes were still closed as he recalled details, but Ren put a hand on her hip.

"How do you know?"

Zia picked up her pack and slung it over her shoulder, readying herself for departure. They would have to move quickly.

"The first dream I had, that same owl led me to Aaliyah's. I was in a garden with her and she showed me the stone."

Ren rolled her eyes.

"That's great and all, but the last time someone saw Aaliyah was when dragons roamed the realm."

Zia was about to protest, but Jace hushed them both.

"Black pearls only grow in the siren court, where Katya's body is. The second stone must be with her."

Ren sighed and looked up at the sky.

"That means we'll need Ash, then."

"Ash?" Zia asked.

"The last living pirate. He has a ghost ship that can sail through siren waters."

Zia pinched the bridge of her nose. They talked over the best course of action, arguing back and forth until the sun had fully risen. Finally, they all agreed they would stay on track with finding Aaliyah. Even if she didn't have a stone, she was their best bet in terms of survival. It was too much of a risk to enter the royal city and try to find the pirate.

The unfortunate part was that following the river upstream would lead them directly through faerie territory. Without Hiro being able to fold them for more than a few feet, they had to travel on foot. Ren fell silent, not wanting to go anywhere near the court. Zia didn't press her on why, but she could feel that the wound ran deep. Jace didn't seem keen on going back to the place that reminded him of Meaghan, either.

They gathered their remaining supplies, filling up their water jugs and stocking up on fruits and nuts before they left. They buried the firewood in the ground, covering their tracks before making their way back to the river. The forest only became more and more lush as they moved deeper within it. The climate changed, becoming even more humid. Everything felt wet. Water poured from the leaves of the trees, as rain constantly fell. Zia's clothes were soaked through.

Ren was staring at Hiro, eyeing him up and down. He fell into stride beside her.

"Planning on going for round two?" he grinned. The faerie shook her head.

"I can change you back, you know. To how you would look as a Lemurian."

Hiro smiled slightly.

"I had the option to change my appearance in The Trials too, but I didn't want to. I feel honored to have grown up in the human realm, watching over Z. I wouldn't change it for the world. This is the body I was given for this life, and I still have an immortal soul. Why would I change it?"

Ren frowned, looking at him like he had three heads.

"What?"

"Nothing, it's just that in a thousand years I have never met someone who didn't wish to change themselves."

Hiro winked, "Like I said, I'm rare."

Misty fog swirled around them, and it was difficult to see straight. All they had to guide them was the river. They moved in silence, and Jace remained on edge, constantly listening for anyone who might be following them. Zia did the same, using it as training to further sharpen her senses as she tried to sense the different energies.

They walked for miles without stopping. She went over everything in her mind again. The dreams. The prophecy. It felt like the answer was right in front of her face, and she was somehow missing it. Zia sighed. She had been the top player in The Trials, and one of the best fighters in Periculum. Yet in the *real* Lemuria, she was barely able to keep herself alive. She needed more training.

Zia touched her forehead, feeling the three dots that now rested there. The first thing she would say to Aaliyah was how completely rude it was to mark someone's face without asking and then shove a dooming prophecy down their throat.

Three stones. Three marks. What did each stone mean? And how was putting them together meant to help anything? Perhaps Aaliyah was the one to teach her to master them. After all, she had been alive for nine thousand years. The healer had to know *something*.

Zia put her hair into a bun to keep it from sticking to her neck, her hair still in the hundreds of little braids Ren had woven. She felt a tightness in her chest. She wasn't exactly a hero in a cape. Her mother was probably expecting a daughter like Ren. Powerful. Feminine. Likable. Someone worthy of leading. She was none of those things. The thought of disappointing her mom made her feel nauseous.

Yet Zia refused to believe those thoughts. She *trusted* herself. It was how she had risen in the ranks so quickly, and she wouldn't hesitate now. Hesitation drew in failure like fire. Far worse than failure was sitting on the sidelines, too fearful to step forward. No, her mother had been right. Her destiny was her own to choose, if she dared.

"Are we there yet?" Hiro whined, interrupting her thoughts.

They all hushed him at once. There was something about the forest that felt off. It made Zia hesitant to make any sound—even breathing too loudly felt like a disturbance. Ren grabbed his shirt with her fist and whispered.

"We're in Morganna's forest now. Faerie territory. You don't want to attract their attention, trust me," she said gravely. Hiro put his hands up innocently and nodded in understanding. The forest was quickly turning into a jungle—enormous vines draped from the tree-tops and there was a constant drizzle of rain. Zia could hear what sounded like frogs in the distance. She noticed an enormous centipede the size of three fingers inching its way up one of the branches. It was a bright violet color with yellow spots.

"You'd be dead within minutes," Ren whispered, following Zia's gaze.

Zia swallowed, watching the centipede disappear behind a leaf. Everywhere she looked, there was something that could kill her. Her eyes darted in every direction. She recalled the stories Ren told her of the faeries, whose currency was in bargains that enslaved the soul, or trading in the blood of magical creatures they collected. Anyone who consumed their food or wine went mad. The king had slaughtered all other courts save for Morganna's. How ruthless had the queen been to survive his reign of terror, her court untouched?

"What are the faeries going to do, sprinkle dust on me?" Hiro snorted.

"You'll be begging for death if you ever face one," Jace murmured in response.

Despite Mei educating Hiro, he was as new to the realm as Zia was. Feeling the weight of Jace's words, they picked up their pace, moving as swiftly as they could without slipping on the wet rocks. Zia's eyes burned from poor sleep, but she could feel her body getting stronger. Every day she could run farther without needing to rest.

The sun fell quickly. The thick layer of fog made it impossible to watch it set, but the sky was growing darker. Zia was afraid to ask how much further until they were out of faerie territory. They were on the outskirts of the court to remain hidden, but there still would be sentries patrolling the border.

Zia shivered despite the hot, humid air. As night fell, the forest came alive. The vines on the trees shimmered. Though they could not see the stars, the glowing river illuminated their path. The water was shallow beneath their feet, and everywhere they stepped left an iridescent footprint.

Ren stopped them all. Her golden wings shimmered as she flew up into a tree that curled over the river. From its branches hung large fruit the size of their heads that looked like apples. They were every hue of the rainbow, varying in color and shape. Ren took out a golden chopstick, switching it into a blade as she cut a few pieces from their branches. Jace caught two of them below in his arms. Ren gracefully fluttered back down from the tree, landing soundlessly on her feet.

She placed the apple-like fruit on the ground and sliced the fruit in half, offering a piece to each of them.

"What are they?" Zia whispered, inspecting it in her palms.

"We have a name for them in Old Lemurian that means 'fruit of the gods.' One bite replenishes all your strength."

Zia took a bite of the strange fruit—the outside was crunchy, but the inside was soft as a marshmallow. Sweet flavor exploded in her mouth. The juice of the fruit dribbled down her chin, and she wiped it with her forearm, smiling broadly at the others.

Hiro had already gotten through his piece, practically inhaling the fruit. The gentle sound of the river was calming as they ate. Zia felt her fatigue and exhaustion dissolve. Her mind completely cleared. The muscles that had been so sore felt loose and relaxed now. No wonder the Lemurians rarely had disease or illness—their food was their medicine.

Ren stuffed the remaining apples in their packs, ordering Hiro not to eat all of them. He rolled his eyes and told her to stop spouting nonsense, but they all knew it was just a matter of time before he wolfed them down.

She then pulled out Zia's cloak, which she had cleaned with her magic. There wasn't a single mark or tear. It looked brand new. Zia beamed at her as she shrugged it on. The one item she had left of her mother.

They continued walking for a few more miles, holding their breath the whole time. There wasn't a single faerie in sight, except for Ren. Will-o-the-wisps bobbed in between the trees. Zia couldn't ignore the uneasy feeling that crept into her gut.

The fog was lifting, making it much easier to see. Little pockets of stars peaked through the cloudy sky. No longer feeling the need to rest, they pressed on without complaint, wanting to make it somewhere safe.

Zia stopped walking. She heard a buzzing sound ahead, like wasps or bees, but far worse. She tried to find the source of the noise. Ren grabbed her arm with a painfully strong grip and put a finger over her lips. She pointed toward an enormous tree. It spiraled upwards, and on closer inspection, Zia realized it was hollow.

The glowing, lilac vines that wrapped around the tree illuminated what appeared to be little moving fireflies. Not fireflies, Zia realized. Ren's fearful expression was confirmation enough.

Nymphs. Ren had told her about the faeries that were so small they were nearly the size of a thumb. They were used to guard the border for Morganna for their keen eyes and lethal venomous arrows.

There was only one path forward. The river was their safest bet, as it was concealed by the other trees and would block out any sounds they made. The faeries didn't seem to notice them, mercifully. Jace moved slowly. Zia kept her footsteps soundless like she had been taught.

Step by step, they made it past the enormous tree. Zia almost let out a sigh of relief, but they weren't in the clear yet. They quickened their pace. They were so close to the border.

And then there was a loud *crunch*.

Zia whirled around and looked in horror.

Hiro had taken a bite of the apple.

The buzzing stopped as all the faeries turned their attention to Zia, Hiro, Ren, and Jace.

They were going to die.

In one long line of wings, the faeries headed straight for them.

Ren broke into a sprint, and they all followed suit. But it was no use. The faeries were faster. Within seconds, Zia felt sharp pain in her back and her arms. She yelped as she saw tiny arrows buried in her skin.

Hiro went down first, his eyes rolled to the back of his head as he hit the ground. Next was Ren. Jace bellowed in horror as he hit the ground. When he shot Zia a defeated look, she realized there was no way out. He mouthed for her to run, but she was frozen.

The world began to spin and Zia was immobilized. Her knees smacked onto the rocky river as she hit the ground, making her eyes water at the pain. The poison was spreading quickly. She fought to stay awake, but all she saw was a blur of wings.

Jace screamed her name just before darkness tugged her under.

CHAPTER 13

The truth is, the ones who try to overpower you are the ones who believe in your power the most. Her real power had nothing to do with her magic. She had a way of making you feel like you were the most special person in the world, like she believed in you before you even believed in yourself. If someone she loved was threatened, hell itself cowered from her as she emerged raging, ready to burn it all to the ground for them. Love could be dangerous. Destructive. I think in the end, the only thing she was really afraid of was herself. —Ren

"They would fetch a high price, my queen. A folder, the first human to ever enter our realm, and the banished prince…" a voice said.

"Nay, it will bring us only trouble. We should kill them, my queen. I would be honored to harvest their blood for you," another voice said with delight.

Zia kept her eyes closed and her breath even, still pretending to sleep. She took note of the sound of running water. The cooler temperature. She was lying against something hard and cold. Her hands weren't bound, which meant they either didn't think her dangerous, or there was simply no hope of escape.

"Enough. I will decide their fate," a cruel female voice snapped. The others were immediately silenced.

Jace's scream echoed in her mind. Where were her friends?

"Shall we wake them up, your majesty? Perhaps we can feed one of them to the black lake," the first voice asked again. The desperation for the queen's approval was all too apparent in his voice.

"There is no need, Silas. The girl is already awake."

A pang of terror hit Zia. She cracked an eye open, and it took everything in her not to scream. She covered her mouth with her palm. She lay on a stone table in the center of a lake. Will-o-the-wisps bobbed above the water, encircled by thin swirls of mist.

The faerie queendom wasn't what Zia would have expected. An enormous, rotund green faerie was sitting on the edge of the lake playing the saxophone, while two little pixies sat next to him playing cards. Many of them were smoking out of thin pipes made from vines, blowing rings as they lounged on the outer edge of the lake. And the *wine.*

Several servants strut about the court, refilling glasses of pink sparkling wine and making sure no hands were empty. There was a powder blue faerie with auburn hair that sang to the royal court, her husky voice amplified by the strange flower she sang into. Four pixies danced in front of her, wearing silk dresses that hugged their curves and pooled onto the floor.

It was perhaps the grandest, most lavish party Zia had ever seen. It reminded her of Mei's VR library, but that had been a meek imitation in comparison. The court appeared completely oblivious to the fact that she was their prisoner, sitting in the middle of a black lake observing them. She wanted to scream, but the longer they were distracted the more time she had to formulate an escape.

Faerie lights dangled from the silhouette of the trees, the light streaming over the crowd beneath the starry sky. The court was almost too beautiful. Like when she ate too many sweets and felt sick to her stomach. Despite the glamor and shimmering riches, it all felt wrong somehow. Like a mirage.

It was not difficult to discern the servants, sentries, and royal court. The servants hustled about, never pausing for a moment, making sure everyone's needs were met. The sentries stood still with their weapons. In fact, Zia would have thought they were statues had their eyes not slowly moved back and forth, scanning the room.

There were three royals that were lounging in a pool of strange, silky water, a *moon pool.* It looked just like the one Aaliyah had in her dream.

The royals cackled with glasses of wine in their hand, ignoring her existence entirely.

Though the faeries would have been beautiful, everything about them felt unnatural to Zia. From their iridescent skin to their overdone hair to the unnatural youth of their features. It was only their pointed ears and fanged teeth that revealed the monster she knew prowled beneath.

The court was dressed lavishly, covered in rich metals and gems while the servants looked ragged and half-starved. They avoided eye contact entirely, except for a violet-eyed servant faerie who observed her closely with a strange curiosity. He was the only one who acknowledged her existence. He had curly hair and moved with such grace she could tell every movement was calculated.

Finally, Zia spotted their queen to whom that cruel voice had belonged—a female faerie sat atop a golden throne covered in vines. Dark, glittering crystal grew from her seat. Her long hair was golden as the sun, and it glittered in the light. Her unnaturally white teeth came with sharp fangs, accentuating her viscous smile. The most spectacular part of her was her wings—they were enormous with fractal patterns in them. Where she was golden as the sun, her wings were a daunting shadow. Her and Ren could have been related, but there was nothing of Ren's kindness or warmth.

There were no sentries surrounding the queen, which meant she was probably more dangerous than an entire army. Two male faeries sat below her, one with dark hair and golden eyes, the other with green skin and yellowing teeth. The latter had a brutal scar slashed across his face. It looked like someone had clawed him.

The Queen of the Faeries held up a hand, and the entire court fell silent. The laughter, the music, immediately cut into a horrifying quiet. Zia stood tall on the stone platform, trying not to stumble from how lightheaded she felt from the poison. Still, she held her chin high, attempting to maintain a semblance of dignity.

The darker faerie at the queen's right hissed, revealing his rotting teeth. "Bow to the queen, if you value your worthless life."

The faeries all murmured in agreement, glaring at her. There was a wicked delight to them that chilled her bones.

But Zia did not bow.

Bow to no one but your heart.

The queen smiled at her with mock sweetness. Her nostrils flared as she took in Zia's scent.

"Where are my friends?" Zia managed to keep her voice steady, her eyes darting around the room.

The queen tilted her head to the side, looking at Zia like a new toy. All of the faeries seemed to hold their breath as the queen decided what to do with her. Zia knew they would not make it out alive unless it was advantageous to the queen.

"Let's not be rude. I believe introductions are in order. I am Morganna, Queen of the Faeries."

The entire court clapped at her introduction, like she had just said the most marvelous thing. Zia had to force herself not to gag. She was still scanning the room, looking for any possible escape.

"I'm Zia. Just a human," she replied with mock pleasantry.

Morganna inhaled her scent again and shook her head.

"Let's not bother with lies, Zia."

The green faerie cackled and whispered something in Morganna's ear. She nodded and looked at Zia with piercing eyes.

"Where are my friends?" Zia asked again, unable to keep the edge from her voice.

She tried to take a step forward on the platform, but her limbs were stiff from whatever poison the arrows had been laced with. Running would not be an option then, it seemed. Especially while she was surrounded by water.

Morganna rolled her eyes.

"They're safe. For now."

The words set Zia's teeth on edge, but she leashed her rage. The way to survive would not be through weapons or combat. She had to be clever. Cleverer than the faeries, who had thousands of years to master bargaining and trickery. Fantastic.

Then she thought of The Trials. She had risen so highly in the ranks not because of any magic, but out of sheer will. Zia had paid close attention—learned a player's strengths, weaknesses, and desires. It was never about the cards she was dealt, but how well she played them.

"How did you survive the entrance? No one makes it past The Guardians, much less a filthy human."

And there it was. Arrogance. That would be her weakness, then. She had lived for thousands of years with the world at her fingertips, indulging in wine and music and trickery. The thought of a mere human being able to challenge her was inconceivable. For the second time, Zia realized the power in being underestimated.

The queen twirled a piece of golden hair around her finger. She wore a necklace with a vile that rested over her heart. It was a vile filled with blood. Zia's stomach churned, not wanting to know whose it was. She willed her face into neutrality. If Morganna knew she was scared, she would have no chance. She reached inside of herself for the confidence and wit that had saved her life many times. She had to play the game.

"Was it supposed to be difficult?" Zia smiled nonchalantly, tilting her head to the side in challenge. The green faerie, Silas, snarled. The queen hushed him with a warning. She was enjoying this. Zia's brazen attitude was amusing to her.

"How is it possible you reek with human stench, but there is also a trace of Lemurian blood? Who sired you?"

Zia had to be delicate in her response. Too much information, and it exposed her and her mother. Too little, and her friends would be killed. All she could do was trust her instincts. The crowd of faeries never took their eyes off Morganna. All of them, except for the one peasant faerie with the violet eyes.

"How about a question for a question, Your Majesty?" Zia grinned at her in challenge.

The queen leaned forward on her throne, her hands gripping its edges. Her endless black eyes sparked with interest. If she were as old as Zia suspected, then boredom was one of her greatest struggles.

"You're clever for a mutt, aren't you? Very well, then. A question for a question, until I decide whether to kill you or sell you."

A mutt. She had certainly been called worse. Zia kept her breathing steady. She looked around for any sort of exit, but there was nothing. Only the murky black lake, and she wasn't willing to find out what lurked beneath those waters.

"I am The Bridge," Zia said, answering Morganna's previous question. The queen's eyes flashed in hunger as understanding dawned on her. Zia felt a small bit of satisfaction—to surprise an immortal was not an easy feat.

"The prophecy," Morganna whispered. Her knuckles turned white as she gripped the chair, and her nails actually dug a *hole* into the arms of the throne. Her eyes were an icy blue now. Perhaps they changed with her mood. The other faeries gasped.

It was Zia's turn.

"Do you know about the three stones? What they do, and how to put them together again?"

Morganna's breath was shallow. The prophecy meant a great deal to her. Whether that was in Zia's favor or not, she was uncertain.

"That was three questions, not one," the queen quipped.

Zia tapped her foot as she stood there, waiting patiently for her answers.

Silas coughed pointedly, but the queen just glared at him. His eyes darted to Zia, and he looked at her with disgust. The other faeries whispered amongst themselves, placing bets on how long Zia would survive, and in what way she would die. Some of them even returned to playing cards or smoking out of their pipes. They were so unphased she wondered how often Morganna used her prisoners for entertainment.

The queen gestured a hand toward the black lake, and it rippled into a picture clear as day. Not a picture, Zia realized. A memory. It was of a golden goddess who sat in the void. Her eyes were made of stars.

"In the beginning, there was only the first goddess, Rhea. Though she possessed powers beyond comprehension, she was very lonely in the emptiness of the void. Wanting more out of existence, she created the first god, Ra. To please his beloved, he made the entire universe in a single breath. They danced together for three days, celebrating their love, and watching galaxies unravel beneath their feet. On the third day, earth was made, and it was Rhea's favorite creation.

"Earth was covered in water, until the mighty continent of Mū rose to the surface. It is said many spirits roamed freely there, visiting from various worlds. The earth was a living library for them to store information and wisdom. Then Lemurians were created. The very first to have bodies. Katya, the original queen, was beloved by all. She deeply respected and honored all life. Especially the faeries," Morganna winked.

Zia stood frozen in wonder. There was Katya, her eyes blue as the sea. Every cell in Zia's body screamed again, *I remember you.* It was like she had seen her face a thousand times before.

Many other creatures surrounded Katya in the memory. Faeries, dragons, sirens, and Lemurians.

"She dreamed of a world where every creature would have a voice. Impressed by her fair heart and wisdom, Rhea and Ra offered a drop of their godly power and ordered the faeries to forge three stones that would represent this dream of unity and balance."

The water rippled, and where Katya's face had been, three stones were now shown.

"The first stone represents Time. With this stone, one can travel time-lines, change the past or future, move through different dimensions, and even walk through worlds."

It was the emerald stone. A shiver snaked down Zia's spine. Morganna smirked, enjoying her discomfort. She seemed to love hearing herself talk.

"The second stone represents the heart of the gods—the stone of love. It is the only force in the world that outlasts death..."

It was a ruby. True to Morganna's words, it looked like a raw heart.

"The third stone is perhaps the most dangerous of all. It is the stone of death. Anyone who attempts to master it can lose their soul in the process, forever wiped clean from eternity. With this stone, the wielder could rip away the veil that separates this world from the next."

Zia didn't fail to notice the desire that was plainly written across the faerie queen's face. The stone was an indigo color, like the Milky Way.

"Together, these stones represent the three most uncontrollable forces in existence: Time, Love, and Death."

Zia stared at the reflection in horror. How was she expected to wield such a power? A sinking feeling hit her gut like rocks falling to the bottom of the sea.

"Then the Atlanteans arrived. Though they possessed no magical gifts, they were cunning and ruthless. They developed technology strong enough to enslave and kill the Lemurians. Disgusted by their greed and bloodshed, Ra created a wave so great it would wipe them out forever. Katya separated the stones from each other, so the king could not wield them, and the world fell out of balance. Individually, the stones are lethal. But together, the wielder becomes a living god. To put them together again, you must walk through the darkest corners of your soul and return again, without losing yourself to attachment and desire."

No wonder Morganna had never gone after the stones herself. There was no way she would risk her power.

True power can only be held by humble hands.

The prophecy echoed in her mind. The lake of memories returned to black water once again. Zia tried to ignore the despair that was now blooming in her chest.

"How do I know you're telling the truth?" Zia asked skeptically.

"Because I am the faerie who forged them," Morganna replied smugly.

Zia mulled over the priceless bit of information she had just learned. The knot in her stomach loosened. Morganna was telling the truth, but it felt like something was missing.

"I have answered *four* of your questions. Now, who sired you?" Morganna snapped. Zia kept her face expressionless. If Morganna knew who her mother was, she could easily sell that information to the king. He still didn't know that Sahara had a daughter.

The queen's eyes flashed red at her lack of response. Their color changed with her mood.

"Keep in mind, mutt, that I hold the thread to your friends' fate." She snapped her fingers. Silas scurried away, his wings flapping viciously. Zia glanced over to the violet-eyed servant faerie, whose eyes were now wide with fear. He shook his head in warning.

Within seconds, Silas returned with Jace, Ren, and Hiro.

The bloodlust was clearly written all over Silas's face as the faerie shoved them onto the ground at Morganna's feet. They were all bound together with dark green vines. They seemed unharmed, despite the purple shadow around Jace's eye. It must have been a strong punch for his magic not to heal him.

"Don't try to escape, clever girl. The more you move, the more the vines will tighten around your wrists until you find yourself without hands." Morganna smiled sweetly at Ren, who had been attempting to shimmy one of her golden chopsticks free.

"I haven't seen you in decades, Ren. I assume guard duty was treating you well," she snickered. Ren's face twisted into fury. Silas knocked her back to the ground and grabbed her by her hair, chuckling. Zia took a step toward the edge of the lake.

Morganna held up a hand and Silas froze.

"It's really too bad, what happened to your sister. It must be so difficult for you, to know her death was your fault, Ren. And you couldn't even stand there with those old bores and guard the entrance successfully. No, instead you pledged allegiance to a human. What a waste of talent." Morganna sighed.

Hiro looked at Ren, and then toward Zia. She knew he could fold himself away and find help. Why wasn't he?

Morganna took note of their exchange.

"Did you think I couldn't smell the magic on your little friend here? I am the oldest faerie in existence. You can't think me so daft. The vines render him unable to do magic."

Morganna tilted her head, looking at Zia like she was her next meal. "I'm growing bored of you all. *Who* sired you?"

Zia pressed her mouth into a hard line. The whole court was paying attention to her now, but her eyes couldn't help but follow the violet-eyed peasant faerie that slowly walked toward her friends. She wouldn't have noticed him, but her intuition was going off like an alarm bell.

Perhaps she would get lucky, and he would help her.

"Silas," Morganna ordered.

Silas slammed Ren's head into the stone ground and it made a terrible *crack* sound. When Silas pulled her head back up, blood was gushing out of her face like a fountain. Zia shuddered.

"Wait!" Zia yelled.

Morganna paused, looking triumphant. Some faeries snarled in protest and the sound of coins clinking rang out. Their lives were nothing more than something to gamble on.

"Sahara. My mother is Sahara," Zia said desperately, praying that Morganna wouldn't sell the information. All she could see was her friends, bound together and helpless.

Morganna's red lips curled into a smile.

"*Sahara.* The most powerful healer the realm has seen, mated with a simple human. How delightful," she threw her head back in laughter. Her golden hair shimmered.

Rage burned beneath Zia's skin.

"What will it take for you to let us leave here alive?"

Morganna stopped laughing and pretended to think about it. Different faeries shouted suggestions.

"*Harvest her blood!*"

"*Feed one of them to the creatures of the black lake!*"

"*Sell them to the king!*"

Morganna held up her bony hand, silencing them all.

"I'll make a deal with you," Zia offered, knowing the queen wouldn't be able to resist.

Ren's eyes darted to her in fear, even as blood gushed down her nose. They were unable to speak, bound by some invisible magic. Zia remembered Ren's words: death was better than a faerie's bargain. Yet she had no choice. They were getting out of there alive—Zia refused to accept any alternative.

"A human mutt wishes to make a deal with a faerie? Perhaps you aren't as clever as I thought."

The other faeries all cackled in agreement. Some exchanged gold coins and gems. Clearly, many of them thought Zia would be dead by now.

"I promise not to harm you, to let you leave, on one condition," Morganna said.

The whole court held their breath, waiting. Zia held the queen's stare. She didn't dare look at her friends sitting on the floor, fearing she would lose her nerve.

"Find the three stones. If you survive mastering them, then you will owe me a favor. Any favor of my choosing." The Queen of the Faeries looked at her in a way that said the favor would most likely be the last thing in the world she would want. She was stroking the blood vial around her neck with a finger.

It was an odd request, since Zia doubted she would be able to even master one stone. But if promising the unlikely long-term saved their lives in the short term, then she would do it. She would damn herself to save them. If she did master the stones and bring them back together, then Morganna would have the power of a god at her will. It was a terrifying thought Zia quickly shoved away.

Zia nodded, "Agreed."

"Every word is a verbal spell, so your agreement is a magical binding contract," Morganna said.

Zia tasted bile in her throat, shoving away the sinking feeling that she had doomed them all. Morganna waved her hand nonchalantly, and a stone path rose up from the waters of the lake, giving her a way out. It created little waves and ripples in the lake. She hesitantly began walking along the path, the poison from the arrows that froze her body in place had subsided. Hiro, Jace, and Ren were still bound.

"You swore to let them go," Zia said as she cautiously approached. Faeries couldn't break a bargain, could they?

Morganna snickered.

"I said *I* wouldn't harm *you*. I said nothing about your friends. Be more specific next time."

As she said that, the sentries closed in around her friends, holding up arrows. The whole court began clapping and dancing, enthralled by their queen's trickery. Music started playing— syrinxes, lutes, and drums. It sounded like a symphony of hell. It wasn't a trial at all. It was an execution.

The Queen of the Faeries smiled dreadfully.

Zia wanted to scream, but no sound would come out.

She was sprinting along the stone pathway, seconds away from her friends. If she could just get to them and cut those vines, they had a fighting chance at escaping. Her eyes met Silas's, and he snapped his fingers just as the stone pathway beneath her feet crumbled. The last thing she saw was the violet-eyed peasant fairy lunge for Silas. She nearly choked on her own hope that maybe, just maybe, his help would be enough.

Icy water bit into her skin, and as she looked up at the surface, she saw a thousand arrows being shot at her. Since it hadn't been Morganna herself who directly harmed her, the bargain wasn't broken. Ren had been right—Zia was a fool to ever make a deal with her, especially without understanding how magic worked.

Her lungs burned as she wasted precious seconds debating what to do. She looked around, until she saw an underwater tunnel that led to a cave. If there was a way out, it would be through there. There was no chance of her making it to the surface with so many arrows being fired at her. A tugging feeling in her gut pulled her through to the cave. She followed it.

The water grew even colder as she made her way to the cave. There was nothing to suggest any sort of air pocket or passageway. It was completely pitch black. She turned to swim back toward the surface and take her chances, but that feeling tugged at her again.

Zia didn't let herself think about what kind of monsters were at the bottom of the lake until she began to hear horrible whispers. She whipped her head around and saw shadowed silhouettes. They looked like sirens but weren't. There was something wrong about them.

One of them lunged for her, grabbing her throat with its bony hand as it shoved her down, down, down into the icy lake. It was a ghoul—the skeleton of a mermaid. All she could see was the empty pits of its eyes as the ghoul shoved her into the darkness of the cave. She kicked and fought with every last bit of strength, then shrugged off her mother's cloak. It forced the ghoul to lose its grip on her. She watched the last piece she had of her sink to the bottom of the lake.

She swam as hard as she could toward the surface. Then she felt a burning *slice* across her back. The ghoul had dug its sharp fingers into her flesh. Even if she survived the encounter, infection would kill her quickly. Especially in those murky waters.

She could sense death hovering near again, that dark angel she had known her whole life. The same one she had felt in the diner in Mount Shasta.

The ghoul opened its jaws to close its mouth around her throat and then hesitated. It pulled back slightly. She felt fear shudder through it. The ghoul immediately released her and swam away, taking her mother's cloak with it. All she could see was its rotting, moss-colored tail creating bubbles as it disappeared. It took her a few seconds to realize that it was not her that made the ghoul flee. It was what was behind her. She felt the ancient presence before she saw it.

Zia turned around to find a pair of enormous, bright yellow eyes staring back at her.

Her lungs burned as she fought the urge to scream. She swam backward into the dim light of the lake, but the eyes followed her until its body was revealed beneath the shadows of the will-o-the-wisps. It was nothing short of a living legend.

It was a dragon. She was surprised the lake was home to such a godly creature. Hues of blue and white blended into its iridescent scales. Then she saw its claws, which were sharper than any weapon. There was no way they were escaping alive. She suddenly wished she was fighting off a ghoul again. Or the phantom panther. *Anything* but this.

The dragon grasped her body in its claws, and she couldn't help but look at it in awe. It was the first time in her life she wanted to bow to something. She felt so small in comparison. Her heart was pounding in her ears.

Zia's magic seemed to rise up out of panic, taking control of her entirely. When she locked eyes with the dragon, her whole body began to vibrate. Within seconds, she was looking out at herself *through* the eyes of the dragon. Her consciousness had linked to the dragon—she could feel what it was like to be in its strong, ancient body. This lake was its home. It had lived there for thousands of years, slumbering. Morganna had no idea the creature dwelled just beneath her court. Zia quickly saw flashes of other dragons, and then their disappearance entirely. The king would have hunted them to extinction, so they hid. Biding their time. For what?

She looked at herself through its eyes. Her lips were blue and pale. She was running out of time. What had felt like frigid water to her human body felt warm and comforting to the ancient dragon. She could feel the well of the dragon's magic. It was a well she could tap into, at least temporarily. She began to reach an invisible hand into that well...

The dragon's roar echoed across the lake. It knew what she was doing. *Who are you?*

The dragon asked, mind to mind. The voice was female. And angry as hell.

My name is Zia Alexander. I'm here to find the stones...

The dragon hissed angrily.

The last person to seek the stones conquered our world and enslaved us all.

The king. She could feel the grief beneath that cold, deadly rage.

Please. I just want to find my mother, Sahara. She's a healer...

Zia trailed off, not knowing what else to say.

The dragon froze in hesitation, weighing her words.

You are The Bridge.

It was Zia's turn to freeze. She hadn't believed the prophecy to be true. Yet the dragon had already known who she was by the mere mention of her mother's name.

Yes, she replied.

It has been a long time since anyone has been able to talk with me. The last one whose heart was pure enough to hear the voice of the voiceless was the first queen, Katya.

Zia shook her head.

How does Morganna not know you live beneath her court?

We dragons have been in a slumber for nine thousand years. The moment your body hit the water, I woke up for the first time in eons.

Why?

The dragons will not return without the true queen.

The words of the prophecy. Zia didn't have time to debate what they meant. Her human body didn't have time.

Please. I'll give you anything. Just help me and my friends.

The dragon seemed to debate her plea. There she was, flirting with death again as she awaited a decision.

Do not promise what you don't have. Words are their own source of magic here, shaping the way your reality unfolds.

Please, she begged again, not having time for fortune cookie wisdom.

You do not yet know what you are. When you remember, do not forget your first promise.

What promise?

The dragon didn't answer. She kept Zia grasped in her claw but blew an icy breath behind them. It propelled them to the surface. What had felt like hours of their interaction had been a few short moments. She squeezed her eyes shut just before they emerged from the surface.

The court was in chaos. Jace had never felt such terror in his life. Before he could even attempt to free himself, a faerie dressed in rags was standing above him with a crescent-shaped knife. He thought the faerie had been about to stab him, but he cut straight through the prince's vines. He freed Hiro next, but it was too late for Ren. Silas had grabbed her and dragged her up toward Morganna's throne, slamming her to the ground beneath the queen's feet.

Silas was about to cut through Ren's wings when Hiro folded straight to the top of the throne, bypassing the twenty sentries. Jace held them at bay while Hiro and Silas went toe to toe. He had to give it to Hiro, he was a swift fighter. Yet none of that mattered once Morganna stepped in. She lifted Hiro into the air with her magic and began choking the air out of his lungs. Jace cut down sentry after sentry, but there were too many to get to him in time. Just as Hiro's eyes began rolling to the back of his head, they heard a loud roar, and the ground beneath them rumbled.

Everyone paused. The court fell silent. Small ripples moved across the lake. Morganna held up a hand and ordered them to stop. For the first time in many eons, since the king had overtaken their continent, there was genuine fear in her eyes. They turned white as a ghost.

"Impossible," she whispered.

As though in answer, water sputtered and exploded out of the lake as nothing short of a legend emerged. All the court could see was a flash of blue scales, and then icy daggers that turned half the court into frozen statues with a single breath. A water dragon.

On the back of the dragon was none other than Zia, a hellish grin on her face as she glared defiantly at Morganna, who for the first time in her life shrunk in her throne. Zia rode on its neck, gripping tightly onto one of the horns. Her eyes flashed yellow as the dragon circled above the court. She ducked off the dragon and rolled, landing right before the queen. Her skin was beginning to turn scaly in a partial blue as though Zia was becoming a dragon herself. She whirled her head to Jace, but there was nothing familiar on her face.

"Get them out," she said coldly.

Jace obeyed. Hiro picked up Ren in his arms and folded right onto the dragon's spine. Jace was about to leap up after him when Zia said, "Him too."

He knew who she meant. He walked straight through the guards to where the violet-eyed faerie stood. His lip was split open—they had been beating him for cutting their binds. Jace slung him over his shoulder and made his way to the dragon, never taking his eyes off Zia.

Zia was standing before Morganna, who didn't dare move. Zia smiled with horrific sweetness as she turned her head toward the throne. Her blood ran cold with icy rage that death itself would have shrunk from. Slowly, that power rose up inside of her until it was too much to contain. Suddenly, she tipped her head back and felt something unfamiliar building in her and finally let out a roar. Ice blew out of her mouth, encasing the throne in shards. The stone ground froze over. She took her blades out from behind her back and sliced into the throne, shattering it into a thousand tiny pieces.

She turned back to the queen.

"Not bad for a mutt, huh?"

The queen sneered at her.

Zia's ice crept up from Morganna's toes, to her torso, all the way to the top of her shoulders until she was entirely restrained. Zia formed a frozen dagger, aiming it at the queen's exposed throat.

It was a strangely alluring power, to hold a life in her hands. The realm's most ancient queen, at her mercy.

For a moment, Zia considered ending her life. She brought the tip of the dagger to Morganna's chest. It would make their lives easier.

"Z!" Hiro called behind her.

His voice shook her out of the frenzy. She threw the dagger onto the ground, shattering it.

"Touch my friends again, and I won't hesitate to run my blades through your heart."

She kept her chin held high as she climbed on top of the dragon. Jace sat directly behind her, then Hiro, Ren, and the faerie. Zia gave one last terrifying look to the faerie court before the dragon tilted its head back and roared.

Before she knew it, they were airborne, flying toward the full moon as they blended with the night sky. Zia tried not to think about how the Queen of the Faeries would reprimand her.

She had borrowed the dragon's power, just barely scratching the surface of its magic. With a little training, there would be no limits to what she could do. All she felt as the magic faded was exhaustion and terror. She had tried to save the life of the assassin in Shasta, yet with a little bit of magic, *wanted* to end Morganna's life. It shattered all her ideas of what it meant to wield magic, and underneath it all, the foundations of who she believed herself to be began quaking. The Zia she had been in Periculum, in The Trials, was gone.

Harsh wind whipped her hair back and forth. The treetops below glowed in the moonlight. The sky was growing brighter now, and a sliver of orange peaked above the mountains as dawn finally rose.

She looked back at her friends. A mix of awe and horror was on their faces. She knew they felt it, too—that maybe, just maybe, they could actually survive.

Morganna had given her a priceless piece to the puzzle. She would think about that later. Zia shifted her attention to the mighty dragon beneath her and could have sworn she saw a single tear well and fall from its eye as it soared through the sky.

All that mattered as the rising sun lit up the sky in greeting was one truth.

They were free.

CHAPTER 14

What truly carries us through suffering is not faith in some god up in the sky or a righteous ruler promising to save us all. It is faith in ourselves—that we are resilient and capable of coming back from even the worst of experiences. This world is a lot to swallow, but if I know one thing, it's this: it takes far more strength to respond from love. So, if you're ever questioning what the "right" thing to do is, know this: if it is done from love, it will be done right! —Aaliyah

Every certainty in life Zia clung to was shattered by the winter winds as she rode on the spine of a dragon. There was no room for logic in a realm ruled by magic. People who played in The Trials wanted to believe anything was possible. What they didn't realize is just how true that is, and just how paralyzing that truth can be. Once Zia found the power slumbering within her, she felt herself longing for the ordinary for the first time in her life. She understood why most people chose to sleep-walk. Living up to her potential was impossible if that potential was endless.

Time and time again, she went over her own edge only to find that there wasn't one.

The air was frigid and sharp. She had nearly slipped off the dragon attempting to tie her hair in a messy knot. Jace had gripped onto her waist, holding on a little longer than necessary. She would be lying if she said she didn't lean into his warmth.

The true terror set in when she spotted several strands of silvery white hair amongst her thick, dark curls. Ren had said it was the cost of accessing so much power at once—*that* was the price the Mortemys had referred to. By taking from the well of another's magic, she had to give up years of her life in return. Zia would have thrown up had there been any food in her grumbling stomach. There were three strands for each time she had used too much at once—the firebird, the Mortemys, and the dragon.

The dragon, whose name they learned was Inka, looked magnificent hovering above the cotton candy clouds. Her scales were a gradient of sea blue, fading into a deep indigo at the tip of her wings. They had been flying all day to put as much distance between them and the faerie court as possible. Dragons happened to be the best trackers in Lemuria because of their unparalleled senses. Inka had come across Aaliyah long ago, and still had her scent committed to memory. Finding her no longer felt like an impossible task.

Zia's back was infected—some of the flesh was already decaying. The ghouls had poison in their touch that bred more of the undead. Ren tried to heal the infection as best she could, but it was difficult while flying. The wound was too deep for her magic, and with Zia having drained most of her energy, her body had little left for healing. The best the faerie could do was stop it from spreading until they found Aaliyah.

They were chasing the sun. It nearly blinded them as it faded from a reddish-orange into the full light of day. Hiro had his mouth open, trying to taste the clouds, until a bug flew into his mouth and he nearly fell off Inka's back. Ren drew blood with her nails as she gripped onto his neck, and said if he didn't shut his mouth, she would be the one to shove him off. She was clearly still upset he got them captured by faeries. Zia would have been too, but they needed the information they gleaned. Understanding the stones was vital.

Faeries. Zia wasn't sure what was more alarming—that she might reunite the stones and owe Morganna a favor or that she would die trying. Either way, her odds weren't looking good. Her goal remained the same, though. If she could just see her mother once, to hear her voice and feel her warmth, that would make everything worth it.

Zia savored the brief moment of safety as they flew. Not having some-one trying to kill them at any given moment was a luxury that was be-coming scarce. Hiro emitted a great howl with his arms out to the sides and his eyes closed. At least *he* was enjoying himself. His mood was infectious—even brooding Jace couldn't help but smile.

The violet-eyed faerie didn't speak the entire time. He still had marks from being whipped and beaten. They gave him space. There would come a time for questions, but for now he had saved her friend's life, and that was enough. Besides, hovering thousands of feet off the ground wasn't the ideal location for an interrogation.

Inka began her descent. They flew beneath the clouds, revealing the breathtaking view of Lemuria. Sunlight stretched over the glittering lakes and rivers. The Redrock Mountains were still covered in fog, as they always seemed to be. There was something about them that made Zia's skin crawl, and she wondered what resided within them.

Bright green birds with forked tongues and translucent wings flew below them. They were circling, hunting for prey, completely unaware of the winged nightmare that hovered above them. It amazed her, how rarely anyone bothered to look up.

Zia squinted as she inspected the mountains further- there was some-thing off about them. A sort of unnatural repetition to the ridges. The trees were arranged in identical patterns. It reminded her of The Trials, when there had been repeating sequences in certain areas of the game.

It is a veil, Inka said to her.

How do you know? Zia asked, scrunching her nose as she tried to piece it all together.

Always look for the blind spot in order to see, Inka replied.

Without warning, Inka nose-dived straight for one of the mountain ridges, just where the pattern repeated. Zia could hear the faerie yelp behind her. She turned her head to make sure everyone was still intact, only to see Hiro gripping onto the faerie by the shoulder—the closest thing to a seatbelt he would get.

It was too fast for Zia to even scream. The ground was quickly ap-proaching. The chilling fog enveloped them, until suddenly they weren't surrounded by the dense, lush forest anymore. The veil was ripped away, revealing the heart of the mountains. They landed with surprising gen-tleness. Inka didn't make a sound as her feet touched the ground and she tucked her wings in, barely fitting in the clearing. Rich, ruby-colored dirt swirled and kicked up with the wind from the flapping of Inka's wings. They all coughed, trying to see through the dust.

When Zia closed her eyes, it still felt like they were airborne. She took a few deep breaths in through her nose. The mountains were different terrain. It was much colder, and the ancient bristlecone trees of the forest looked like sculptures. The trunks twisted in various knots toward the sky, like they had spent their existence dancing with the wind.

Jace leaped off Inka's back and helped them all down, except for Hiro, who somehow managed to tumble off and fall face first on the red dirt. When Ren gave him an incredulous look, he tipped his hat toward her.

"Someone has to be the entertainment around here."

Zia's thighs were quaking from remaining in the same position all night and day. She forced her body to take a few steps but felt like a wobbling fawn learning to use its legs.

Hiro clapped Zia on the shoulder and she almost fell over.

"I'm proud of you, Z. You managed to be high up in the sky without getting sick."

Ren interrupted him and poked him in the chest.

"*More* impressive is that she managed to harness the power of a dragon and save us. No thanks to you endangering all of our lives because you were *hungry*."

"Now we have a great story to tell, though. Right guys?" Hiro smiled sheepishly.

Ren actually *snarled*, preparing to lunge at him just as a black owl swept directly between them, landing on a nearby branch. It instantly diffused her anger and her hair returned back to its normal golden color.

They eyed the bird curiously, but Zia had already encountered it before in her dreams. Those silver eyes would haunt her for years to come. It remained perched, watching all of them curiously. The expression it bore was too intelligent to belong to a mere animal.

Zia took a step toward the owl and smiled, her blue eyes twinkling as she knew in her heart that they had somehow made it.

Jace stole a glance at Zia—her hair was a mess from the wind, loose strands stuck in every direction. Yet there was a wild beauty written across her face—like she was born to ride dragons and go toe to toe with ancient faerie queens. Ren caught him staring at Zia and smirked. He flipped her off and turned his attention back to the owl.

"Alright, so where is the old healer?" Hiro cracked his knuckles and yawned.

Even Inka glared at him in warning with her iridescent yellow eyes. Right when he said it, the owl leaped from the tree and erupted in white flames. They all jumped in surprise. The only ones who remained un-phased were Zia and Inka, who had known what the owl was.

Standing before them was Aaliyah, with joy twinkling in her hazy eyes. She looked exactly as she had in Zia's dream, but she was shorter than Zia anticipated. She carried a wooden staff with two snake carvings wrapping around it, and a silver orb perched atop it.

Everything about Aaliyah felt oddly comforting—her broad, childlike smile, her natural beauty, her eyes that, despite being blind, saw every-thing. Though her body was small, her spirit felt larger than a god. She reminded Zia of Mei a bit, and Zia understood how she had come to be the first Elymental of the realm.

They all stood there, speechless.

"I may be older than dust, Hiro Sato, but I still got it," she winked. His eyes widened at the mention of his last name. At the realization that she most likely knew everything about them.

Aaliyah walked toward Inka and stroked the side of her scaled face. "Hello, old friend."

Much to Zia's astonishment, Inka *purred* in response. Inka bowed her head to the healer, and they pressed their foreheads together. Aaliyah's silver hair fell onto the forest floor like a glorious moonlit waterfall.

"Why did Inka only awaken now?" Zia asked, though part of her knew the answer.

Aaliyah turned toward Zia, acknowledging her for the first time. She gazed just above her head thoughtfully.

"The dragons were our realm's fiercest protectors. With the fall of Queen Katya's empire, the king or Morganna would have enslaved or used their power for their own sadistic gain. The dragons disappeared, only agreeing to return with the rise of the true queen. Most in Lemuria don't believe they exist."

Aaliyah took pink meat out of her pouch and fed it to Inka. The dragon's eyes softened in gratitude as it gobbled it up. When was the last time the creature had eaten?

Hiro swung his arms, stepping toward Inka, "I can't believe a dragon was hiding in the faerie court. Thank the gods they didn't know. You should've frozen that evil queen to death, Z" Hiro cracked his knuckles.

Inka growled in agreement, her nostrils flaring.

Aaliyah chuckled as she turned to Hiro, still gently stroking Inka's side.

"Wouldn't it be so easy if we could just categorize people as good or evil? The sun and the moon are opposites, and yet neither would exile the other. This is how nature has kept its balance since the beginning. Darkness is the womb of potential. It is where we all come from and where we will all return to. If you only yearn to know the light, you'll never understand how sacred darkness can be. Take it from an old blind woman."

Hiro rolled his eyes at that.

"Yes, but aren't some people just *bad*?"

Aaliyah shrugged.

"In the eyes of the king, he is a liberator to his people, not a tyrant. He will not stop until the entire world is 'free.'" She turned toward Zia, "And you, my dear, are a threat to that—a power-hungry thief come to steal his throne. Every leader has a way of justifying their way. If you want to know the truth, look to the people."

"The *last* thing I want is to rule," Zia scowled.

"Which is precisely why you should," Aaliyah winked. The orb atop her staff gently bounced up and down. It looked like a storm churned within it.

"Well, I don't know about you lot, but I've always had one foot in heaven and the other in hell." Jace leaned against the trunk of a tree, his eye still bruised.

Aaliyah's back stiffened at the sound of his voice. She turned away from the dragon to face him. Her breath hitched. Jace noticed her discomfort and stepped toward her, taking her palm in his.

"I'm Jace, son of—"

"You're the Prince of Atlantis, banished and stripped of your titles."

Jace frowned at her boldness. Aaliyah was staring just above his head, running her fingers over his palms and arms, then his face. She closed her eyes, breathing sharply through her nose.

"So, it's true. He burned you," her voice was heavy.

"Do you two know each other?" Hiro asked, scratching his head.

Jace's eyes trailed over her face, studying her wrinkled hands that clasped his own. Aaliyah blinked, and the emotion on her face was gone, replaced by a cheerful smile.

"I ask my birds to bring me stories of the realm, since I haven't left this land in a few thousand years. They told me of the legendary Prince of Night—a warrior banished for standing up against the tyranny of his own family."

"That makes it sound romantic," Jace snorted.

Aaliyah's smile turned sad.

"There is nothing romantic about doing what is right at great personal cost."

No one knew what to say after that. Zia cleared her throat.

"Aaliyah.... I bargained with Morganna," she swallowed, nearly choking on the words. She told Aaliyah the whole story, from getting captured to nearly freezing the queen over. Her cheeks reddened with shame. She had been desperate, and now it could very well cost them all their future.

Aaliyah's silver eyes narrowed.

"You also spared her life, child. Whether she wants to admit it or not, she is indebted to you."

Fireflies swarmed around Aaliyah, and they created a lit pathway, hovering just above the ground. It was dusk, and the forest looked like something out of a storybook, brightened by the firefly pathway. The knotted trees hugged the winding path, and the thin layer of fog was dispersing.

"Come, we need to get to my hut. No one will find you there," Aaliyah said comfortingly. She walked slowly along the path, fireflies guiding her with their perpetual humming.

The red dirt was soft and cooling beneath Zia's bare feet. Exhaustion slowly sunk into her as she began to realize that she was safe. Her thighs were sore from flying, but she shoved away the feeling with the hope that rest would come soon.

The forest began to glow with nightfall again, and she could see the network of energy that moved between the plants. The walk was only a few minutes. Inka flew above the tree canopy, following them. The hallway of trees opened up into a wide meadow. At its center, a waterfall pooled into several small bioluminescent lakes that rested on top of each other like a staircase, then squeezed into a narrow river.

Follow the river upstream, Aaliyah had told her.

Zia was suddenly grateful they didn't walk the entire journey—it would have taken weeks, perhaps months to find this place. As they walked closer to the waterfall, Zia noticed there was a cave behind it. Her curiosity peaked as she wondered how deep it went. She could see the faint light of glow worms, the same that had been in the cave by Lemuria's entrance.

Inka hovered in the air and then landed softly by Aaliyah's hut, tucked below the largest tree Zia had ever seen. It had chandelier leaves and blossoming orange flowers that dangled from its branches. The vines were various hues of green. Zia felt a reverence for the ancient tree, which was perhaps more ancient than the woman who resided beneath it.

Aaliyah's hut was small, and there was a lovely garden just outside of it in the shape of a spiral with a single stone in its center. The soft breeze carried the scent of herbs—basil, rosemary, oregano, thyme.

It was obvious why no one had ever found Aaliyah. She was hidden by the ridges of the mountains and the twisting trees, not to mention the magic she warded the property with. Aaliyah lived there for thousands of years. To be alone for so long without anyone knowing whether she lived or died...Zia felt a pang in her heart at the thought of such loneliness.

Inka curled up like a dog amongst the wildflowers and closed her eyes, looking at peace for the first time. Zia was unsure of what she should do first—bathe, eat, sleep, or ask Aaliyah the endless list of questions that rattled her mind for the past week.

They walked along the stone path to the hut. Hiro ditched his shoes, as they had finally fallen apart. He was infatuated with the feeling of the red dirt between his toes. He seemed to blend into Lemuria more each day, aside from his top hat. The violet-eyed faerie watched Hiro curiously, like he was an unsolvable puzzle he had never seen before.

Jace clenched his jaw as he assessed the land, examining all exits and potential dangers. Zia rolled her eyes—a warrior, through and through. When Aaliyah sensed his tension, she laughed and poked him with her staff.

"How serious you are! This is the safest place in any realm. Now come, let's feed you and put a smile on those faces before you're as wrinkled as me." She cackled as she said it, revealing a few of her missing teeth.

Hiro's head snapped up and he grinned.

"I always tell them that! Brooding is their favorite pastime."

Aaliyah winked and led Hiro into her home, the two of them laughing like old friends. Their chatter trailed off in the distance. Zia paused before entering the hut. Jace stopped beside her, eyeing the waterfall staircase beyond.

"No one ever thought she was real. Even my father never spoke of her, but he must have known her. She was Katya's closest friend. He executed the other Elymentals." He clasped his hands behind his back. The two of them stood there, watching the waterfall tumble for a few minutes. They were both lost in their own thoughts.

"Jace, what if I can't do it?" Zia interrupted.

Jace's eyes slid over to her. They looked like emeralds beneath the silvery moonlight.

"I think you're more afraid that you can do it." He playfully elbowed her, "I bet on you in The Trials, and I'm betting on you now."

She stepped in front of him, close enough for their breath to mingle. He looked like he was about to say something else when they were interrupted.

"Excuse me! Are you going to just stand out there and let the infection in your back spread?"

Zia's eyes widened at Aaliyah's booming voice from inside.

"How the hell did she know? I swear she's psychic or something," she whispered.

"It doesn't take a psychic to smell your rotting flesh, girl." Aaliyah interrupted.

Zia gave Jace an exasperated look. He rubbed the back of his neck and grinned, shaking off their tension.

"She's right. You should probably get that fixed," He jerked his chin toward the entrance of the little hut, and a few curls fell in front of his face. She fought the urge to reach up and interlace her fingers in them.

Zia curled her fingers into fists and walked toward the small wooden door. Both of them had to duck to enter.

The hut was enormous inside. It may as well have been a house. The walls were made of wood with colorful vines snaking up every corner and nook. There were hand-made carvings above each door. A wooden staircase spiraled up the center, leading to several levels with various rooms. Every manner of plant and herb hung in the kitchen. To the far side of the room was a small dining area with handwoven cushions, and a table that looked more like a wooden slab. There were a few larger crystals in the corners, but that was the only decoration. No art or extra trinkets. No frills or furniture a normal human home would have.

"You each have your own room. The house becomes what the guests need it to be," Aaliyah smiled as she twirled a brown gel around in a jar.

The clanking sound against the glass bounced off the walls. Ren and the other faerie excused themselves to their rooms. The other faerie hadn't spoken a word since they left. It made Zia uneasy. When they noticed there wasn't a room for Aaliyah, she told them that she never slept. She spent her nights in deep meditation by the stone in the garden. Everyone was too exhausted to question her.

"Sit," Aaliyah commanded. It reminded Zia of the first time she had commanded that when they sat by the moon pool in her dream. Zia lifted up her shirt around her neck, her small bra the only thing covering her. Her cheeks heated at the thought of Jace still being in the room. She heard his throat clear and the sound of heavy footsteps walking up the wooden staircase. He muttered something about needing to bathe.

Aaliyah rubbed the gel into Zia's back. It smelled like tar. She wrinkled her nose and winced at the pain. The only relief was the cool breeze that wafted in through the kitchen window, kissing her cheek.

"Sorry, girl. Before I can do any sort of magic on you, I need to get rid of the bad flesh and stop the poison from spreading."

The pain was excruciating. It felt like her skin was boiling and bubbling alive. She clamped her teeth together, lying still on her stomach as best she could. She swore with the foulest language she could possibly think of, until Aaliyah threatened to let her turn into a zombie if she didn't watch her mouth. Hiro came and sat next to her, letting her squeeze his hand off.

"How long has it been?" Zia asked through gritted teeth.

"Ten minutes."

Zia hissed as she felt Aaliyah's magic begin to work all the way to the bone.

"Oh, hush now, I know it feels longer than that. That's how time works, you know. A few seconds of pain feels like an eternity. An eternity of pleasure feels like a few seconds," she chuckled to herself.

"Speaking of time..." Hiro's words hung in the air. He was leaning back against a chair with his feet on the wooden table. His hat dipped over his eyes slightly, and a lazy smile spread across his face.

"Straight to the point, eh?" Aaliyah said. Zia's eyes nearly rolled to the back of her head as she felt her flesh closing up. It was taking everything in her not to scream.

"I mean, we don't have a lot of *time*." Hiro said, crossing a different ankle over the other. Zia wanted to whack him upside the head for the way he just nonchalantly sat there while she suffered. She squeezed his hand until he yelped in pain and tore it away.

Aaliyah rested a hand atop her back and she nearly cried in relief as the magic began to soothe her, coaxing her into a deep relaxation.

"Of course, you do. The pressure of time is the fear of death," Aaliyah replied. She picked up her healing supplies, the bloody bandages, and bowl of dirty water and rushed off to the sink. Zia heaved a sigh. She couldn't stand having another person around who spoke in bumper sticker. Hiro was enough.

"*That's great*, but do you have the stone?" Zia asked impatiently, her whole body was covered in icy sweat.

Aaliyah turned her head over her shoulder, her eyes staring at the floor in the distance.

"Don't worry about all that. First, we'll get you a hot meal."

She waved her hand in the air, gesturing to the upper levels.

"Why don't you get cleaned up? There are fresh clothes on your beds and I'll have dinner waiting for you when you're done."

Zia stood, feeling lightheaded.

"We've traveled a very, very long way to find you. To learn how to control the time stone."

Aaliyah was already chopping vegetables from the garden. How she did that without slicing her own hand off was a miracle.

"You haven't even learned to control yourself, and you want to control time?" She shook her head.

"But—"

"Go wash off. Make yourself at home," Aaliyah said in a way that made it seem final. Zia's heart sank. She did her best to ignore the panic that was rising with her. She had traveled so far to get here. Suddenly, finding her mother felt very, very far away. She wanted to grab the woman by her shoulders and shake her until she agreed to teach Zia everything she knew. Her palms twitched at her sides. She took a step toward Aaliyah, even though her back was turned.

Hiro stepped between them, bringing a hand to Zia's shoulder.

"Come on, Z," he whispered.

She opened her mouth to snap at him, but she saw the pleading look in his eyes. She nodded, resigned, and followed him up the winding staircase. It creaked with each step they climbed.

Their rooms were next to each other. Jace, Ren, and the violet-eyed faerie were on separate levels. Hiro followed her into her room, shutting the door behind him. It was simple, resembling more of a treehouse than anything else. A small bed with white cotton sheets rested in the corner by the open window. She had a view of the bioluminescent waterfall just outside, and a crystal tub in the small bathroom that was adjacent to it.

The moment he closed the door she whirled on him.

"If that old bat thinks she's going to get in the way—"

Hiro held up a hand.

"Relax, Z. She didn't get the fancy title of 'Most Powerful Elymental to Ever Walk the Planet,' for no reason. Don't you think she might know what she's doing?"

Zia pulled at her hair.

"The longer we take, the closer the king is to finding the other stones. The more time he has to hurt my mom. What if something happens to her?"

Hiro shook his head.

"It won't. She is his only leverage against you, and a talented healer. He would be an absolute moron to kill her. The king may be many things, but he's smart, Z."

She sat on the floor with her back leaning against the wall and hung her head. Hiro sat next to her. She leaned her head against his shoulder the way she had a thousand times. He pulled her hair back from her face.

"Z, she might be the only person alive who can teach you how to control your magic. The only other person who has had powers like this was Katya, and she *knew* her. Being a folder is different, but I still understand that magic is its own living force. The chaos can consume you, if you're not careful."

"That's a bit dramatic, don't you think?"

Hiro's tone turned serious in a way it had only a handful of times in their lives.

"You don't understand. The way you looked when you came flying out of that water. When you froze an ancient faerie queen without half a thought. Your eyes…. it's like you weren't even you anymore."

Cold sweat stuck to the back of her neck. She hated the truth of those words, the genuine fear in her best friend's voice. He was right, though. She barely remembered those moments.

She blew out a breath.

"When did things get so complicated?"

Hiro shrugged.

"I'm glad they did. Things were starting to get boring," he winked. "Besides, now you've got an attractive prince drooling after you."

She froze at the words, and he burst out in laughter knowing he had her.

"He is not attractive. And he is not *drooling* after me."

It was the first lie she had ever said to Hiro, and he knew it. Hiro couldn't stop laughing and placed a hand over his heart.

"*My sweet Bridge, I shall spend my days forevermore looking at you longingly. Your eyes are like twinkling stars—*" Zia tackled him to the ground before he could finish.

He instantly scrambled up, racing toward the door when she hurled a pillow at his face. She could still hear his laughter down the hall several minutes later. Her face burned and her breath shortened. The last thing she needed was some stupid, tragic love story in the midst of all this.

A *prince*. Absolutely not. There was no way she was going to get involved. She had enough to worry about—more important things to focus on than some silly romance. Besides, he was her friend. He had been since the moment they met. That was more precious to her than their...tension.

Yet the way those sea foam-colored eyes burned so intensely when they looked at her...her toes curled at the thought. She shook her head.

"*Enough*, you idiot," she whispered to herself. He was a prince. The son of her enemy, for gods' sake! Not to mention immortal—she would grow into a withered old bat while he continued being a handsome young warrior flouncing about.

Zia grunted and stomped over to the tub, running the hot water until the hissing steam filled the whole bathroom. Zia could vaguely smell dinner being made below. Her stomach grumbled in response. It had been days since they had a proper meal.

There was a small jar of soap that smelled like vanilla just next to the black stone tub. She eased into the water and groaned at the way it relaxed her muscles. She poured a dollop of the soap into her palm and began scrubbing furiously, wiping away the dirt and blood that didn't even belong to her.

Zia clawed at her scalp, peeling away any dirt in her gnarled hair. She could *really* use Ren's magic with the sorry state she was in. She dumped more of the bath oils into the water, savoring the smell of them. It was the first time in her life she had used real oils—not cheap drugstore products. Aaliyah had likely brewed them herself with the herbs in her garden, since she wasn't exactly receiving a delivery service or *leaving* anywhere for that matter.

Zia closed her eyes, sinking her shoulders beneath the water and playing with the faucet with her toes, turning it on and off as the temperature changed.

Hiro was right. Something else had taken over her in the faerie court. Every time she used her magic, she found a new depth to it. It was unsettling to think that her power might be endless. The wet, silver strand of hair stuck to her shoulder. She twirled it around her finger. Everything had a cost, it seemed. How much of her life had she lost in that moment?

A knock on her door sounded. It was Ren, calling to her that dinner was ready. She reluctantly pulled herself out of the tub, wrapping a towel around her and taking steady breaths. They were safe. For now.

Loose white pants, a cotton shirt, and a soft robe were left on her bed. She slipped into it, enjoying the feel of the fabric against her skin. She knew her hair was a lost cause and resigned to asking Ren for help later. She sighed, tying it in a gnarled bun atop her head with the silk sash that had been left on the bed.

By the time she made it downstairs, the others were waiting. They sat on floor cushions around the wooden table, chattering softly while Aaliyah finished with their plates. Aaliyah cooked wildly like it was a dance. She twirled and threw all manner of spices, herbs, and oils into a stone pot. She sang songs in the Old Lemurian language, which sounded so familiar it made Zia shudder.

Jace's head snapped up the moment she walked in. His eyes followed her as she made her way to the table. She swallowed, doing her best to hide the way the weight of his gaze made her stop breathing.

The violet-eyed faerie was the last to join them. He sat down and shifted his weight when he noticed that they all were staring.

"What?" he asked, with a deadpan expression.

Hiro, who was sitting next to him, leaned toward him a bit.

"Well, you haven't said a single word since you rescued us..."

The faerie shrugged.

"Technically The Bridge rescued you."

Ren, who was sitting cross-legged on the floor, tilted her head to the side, studying him.

"We haven't met before. I thought I knew everyone in Morganna's court. What's your name?"

The faerie's mouth quirked to the side.

"We have met before, actually. I was nobility once. Part of Morganna's innermost circle. Until the day she sentenced you to live out your days with the Guardians."

Ren's face shone deathly white, her mouth quivering. She had never spoken about what happened to her in the faerie court.

"Rhoedlyn," she whispered.

Rhoedlyn waved a hand over his face and his appearance changed. His eyes turned golden as the sun. He had several small hoop earrings on each ear, with different gems, and an enormous stone pierced into his nose. Even his eyebrows were golden, and his wings. He turned his attention toward Zia.

"As she said, my name is Rhoedlyn. No idea why my parents decided to bestow such an unfortunate name when they were so fortunately blessed with my existence. Long story short, you can call me Rho."

Zia frowned.

"How do you two know each other exactly?"

Rho looked toward Ren, who shook her head. He clasped his hands over his lap gracefully, with completely perfect posture. In a matter of a few seconds, he had become someone else entirely.

"She's my cousin. I am half sprite, which is why I am considerably smaller than most faeries. Well, most of me anyway," he turned toward Hiro and winked.

Hiro nearly spit out his water in return, his ears and cheeks turning bright red.

Jace cleared his throat, and they all turned their attention back toward Ren. Her lips were wobbling.

"What happened to you?"

"Our family is the last bloodline of faeries who can fully change in appearance. After she shipped you off, she wanted me to become her spymaster. I would prefer death to being her puppet again, so I shifted into the lowest of peasants. You'd be surprised how invisible the help is. Oh, the things I saw..." he chuckled, mischief dancing in his eyes.

"Why not just leave the court?" Zia asked.

Rho tapped his knuckles on the wooden table.

"I was waiting."

"For what?"

"For *you*."

Dead silence hung in the air.

Jace snorted.

"There was no way you knew she existed. Sahara gave up her freedom to keep it hidden."

Rho gave him such a smug expression that Jace's eyes turned murderous.

"My dear prince, who do you think gave Sahara the idea for The Trials? Do you think she coded it all on her own? Do you think mating with a human was an *accident*?"

Ren was still silent in the corner, sitting still as stone. Zia could feel the sheer panic rising up in her. What wasn't she saying?

"So, you're saying that you helped her mom create the world's most popular game and then sat on your ass and waited for her to just magically appear?"

Rho raised a brow, like he was annoyed to be explaining such an obvious thing.

"Do you think it random that we are all together? This is far bigger than some odious king, the world has been waiting eons for—"

All the waters in their cups went splashing into Rho's face like a small tidal wave. For a split second, Zia saw beneath his arrogance. He blinked rapidly, his face flushing. Aaliyah was standing there with a hand on her hip.

"That's enough out of you, Rhoedlyn Hayes. Dinner is ready."

His mouth was hanging open like a fish.

"Beware of the man who thinks he knows more than you. The ones who actually know don't need to go shouting about like a baboon," she huffed before walking back to the kitchen.

Rho was quiet after that. Aaliyah was a force to be reckoned with—he would have been a fool to challenge her. Zia leaned her head back and closed her eyes for a moment, the exhaustion truly hitting her. It had been a week since she slept properly. The sound of a plate clanking made her open her eyes, and she yelped at what stood in front of her.

A small tree with *eyeballs* was staring at her, extending a plate with its branched hand. She looked around and saw everyone else was already eating, acting like it was completely normal to be served by a walking stick.

"This is Laryx. He helps me with the land. He is one of the Tree People," Aaliyah said casually.

Laryx bowed in response. He didn't speak. Zia hesitantly took the plate of food from him.

"Thank you," she said, unsure of what else to do.

Laryx smiled in satisfaction and walked out of the room, disappearing from sight. Zia knew she should really stop being surprised by things like walking trees and dragons.

She looked down at the plate of food, but there was nothing she recognized.

They were all foreign plants steaming on top of what could have been jade rice, and beautifully garnished with a purple flower. The veins of the flower glowed, and Zia couldn't help but wonder how it was edible.

The rest of them had already licked their plates clean, so Zia took a bite with her fingers. Cutlery, it seemed, was not a part of Lemurian culture. She nearly moaned as she tasted the first bite. Never in her life had she tasted so many flavors, all of them new to her. She ate slowly, trying to discern how Aaliyah cooked food like this. Food that made her feel full in far more than just a physical way.

None of them spoke throughout dinner. Eventually the others slumped off to bed, immediately falling asleep. Jace was the last to go, giving her one last glance over his shoulder before climbing up the stairs. Just as he took the first step Aaliyah called after him.

"Jace?"

He paused, looking over his shoulder.

"What became of your brother? The Crown Prince?" she asked.

Jace's brows knit together.

"He never learned to bend the other elements. His fire is still wild and unchecked."

Aaliyah stared blankly at the floor.

"And his heart?"

Jace tapped his finger on the railing, weighing his words.

"He burned my—" Jace's voice was hoarse. "He burned a young faerie named Meaghan alive. She was innocent. That was when I was banished for trying to kill him. I don't know how much of a heart he has left."

Aaliyah nodded stiffly. Jace's gaze shifted to Zia. He smiled, but it didn't reach his eyes. Then he turned around and soundlessly climbed up the stairs, his shoulders slightly curved, like the weight of the past week finally took its toll.

Laryx returned to take her wooden plate and clean it. She argued she could clean it herself, but his grip was surprisingly strong as he ripped it from her hands and smiled.

Aaliyah walked outside to her garden, then a few minutes later returned holding crushed herbs in her hands. She placed them firmly in Zia's palm.

"Eat these. They will return your strength."

Zia winced as she placed them in her mouth without protest. It tasted like dirt and left a dry, cotton taste in her mouth.

"They all admire you quite a bit, you know," Aaliyah beamed at her.

Zia shook her head.

"Aside from Hiro...they are here because they think I'm their only hope. All because of some silly prophecy some idiot wrote thousands of years ago."

Aaliyah firmly squeezed her shoulder and stood up.

"Their loyalty has nothing to do with the prophecy."

Zia was quiet for a long moment, staring at the flames and the dripping wax on the candles.

"I've done nothing to earn it."

Aaliyah gave her a knowing look, the wisdom of her nine thousand years showing.

"Get a good night's sleep, Zia. We have a lot to do. You can sleep in tomorrow, and from there on out we begin lessons at dawn."

Though she was afraid to ask, Zia said, "What will these lessons entail, exactly?"

"Oh, a little of this, a little of that..." Aaliyah began humming to herself. She closed her eyes and gently rocked back and forth.

Zia shook her head, not bothering to figure out what she meant by that. She was too exhausted, unable to process the weight of her new life as she climbed up the stairs. She looked down one last time at Aaliyah over the banister. The woman waved a hand and all the flames of the candles winked out at once, leaving them in complete darkness. Zia had a feeling she knew she had been watching.

Sleep found her the second she collapsed on her bed, the sound of the rushing waterfall and the birds fading away.

CHAPTER 15

We are ruled by what remains buried in us. —Aaliyah

By the time Zia woke up it was already noon. The sun was at its apex and boiling everything in sight apart from the frigid waters of the lake. She had the kind of deep, demanding sleep where she forgot her own name. Rho and Hiro were already off in the Red Grove Forest, and Zia couldn't help but smile a bit for her friend when she heard that.

Light spilled through the windows of Aaliyah's hut. Zia found a fresh change of clothes waiting for her in the kitchen—a high-waisted pair of magenta-colored pants with a matching top that revealed her midriff. Patterns of gold swirled throughout the fabric.

"My very best spiders made them," a cheerful voice said by way of greeting.

Zia looked up to find Aaliyah in the doorway, the backlight of the sun made her hair look like silver fire.

"Your what?" Zia blinked.

"Come see for yourself," Aaliyah gestured as she held the doorway of the hut open.

Zia hesitantly walked out of the hut. Aaliyah led her down the winding stone path, through the spiraling garden. There were rows and rows of herbs, vegetable stock and various flowers. Zia's mouth watered as she thought of all the meals she could cook with such ingredients at her fingertips.

They turned a corner through a patch of yellow Helius flowers and found two enormous spiders spinning thread after thread like they were two humans with a spindle. Zia yelped and leaped back a few steps, never having particularly cared for spiders. They were both around her size, and black as the night sky with bright blue bellies.

They paused and looked up at her, their pinchers clicking together a few times, until they saw Aaliyah standing behind her and went back to their weaving. They were making what looked to be a pair of men's pants, probably for Jace judging by the size.

"Zia, meet the most talented weavers in Lemuria. This is Sabrina and Leah."

Sabrina, with her depthless black eyes, gave her a slight nod in greeting. Leah just stared at her, looking like she wouldn't mind sinking her pinchers into Zia's neck.

Zia cleared her throat.

"Thank you. For the…. clothes," she trailed off, forgetting how to properly formulate a sentence.

Aaliyah's eyes twinkled with amusement.

"They only speak Old Lemurian, which is one of the things you'll be learning today. Come, let's make sure you get a nice meal before we begin."

Zia nodded, scurrying after Aaliyah.

Laryx had an entire buffet waiting for her—porridge, hot toast with bright-colored jams, potatoes seasoned with rosemary, and juices from the fruits of the grandmother tree that hovered above the hut.

Zia devoured it all, feeling sick after eating too quickly, but grateful to have a proper meal after so many days of running herself ragged. After she licked her plate clean, Laryx took it from her with an enormously satisfied look on his face.

"Teach me how to cook like that," Zia insisted as she tried to help him with the dishes. She had always wanted to learn how to cook but hadn't had the money nor the kitchen to properly learn. Her attempts had resulted in quite a few explosions, until her dad forbade her entirely.

He waved her away, but she was fast, and beat him to grabbing the bar of soap. He blinked slowly in surprise. Zia quickly discovered that the Tree People were incapable of speaking. They were stewards of the land, making sure crops thrived that year and the earth was being properly tended to—their magic was directly linked to nature. The Tree People were the one species the king hadn't executed, because they were helpful servants to him and couldn't talk back. Aaliyah recognized Laryx's talent for cooking and brought him back to her land.

It seemed her gift was to bring out the gifts of other people.

Zia scrubbed at one of the copper pots while he watched her with skeptical eyes.

"I'll help you in the garden, or whatever you want. But please teach me, I'll be your best student," she insisted more gently this time. She never had an outlet—something that felt like just hers. Cooking seemed the most useful place to start and would give her an excuse to break up the training a bit.

Laryx looked at her curiously. He shook his head and pointed to her, then made several gestures with his hands. She understood well enough. *Cooking was thought of as a servant's job.*

"Well, whoever came up with that rule had their head up their ass," Zia scowled.

Laryx's eyes bulged in surprise at her language. He put a branched hand to his mouth, and she could tell he was holding in a laugh. Zia crouched down on her knees to be at his height and put a hand on his shoulder. A small rose bloomed from it.

"Well, my friend, I am learning that the rules need to change as we do, so it would be my honor to learn from you."

Laryx's bright eyes glimmered. It nearly cracked Zia's heart in two, to see the joy there. She finished the dishes and stalked up the stairs to get ready but froze halfway up the steps as she realized Jace had been standing there the entire time, watching her with Laryx. His mouth was parted slightly, his brows knit together as he leaned against the banister.

"Were you born frowning?" She asked.

"You asked him to teach you a servant's job," he replied. She could hear the disbelief in his voice. Of course. He had grown up a prince, probably never even noticing the Tree People.

She raised her chin.

"Yes."

"Why?"

Zia pushed past him, stepping up the staircase.

"Because, your highness, cooking is not a *job*. It's an art form. And it's no different than that sketchbook you hide for dear life."

He nodded curtly, then walked out the door, muttering something about going hunting. She scowled, slumping up the rest of the staircase to her room. He was infuriatingly difficult to read.

Zia slipped on the clothes the spiders wove her and shuddered. They fit her too perfectly, like Sabrina and Leah somehow knew every curve and edge of her body. She adjusted the clothing nervously. It was more revealing than anything she had worn in the human realm, but the scorching weather outweighed her discomfort.

She met Aaliyah outside beneath the grandmother tree, where all of their lessons would take place. Aaliyah said their ancestor's wisdom was encoded within its mighty trunk, to which Zia chuckled under her breath because she knew it was really just the only place that had even a sliver of shade on the property.

They began with language lessons. Though Zia could read the *Book of Lemuria*, Aaliyah explained that was only because she was Katya's descendant and needed to learn how to speak the language. She taught her Old Lemurian first. Hiro joined in on those lessons. Mei had taught him the modern dialect, but not the ancient language. He picked it up instantly—with his photographic memory, he had always done well in school without any effort. He was fluent by the end of the week, while Zia was still twisting her tongue just to get the most basic of pronunciations right.

The rest of Hiro's time was spent with Rho, lounging in the meadows and reading to him or wandering off into the forest. Though Zia was happy that Hiro had a connection with the faerie, and saw the way his eyes lit up around him, there was something Zia didn't trust about Rhoedlyn. She didn't bother to hide the fact that she watched him like a hawk.

Aaliyah refused to teach her magic until she learned Lemuria's language, history, and customs, which Zia thought was a complete and utter waste of their time while the prophecy loomed over them. But she said it was imperative that Zia understand the wisdom of where she came from before she could unlock the knowledge of where she was going. Besides, she figured blending in was an asset, which she couldn't very well do in the royal city if she knew nothing of their customs.

She waved off any questions Zia had about the stones—she had a remarkable ability to evade giving a direct answer to anything. Zia began the majority of her days by waking up early and making breakfast for everyone with Laryx. When she wasn't learning magic with Aaliyah, or training with Jace, she was in the gardens learning about permaculture and cooking.

The days were hot and long, which made the waterfall a great blessing. Whenever Zia would get too cranky, Jace picked her up and threw her into the spring waters. It was becoming as easy as breathing to be around him, and with Hiro being occupied most days...he was quickly becoming a dearly close friend.

It terrified her to get used to such a thing.

Aaliyah took a particular interest in Jace. During their dinners, she asked him about his life growing up in the royal city and his time as commander of the Shadow Warriors. She seemed fascinated that, despite who his father was, he had turned out decent.

After dinner, Jace and Zia would stay up after everyone had gone to bed and talk into the morning. Jace propped up on his elbows as he told her stories of his time commanding the Shadow Warriors, and his adventures during his exile. He showed her the scars he had aside from his burns—bite marks from the fangs of a siren, places he had been stabbed, or broken bones after falling off a Zhulu. Zia hung on every word of his stories, because she had never met someone who lived so many different lives within their one.

They were lying on the floor, head to head, and she had clasped her hands over her belly to avoid touching his. His voice grew heavier as he spoke.

"I realized that every court had something to teach me, you know? So, I found a master from every part of the realm and trained. I didn't have magic, so I had to rely on my other skills. I started to gain a reputation, I guess. I had won all of this glory and had no one in the world to share it with." He ran his fingers through his hair. "Even when I won that duel with Leo and became general, it still wasn't enough. It was never enough for him..." He trailed off. His eyes flickered to hers, and they just stared at each other for a moment. She offered him the only thing she could in return—her story. The bits of it that she had kept locked away in the back of her heart and never told anyone.

"I used to start these brawls in school and wouldn't stop until someone pulled me off a kid. I was just so *angry*. At my dad, at myself...I thought I killed her by being born," Zia whispered. "Whatever man my mom fell in love with is gone. The grief broke him. And I...I think I was so narrow minded. I thought I just wanted to escape Periculum, but I think I wanted to escape seeing that look in his eyes every day. To escape this feeling that I don't really have a right to...be here." Her voice cracked.

Jace rolled over to face her, and there was understanding in his gaze.

"I know what it is like...for everything you do to be to prove them wrong. To feel like you have to *earn* your place in the world."

She turned to face him, and breathed in his scent.

"Cheers to bastard fathers," She smiled.

He laughed.

"To bastard fathers, and stubborn as hell warriors."

Her heart leaped at that—the way he spoke to her like she was an equal. She had never met a man who had done so, besides Hiro. She felt a twinge of sorrow that she felt like that was a privilege. She changed the subject.

"Is there anyone in the realm who could kick *your* ass?" She asked.

He whistled.

"Without magic? The only person is The Last Shadow. He's the greatest assassin in the world. I've looked for him everywhere. They whisper legends of him from the Ordos Desert to the deep waters of the siren court. Even the king and Morganna fear him, but no one knows who he is," He arched a brow, "One day, I will find him, and put my skills to the test."

"I hope I'm there for that," Zia smiled.

He interlaced his fingertips in hers, and they lay there forehead to forehead. They fell asleep like that, and it was the most strangely intimate experience she had in her life. He was so easy to talk to, to be around. She felt like there was nothing wrong she could say to him.

She felt like *herself* around him.

And for the first time in her life, Zia Alexander felt the walls around her heart begin to crumble.

The days began to blur together. They found a rhythm and routine within the sanctuary of Aaliyah's property. Even Inka had decided to stay with them, spending her days roaming the skies or lying with her belly toward the sun in the meadows. Ren was able to cloak her with magic so she couldn't be detected on her wanderings.

Her time with Laryx was her sanctuary, perhaps because he couldn't talk, and she enjoyed the rare moments of silence. It was also the only time she wasn't *The Bridge*. Chopping vegetables, harvesting herbs in the garden, learning about various spices and how they all danced together...it was the one thing that was just for her. The tension in her shoulders eased when she was in the kitchen, the knots inside of her started to unwind.

Zia was improving with language and history at a glacial pace. Winter would be on its way soon, and they had to travel to the royal city of Mū before the snow stuck to the ground, or else it would be too difficult to navigate. Aaliyah still refused to speak about the stones with them.

On a particularly sweltering day, Aaliyah forced her to stand in the same position for four hours. Her knees were deeply bent in a wide squat. Her arms were held out in front of her. Anytime she started to slouch, Aaliyah would tack on more time. It was infuriating. Zia's arms were shaking. She felt the hot sun branding her back. Sweat dribbled down her spine.

"How is this supposed to be helping?" Zia asked through grit teeth.

"Tune into your own body. If you don't learn to understand your own energetic subtleties and currents, you'll die getting lost in someone else's." Aaliyah replied cheerfully.

Though Zia didn't want to admit it, she did start to feel it. Almost like energetic tides throughout her body. If she focused enough, she could feel into the currents around her. She closed her eyes. Her own field felt like a still pond on a summer day.

"Good. That's it. Now widen your perception. What do you feel?"

Zia expanded her focus. It felt like she was stretching her skin. Her attention went straight to the nearest person to them, Ren. She was lounging on the grass by the waterfall, soaking in the sun and smoking from her vine pipe.

Ren's energy felt choppy like a riptide during a storm. There was so much anxiety. So much grief. Zia lost control. It felt like she slipped on a banana peel, as she was suddenly falling inside of Ren's mind.

Ren's inner world was an endless whirlpool of memories. She had lived for so long that there seemed to be an infinite string of moments, spiraling deep down. Zia couldn't control where she went. She was free falling down her mind, shelf after shelf.

Memories of Ren's childhood appeared—playing with sirens in the ocean with her two sisters, riding on the back of enormous whale sharks and sea serpents. Memories of her mother teaching her about magic. Memories of that magic growing stronger and stronger. Morganna noticing it and extending a personal invitation to Ren's family. They had arrived at the royal court—all of them, including Rho. Her mother wept as Ren accepted the queen's offer to serve.

Ren's mother had gotten on her knees, begging to take her place instead, knowing that to serve was little more than to be a slave. The queen, insulted by her words, had killed Ren's father, coveting Ren and her sisters for the court. Most of Ren's memories after that were a blur. She spent her days self-destructing. She ate nothing. Drank herself into oblivion with summer wine. Had an endless line of people sharing her bed. Zia's stomach churned as she felt Ren's pain.

Further and further Zia fell, the whirlpool growing darker as she reached Ren's subconscious. She slammed into cold hard ground that felt like ice. There were thick vines growing over the walls with sharpened, black thorns. For someone who had mastered beauty, her inner world was rotting. Zia could barely move. She was freezing, shivering to the bone.

"The prophecy is real, Ren. I swear it. I've met the girl's mother." Rhoedlyn was suddenly standing there, his golden eyes burning into hers.

"Why should I give a damn about some human girl?" Ren laughed darkly, taking a swig directly from the bottle.

"Because she is our last hope."

Ren snorted, walking away from him with a careless swagger. Rhoedlyn gripped her arm tightly.

"You still have two sisters, you know. They'll come of age soon and be little more than Morganna's pets to torture as she pleases. They don't have your magic. She'll find them useless, except for being leverage over you."

Ren froze at that. Her mask of carelessness dropping ever so slightly. She turned toward Rhoedlyn.

"You swore you'd protect them, Rho."

"And I will, but you need to be smarter. Train with me. Rise up in Morganna's ranks. Become her most valuable spy and learn everything you can. Knowledge is the only weapon that matters in this court."

Ren rolled her eyes.

"I'm not her strongest nor her smartest servant. I believe the latter is your skillset."

Rho shook his head, taking one of her palms in both of his.

"You know what trumps brawn and brains in the eyes of men?"

She eyed him curiously, but he didn't let go of her hand.

"Beauty."

Ren rolled her eyes, but he shook his head.

"Learn to use your beauty as a weapon, and you'll find yourself in rooms even the bravest of soldiers or the most intelligent of advisors spend their whole lives trying to gain access to. How do you think the siren court has gone untouched for so long? They are utterly terrifying and yet impossibly alluring."

Ren swallowed.

"I don't want to be anyone's pet. Not the king's. Not Morganna's."

Rhoedlyn cocked his head to the side.

"Then be a predator disguised as prey. You can fast if you know when your next meal is. So long as you have a purpose, a plan, Ren, you can survive anything. Help me prepare for The Bridge, so that when she comes of age, we will be ready for her. Help me protect your sisters. Help us to one day create a world we don't just have to survive in. Please." It was perhaps the first and only time Rho had used the word please.

Ren nodded, and the memory dissolved. More and more popped up, but they were faded. She didn't touch a glass of wine again. Instead, years were spent rising up in the ranks just as Rho planned. She became invaluable to both Morganna and the king, both of them thinking she belonged to them. Her anger honed into a sharpened blade, the loyal servant.

Closer and closer Zia walked to the center of the dark room. There was a book on the table, covered in vines. It opened to a single memory that played on a loop again and again. The sound of Ren's sister screaming echoed.

It was the day for her sisters to come of age. Rhoedlyn had convinced the queen to let her work on the borders, guarding the court instead of being sold. They all attended the ceremony for the young faeries. Her sister, Najwa, was in her prettiest white silk gown. She had sewn it herself. Her golden hair was decorated with lilac flowers—Ren had helped her braid it. They all held their breath as they stood in front of Morganna, waiting.

Morganna surveyed all the young faeries, her eyes landing on Najwa.

"Such a pretty young thing you are," Morganna said, giving her that spider's smile.

"You wish to guard the border?" she asked, tapping one of her long nails on her throne.

Najwa nodded with a soft smile. She had always been the most delicate of the three sisters.

"Ren. Come here."

Ren plastered a neutral mask on her face. She bowed before the queen, lowering at the waste.

"Yes, my queen," she said subserviently. A loyal servant, through and through.

"Did you get that information that I needed on your last mission?" Morganna twirled a strand of gold hair between her bony white fingers. Ren kept her eyes on the ground, speaking carefully.

"No, Your Majesty. Gaining access to the king's private quarters will take some time."

The queen raised a brow.

"I know he must have one of the stones. How else would that fool remain in power without a drop of magic to his name? You're telling me that you have failed your queen."

Ren ignored the blind panic that swept her body.

"I don't think that he does. My queen, I have not failed. I only need a little more—"

"Silas." The queen snapped her fingers.

Silas was instantly behind Najwa, his yellow eyes full of cruel delight.

"Clip her wings," Morganna ordered, smiling at Najwa. Najwa's eyes instantly widened.

"P-please...." she could barely get out, her face turning white. Silas slammed her to the ground, grabbing her by the hair.

Rhoedlyn jolted upright from his seat, walking in front of Morganna.

"If I may, Your Majesty—"

"Did you or did you not tell me that this girl would give Ren the proper incentive to complete her missions?"

Rhoedlyn's eyes darted back and forth from Najwa.

"I did, but—"

"And did she or did she not complete her mission in the time given?"

"Your majesty, gaining access to the most guarded room in the realm is bound to take—"

Morganna held a hand up.

"I have heard enough of this nonsense. Silas, clip her wings and sell them to the highest bidder, then toss her body in the lake."

Ren was running before Morganna could finish the sentence. She instantly lunged for Silas, knowing it was a fool's mission. She managed to slice his face as she knocked him over, but the rest of the sentries were upon her within seconds. She killed a few, her body blocking Najwa, until an ear-splitting scream echoed across the court.

Morganna herself was standing behind Najwa. She had clipped her wings. A pool of blood dripped onto the floor.

"Dispose of her. Now."

The rest was a blur—the sound of Najwa's body hitting the water, the screams of the other faeries. Rhoedlyn disappeared out of sight.

Zia.

She vaguely heard a voice.

Zia! Get out of here!

Zia was ripped out of Ren's subconscious, as though a hand had grabbed her by the neck and yanked her upwards. There was no time to process, to ease out level after level. A bright light blinded her, and she slammed into her own body. She keeled over on the grass, vomiting up her guts and feeling the burning sun on her skin. It took her several moments to understand where she was as she heaved and heaved and heaved.

Her eyes watered as she continued gagging, long after there was nothing to throw up. Aaliyah murmured something soothing in Lemurian, her magic coaxing Zia into a calm. She created a gentle breeze of wind on the back of her neck.

When Zia looked up, it wasn't Ren who was standing there. It was Rhoedlyn.

"You waited for me," she croaked.

He gave her a single nod.

"I told you I did."

"You disappeared—"

He interrupted her.

"There was nothing I could do for Najwa. Ren was tossed in the dungeons to be executed. I convinced the queen Ren's magic was too valuable, and that she should be sent to The Guardians instead as punishment. And then—"

"—and then he convinced me not to kill the entire court, and myself afterward. He convinced me that it would all be for nothing. That there was still hope worth living for."

Zia whirled to find Ren standing behind her. Ren had a hand on her hip, looking as composed as ever with her French braids and flawless skin, but there was great sorrow in her eyes.

"You shouldn't go rummaging about people's minds without permission, you know."

"I'm sorry, I didn't mean—"

"I know," Ren interrupted her, the harsh look on her face softening.

"If Ren hadn't pulled you out of her own mind, you would have been lost. Katya made the same mistake with me once. The subconscious is unknown territory, and yet it rules the majority of all our actions. Like riding a dragon, you may think you're in control, but if that dragon decides to change directions, you will have no choice over the matter. We are ruled by what remains buried in us."

Aaliyah leaned in a bit closer to Zia and lowered her voice.

"There's a reason I didn't want you using your magic too quickly. There was zero control," Aaliyah said gravely. She was sitting in the shade, her hands clasped over her lap.

"Then what are we waiting for me to learn?" Zia snapped.

Rho let out a low whistle.

"Yourself, of course. It's a dangerous thing, empathy. Without a strong sense of who you are, you can very easily lose your way..."

Zia cut a glare toward Rho, then looked toward Ren.

"I'm sorry for your loss. Your parents, and your sister," she whispered.

Ren looked at the ground but seemed to be somewhere else entirely.

"She was so young. And soft. Too soft in such a hardened world. But her legacy lives through me now, and it's my responsibility to make her death mean something."

Her shoulders drooped, like the burden she carried since that day weighed even more heavily on her now. Rho cleared his throat, interrupting them. His hands were clasped behind his back as he walked.

"If I may, Aaliyah. I think I might be of assistance in your lessons. Though my magic is nowhere near as magnificent as yours—"

"Enough with the false flattery," Aaliyah waved her hand away like she could flick him into the next world.

Rho blinked slowly, then started again a bit sheepishly.

"Apologies. Old habits and all."

Aaliyah sighed.

"On with it."

He started again.

"If Zia is to learn her own boundaries, perhaps my mind would be the most suitable to practice on. After all, I have spent a lifetime putting up walls and placing traps for people. She won't be able to fall too deep like that. If she can safely navigate my mind, I guarantee she can navigate anyone's."

Aaliyah pursed her lips, thinking about it for a moment. The sound of wings flapping in the distance flooded the meadow. Inka was landing soon.

"Alright. Fine. We start tomorrow. Everyone else—take the rest of the day off. I need some time to think." Aaliyah stood up, gripping onto her staff. She began walking toward her hut, and Rho had a satisfied look on his face like he had planned for this all along. Even after seeing that he helped Ren, Zia didn't like or trust the faerie one bit.

Just before Aaliyah left, she paused, calling over her shoulder.

"Oh, and Rho?"

He turned toward Aaliyah.

"Yes?"

"Careful, now. Wear enough masks and you'll forget which one is your own face."

Zia saw the fear that flashed in his eyes just before he settled back into a smug calm. Everything about him made her want to knock his teeth in. He turned back toward Zia.

"As you saw...I trained Ren. I have a unique skill set that is at your disposal," he grinned, bowing his head slightly.

Ren hissed.

"Your *unique skill set* really served Najwa well that day, didn't it cousin?"

Rho's face twisted in pain. It might have been the first genuine expression Zia had seen from him.

"There was nothing I could do. I had no idea that Morganna would..." he swallowed loudly, then lowered his voice, "Don't think for one moment Ren, that I do not carry the burden of Najwa with me everywhere. But it was bigger than her. It was bigger than all of us. This is about the future of the realm."

A tear slid down Ren's cheek.

"How many tyrants have we seen sacrifice innocent lives for *'the future of the realm?'*"

She turned on her heel, her boot leaving a scar on the grass as she stomped away, her glittering skirt trailing after her. There was nothing of her usual proud posture as she walked. Guilt gnawed at Zia as she realized the violation of unlocking some of Ren's worst, most guarded memories—that she too, had to relive those in order to pull Zia out.

"I need to bathe," Zia muttered, moving to get as far away from Rho as possible. She hurried over to the waterfall staircase, climbing the mossy edge and being careful not to slip. She eased her body into the icy waters, groaning in relief at the way it washed everything from her mind. She welcomed the way there was nothing else she could focus on.

She settled into the top pool so that she could sit beneath the waterfall, feeling the rapids pound onto the top of her head. It squeezed into four more pools before entering the river stream where the butterfly fish swam. The water was crystal clear, with pebbles and soft sand at the bottom of the pool.

The sun was on its last leg and would dip beneath the mountain soon. Golden light seemed to blow up the mist from the waterfall, carrying it away until it faded into the shadows. Inka finally landed in the sprawling meadows, her glorious, flapping wings creating harsh winds that carried all the way to the spring pools. She eyed Zia, blinking once in recognition before nestling into her usual spot by the garden.

It was difficult to find a moment alone at Aaliyah's. Though they all had their respective rooms, their days were so full of training and planning that they spent little to no time in them. The waterfall had quickly become Zia's favorite place to rest in between sessions. For a moment, she could think of nothing else.

She shuddered. People she didn't even know existed had already sacrificed so much, Waited so long for her. It made her sick, especially because she didn't believe in the chosen one nonsense. If a world was really to change, it was the people who needed to change it, not one single savior.

Though she did have to admit, it utterly terrified her that her life seemed tied to everyone's fate, as Rho had said. The longer she spent in Lemuria, the further away her old life felt—as though that had been the dream, and this had always been real. Her father and Mei's faces were beginning to fade in her mind.

She didn't miss Periculum, but there had been familiarity with life there. It was a complete known. There were only so few paths she could take, unlike in Lemuria. Anything could happen at any point during the day. Their lives could completely flip upside down in an instant. At first it was thrilling, but now...she was beginning to understand the cost of freedom. It felt like being shot out of a cannon, moment to moment.

How long had they been there? Weeks? She traced the moon cycle all the way back to that day they left in Periculum. When she figured out the day, she blinked slowly. It was November already. They had been there for two months. Her nineteenth birthday was coming up on the 11th.

She silently thanked whatever gods existed that Hiro had no concept of time. He wouldn't remember that it was her birthday, and no one else knew. She could silently let it pass without a thought. Her birthday had always felt more like a funeral, since it was the day that she thought she killed her mother during birth. Despite knowing the truth now, her body was still used to carrying that feeling.

Zia began to shiver in the last speck of heat from the sun. Her teeth chattered uncontrollably. She eased her body down to one of the lower pools where the water was far stiller. When she saw her own reflection, she nearly jumped back.

She barely recognized herself. The dark shadows that had always been beneath her eyes were gone. They were a bright, clear blue. Her cheekbones were more defined. Her lips fuller. Her face had filled out. Her hair had grown to her waist and had a shine to it instead of the dull, straw feeling of before. Her body filled out more with a woman's curves. She looked healthy. Pretty, even. Like she had grown into herself more.

"Zia," A silken voice called.

She slowly turned toward him. He was wearing the black pants the spiders had sewn him, with knives tucked all along the sides. And nothing else. It was the first time she had seen him without a shirt, and she wanted to drown herself at the sight.

He noticed her staring at his sculpted chest and his mouth quirked to the side. It snapped her out of it. She cleared her throat and pretended to see something immensely interesting in the spring pool.

When she looked back up, she saw him taking his pants off shamelessly and placing them on the grass. His undergarments left very little to the imagination. Her throat went dry.

"What are you—"

"Had to keep the knives dry," he smiled wryly.

Jace eased his body into the pool, creating little waves that rippled toward her. The water was a glassy pink, reflecting the cotton candy skies that accompanied the sunset.

"I heard. About what happened." The warmth in his voice soothed and settled something within her.

She kept staring down. He lifted her chin with two fingers.

"Are you alright?"

His eyes searched hers, like they might find the answers to more than what he had just asked. She shook her head, looking anywhere but at him.

"Look at me," he commanded.

Anger swelled in her chest. She felt her face as she looked him square in the eyes.

"What do you want me to say? That I'm alright? That all of this is *normal*? That good people have given their lives for me because they hope I'm the answer to their prayers? Mei. My dad. Ren's sisters. People have sacrificed so much! For what? I can barely speak the language. I can't control my magic at all. And they're expecting me, a human, to do what no one else has been able to?"

She went to get out of the pool. He gripped her by the shoulders but said nothing. He just stared at her, holding her there, giving her space to feel what she needed to. The anger turned to grief, and the tears started to fall. Her vision blurred and she blinked.

"They deserved better."

He knew who she meant. He gripped her shoulders harder.

"Then create a world that's better."

She turned away from him to wipe the snot from under her nose. He hooked a finger under her chin, and gently turned her to meet his gaze.

"Hey. Don't turn away from me. I'm here for all of it. I don't respect someone who holds it together all the time like Rho. You're honest. And brave. And so *human*. I've seen you risk your standing in The Trials for a siren. I've seen you take a bullet for a girl you didn't know. I've seen you try to save an assassin who tried to kill you. I've seen you treat Laryx like he's your equal. I've seen you harness a dragon, for gods' sake—"

"I didn't *do* any of that alone," she cut him off.

He tucked a strand of hair behind her ear.

"My point is that I see you. And you won't have to do any of this alone."

There was so much she wanted to say to him but couldn't find the words to—they all got caught in her throat. Crossing that line with him was too much to handle. If he rejected her, or something went wrong... she couldn't take losing another person she cared for.

"I should start on dinner with Laryx," she muttered. Her heart twisted at the disappointment that was so clearly written across his face. She felt the opening between them close. His face turned stony as he backed away, then stepped out of the pool.

"See you later," he said casually before walking back into the hut. It felt like a bubble had popped as she gazed after him, she wondered if what she thought was between them was really just a fever dream. Perhaps he was just trying to help her find the confidence to do what he thought needed to be done. He was a prince, after all—charm and flattery would be the first language he learned.

And yet, she couldn't shake the familiarity she felt around him. The way her body relaxed in his presence. The way his words defogged the windows of her mind. The way she couldn't help but spend the entirety of her days looking forward to their late-night conversations, no matter how exhausted she felt.

"You're in so much trouble, baby girl." Ren slowly strutted toward her, a smirk on her lips. She was balancing a basket of grains from the garden on her hip, looking down at Zia in the pool. Her amber eyes looked rosy in the setting sun. The grief that weighed on her from earlier had lifted.

"I don't know what you're talking about," Zia's face heated.

Ren shrugged a shoulder, her golden hair pooling down her back.

"*Right.* Well, when you do, and you want a woman's advice, or wardrobe for that matter, I'll be here." She winked and walked off toward the hut, her hips swishing with each step. Zia couldn't help but admire the way her friend carried herself. Everything Ren did, she did with a lightness of touch, no matter how many burdens she bore.

Zia dunked her head under the icy waters. The last bit of color leached from the sky. All she could see when she closed her eyes was Jace's disappointed face.

Ren was right: she was in so much trouble.

CHAPTER 16

It's difficult to explain. I spent my life having an agenda for everything. I was always several steps ahead. I had a clever answer at the ready. People came to value my perspective and guidance, trusting it over even theirs, simply because I bent over backward to understand their desires and their blind spots so they would need me. It was a dangerous game I was playing. It still is. What I didn't see coming is that there would be someone who didn't value that sort of control. Someone who was willing to be nobody when I spent every waking moment proving I was someone. —Rhoedlyn

The kitchen was a madhouse. Normally, everyone ate at different times—it made the cooking and cleaning aspect far easier. This wasn't one of those days. The sun was just starting to rise. The owls hooting in the distance all sang to each other. Zia wondered if Aaliyah could communicate with them, since that was her other form. She never explained how she was able to shift. In fact, she rarely explained anything at all.

Her arms felt wobbly from training the previous day as she chopped as many potatoes as she could, knowing that Hiro and Jace alone could scarf down the entirety of the kitchen. Though Jace hadn't been cold toward her, he remained closed off. Distant. It drove her mad, and unfortunately, his mood seemed to come with even more grueling exercises. In addition to their sparring, Jace now taught her hunting and tracking, how to use different weapons more skillfully—knives, a bow and arrow, her fists. Zia's twin blades were still her favorite, but she rarely used them because Jace considered them a crutch.

She slid the potatoes off the cutting board and into a bowl, handing them to Laryx. He seasoned them with rosemary, salt, and other spices she didn't recognize, then placed them on a stone pan. He made his way over to Aaliyah, who had been sitting by the window humming to herself and tugged at her robe. She gave him a nod, slid off the stool and made her way over to the kitchen.

Her cheeks puffed out like two balloons and she breathed fire out of her mouth, roasting the potatoes to perfection. The heat nearly burned Zia's face, but she watched in awe. The chatter in the living room ceased as she did it, until an *ooooooh* from Hiro shattered the silence. They continued cooking—porridge, toast, fruits, and eggs from the chickens by the garden. Piles and piles of food, wiped away within seconds.

Zia wiped the sweat from her forehead, taking a moment to stand by the window and enjoy the chilled breeze. The sweltering days were done. Lemurian seasons didn't happen slowly the way they did in the human world. One week, they had barely been able to stand being outside for more than thirty minutes without hopping in the river, the next, the spiders were weaving them winter coats. They didn't have long until snowfall. Zia dreaded the day it would first stick to the ground.

Aaliyah took her breakfast outside. Zia could hear the distant music of the flute floating over—she always played it in the early mornings. Sometimes, she wondered about Aaliyah's long life before they arrived. Nearly nine thousand years in solitude, with Laryx and the spiders. Had she had no other visitors?

"We've come a long way since my pancakes, Z." Hiro was making a mountain of toast on his plate, one arm draped around Rho. They hadn't outright declared anything, but they spent many dinners making out without a care for who sat next to them. The two were big on public affection. When she asked him about it, he would just smile and say that he felt understood. Seen. Like Rho was the first boy to care for him without demands or expectations. It was the only thing keeping her from pummeling the faerie or feeding him to Inka.

"Maybe in the cooking department, but it's not like I've made much progress in other areas," she looked pointedly toward Rho. Rho had proved to be the worst teacher she ever had. Mei had been tough. Jace challenged her. Aaliyah was just outright frustrating. But *Rho*? They had spent the entire week sitting across from each other while he just stared at her with unfailing arrogance. Every time she tried to link her consciousness with his, she'd face a different obstacle—an endless hall of mirrors, an unclimbable stone wall. One time, he even had a spider chase her out of his mind. He laughed about it for days.

She had never met anyone more capable of amusing themselves to the degree that he did. He gave her zero tips or helpful corrections other than asking asinine questions like, "Who are you *really*?" over and over and over again. She'd always give him the same response: "Zia Alexander, you idiot." He'd just shake his head and kick her out in a new torturous way. She wanted to complain to Aaliyah and beg her to be her teacher again, but she knew that would be giving up. She also knew that there wasn't a single thing that happened in the meadows Aaliyah wasn't aware of, and despite the short while they had spent together, Zia trusted her. If she was letting Rho train her, it was for a reason.

"Go easy on her, would you?" Hiro handed Rho a plate and nipped at his ear.

Rho never took his eyes off Zia.

"Easy makes for a bland, incapable person. Zia is neither of those things."

He took the plate and grabbed Hiro's hand, pulling him outside. They liked to eat by the waterfall together, wrapped up in blankets the spiders wove. She gave Hiro an exasperated look. He just tipped his hat as if to say *good luck*.

Zia went to sit down and eat breakfast next to Ren. Ren was half awake, still wearing her pink silk robe, her hair in twin braids on either side of her face. Her eyes were heavily lidded. Ren hadn't touched her food yet, despite having taken a larger portion than both boys combined. She kept yawning into her cup of tea, barely acknowledging Zia when she sat down. They ate in silence.

Jace entered the kitchen without a sound. He took a heaping pile of food for his plate. He was dressed in a black, formfitting jacket and pants with black boots. His skin had tanned quite a bit the past few weeks, and his curls had highlights from the sun. Zia grumbled into her plate as she ate. She cursed herself for the way she noticed the smallest of details about him.

"Ladies," he gave a curt nod before stomping out the door.

"Where is he going?" Zia turned to Ren after the door swung shut.

"Probably to brood over why you don't love him," Ren smirked.

"What? That's not true I—"

"So, you do love him?" Ren sang in response, holding her head lazily in her palm. Zia shook her head.

"No, I—"

"Look, baby, you've clearly only had Hiro in your life. Which is *not* the person I'd be asking relationship advice from, since he's mooning over my cousin." She made a gagging noise.

"The point being, I am your friend. Which means I am your second brain. And so, if *we* are having issues in matters of the heart, then *we* should talk about it so that it doesn't distract us, thereby ruining *our* chances of taking back Lemuria."

Zia leaned her back against the wooden banister and sighed, sinking into the floor and letting her shoulders slouch. Ren was right. Hiro was all she ever had, and he was the best friend she could ask for. Yet, without her mother, she desperately needed a female presence in her life for advice.

Ren poured some tea for Zia, gently nudging it to her side of the table. "Spill."

Zia looked around the room, making sure they were truly alone. They were. Even Laryx had vacated the hut. She leaned forward, keeping her voice at a whisper, and spilled. She told Ren of how she saw Jace and the time stone in her dream before she even knew they existed. She told her of The Trials, and how even the NPCs like Alita and the siren in the game helped her, all because her mother was The Architect. She told her of Jace betting on her, of Mei sacrificing herself, of the last time she saw her father. Her voice cracked at that memory, and she moved on as quickly as she could, not yet ready to face the fact that he might not be there if she ever returned.

She told her of Jace, and how she was feeling things that she never had in her life, and the way that terrified her more than the king or stones. Zia even told Ren what it was like to be inside of *her* mind, falling down endless memories that were overgrown by wilted thorns. How she failed again and again with Rho, and that she didn't trust him.

The entire time she spoke, Ren listened. She didn't interrupt. She didn't do what most people do, which was pretend to listen while she thought of what she would say. She just sat there, gently nodding at times, patiently hearing every word of Zia's unbelievable journey.

When Zia finished, and it felt like a thousand weights had lifted from her, she sighed, burying her face in her hands. Ren tilted her head to the side, looking off in the distance to think for a moment. She threw her head back to drain the last of her tea and snapped her fingers at Zia.

"Alright sit up. Don't give me that hopeless, poor me I'm the chosen one nonsense. As you said, it's not *you*, it's all of us. As Yetiri pointed out: the world has suffered enough in the hands of heroes."

Ren interlaced her fingers and stretched out her arms, yawning one last time.

"Let's start with the guy, because that's obviously what we care about the most. No matter how important the mission, how grand our lives become, love will always remain the priority in our hearts."

Zia's brows knit together.

"How is that the priority after everything I just told you? What if love gets in the way of destiny? Shouldn't I do what needs to be done *first*, and then maybe see..."

"No," Ren waved a dismissive hand.

"If he 'gets in the way of your destiny,' then it's not love. Love helps you become more of who you already are."

Zia snorted, rubbing at her temples.

"The spiders should build you a soap box. I just think that all of this can wait. Besides, he doesn't seem to care about anything at all right now," Zia replied.

Ren grunted.

"Are you really so dense? Men are just as emotional as we are! Oh, sure. Perhaps they show it less. He's a warrior who is protecting his own heart, because for the first time in his life he has met someone who could truly break it."

Zia shook her head.

"He's the son of our enemy."

"Exactly. He's giving up everything. His titles. Any semblance of security and comfort. Everything he has ever known. Why? Because he believes in you. Haven't you questioned why he was in your dreams before you even met?"

Ren sighed like she was talking to a child, and finally bothered to dig into her food. She ate a few bites of fresh fruit, mulling over all the information Zia had just given her.

"What do I do?" Zia finally squeaked. She was so embarrassingly out of her depths when it came to him. Taking back the realm seemed an easy feat in comparison.

Ren shrugged.

"Wish I could tell you. You don't really decide the way in love. If it's real, love will show you the way. And the bravest thing you can ever do is follow it."

Ren stuffed a pile of potatoes into her mouth, eating with as much grace as a rabid street dog. Zia's lips twitched into a smile. She stifled a laugh that the graceful, perfect faerie could eat them all under a table.

"We're having a bonfire tonight. Let me help you get ready," Ren said through a mouthful of potatoes. Zia knew what she meant—she would dress Zia, do her hair, and prepare her emotionally as best she could. Tonight would perhaps be her only window to tell Jace how she felt. They would need to leave soon before snowfall.

She had yet to master anything. Not her own magic. Not the time stone. Nothing. Her lesson with Rho was in an hour. Every day was the same: *"Who are you, who are you, who are you?"*

It felt like taking a hundred steps backward. It didn't matter that she was nearly fluent in the language now, and her combat skills had improved drastically, if she couldn't harness her own magic enough to use the stones.

Ren licked her plate clean, then sauntered over to the sink and delicately placed it there.

"When it comes to my wretch of a cousin, he doesn't do anything without reason. Every action, every word is thought through a thousand times over. Which means there's a purpose to it all."

Zia wasn't hungry anymore. She had a vulnerability hangover from discussing her innermost thoughts. She groaned.

"We sit there and do nothing. I try to crack into his mind, to link my consciousness with his. It doesn't work. His mind is too well guarded. I can't feel his emotions at all. Every day it's the same. He asks, *'Who are you?'* I answer with my name. He calls me an imbecile, kicks me out, and the lesson ends."

Ren looked out the window, watching them all outside. They could hear Hiro's laughter in the distance. Aaliyah was still playing the flute.

There was more wind than usual, knocking the chimes together. Ren walked around the counter and propped herself up on the stool.

"You answer 'who are you?' with your name?"

Zia twirled her fork mindlessly.

"Yes."

"What if you didn't?"

"What else is there?"

"Nothing," Ren said the word slowly as the light danced in her eyes. Zia scoffed.

"Thanks. That is supremely helpful."

Ren stood up and tossed her hair over her shoulder.

"*I've* already solved your love life. A girl can only do so much," she winked, and then began to climb the steps up to her room. Zia could hear the door gently shut, and a bath being drawn. She blew out a long breath, tugging on her frizzy hair. Ren was insane. Or genius. It was unclear which was true. Zia shoved aside any thoughts of Jace—it would do her no good to get distracted today, mulling over Ren's philosophical nonsense.

Later. That was a later thing to deal with.

She did, however, bring up a good point about Rho. He was far too calculating to just mess with her for a week, and they were running out of time. Aaliyah was waiting for Zia to master herself before even being allowed to touch the stone, and Zia had the horrible feeling that they would leave empty-handed.

Zia cleaned all of the dishes in the kitchen, enjoying the feeling of the warm water on her hands as she scrubbed the copper pots and pans. It was a chilled day, so she slipped on an extra coat and her warmest boots before walking outside. During their time, the spiders had given them all new wardrobes. Apparently, they never stopped weaving. Aaliyah said they wove tapestries that told the future, though Zia was hard-pressed to believe that. It was why there were so few spiders in the land—the king kept most of them in the castle as oracles. Aaliyah had a tapestry hanging on the wall of the living room, which Hiro had spent many days squinting at. What he understood within the weavings, he didn't say.

Zia walked outside, instantly feeling the frigid wind wrap around her. The sky was overcast, with a thick blanket of cloudy mist covering any speck of blue. It made the rest of the land look gray, too. There were far fewer birds and animals than usual. Even Inka decided not to roam the skies that day, preferring to cozy up by the hut. Smoke puffed out the chimney from the endless fire that never stopped burning, thanks to Aaliyah's magic.

The weather reminded her of Periculum—of days spent riding around in Betty, desperately racing to get to the refrigerator door and climb into Mei's VR library to escape their crumbling, bleak world. They had come so far. Farther than Zia could have even dreamed.

She would not let this be where it ended.

Zia strutted over to Rho with a formidable look on her face. He was lounging lazily by the river with Hiro, popping cotton candy grapes into his mouth. His golden eyes slid over to her, studying her as she approached.

"Back for more fruitful lessons, my sweet Bridge?" He chuckled. His thick, curled eyelashes fluttered.

Zia crossed her arms, tapping a foot on the ground.

"Get up. We start early."

Rho hummed gleefully.

"I'd rather not waste my time on a girl who doesn't even know who she is! Especially when I have such a handsome view," he winked at Hiro, bringing his palm to cup his cheek.

"Get up." Zia said flatly.

"Come on, Rho. Z's my best friend. You said you'd help," Hiro muttered to him, stroking his hair.

Rho opened an eye, his attention snapping toward her. He sighed. It appeared Hiro did have some sway over the cunning, selfish faerie.

A cat's smile spread across his face as he sat up, dusting his hands off. He was wearing a silk button-down shirt that was cut perfectly for his delicate, shimmering wings.

"I've given up quite a lot for the idea of you, you know. It's a shame the real thing isn't holding up."

Her head roared as the words struck home.

They stared at each other. His smarmy smirk tipped her over the edge. Zia's breath shortened. She began to see red spots. He had cost them so much time. Every day counted. She grabbed Rho by the neck of his shirt, hauling him up into the air.

"Z! What are you—"

Splash. Before Hiro could even finish his protest, she tossed Rho into the freezing spring pool. He gasped for air, complete shock on his face. She glared at him.

"Sorry to disappoint, but since we're being honest today: I don't trust you. I don't like you. And, if you hurt my best friend, I will slice the points of your ears off."

Rho didn't break his composure for even a moment. He had been provoking her, testing her edges, determining how much control she had over her temper.

"Charming, but you won't be doing much of anything at this rate. Magic is linked to your emotions. It's why Aaliyah won't let you touch the stone. If you don't even understand your own chaos, how could you possibly hope to serve anyone at all?"

"I just served you your ass just fine."

Rho chuckled, stepping out of the spring pool. He waved a hand over his face and was instantly dry. Zia stomped over to the grandmother tree. She heard chuckling from the garden, and turned to see Aaliyah, rocking back and forth on a wooden chair. Blue lotus flowers bloomed behind her, growing from the mud. Zia's face heated.

The clouds were becoming pregnant with a dark gray color. Hopefully it wouldn't storm soon. She sat cross-legged on the ground and waited for Rho. He was purposefully taking his sweet time. Her resolve was wearing thin with each passing moment.

Today was her birthday—nineteen years old. She didn't feel any different, just the familiar grief that came with each passing year. A strange loneliness enveloped her, despite not being alone. It gnawed at her heart. Rose up as a lump in her throat. She picked at the emerald grass, feeling the soft blades between her fingertips

"Are you ready, Bridge?"

Rho stood above her. She hadn't heard him approach. Jace would have walloped her for not noticing such a thing. He had blue hair today that fell in little ringlets around his face. His wings matched perfectly, though their color was muted by the gray sky.

She slowly lifted her head to meet his golden eyes. Every look was a challenge. He didn't care if she was human or Lemurian—Rho's game was one of the mind. If she could outsmart him, then maybe she had a chance at beating the king.

Rho sat down cross-legged in front of her. They were knee to knee. She could smell the forest on him. Perhaps he would always carry the scent of his home no matter what form he took, or how much he despised where he came from.

"Do you remember the riddle about the stones from the prophecy?"

His lips curled back revealing his sharp, pearly teeth. It reminded her of a shark. She searched her mind again and again. Nothing. Completely blank.

"No," she admitted.

He smirked.

"That's a shame. It would have been most useful to you. Oh well, let's begin."

Again, she felt her anger bubble up, but there was no time for that. She would only prove him right by reacting. Today was her last chance to get this right. She had no other option.

Zia stared into Rho's eyes. His pupils were a black hole she suddenly fell into. He *let* her fall into them. It was an endless void with no bottom. There were no memories, only darkness. And then the falling ceased.

"Who are you?"

She whirled around to see Jace standing there. He was dressed in black, but his figure was see-through like a ghost. Rho was playing a trick on her in the landscape of his own mind.

Jace walked toward her, hands clasped behind his back. His strong chin jutted upwards, a ghost of a smile on his lips. When he was only inches away from her, his head fell to the side.

"Who are you?" he asked softly.

"Zia Alexander," she answered with every amount of confidence she could muster. That had been Rho's point, right? To maintain a sense of self even as she wandered through the labyrinth of another.

His face fell. Maybe she didn't say it right. He turned around and silently walked away. Her heart twisted in pain watching him leave.

"Wait!" she called after him, but he was already gone. She was alone in the dark.

She sat down, letting her head hang between her knees.

"*Think, think, think!*" she whispered to herself. What had Rho wanted her to understand?

"Zia." It was her father now. He lifted her up onto her feet. She broke into uncontrollable sobs at the sight of him, despite knowing it was an illusion. It felt so real. Those deep wrinkles between his brows where they usually knit together. His muddy brown eyes. The old, beat-up jeans he wore when he did construction work. He was exactly how she had left him.

"Who are you?" His voice was harsh, the way it was when he usually scolded her.

But she couldn't answer. She couldn't stop crying.

"I'm so sorry..." the words tumbled out. She went to grasp his hands, but he took a step back, narrowing his eyes at her.

"You are a disappointment. You always were. Your mother and I could have been happy, if it weren't for you. And now you're letting everyone else down, too."

She sank to her knees. The words shattered something in her. It was her greatest fear—to let down the ones that she loved most, to never, ever be enough no matter how hard she tried.

"I'm trying, I swear I—"

"Who are you?" his voice was cold.

It took every last ounce of strength to respond.

"Zia Alexander," she whispered. The resolve and fire that normally burned in her belly was gone. When she looked up, he had vanished. She did not call after.

And then she was falling again, the ground disappeared out from under her. She didn't have a voice to scream. She felt like a floating speck amongst the endless ribbon of time.

But there was a small circle of light she was approaching.

The circle got bigger, until she realized it was an enormous door.

She fell through the door and into the open sky. It was the city of Mū, just as it had been shown in The Trials, only ten times more beautiful—pastel painted skies, a wild sea crashing against black sand, circular homes made of crystals and winding rivers, tree highways and hover cars. Loud music played below—violins and lutes and fiddles. Art filled the streets. All of the vibrant, unique quarters. It was one brilliant, beautiful symphony.

Then there was the pyramid-shaped castle. She winced as she kept falling all the way to its point, straight through the walls.

Then directly into the king's chambers.

He lounged on his throne, eyes an icy blue that bordered on white. He had cropped, gray hair and unnaturally smooth skin.

A row of guards stood on either side of the room's hallway. The castle was dead silent. Void of life. It felt like a tomb. She landed right before his throne made of crystal—the throne that had once been Katya's. The king's eyes slid toward her, unphased by her grand entrance.

He did not acknowledge her. He nodded toward one of the guards. They exited the double doors. The king finally focused fully on her, and a sense of dread filled her whole body. Was this still a dream? Or had she somehow folded like Hiro on accident? It felt too real.

"Who are you?" he asked in a bored tone.

"Zia Alexander."

The king's eyes danced with delight. He had won. The double doors opened, and whatever dream this was quickly turned into her worst nightmare.

Her mother was in chains. The guards hauled her toward him, then slammed her onto her knees before the king. She did not speak, only looked at Zia with unwavering strength in her eyes. No fear.

"I'll ask you one more time..." he said, amused.

The guard brought a blade to her mother's throat.

"Who. Are. You?"

Zia started panting.

"NO. P-please—"

"WHO ARE YOU?" the king snarled, leaning forward. The blade inched closer to her mother's throat, touching skin now. It drew a bead of dark, red blood. Her mother looked at her with complete trust. Complete compassion. More than she had ever felt she deserved. She wouldn't let another person down. Not now. Not her.

What had Rho said? Remember the prophecy. Some nonsense about restoring balance and finding a key. No, he specifically mentioned the part about how to wield each stone. Hiro had relayed the riddle to Rho, which meant it was somewhere in his memories. She had never chosen what part of someone's mind to enter before, but she had to try.

Time froze as Zia focused all of her energy like a magnet, doing her best to call the prophecy to her. The room began to vibrate like an earthquake, and a piece of paper fluttered toward her.

Nobody can master the first stone
Most lose their minds
And never return home...

She panted. Nobody can master the first stone.

Nobody.

No. Body.

That was what she became when she entered someone's mind. Formless. Consciousness without a body. It was why the stones needed to be wielded by a Psukhē. The magic allowed her to wield the stones without losing her essence. Only her body.

She had to be willing to let go of everything she was, not clutch so tightly to who she *thought* she was.

"I'm nobody," she whispered.

"What was that?" the king snapped.

Zia tilted her head up in defiance. It didn't matter what he tried to do to her or take from her. Not if there was a place inside of her that even he couldn't touch.

"I am nobody," she said with a wicked grin.

His face twisted in anger, but he held up his hands for the guards to drop her mother. Zia went to run directly to her, but the scene dissolved. Her mother fading into the black void.

She was in the darkness once more.

Laughter echoed in that darkness. In the distance, a candle flame neared. She could see the outline of small, delicate hands. It was Rho, carrying the candle flame. He was in his original form—golden hair and eyes. He was chuckling.

"Perhaps you're not as slow as I thought."

She snarled and went to grab him, but he was made of mist. It was pointless while they were in the subconscious plane. Rho smirked, walking around her in circles.

"Old Lemurian is far different than English. Your definitions are quite simple, you know. It's why Aaliyah forced you to learn, aside from the convenience factor. I knew exactly what she was doing. What's the first line of the prophecy, little thief?"

He was referring to her stealing the prophecy right out of his memories. She had zero qualms about rummaging through his mind, considering the horrific scenes he had just subjected her to.

"True power is held with humble hands."

"And do you know what '*humble*' translates to in Old Lemurian?"

She shook her head.

"I must have missed that in my endlessly boring lessons."

He stopped circling and leaned in close toward her until he was inches away. She should have been able to feel the heat of the candle beneath their faces, but this was an illusion. Light bounced off his face in the dark, the fire twinkled in his eyes.

"Most people think to be humble is to be less than or to deflect praise. In Lemurian, it translates to: 'one who has the confidence to be nothing despite a world that constantly demands they be something.' That is true power."

Before she could react, he winked, then blew the candle out.

The moment the flame snuffed out, she fell back out of his mind and into her own body. He had kicked her out. She ran her hands along her body, panting to make sure she was really back. The blinding light that burned her eyes. The sound of the waterfall. The wind. She felt the grass beneath her toes. The disorientation dissolved after a few minutes.

"You've been planning this," her voice rasped.

"As I said, I sacrificed a lot for the idea of you. I wanted to ensure you were worthy of my help. Turns out, you are." He stood on his feet, letting her keel over herself in the dewy grass.

"She was always worthy, Rhoedlyn," Aaliyah's cold voice boomed. She was by Zia's side, instantly soothing her with her magic.

Rho held up his hands and bowed.

"My work here is done. You're welcome."

Zia's head snapped up.

"Wait. Don't we need to practice more? We only have one day and—"

"And you are ready, Zia." Aaliyah pulled her staff out and stomped it on the ground three times. The bobbing, silver orb opened and within it was a familiar, glittering emerald stone.

Time.

Aaliyah pulled the stone out and gently placed it into Zia's palms.

Zia held the rough edges within her fingertips. It was hard to fathom that such a small, tiny thing could change the fabric of their very existence. Her ears rang as she tried to reign in her focus. Thunder cracked overhead as the looming threat of the clouds grew darker.

Most people spent a lifetime letting time slip through their fingertips. She held all of eternity between hers. It was completely terrifying for one person to hold so much power. She understood why the prophecy would call for a human—for someone who could not live and rule forever. To master it was to let go of it.

As she had let go of herself.

"Do we start now?" Zia croaked.

"Gods no, child! I need to fix this weather for our celebration tonight. You've done enough for the day!"

"Celebration?" Zia formed the words slowly, dread filling her. Aaliyah gently took the stone from her hand and placed it back in the center of the orb. It closed, concealing the glittering green entirely.

She winked at Zia.

"Happy birthday, dear."

Before Zia could protest or ask her how the hell she possibly could have known, Aaliyah was already making her way to the center of the garden at a surprisingly fast pace for a nine-thousand-year-old.

She needed to find Hiro and whack him upside the head for revealing her birth date. Of course, the one and only time he bothered to remember a date was her birthday. Traitor. Zia looked up at the sky and sighed, forcing her limbs to move as she made her way toward the hut. She needed a nap. Desperately.

Zia nearly melted at the hot air that enveloped her when she opened the door. The fire at the hearth was on full blast, its flames dancing wildly creating *crackle pop* sounds. Hiro was cozied up by the fire with Rho already. He was reading a book to Rho in Lemurian, his accent absolutely perfect. He finished the chapter, and proudly plopped a toothpick between his teeth.

"What is the point of this?" Rhoedlyn asked.

Hiro pulled it out and playfully stabbed him in the shoulder with it.

"*That* is the point."

Rhoedlyn narrowed his eyes.

"Hiro."

Hiro gave him a sheepish grin.

"I was a scrawny kid growing up and got bullied a lot. One day, these three kids cornered me and started calling me toothpick. Right as they were about to pummel me, Zia beat them over the head with her lunchbox until they limped away crying. We've been best friends ever since," He shrugged, "I guess it's my way of reminding myself that our greatest shame can become our greatest strength."

They didn't notice her when she first walked in. Rho's head was gently resting on Hiro's shoulder, with Hiro's arm draped around him. It was such a simple moment of intimacy, curled up by the fire together. She was happy for Hiro. Truly, she was. He deserved that more than anyone she knew. Yet, she couldn't help but feel a sense of dread—how many of those precious, simple moments together did they have left?

She slumped her way up the stairs.

"Z!" Hiro called excitedly.

"Don't say it," she snapped, instantly feeling guilty as she dredged her way up the wooden staircase, moving all too quickly into her room. She locked the door before he could come console her or ask what was wrong. She needed a minute. Or an hour. Or perhaps a lifetime to sort through the absolute emotional mess she felt like.

As always, when not knowing what to do, she drew a bath and plopped her body in the tub, closing her eyes and letting her problems melt away in the hiss of the steam. She felt empty. Hollow. Like everything she was had been drained to the very last drop.

Her shoulders sank below the scalding water, and as she closed her eyes, she could barely bring herself to care about anything at all.

CHAPTER 17

I couldn't help but feel that no matter how grand the quest or vital the task, it was still those tiny perfect moments that we stayed alive for. I began to measure my life in memories, not milestones. Experiences that I would remember 5, 10, even 100 years from now. Little by little I stopped searching for power, or love, or purpose. Little by little, I stopped searching for anything at all. I spent my time noticing the way dawn broke that day. Or the light in his eyes when he laughed. Or the exploding flavors of a warm, cooked meal. These were the small moments that I knew would carry me through the big ones. —Hiro

Zia had fallen asleep in the tub. She woke up to banging on her door, jolting upright. The water had turned cold, yet the heavy weight of exhaustion had lifted. Her muscles had loosened a bit.

The banging grew louder.

"Open this damn door *right now* or else I'm going to kick it down and ruin my favorite pair of heels!"

Zia gulped. Only an idiot would ruin something from Ren's wardrobe.

"Coming!" she called, her voice still raspy from sleep.

She wrapped a black towel around her body and her hair, ignoring the way water still dripped down her neck. Goosebumps covered every inch of her body. So much for the bath warming her up.

She wrapped her hand around the cool, brass handle. Before she could even twist it all the way, Ren was already barging in.

"Do you have *any* idea how much work I had to put in to make everything perfect for you tonight? I even went and talked to those wretched spiders! Whatever their names are—Nightmare #1 and Nightmare #2."

"Sabrina and Leah," Zia coughed pointedly.

Ren waved her off as she set down several bags on Zia's bed. She was wearing a red silk gown that was form-fitting, but seemed to move with her as she walked. The back of the dress was low cut, all the way down to her tailbone, and revealed two dimples on her lower back. Her hair was pulled back in a sleek, tight bun and her eyes were framed by dark liner. She had several gold bracelets that all clinked together when she moved, and twin rubies dangling from her ears. Zia wondered how many men would lay down their lives just to get near her.

"The spiders were so frustrating. They kept wanting to put their own designs into it, and then threatened to *eat* me when I told them they had poor taste! So, I had to have Laryx help me. He's the best, really. I hope we get to take him with us when we leave. They did what I wanted straight away, though the beading took a while."

Zia's jaw dropped as Ren pulled out a dress that looked like a work of art. It was an electric blue color with long sleeves made of silk that would wrap all the way around her middle fingers, secured by the beaded rings on the end. The neckline plunged, and glittering beads wrapped around the bodice. It flowed all the way to the floor, with a very small train in the back. It looked like it belonged to a princess or a queen.

"I knew you'd love it! This is how I see you," Ren winked, hanging up the dress.

Before Zia could protest that she was completely delusional, Ren was already grabbing her by the shoulders and ushering her into the bathroom. She forced her to sit on a stone chair by the vanity. In the flash of an eye, Ren had already dumped out the remaining contents of her bag—red powder made from tiger lily flowers for her cheeks, small little jars of eyeliners, and hair gels. Zia didn't have the slightest clue what most of it was.

"Please don't change too much. I still would like to look like me," Zia said, daring to look at herself in the mirror. She pulled the towel off her head and let it fall to the floor, suddenly feeling shaky.

"I'll repeat what I said when we first met—beauty is not meant to hide who you are, but accentuate more of who you are! Trust me."

Ren flashed a smile that Zia was certain no one had ever said no to. She conceded with a small nod. It was enough for Ren. She began work on her hair, first brushing it out by hand and squeezing out the wet drops. Then Zia felt a tingling sensation on her head. Magic dried and curled it, waterfalling in perfectly crimped waves that fell all the way down to her tailbone. It was the longest her hair had ever been, and a far cry from her frizzy curls.

Ren worked on her in silence. When Zia moved too much she'd snap at her to hold still so as not to ruin her art. She braided half her hair in a crown atop her head, adding tiny butterfly pins of silver in the back. Then she went to work on her face.

She added a glow to her cheeks and painted her lips. Zia's face looked natural, aside from a liveliness and glittering glow to it now. Ren had somehow made her eyes look an even brighter blue with light liner, her lashes long and curled. A sprinkle of glitter across her lids looked like the starry sky.

Zia's eyes slid toward her open window. Violet roses were blooming, their vines beginning to wrap around the windowsill.

"Okay, one last finishing touch!" She interrupted Zia's thoughts by pulling out a necklace. Zia's first thought was that it could have fed half Periculum.

An enormous, blue sapphire hung just above her collarbone in a tear-drop shape. Ren finished fastening it. Little white stones glittered all along the silver chain.

"Are they diamonds?" she asked.

Ren rested her hands on Zia's shoulders, admiring her work.

"No, they are a very rare Lemurian stone made from the tears of mermaids. This necklace was a gift, and worth more than that stuffy, ostentatious castle the king sits in."

Zia touched the blue stone lightly with her fingertips, barely believing her eyes. She didn't miss the flash of pain in Ren's eyes.

"Who was the necklace from?" Zia asked softly.

Ren walked over and got the dress from the hanger, unzipping the back to help her into it.

"Her name was Serena. A siren. She had long dark hair and eyes of gold. Not like Rho's, though. They were warm like the sun. She had this glorious, lilac-colored tail. We spent a summer falling in love."

Zia arched an eyebrow. Ren smirked.

"Don't look so shocked."

"No, it's not that. I shouldn't have assumed. I just…. wow. How many men have cried for not being able to be with you?" Zia half-laughed.

Ren snorted.

"Many, but not for that reason. It's about the soul for me. Gender never mattered so much. Neither did what breed of creature they were. Faerie, siren, Lemurian…my heart chooses what it wants."

Zia dropped her other towel and stepped into the dress slowly, not wanting to rip the fabric. Ren gently pulled it up, helping her arms through and looping the beaded rings around each middle finger.

"Where is Serena now?" Zia asked gently.

Ren zipped the dress up slowly. It fit Zia like a glove.

"She is…. very high up in the royal court of the sirens. The queen didn't approve of her being with someone like me. So, she gave me this necklace, and I gave her my most prized dagger, and we parted ways. Now I am giving it to you."

Her voice was heavy. She cleared her throat, fastening the last of the dress. Zia brought a hand to her collarbone.

"Ren, this necklace is beautiful. But I can't accept it. It means too much to you." She turned to face Ren and grabbed both her hands.

"That is exactly why you must accept it. I can't look at it anymore, and I honestly can't think of anyone else more deserving of wearing it. The dress, the necklace, it's all yours, Zia. Because I see the woman you are becoming, and I believe you deserve pieces that remind you of that."

The full weight of Zia's gaze settled on her. Ren wiped small tears beneath her eyes.

"Don't ruin my makeup with your pity! You get to be as old as me, and you fall in love and get heartbroken too many times to count. Besides, I have enough jewels and dresses. It's time we start *your* collection."

Zia pulled her into a hug, wrapping her arms around tight.

"Thank you, Ren. For this, and for being my friend."

Ren seemed to collapse into the hug for a moment. The faerie who had a presence that filled the entire room suddenly felt small in her arms. It had been a long time since she felt held—supported by someone. By the time she pulled away, she had already gained her composure back.

"Happy birthday, Zia."

Zia felt such a strange, fragile joy sweep through her heart. She walked over to the shoes Ren had made for her—blue, strappy sandals that laced around her ankles. Her friend really did know her. She despised heels because she looked like a baby fawn trying to use its legs. The flats were mostly hidden by the dress, and they were comfortable.

Ren opened the door and twirled her hand in a mock bow.

"After you."

Zia took a deep breath, knowing these were her last moments before everyone saw her more dressed up than she had ever been in her life. Even in The Trials, there was still a fierceness to the way she dressed herself. Everything about this felt feminine. Vulnerable. Her palms were sweaty as she walked out, approaching the staircase.

Jace was already standing by the door, leaning against it the way he had when they first met. Except now, the confident warrior was nowhere to be seen. Jace's breath hitched when he saw her, eyes widening with awe. Ren chuckled darkly, taking pride in her success. That reaction was exactly what she was gunning for.

Zia prayed he couldn't tell just how close she was to turning around and running back to her room. Her whole body shook. She gripped the banister with one hand and her skirts with another, needing something to do with her arms. Every step down took more focus than any of her lessons. Tripping would be a nightmare at this point.

She finally made it to the bottom, letting the silk train fall behind her. She was doing her best not to fidget or mess with her hair, mainly so that Ren didn't kill her. Time slowed as she approached him, every step feeling like a thousand years. He was dressed in black, as usual, except his outfit was far nicer. His dress pants and black jacket were form fitting enough that she could still see his broad shoulders, his muscled legs. His black, curly hair was tied back in a bun. Thick brows, for once, not in a frown. A warm smile played on his lips. He blinked several times, taking in every inch of her.

Zia finally stopped a few feet in front of him, not daring to move any closer. His lips parted.

"You look—"

"Ravenous? Dazzling? The most perfect woman to ever grace Lemuria's lands?" Ren interrupted him, placing a hand on her hip. He glared at her slightly.

"I was going to say, 'devastatingly beautiful,' but sure."

Ren rolled her eyes.

"You're an immortal with all the time in the world, and that's the best compliment you have come up with for a woman?"

"Don't you have somewhere to be?" Jace said pointedly.

"Yes, of course, your royal highney." Ren bowed before exiting the hut. Just before she closed the door, she looked over her shoulder one last time at Zia and wiggled her eyebrows. Zia wanted to pull her hair out. Her face heated.

Ren had taken her as far as she could. It was on her now to tell him the truth, but words were lost on her lips at the moment.

Jace eyed her up and down.

"You really do look devastating."

"Um, thanks," Zia squeaked. *Really? Um, thanks? He's going to think you are the biggest moron to ever walk the planet!*

"Shall we?" he extended an arm.

"Where are we going?" she asked.

"You'll see, birthday girl. You'll see."

Her heart pounded in her ears. She was definitely going to exact revenge on Hiro for telling everyone. Despite her nerves and embarrassment, nothing seemed to matter more than the fact that he was smiling at her.

She looped her arm through his, and he opened the wooden door with his other hand. It was pleasantly warm outside like a summer night. She raised a brow, looking around her.

"Aaliyah spelled it so you'd be warm," he explained. Of course, she had.

The pathway was lit with hundreds of tall candles, the wax dripping slowly. Fireflies swirled around her as if to say hello, beckoning them forward. They walked slowly along the path, taking in the scent of the flowers and the way the flames danced, guiding their way. She looked up at the night sky and paused.

It looked as though a mage had tipped his hat and all the stars tumbled out, nearly covering the darkness. The high tide of night swallowed the rolling hills and mountains. The moon was nowhere to be seen.

"It's beautiful, isn't it?" she said, tilting her chin up so high it craned her neck.

When she looked back down, Jace was staring straight at her. Unflinching. Inches from her face. She felt his warm breath as he said, "Yes."

It didn't take a genius to realize he didn't mean the stars. He hadn't looked at them once. In fact, ever since she walked down the stairs his eyes hadn't left her.

They continued onwards, following the fireflies through the garden until they turned a corner to find Laryx. He was dressed in a tux, his branched hands poking out through the sleeves.

He walked up toward Zia, holding a glowing blue lotus flower he had picked and cleaned from the mud. She bent down so he could reach her and place the flower behind her left ear. His dark, black eyes watered with pride. It broke her heart.

"Thank you, my friend." She clasped his branched hand between both her palms.

The smell of food wafted through her nostrils. He tugged her onwards, Jace remaining closely beside her. They walked through the rows of violet rose bushes and into the center of the garden. She froze in place. The entire garden was transformed.

In the center was a bright, burning bonfire with stones surrounding it. Wooden benches had been brought out with thick, warm blankets. Rho and Aaliyah sat by the fire, playing music. Hiro was dancing in circles, holding sparkling wine in one hand and his hat in another.

An enormous buffet ran from either end of the garden with enough dishes to feed a village. Upon closer approach, she realized they were her favorite meals—some of them even from the human realm. Mac n cheese with crispy mushrooms on top. Lemurian delicacies she had enjoyed making over the past month with Laryx. Enough wine for them to drink themselves into oblivion. At the end of the table was an enormous, chocolate cake dripping with a raspberry sauce. Hiro must have spent hours in the kitchen with Laryx explaining how to make it all.

The moon pool to the right was even decorated with blue lotuses gently bobbing up and down on the water's surface. Strings of lights had been dressed around the surrounding flowers. Hundreds of candles framed the garden.

"You guys did all of this...for me?" she breathed, unable to properly take it in.

Hiro cackled loudly in the distance, sauntering toward her to take her hand.

"Happy birthday Z!"

He spun her round and round until dizziness took over her and she nearly fell over. He caught her, and they both laughed until their ribs ached.

"I can't believe this," she said with a hand to her heart, looking around the garden.

Laryx tugged at her skirts, holding a glass of wine. He placed it in her hand.

Hiro grinned.

"Laryx did most of it. He needed to create a proper birthday for his first friend."

That broke the dam inside her. She burst into tears and threw her arms around Laryx. The wine spilled onto the ground and he squeaked in surprise, then brought his arms around her waist. They sat there hugging for a few moments.

Someone was already pressing another glass of wine into her hand. Ren.

"Drink. For once in your life, enjoy a night of not being so tense you could squeeze a diamond out of your ass!" Ren threw her own glass back down her throat, making her way to the moonpool to swim beneath the stars.

Laryx wove her off to go dance and made his way to the buffet to do a few finishing touches. She realized Aaliyah was holding a fiddle and Rho a violin. Sweat dripped down his forehead as he played a tune that made even Zia want to dance.

She stood there for a moment, seeing the love from her friends in every detail of the celebration. This is what Aaliyah had meant—their loyalty had nothing to do with the prophecy. It was friendship. Only true friendship could inspire such care and beauty.

Zia was uncertain of how long they had together, this chosen family that they had built. The only guarantee, really, was the breath she was taking. A night spent with her friends dancing to music beneath the open sky. She would not let it slip through her fingertips. Like her mother had told her in her dream, she would seize it—every last drop of joy and humanity in her heart.

She chugged the wine, feeling the bubbles sing on her taste buds. A deep belly laugh escaped her as she picked up her skirts and made her way to the fire. She looped her arm around Hiro's, and the two of them danced together into the long night.

Aaliyah and Rho played their music for hours, until they were both soaked in sweat and had a looseness in their bodies that only came from giving oneself over to their art. The music flooded their souls. Zia didn't feel tired anymore as she swirled to each song.

Ren slid out of the moon pool, and after several glasses of wine, sat next to Rho. For the first time, she looked like an absolute mess. Her hair was wet and all over the place. Her makeup had slid down her face. But when she opened her mouth to sing, they all fell silent. Her voice was earth shattering. Having lived for so long, it was as though the depth of her experiences tumbled from her lips.

Aaliyah and Rho found the perfect tune to go with her song. She sang in Old Lemurian. Hiro and Zia kept on dancing. She didn't fail to notice that Jace had sat by the fire, watching her the entire night with an emotion on his face she couldn't quite read.

When Zia was panting and her hair had fallen out, she went to sit down. But before she could, Jace was already up and extending a hand. The firelight danced in his eyes, the warm glow illuminated his face.

"May I have this dance?" he asked with such formality she would have normally laughed, had her heart not been about to leap out of her chest. Tonight, she would let herself do what she wanted without a second thought.

"Always," she replied, taking his hand.

As though they had been waiting to play it for them the entire night, Rho and Aaliyah slowed the music. It was a romantic song. The violin building in its intensity. It was what love sounded like. Ren's voice was like honey. It started low, building and building until her voice boomed, flooding the meadows with pain and pleasure. Joy and sorrow. Love and loss.

Jace's arm wrapped around her waist, his other hand interlaced in hers. They were nearly nose to nose. He gazed at her like he wished to give her everything he was and would be. She couldn't shake the feeling that he never looked at her, but into her. It stripped her bare. Terrified her. Yet, she had never felt more alive.

He spun her around gently, then drew her close. She ached to touch him, like they couldn't get close enough. She yearned to feel his arms around her. To know what it would be like to kiss him. Their breath mingled. His hard body pressed against her soft one. He was a strong, unwavering mountain and she was the wild sea whose waves crashed against him in breathtaking chaos. Their dance unraveled her, and when it ended, when the last note the violin played rang out into oblivion, they remained standing still. Gazing at each other for what felt like forever.

Then clapping started. Hiro. The rest of them broke out into applause. Zia didn't care. She didn't feel embarrassed. She didn't make herself wrong for wanting him. Her heart dreamed of him before understanding what he was to her, and for once, she would let her heart hold the reins over her mind.

He brought her hand to his lips, never taking his eyes off her. He kissed her knuckles with such tenderness, she felt her core heat. Her cheeks flushed. Shivers ran down her spine, rattling her to the bone.

He released her hand, then jerked his chin toward the buffet.

"You should eat something. Sit by the fire with your friends."

She tilted her head to fully take him in. He could see the impatience, the longing and yearning that yanked at her heart. It mirrored his own. He dipped his head low and brought his lips to the shell of her ear.

"Later, Zia. We'll have our moment. For now, I want to see that bright smile of yours. I want to see you laugh with your friends. I want you to know how loved you are."

She swallowed loudly. Unable to respond, she nodded slowly. Then made her way over to the buffet. The rest of them were exhausted from dancing and playing music, so stuffing their faces was a natural progression. They all piled heaping amounts on their plates and went back for seconds and thirds.

The mac 'n cheese was the first dish to be wiped clean. Aaliyah, in particular, marveled at how human food could be so delicious. In her whopping nine thousand years, she had never tasted such a flavorful meal. Zia and Hiro laughed until hot tears streamed down their faces. If only she knew.

By the time they were done with dinner, they all lay on the logs. Zia had a hand on her belly. It was so full she was sure it would burst. Luckily, the fabric of the dress was stretchy. She closed her eyes, listening to the crackle and pop of the logs and the stories exchanged around the fire. It was mostly Rho, boasting about his clever adventures. He droned on, until Hiro interrupted him by grabbing his face and kissing him just to shut him up. Then he spoke.

"Alright, I know Lemurians do birthdays a tad different—"

"You mean getting so drunk and dancing until we don't remember our own names? I think we've done that." Ren interrupted.

Hiro's mouth quirked to the side.

"Yes, *that*. But in the human realm, we sing a song and blow a wish out on candles."

Zia propped herself up to protest, but Laryx was already carrying the giant chocolate cake with 19 little candles all lit up. The flames twinkled. Hiro, being the only one who knew *Happy Birthday*, sang it in his horrible tone-deaf voice.

Laryx brought the cake before her, and as she looked out at her friends through the candle flames, she realized she had everything she ever could have wanted. She found something more precious than any stone. And all she could hope for was more moments like this—that they would get to see a world where these nights weren't a rarity, where everyone could know such safety and comfort and joy.

She blew out the candles, the smoke curling and dissolving into the night. Everyone clapped, and as she looked up at Jace, he smiled broadly. Despite how full they were, they all devoured the chocolate cake. Chocolate had always been her favorite. The fact that Hiro and Laryx had put so much effort into the night...she felt like the luckiest girl in the world.

Hiro and Rho fell asleep on each other. Ren was barely coherent—she would surely be hungover by the morning. Laryx took all their plates, already cleaning up the garden. Zia sighed in satisfaction.

"Zia," Jace's voice warmed something in her. He held out two hands to help her up.

"Jace," she replied.

"It's time," he said.

"For what?"

"You'll see, birthday girl. You'll see," he winked, echoing his earlier sentiment. She took both of his hands, which seemed to lace perfectly in hers, and allowed him to lead her through the garden. He took her out into the meadow, which was completely dark, and they stopped by the ancient tree.

Their eyes locked for a moment, and a magnetic current passed between them.

"It's strange," She said.

"What is?" He brushed his knuckles along her cheek, and she leaned into the touch.

"I can't explain it. I just feel like I've known you before..." She trailed off, trying to muster up the courage to tell him about her dreams.

His lips parted like he might say something, and an expression she couldn't quite read crossed his face. It felt bittersweet, like a strange sorrow. Within a few seconds it was gone, and he hooked a finger under her chin.

"Look up," he smiled.

She gazed up, unsure of what she might find. It looked like a cloud at first, dancing across the sky. Then the cloud began to glow a bright green color. Then purple and rosy pink. The lights danced and swirled across, covering the sky in color. She had seen it once, in The Trials, but it did not compare to this. Not in the slightest.

The entire world seemed to pause. Nothing else existed but those lights that were putting on a show for them.

"Some believe they are our ancestors."

"Why do they appear tonight?" she asked.

He cupped her cheek with his hand.

"You were born on the eleventh day of the eleventh month. When the hour is darkest, the veil becomes thin enough for them to pass through, reminding us they are with us."

It was a strange feeling, knowing that she may never see a moment so perfect as this one again—standing with him, watching the sky dance for them in every hue. She wanted to drink in every last detail, and yet there was a bittersweet sorrow knowing it would pass.

He brought his forehead to hers. Even the lights couldn't pull her attention from him. From that familiar smell of sandalwood. From the feel of his arms wrapped around her.

"I couldn't keep my eyes off you tonight."

She breathed him in, letting the scent settle her nerves.

"There's so much I want to tell you, Zia. So much I need you to know. Every time I see you, you stump me. I think you're going to do one thing, and then you do the opposite of that." He ran his fingers through his hair, chuckling softly.

She interlaced her fingers around his neck, nudging his nose with her own. Now was the moment. The words rose up in her throat.

"Jace, I—"

And then he was kissing her. Soft. Patiently. Like he had all the time in the world to learn the curves of her mouth. Her heart didn't explode or burst into fireworks. For the first time since she met him, she felt calm. Completely at peace. Like she had been walking toward this moment for an eternity.

The kiss deepened. It became urgent as he pulled her in tightly. His tongue slid into her mouth and she nearly moaned at the taste of him. It didn't feel like their first kiss. Not at all. Their bodies just seemed to fit.

Wings flapped and a harsh wind almost knocked them backward, interrupting the moment. Inka was landing in the meadow, and she had two small seats fastened atop her spine. Laryx had crafted a harness, so the two of them could have privacy together and find freedom on the winter winds.

Inka landed, and dipped her head before Zia, bowing slightly. She held her wing to the ground so they could climb atop her. It was the first time anyone would ride her since they had arrived at Aaliyah's—and likely the only time the dragon would allow a harness and seat atop her.

Jace smiled down at her and tucked a strand behind her ear.

"Care for an adventure, Zia Alexander?"

She shook her head, disbelieving that any of this was real. She was fairly certain she would wake up to it all being a dream. Especially him. But tonight, she had promised to let her heart lead. And her heart wanted to *fly*.

Jace got on Inka first, extending a hand to help Zia up with her skirts. She ditched her strappy sandals in the meadow, preferring to be barefoot. She rode in front. He wrapped his arms around her.

Where to?

Inka asked Zia silently, mind to mind. Zia turned back to see Jace's face before they took off, not really caring where they went so long as they were together.

Show me Lemuria, she replied with wonder.

As you wish, the dragon responded. It was perhaps the only command the creature would ever take. Only for Zia, who had woken her from her long slumber. Zia could feel the scales of the dragon beneath her feet. She held on to one of the horns as Inka's great, godly body began to move. In one large huff, they sprung from the ground and were off.

She was growing fonder of heights every time. Inka flapped her wings, sailing toward the stars until the bonfire and her friends below looked like little ants. Zia whirled her head around, looking at the swirling lights as they grew closer and closer. She held out her hand like she might touch them—grasp them if even for just a moment.

Zia threw her head back and howled with everything she had, feeling a freedom and ecstasy so rare she thought she might die from it. As Jace chuckled and wrapped his arms tighter, his nose nuzzling her neck, a single tear slid down her cheek.

It was the happiest moment of her life.

Thanks to Ren and Rho's magic, they were invisible to all below them. Safe to explore the entire realm, should they wish. The lights grew brighter as if to say hello, not a single cloud in sight.

Inka flew lower, so Zia could glimpse the world she dreamed of her whole life. They passed an enormous glittering lake. Its glassy waters reflected the sky. Faster and faster, she flew, sailing through the mountains. For hours they rode, exploring the vast territories. They flew over the sand dunes of Ordos. Jace said there were sand bandits there—assassins trained to be invisible and thrive in the harsh conditions of the desert. It was rumored that was where The Last Shadow lived.

They passed over the Black Salt Seas, where the siren court ruled. The waves were enormous and chaotic. She could feel the sea spray on her skin. Something about it frightened her, not being able to see what lurked beneath those depths.

They flew everywhere except the faerie court and the city of Mū, since Morganna would likely be able to see through the veil Ren and Rho had cast. The world was so beautiful—so raw and wild it broke her heart to think of Periculum.

Something worth living for.

She had found it. The people and place she would cherish above all else. A word that had felt so foreign on her tongue, but now was the only thing that made sense: *home.*

"Jace, there's something you should know." Zia squeezed his hands.

He nuzzled her neck.

"Hmm?"

She sucked in a sharp breath, finally letting go of the words she should have said the moment they met.

"I dreamt of you before I met you. I was in a forest, racing away with the time stone. You were trying to stop me from leaving, but the king's guards were after us. The last thing I remembered was your face—your eyes before I tumbled over the edge of a cliff and hit the water."

He froze, his entire body going rigid. There was no turning back now.

"That wasn't the first time I dreamt of you, either..." she said quietly.

She stared blankly at the mountains below, waiting for him to reply. They were almost back at Aaliyah's. Dawn was approaching—she could tell by the way the black night was lifting into a sapphire blue.

His voice was hoarse as he spoke.

"Zia, I've known—"

His words were cut off by a loud screeching noise followed by a *crack* sound. Inka was roaring in pain. Someone had shot a spear and it was now stuck in her right wing. Zia could barely register what was happening.

And then they were falling out of the sky.

Falling, so fast that she watched the greatest dream of her life turn into a horrible nightmare.

Falling, so fast she could barely hear Jace screaming her name like a frightened prayer on his lips.

Falling, until they hit the ground so hard through the trees, her teeth rattled in her skull. The impact so harsh her body couldn't even feel the pain of the crash. The adrenaline coursed through her veins.

She could see torches lit in the distance, hear the voices of men all around her. Her head was on the ground, her eyelids fighting to stay open. Her blurred vision desperately tried to focus as she spotted a pair of leather boots, walking toward her.

"Tell the king we've found her." His voice was cold and unyielding. Where was Jace? How had they seen them through the cloaking spell?

The man crouched on his feet, tilting his head to look at her like a hawk. She vaguely felt the sensation of warm blood sliding down her temple. His long, red hair went to his shoulders. Freckles sprinkled across his nose. His eyes were a cold blue. She had seen those eyes before in the king. But this wasn't the king.

This was Jace's brother.

The Crown Prince of Lemuria looked at her the way a predator does before devouring his prey. He smiled coldly.

"Hello, Zia."

PART III

QUEEN OF HEARTS

Death is stronger than life, and life is stronger than time. Yet love, in all its mystery, is stronger than all these forces combined.

—LEMURIAN PROVERB III

CHAPTER 18

Fear is its own force. It can warp who we are and wipe away our values. The need to survive is woven into our very cells. Yet to live without fear is to live without care—to never truly let the world in, at which point, you are nothing more than an empty shell. I spent a lifetime in the shadows, making friends with my fear. Learning every inch of the hidden corners of my soul. Understanding the ugliest of my desires. The purest of my intentions. By the end of it, fear no longer had any hold over me, because I truly knew myself. And if you know yourself, you cannot be manipulated through fear. —Kali

The first thing Zia noticed were the voices—hundreds of voices, all buzzing around her in Lemurian. She could barely pick up bits and pieces of their conversation, but suddenly felt immense gratitude for Aaliyah forcing her to learn the language. She had forgotten, for a brief moment of peace, exactly what happened.

The second thing she noticed was that she was lying on a soft bed that felt like a cloud. It was too soft and felt like it might swallow her body whole. Blankets were draped over her. She brought her fingers to the side of her head. The wounds were all gone. Someone had healed her. Upon further examination, she saw her dress was torn at the shoulders—the only proof that she had fallen from the sky. Ren's necklace, mercifully, remained perfectly intact at her neck. She would never have forgiven herself had it been lost. The glittering sapphire seemed to mock her—a promise of what she almost had.

Zia blinked a few times, sitting up slowly to look around. She was in a large tent. There were few things in it aside from beaded pillows and silk blankets. A singular, wooden table with a pitcher of water was next to her bed. Though her mouth was dry as ash, she refused to drink it in case it was poisoned. She did check to see if the table had legs that she could rip off and fashion into a weapon. It didn't.

All along the tent was an embroidered insignia—two pyramids on top of each other, one facing up, the other facing down. The king's symbol. It was a far cry from the usual structure of Lemurian homes, Aaliyah had once told her. They were always built circular, until he had his castle made. The nobility who lived in the outskirts of the castle had decided to build their houses in a similar pointed structure. Apparently, it was how every building in Atlantis had been done.

She stood up, realizing that she wasn't wearing any shoes as she felt the rough rug beneath her callused feet. Her hair was sticking in every direction. All the glamour Ren had carefully done was washed away. She inched along the wall of the tent, straining her ears to see if she could pick up on a conversation. She needed to find out what happened to Jace and Inka.

Spindly, branched fingers curled around the tent flap and opened it. The light from outside was blinding. It must have been around noon. One of the Tree People walked into the tent. It looked so much like Laryx she froze, but this one was taller. Thinner. The squeaking noise the creature made when she realized Zia was awake sounded female. She was dressed in what appeared to be a servant's uniform. They stood still, watching each other.

"The man who fell from the sky with me. Where is he?" Zia asked, doing her best to keep the panic from rising up in her voice. If Laryx had been kind, perhaps this creature would follow suit.

The tree person blinked a few times, her thick lashes visible even from the other side of the tent. She shook her head and immediately waddled out.

"Wait!" Zia called. But it was too late. She had gone as quickly as she had come, probably to rat on her to one of the guards. Zia grunted and stood, searching around the room for any sort of weapon. All they had were stuffed, frilly pillows. Even a tent pole would have been useful. She started tearing the room apart, desperately looking for even a dinner fork. Though she had done well in her lessons with Rho, she wouldn't dare use her magic here. They probably thought she didn't have any, which was far better than them abusing it. So, she'd have to rely on her other skills.

"If you're planning to kill me, I suggest using something a bit sharper," a smooth voice broke her frantic search.

Zia whirled around, a torn-apart pillow in hand, panting. She probably looked like a rabid animal. The Crown Prince stood there, his hands clasped behind his back, with amusement dancing in his eyes. The light from the tent streamed through, illuminating his red hair and making it look like it was on fire.

He had nothing of Jace's swagger. This man was calculating—his spine straight, his clothes buttoned up, and not a single hair out of place. He was wearing fine pants tucked into his long, leather boots, and embroidered jacket with his father's crimson insignia on the chest. Yet no weapons that she could see. Though she supposed that, if he could incinerate her on the spot, he wouldn't need them.

"Allow me to introduce myself to our most esteemed and lovely guest. My name is Leo, and I—"

"I know exactly who you are, and I know exactly what you want," she snapped.

Despite having no weapons, and being in the middle of an enemy encampment, Zia kept her chin high. She allowed herself to settle into that indestructible calm she had touched when she was in Rho's mind—the calm that had gotten her through Periculum.

A crooked smile spread across Leo's face. She noticed he had freckles everywhere. His features were harsh and honed to perfection—a strong, square jaw, thick, groomed eyebrows, no stubble, as Jace had. Even his hair, which fell on his shoulders, had clearly been brushed out and gelled.

He took a few steps toward her, pacing around the room slowly.

"It's been ages since anyone has spoken to me like that."

"How boring for you," she remained where she stood, doing her best to not let him intimidate her. He halted his pacing, raising his red, arched brow. He lowered his voice slightly, like he was telling her a most precious secret.

"You have no idea," his voice was husky. His eyes fell to her necklace, her dress. He was examining her with a soldier's assessment, to see how dangerous she was. She supposed it was in her favor that they would assume she had no skill in combat and couldn't speak their language. People were far more revealing when they thought you to be beneath them.

"They didn't tell me you were beautiful," he said.

She snorted.

"Don't start with that bullshit, prince," The words tumbled out harshly.

He paused, slowly turning toward her. It reminded her of a snake coiling before it strikes. One day, she would learn to shut her mouth before it got her killed.

"I can tell you're an honest girl. So, in the spirit of honesty, I'll be frank. Zia, you see, I'm in a bit of a predicament," he began his pacing again. Even without him showing it, she could feel the magic that surged within him. It wasn't like Aaliyah's—contained and deep, like an infinite well. He was wild and unpredictable. She wasn't sure how in control of his own chaos he was. If his temper spiked, his magic would too. Being burned alive was the *last* sort of death she wished to face.

"My father would prefer to have your mother tossed in the dungeons, kill my brother, and torture you until you unite the stones for him. As you know, he needs The Bridge, Katya's descendant, to use them. So, he wouldn't kill you. But your reality wouldn't be...pretty," his eyes darted to her at that, looking at her through his thick gold lashes. It was taking everything in her not to react to his threats. His face softened, the threat in his tone gone.

"And that is a shame, for a girl as lovely as you. You see, I want us to be friends." Leo stopped a few feet before her. He tilted his head with a hawk-like gaze. This was a man who had never known what it felt like to be powerless, or hungry—a man who had spent his entire life being bred to rule by charm or force. She did not want to admit how much it terrified her, nor how completely out of her depth she had been to think going toe to toe with his father was a good idea. Yet still, she had to *try* not to piss him off. At least until she found Jace.

"Friends," she said through her teeth, her whole body went rigid.

His full lips twitched into a smile.

"Yes. I don't have many friends. Not any real ones, anyway. And I believe your value lies far beyond your blood. Wouldn't you say?"

The question was veiled, and she had the horrible instinct that he somehow knew about her magic. All it would have taken was one of the faeries from Morganna's court to send a message. Perhaps the queen herself had sold her out.

She took a step back and bowed her head slightly, doing her best to appear submissive.

"I'm just a human girl."

Leo chuckled darkly.

"That act might work on our court. It might even work on my father. But I can see it in your eyes, Zia Alexander…"

He gripped her jaw and lifted her eyes to meet his. His touch felt cold and unyielding. Everything in her was screaming to *run*—to get as far away from this man as possible. His energy felt magnetic, as though she might lose herself entirely if she remained too close to him.

"We're more similar than you think."

"I have *nothing* in common with you," she growled, taking a step back.

A ghost of a smile played on his lips. This was nothing more than a game to him, as it had been to Morganna. The cruelty and greed of an immortal were more infinite than the cosmos—they had forgotten the preciousness of time.

"Is that so?"

The candles in the tent suddenly blew up into wildfire, and an insufferable heat consumed the room. The flames were contained, never so much as coming close to harming Zia or burning the canvas walls. Fire danced in his eyes as he took a step toward her.

"Does the same rage that drives me not *burn* in you? Do you not, deep down, beneath your false deflection of your destiny, feel the power that aches to be let out?"

Leo got so close, she backed into the wall of the tent and stumbled. Flames danced at his fingertips. He lowered his mouth to her ear and whispered.

"You were an extraordinary girl who found yourself born into an ordinary world. But you refused to accept that, didn't you? So, destiny brought you here. Destiny gave you, a human, the power to reshape the world. The magic people have killed and sought for eons, runs in *your* veins."

The flames in the tent all winked out. Smoke from the wick curled around the air. He backed away from her. She hated the way she froze, unable to move, shaking. He dipped his chin.

"As my friend, Zia, I'll tell you: I want it all. I want to remake the world. And I want a true queen by my side. My brother cannot offer you the world. He cannot give you the opportunity to create real change. He will not beat my father, who has ruled for eons. He does not understand the darkness that you shove down in yourself. But I do. I can feel it calling to me."

His breath shortened. She thought he might burn the whole tent to the ground. Then she saw the invisible leash he had over himself tighten. Leo abruptly turned to leave the tent, pulling open the door. He looked back at her over his shoulder, and she could have sworn she saw a flash of sorrow in his cold, blue eyes. It occurred to her that the prince was…lonely.

"You would be wise to think before you react, Zia. I am your best shot at survival from my father. I intercepted the spies from Morganna's court before they passed information to him of your magic, or of your…close relations with my brother."

She felt dizzy. He had all the leverage he needed over her. For whatever reason, the Crown Prince had his own games to play right under his father's nose.

"We wouldn't want our lovely guest finding herself in…less than ideal circumstances." The prince winked and left the tent. Whatever humanity she saw in him was gone—perhaps imagined.

The moment he left it was like her entire body unfroze. Her shoulders slumped. Her ears heated. She had felt *paralyzed*. What good was all of her grueling lessons and careful training if all she could do was freeze?

She hadn't even asked about Jace or Inka. What the hell just happened? The worst of it, she supposed, was that there was an incredibly small part of her that wondered if he was right to some degree. She refused to let herself look at that now. He knew exactly what he was doing, messing with her mind. She hadn't faltered with the Hantu, or Morganna, even. There was something about Leo that truly terrified her.

Escape. That was what she needed to focus on. Find Jace, figure out what they did with Inka, and escape. With no weapons and surrounded by magic wielders, it would prove difficult, but she had faced worse odds. Aaliyah must have realized they weren't coming back by now. Maybe she would find them. It would take weeks to travel to the city of Mū— perhaps she would find them before they arrived, and the castle was impossible to infiltrate. They were in the mountains, miles and miles away from the Black Salt Seas. At least Aaliyah had kept the time stone. If she had given it to Zia when she wanted it, Leo would have it in his clutches by now.

Another man walked into the tent. He was tall and lanky, with thick gauges all along his ears. He was dressed in all black, clearly very high up in rank since he was not in the royal uniform. He wore a cloak with a hood over his head and had a bow and arrow at his back. His mouth a thin, flat line. She could barely see his features, but there was something familiar in the way he moved.

"I have come to take you to the castle," his voice was low and cold. He didn't bother to introduce himself. Where did she know him from?

He walked over to her, placing a hand on her elbow. She jerked her arm away.

"Keep your hands off me or I'll rip your eyeballs out."

He gripped her elbow again, and she kicked him in the shins. He twisted her arms behind her back so hard that her eyes watered. The man was fast.

"I suggest, Bridge, you do not fight me."

When she turned to look back up at his face, his hood had fallen off his head. Standing above her were the features she had known all her life—the thick, bushy brows, the thin, almond-shaped brown eyes, the high cheekbones. Only this man was bald, his face older and crueler.

"You're Zayne Sato. You're Hiro's father," she breathed.

The man looked down at her with cold fury, and then she felt the familiar zap of magic run through her. Within a few seconds, she was disoriented, moving through time and space faster than she could understand what was happening. It felt like being on a train going three thousand miles per hour.

She landed on cold hard ground, her knees barking in pain, panting. She was soaked in cold sweat. The man had vanished, leaving her alone. Zia stood up to look around. Her ears were ringing from the jarring space travel. She blinked several times, her vision coming into focus.

The ceilings were enormously high but slanted, moving toward a pyramid shape. The walls were made from a crystal that was transparent from the inside out, but opaque from the outside in. There was a large bed that could sleep five people with curtains draped over it. Silk sheets with crimson curtains draped all around like a fine cocoon. To the left, there was a bathing room with rose gold accents, an enormous vanity that Ren would have died for, and a closet. She frowned and walked toward it. There were only dresses—big, frilly dresses that looked to be exactly her size. Her throat ran dry.

"They have been preparing this room for you for a while now," a girl's voice shook her.

Zia whirled around to find a girl that could not have been older than fourteen standing there, patiently. She was a brown-skinned Lemurian girl with light, coffee-colored eyes. The girl wore a powder blue dress with an apron, her hair swept up into a delicate bun.

"Think of me as your...handmaiden. I'm here to look after you. My name's Kali, by the way."

Zia squinted, eyeing the girl further. Though she spoke formally, there was something off about her accent.

"Aren't you a bit young to be a servant?"

The girl's eyes were like steel. There was a harshness to her face that made Zia wonder how she ended up in the castle. Nothing about her felt like it belonged to the court.

"Aren't you a bit human to wind up here?" she raised a brow in question.

Zia put a hand on her hip.

"Fair enough."

Kali looked around the room, making sure that no one was there. When she was certain that they were truly alone, she spoke quietly.

"A word of advice, Zia. Everything in this room was designed for you. To make you comfortable. So comfortable you lose your edge."

Kali lowered her voice to a whisper.

"Before you try to escape or fight them, *learn* them first. They have an advantage over you. Their spies have been reporting since you first stepped foot in our realm. You cannot beat them. Not by force. Only outsmart them."

The girl reminded her of Rho in that moment, and Zia knew without a doubt she wasn't there by mistake. Whatever her agenda was, allies would be hard to come by in the castle.

"The Crown Prince...he said he wants to protect me from the king." It was a question. She still wasn't sure the best way to handle Leo, but he did have vital information on her.

Kali rolled her eyes.

"Protect you, or muzzle you? Be smart. Look around you—the expensive dresses, the lack of weapons. The Crown Prince has a dream, and you have a role to play in it, so play it long enough to survive."

Zia grunted. That answered that. Kali moved over to the bathing room to draw her a bath. The spout creaked before the water began to flow, making her think it had never been used. They truly had constructed this room for her.

Zia followed her, staring blankly at the rose gold tub. Kali sat on a stool, her eyes locked on Zia. The girl could tell that there was more left unsaid, so she patiently waited.

"He said he wanted it all. Not just the stones. Me." Zia swallowed, bringing her eyes to meet Kali's. The girl remained silent, and Zia frowned at how it somehow forced her to say more.

"He offered me the world," Zia despised the way it came out like a question again.

Kali rose, moving with a swiftness to leave her with some privacy. Before exiting the room, she turned to Zia with a wisdom on her face that went far beyond her age.

"Be careful of men who offer you the world when you were always meant to create your own."

The words sent goosebumps blooming all over Zia's body—a warning from a potential ally who knew the prince and understood the games that ran within the castle. Zia hesitated before climbing into the tub.

"Wait. My…." Zia drew a blank, unsure of what to call him. She wiped her skirts with her palms. "Jace. The other prince. Can you please find out what happened to him? And the dragon, Inka."

Kali gave a slight nod.

"I do not know what happened to your prince, but the dragon was brought beneath the castle in chains. Only those in the king's inner circle are allowed beneath the library floor."

Zia's mouth went dry. Her eyes darted around the room, suddenly feeling like a thousand eyes were watching her. There was nowhere safe for her here.

"Thank you," she whispered, staring off blankly.

The girl left without another word, leaving Zia to have a moment alone. The sound of her heels clacking on the stone grew quieter and quieter, until disappearing entirely. Zia loosened her breath. She needed to collect herself before she was to play their games. It felt like the walls were closing in. She was trapped—a beautiful ghost, to be molded and shaped as Leo willed, or beaten into submission if she refused.

Yet even in Rho's mind, when the odds had been stacked against her and terror threatened to claim her, she had found a way—through the part of her that dwelled beneath her fear, the way the ocean floor is calm beneath a storm's relentless waves. There were benefits to being in the king's castle, and she would leverage them. The very least she could do was pave a clear path for Ren, Hiro, and Rho to walk.

Kali knew she was no doll. She risked a great deal to warn her even on their first meeting. She didn't tell her to become what they wanted, only to play a role long enough to survive. First and foremost, her mother was in the castle. She'd have to be careful in the way she approached finding her. The king would anticipate that.

Secondly, there was a very large chance that he had one of the stones. If no one was allowed beneath the library, perhaps it was a good place to start. Leo seemed to be his greatest weapon, being one of the last remaining full-powered Elymentals. The prince could incinerate half the Shadow Warriors without a second thought if commanded. That kind of magic was vital in a war. Yet he was no pawn, since he was already concealing secrets from his father.

She needed to know how loyal the Shadow Warriors were to the king—if there were some who still believed in Jace. People were willing to do great and terrible things to survive if they didn't think they had another choice. If they knew that there was another way, perhaps they'd choose differently.

She got in the bath and scrubbed at her skin furiously. The tub was enormous and could easily fit three people in it. Everything in her room was overdone. Kali had been right—too much comfort dulled the edge.

Yet she had to admit, it was the first time she had ever experienced true luxury—the kind of luxury that made The Electi look like they were living in squalor. Atticus Ashwood would have sold his soul to have a room like this. She scoffed, thinking of just how far away that world seemed.

Zia climbed out of the tub and dried off, then walked over to her new closet. The dresses were lovely, she had to admit—various colors with intricate beading and fine fabrics. But they weren't *her*. They felt like someone else's idea of her. The one Ren had made felt like a dream—she couldn't have designed such a perfect one for herself in a thousand years. Yet these…bile rose up in her throat at the thought.

When Kali returned, Zia immediately told her to go and locate some pants. The girl replied that the prince would not be pleased. When Zia responded that the prince could wear the dresses if he liked them so much, she could have sworn she saw pride swirl in Kali's eyes before she disappeared. She then spent an hour brushing and braiding her hair, pulling it back from her face.

Zia walked over to the window and pressed her forehead against the glass. She could see the city from her room and wondered if that had been intentional. It looked so full of life—crowded markets of buyers and sellers, artists painting on the streets, the great river running through the quarter. Her mother and Rho really had done a fantastic job of replicating it in The Trials. Yet even so, reading about a place and experiencing it with one's senses were entirely different things. Nothing could have prepared her for it.

She touched the glass with her fingers, feeling like she might be able to reach far enough into the heart of the city. Were the citizens struggling under the king's rule, resenting his reign? Or had he brainwashed them all so thoroughly that they had come to love their cages?

"I have found everything you need." Kali was standing right behind her.

Zia jumped and yelped.

"How do you *do* that?"

Kali was already draping the pants over the bed. They were clearly men's pants, but small enough to fit her. It looked similar to what Jace wore every day—a black shirt, jacket, and boots.

"Do what?" the girl asked mindlessly, though Zia knew there was nothing mindless about her.

"Appear in and out of places like you're invisible. Are you a Folder?"

The girl turned her head slightly, though remained staring at the floor.

"No. I don't have a drop of magic in me."

Zia walked over toward the bed and ran her fingers along the fabric. She hoped they wouldn't get Kali in trouble for helping her. She slipped on the pants and shirt. The girl dropped to her knees to tie her boots strings. Then Zia felt something cold and hard slide into the boot against her calf.

"What—"

"As I said, I have found everything you need," Kali said slowly, her eyes darting to the walls.

The girl had slipped a knife into her boot. This young, strange girl who had already risked so much within the first few hours of meeting her. Not a drop of fear in her eyes. She had the most unwavering gaze Zia had ever seen.

"Who are you really?"

The girl smirked before rising.

"I'm your handmaiden."

A knock sounded at the door before Zia could question her further. She jumped out of her skin at the interruption.

Kali dipped her chin.

"I believe that's the Crown Prince."

The girl went to open the door. Even the way she walked had weight to it. Strength. Like the soles of her feet were somehow rooted to the earth.

The large, wooden door yawned open and Leo was standing there, waiting. He had changed now, dressed in an outfit more suited for court than hunting her. He had a dark brown coat with gold buttons that hung open. His boots were far nicer and less practical. His hair was pulled back into a sleek bun. When his eyes beheld her, and the men's clothes she wore, he looked more than displeased.

"Those dresses were made by the finest fabric makers in the realm. Were they not to your liking?"

Zia strutted right up to the door, her arms folded across her chest. Her braids slid behind her shoulder, draping down to her lower back. She wanted to tell him that the finest fabric makers were two spiders that were miles away from the castle, but that would require giving him an ounce of information.

"They were to *your* liking, your highness."

A strange delight illuminated his eyes. Perhaps he really didn't have any other friends in the court. The way she spoke to him would have gotten anyone else tortured and killed, yet he seemed amused by it.

"I suppose it would be much harder to kill us all in skirts, hmm?" he winked. His tone was patronizing, like he didn't believe she could really do any damage—an adorable house cat hissing at him instead of a wolf.

She narrowed her eyes at him.

"I would still manage."

She heard a half chuckle behind her and saw Kali bring a hand to her mouth.

"You have clearly met Kali. She's pure trouble, but the absolute best of our servants."

Leo's eyes settled onto her. She suddenly looked quite uncomfortable, like she preferred to blend into the shadows, because any attention might cause her to combust.

"Is there a reason you're here?" Zia snapped.

The Crown Prince stepped in front of Kali, blocking them from each other. His eyes darkened.

"Careful how you speak to me. Your honesty amuses me, but one word from me and—"

"And you'll have me tortured and thrown in the dungeons? I don't believe you." Zia stepped toward him until they were toe to toe, her anger a familiar comfort. She despised the way the prince who was so opposite of his brother—the way he made her freeze like a half-wit, so cruel and calculating. "I know what it looks like when a man needs something from me. So whatever it is, you may as well be honest about it."

She poked him in the chest. The guards around them gasped. She had barely noticed them before, as they had stood so still against the walls that they seemed a part of them. One look from Leo silenced them all. He held a hand up as one of them had taken a step forward to reprimand her. Then slowly lowered it.

"What I want..." He let out a breathy laugh. The torches that lit the hallways surrounding the garden suddenly went up in wild flames. She could practically smell the fear on the guards. Kali took a step toward her, but Zia blocked the girl with her body.

"What I *want* is for you to—" He stopped himself, and the torches winked out entirely. Smoke curled around the wicks. Leo plastered a close-lipped smile on his face, "I have come to escort you to my father. He would like to meet his new guest."

Zia's face leached of all color.

"Don't you mean prisoner?" she countered.

"That depends on you."

Leo held out his arm, and she knew that gesture was a silent offering. Walk by his side, play his game, and she was a guest. Reject him, and the consequences would be severe. She wasn't afraid of the dungeons and had faced harsh conditions before, but Leo knew too much. He would tell his father the truth, and they'd force her to use her magic on the stones, or they would torture the list of people who had come to be her family. She couldn't even bear the thought of it.

And so, Zia swallowed her disgust, looping her arm through Leo's. She looked over her shoulder at Kali one last time and saw the warning in the girl's eyes. *Play the role long enough to survive.* As she walked through the open hallways with the Crown Prince, it felt like she was stepping toward her death. They strolled in silence, the guards trailing behind them.

The castle gardens were nothing like Aaliyah's. They were groomed to perfection, the roses trimmed and stripped down to be without any thorns. The Tree People all tended to them in unison, wearing their ragged uniforms. She looked up at the gray sky, savoring the seconds of open air before she met her fate.

They climbed the spiraling staircase that led up to the pyramid's point, where the king's throne room was. Up and up they went, climbing hundreds of steps. She could see everything, from the sea that stretched on to the horizon, to the bustling city below, to the forest cloaked in mist. Her breath shortened, her body tensing as they climbed the final flight.

Leo brought a hand to her shoulder and squeezed.

"I won't let him harm you," he said so quietly it was barely a whisper.

"Don't talk back to him, and don't let him see that you're afraid."

Sound advice. If only the prince knew she was incapable of speaking, that her throat was closing up. She repeated the words her mother had said to her in the cradle, again and again. The words Katya had uttered to the king long ago, before he destroyed everything she loved.

Bow to no one but your heart.

They climbed the final step. The well-threaded rug was rolled out in the middle of the room. There was no art, no crystals. It had felt as it did in Rho's mind—like a tomb. Burgundy curtains were pulled over the windows, though Zia could see the Black Salt Sea through a sliver of them. She desperately wished someone would open the windows. The air was stale- lifeless.

In the center, sitting on the crystal throne, was the man who had taken everything from her—the man who had destroyed her life before she took her first breath in the world. As her eyes fell upon his face for the first time, she decided that she would give all of herself to see that crown ripped right off his head. Even if it took her last breath.

Leo strongly nudged her foreword as they walked right up toward the throne. At the bottom of the steps, he kneeled, bowing his head before his father in subservience. The king looked at his son approvingly, then turned his attention toward Zia, who remained standing.

"So, this is the human," the king said in Old Lemurian.

The light caught the jewels on his crown. There must have been hundreds of little clear gems adorning it, with a giant pointed crystal in the middle—a mermaid tear. There were two gems resting on either side of the larger crystal. One black. One red. His colors.

Leo nodded, glancing at her like she was game he brought in after hunting.

"Yes, father. We intercepted her riding the first dragon to be seen since the floods. With Jace," he added.

The king waved a hand.

"Yes, yes. Jace has been tossed in the dungeons, along with that beast."

Zia's heart began pounding so loud she was certain they could hear it with their Lemurian senses. The dungeons. At least he was alive.

"She doesn't know where the stones are," Leo added.

She had to do her best not to react to his words, since she technically wasn't supposed to speak their language. Not to mention, Leo had never asked her if she knew where the stones were. Why was he helping her?

"I didn't think that she did. She's a human, Leo. They don't have the minds that we do." He waved a hand lazily in the air, "Oh sure, they look like us. But they are no different from the rest of the animals we hunt. Even their ignorant governments need our guidance in their rule. I have stopped them several times from destroying the entire planet with their weapons and world wars. I was gracious enough to help them, but this one is no more special than the rest of them. She was merely born into a magical bloodline, thanks to her traitorous whore of a mother. Mating with their disgusting breed. Diluting centuries of—"

"Don't talk about her like that," Zia snarled, lifting her eyes to meet his. She spoke in Old Lemurian, jutting her chin upwards. Leo remained on his knees like a coward.

"And my *name* is Zia. Zia Alexander. Not 'the human.'"

The king's mouth parted. He blinked in surprise, as though he didn't expect she could speak full sentences. His cold, depthless eyes narrowed in on her.

"I've had men executed for less than a sharp tongue, you know," he said cruelly.

A wicked grin spread across her face.

"Then execute me."

The King of Atlantis and the Bridge of Lemuria stared at each other as the entire room held their breath.

"If I may—" Leo started, trying to smooth over the situation.

"You may not," the king snapped.

Zia rose to her feet. It was a gamble, what she was about to do. Yet, in order to remove the king's leverage, she needed to tell the truth. Honesty was all she had.

"You need me. Not just my blood, but *me*. My magic. You can't speckle a few drops of my blood on ancient stones and think you'll be the conqueror of the universe."

The king scoffed.

"You don't have magic beyond your blood. It's impossible for your kind to—"

It was perhaps the most moronic thing she had ever done in her life, but it was the only way. The only way for her to gain her own leverage. To protect the ones she loved, she needed to have something over the king, so he would know that they were on even footing.

Zia Alexander cast herself into the king's mind, blowing past every single barrier he had. The last thing she saw was his eyes bulging in shock before she sailed down into his consciousness like a pirate in a storm, into the depths of the darkest place she had ever been in her life.

CHAPTER 19

We want free will, but not the responsibility that comes with it. We want change but are scared of it. We ask for better leaders, but don't think to lead. We over-consume, then wonder why there is no space to create. We yearn for connection, yet isolate ourselves. We seek love yet fear loss. We wish for a better world, but not at the cost of comfort and convenience. When someone comes along, unwavering and unfaltering in their resolve, no matter how ludicrous their plan may seem, they will it into existence because it's not a far-off dream or an ideal for someday: it's a plan. And that was what truly terrified me. He was without a doubt the most certain man I ever met. —Zia

Zia could feel the king searching through his own mind for her. The gateway to his consciousness was blocked by walls of icy fire and steel, darkness that could swallow a person, but she obliterated every barrier with ease. The king had tried to trap her before she made it through to the deeper parts of his consciousness, but his attempts were feeble.

After all, she was nobody.

The setting of his psyche shouldn't have surprised her. She knew from training that the interior of a person's mind always reflected the state of their subconscious—Ren's had been a garden of wilting flowers from years of neglecting her grief, Rho's had been blank and empty, shaped into what everyone else needed. The king's, however, was the perfect picture of irrelevance—it was a mirror image of the castle, but cold and dark, with no one around. It looked like an abandoned home with no warmth, no life. Spiderwebs blanketed the unlit torches. The stone tiles were covered in dust. All of the vines and flowers that grew throughout the castle had wilted, allowing the weeds to fully take over.

Zia rose fully, assessing her surroundings. Even the pigment of the hand-sewn rug had faded. For a moment, she felt a pang of pity for the king. This place was lonely. Dead. Like being frozen in time, forced to look out at the world through a one-sided mirror.

She walked silently, blending into the shadows. She was nearly invisible, her body more of a shimmering outline than anything with density. She could still *feel*, but her sense of self was stripped- a drop in the vast ocean of the king's psyche.

The winding crystal staircase beckoned to her. Step by step, she carefully walked, feeling that familiar tug that had been her intuitive compass her whole life. The staircases creaked, and despite it not being real, she couldn't help but feel like she might fall right through.

Zia made it to the bottom and turned down several hallways, each archway shaped like a pyramid. Her footsteps were soundless. The thread led her down a familiar corridor, and it suddenly clicked in her mind where she was.

In Katya's necklace, she had seen a memory of the queen running through these same halls to get to the castle's secret Lost Library. There was a library open to the public that contained history books the king approved of, specifically, books that were told in *his* favor. But all of the real books, the ones that contained magic spells, healing potions, and the truth of Lemuria and Atlantis's bloody history, were sealed within the castle walls.

Zia rounded a corner and saw the very same wall Katya had walked through. There were two sculptures of Zhulu birds on either side. The paint was chipped away.

Everything about this place felt forgotten, and she couldn't help but wonder if that was the king's true fear: insignificance.

Zia brought her hand to the same Zhulu head Katya had used to enter and pushed down hard. The wall yawned open slowly, and an enormous gush of wind pushed her backward. The moment Zia stepped through the door, the walls of the library shook like an earthquake. She gripped onto a nearby railing, squeezing her eyes shut as dust poured from the ceiling. Mercifully, no bookshelves had fallen and squished her.

She could hear the king's roar in the distance, angrily searching for her. They were both imprisoned in this dream-like state. He couldn't harm her in real life, nor she him. The guards could pose a threat, but she was betting on Leo helping her. He had already lied to his father about his suspicion that she knew the whereabouts of the time stone. Perhaps their agendas were more aligned than she originally thought.

The library was built like a dome, with a spiraling staircase winding down the center. A small, triangular-shaped skylight provided a sliver of moonlight that illuminated rows of mahogany shelves and leather-bound books. It hurt her brain to look at. How much knowledge was being lost in here? Restricted from the people.

Hurry now.

A voice spoke to her. She had heard it before, on that wobbly bridge at the realm's entrance. Zia picked up her pace as she descended the staircase. It seemed to go on forever. Down and down, she went, spiraling to the bottom. All of the oil lamps and torches were burned out, yet she could see the silvery outline of everything, her eyes adjusted to the darkness.

It was strange to be in a body that could not tire. She made it to the bottom floor. The temperature dropped significantly. When she walked across the stone, it sounded hollow. She jumped up and down to test her theory.

Zia knew there was a network of tree tunnels that Aaliyah and Katya's daughter had used to escape, but she couldn't help but wonder if there was something beneath the castle. She inched along the stone walls and noticed carvings in the ground. Not carvings. Little holes. There was a draft moving upwards from the floors.

Zia walked along the perimeter of the room, searching. She ran her hands along the icy walls, trying to feel anything. Devoid of her sight in such consuming darkness, she had to see with her other senses with it being so dark at the bottom.

The walls rattled again, sending pebbles tumbling to the floor. The structure wouldn't hold much longer. His voice was getting closer. She needed to find what she was looking for.

To your right, the voice said urgently.

She looked over to her right, squinting her vision to focus. The small, royal insignia of two pyramids was painted on the wall. One facing up. One facing down. She prayed she was right about her hunch.

Zia brought her hand to the insignia and felt the bottom pyramid was indented. She pushed it inwards, slowly, and it creaked. The whole library tremored, and she knew the king felt where she was, and what she had found.

The floor beneath her groaned open. She kept her back against the wall, barely standing on the edge so she wouldn't be swallowed whole by the pit below. There was an identical spiraling staircase to the one she had just climbed down. How far it went, she couldn't tell. The draft wafted upwards like a haunting wind.

"*STOP!*" she heard the king yell. He was several floors up, shouting at her over a railing.

She broke into a sprint down the stairs, and the floor shut above her. As she moved, another earthquake happened. She held onto the railing with all her might as the room began to tip upside down, gravity inverting itself. Her palms were sweating, but she maintained her grip. Suddenly she was no longer walking down, but up. No matter how long she spent in Lemuria, she would never get used to the magic.

The insignia wasn't just a symbol. It was a map. The king had built a second castle beneath, and a part of her really did not want to know what he kept there. Yet still, that tugging sensation pulled her upwards. As she walked up the steps, she began to hear whispers. It sounded like the dead, all desperately talking to her at once. Hundreds of whispers, talking so fast she couldn't understand them. It was taking everything in her not to rip herself out of his mind and back into her own body. Everything about this place felt *wrong*.

Zia hurried, making it to the top floor. The whispers stopped. Red light flooded in through the windows, pooling on the marble floor. She looked outside to see a blood moon hovering just above the forest. It was the closest she had ever seen the moon before, like she could reach outside the window and touch the cratered surface.

Zia surveyed the room around her. It was cluttered with advanced technology and weapons beyond her imagination. She scanned the walls, able to identify what appeared to be flying hover ships and blaster guns, but the rest was foreign. If humans had advanced in weaponry so vastly in just two hundred years...what had the king built in over nine thousand?

That horrible sinking feeling in her gut worsened. The largest machine she saw was in the shape of a hexagon. It was matte black, with markings in a language she did not recognize over it. Atlantean dialect, perhaps. Everything about her was both drawn to and repelled by it.

Zia's eyes flickered above the machine to an oil painting of a woman. She recognized her instantly. Queen Katya. Zia stepped forward to run her fingers over the frame of the painting. That face. Every time Zia saw her face, she felt like she was staring at an old friend. This was equal parts shrine and weapon room.

"I had never seen anything like her," a voice said softly.

She whirled around to see the king standing there.

"She was the most powerful person I had ever met. Her magic was that of a god's."

He did not take his eyes off the painting. The silence between them stretched on for too long. Zia cleared her throat.

"You only wanted her so that your lineage would have power you could manipulate for your own gain."

The king scoffed, his eyes finally sliding to her.

"Of course I did, but it went beyond that. We were meant for each other. One of my finest oracles told me of a woman that would be my match. My equal. I sailed through the seven seas to find her."

Zia's palms twitched at her sides.

"You weren't her equal though. Not even close. And when she refused to be manipulated by you, you killed her and wiped out an *entire* civilization."

The king chuckled darkly, strolling around the room. His robes trailed behind him, the silk flowing over the dusty tiles. He slowly shook his head.

"It's strange. Despite being human, you have so much of her in you. Of course, you're her descendant, but your ancestors didn't have her spirit the way you do. Or the magic, for that matter. I underestimated you, it seems."

"I'm used to it." She gritted her teeth.

He paused by the windowsill, looking out at the blood moon with his hands clasped behind his back.

"The Great Wave wasn't my fault, you know. Despite what that absurd book says. The gods weren't punishing me for her death."

"Then what happened?"

The king heaved a sigh.

"We were destined for one another," he began again.

Destiny. How many times had Leo used that word as an excuse in their first meeting? She was growing to despise the sound of it.

"The union of Atlantis and Lemuria through our bloodlines would have reshaped the world. Our child was meant to be The Bridge they wrote about. Half Atlantean. Half Lemurian. The most powerful child to ever be born." The way the king spoke sounded disconnected, like he had shared this same exact story a hundred times to the point where the words lost all meaning.

His eyes darkened.

"But Katya did not want to share her throne. She did not see that, together, we would remake the world. She cursed us all when she ripped apart those stones. They were a gift from the gods and she practically spat on it. The stones are the power source from which Lemuria's magic is derived. *That* was what triggered the Great Wave. It created a massive disruption in the earth's core...."

He heaved a resigned sigh, like he had no choice in the matter. "I killed her to save us all. Drove a knife right through her selfish heart and had an Elymental named Aaliyah seal our realm in another dimension as we moved into Middle Earth. The majority of us were wiped out. There used to be millions of Atlanteans and Lemurians. We would have been extinct, if *I* hadn't preserved the survivors."

Zia tucked that bit of information away. The way he referred to Aaliyah made it sound like he believed her to be dead. Perhaps his spies hadn't learned everything. It would certainly give them the element of surprise if she assisted them in a fight.

The king turned on his heel to face her and frowned.

"For those who survived on the surface, repopulating, their magic diluted because the stones were no longer near. Then the humans arrived. You're no better than parasites. Breeding faster than you can sustain. I had hope for your kind, but I was disappointed. We've always been watching, you know."

He began pacing around the room again, looking fondly over his many weapons.

"The number of times we have intervened in humanity is embarrassing, really. Your leaders are little children playing God. We taught you about weaponry, and you started world wars that almost obliterated the entire planet. We taught you about technology, and you depleted earth's resources. And then came the famine. Plagues and viruses. Instead of helping you reach your potential, your rulers distracted you. They fed you food that had no life. Television and games and social media and drugs that dulled your senses and weakened your minds. Created a system you didn't even *know* you were a slave to. All the while, they were draining you of your most precious, mortal resource: *Time.*"

The king interlaced his fingers and grimaced. The crystals on his crown looked like blood rubies in the moonlight.

"You are hamsters on an endless wheel in a silent, desperate search for meaning. Parasites, destroying the very world you call home. We are done intervening. We are done helping."

Angry, hot tears swelled in Zia's eyes. She stepped away from the painting, doing her best to put as much distance between them as possible. Her heart sank to her stomach as she thought of her father and Mei in the human realm.

She had to get out of this cruel man's mind.

Wait. That voice said again.

"What is this place?" she asked, rubbing at the back of her neck. The best she could do was keep him talking. Her eyes darted around the room and she eyed the exit. The moment the voice allowed, she was getting the hell out of there, but there was something else she needed to know.

The king strutted over toward the larger machine. He ran a hand over its hard, smooth surface and admired it in the way a parent would a newborn child.

"This? This is the *real* castle, girl. Since Atlantis didn't have magic, we developed technology. Weapons that would make even your best look like toys. I've been developing this machine for many years, waiting until I had the stones to use it. No one knows, save for Leo."

"And what exactly do you plan to *do* with these weapons?" It was a stupid question, but she needed to hear him say it.

The king looked up at her slowly, dropping all bravado. Unlike Leo, this man had no interest in pretending to be anything other than who he was. He walked slowly toward her until she could see the shine on his forehead and the details of his icy, white-blue eyes.

"I'm going to remove the parasite. To disrupt the tides and use the very same wave that created our fall from grace to wipe out your civilization entirely. Then, we can return home to the surface and mold a new world."

Zia went rigid. Her breath quickened. It was so much worse than just wanting the stones for his own rule over Lemuria. It was the fate of her world. The fate of the entire planet. She was helpless to do anything in here. None of this was real. She needed to find Jace and blow this weapon to smithereens. It was more important than the stones now.

"You can't do that. Not without my magic. And I won't help you."

The king laughed.

"I can. And you will. You see, I've had my spies on you for quite some time. To learn your weaknesses and your desires. I originally was going to just imprison you and drain you of your blood, but my son convinced me there was another way. Your magic is most impressive. If you're properly trained, you might even be as good as Katya one day. A skill we can certainly use in our great kingdom. I am not a man without mercy, girl. I will make you a deal."

Zia clenched her fists.

"Why would I make a deal with some lunatic with a messiah complex?"

The king ignored her question and fixated on Katya's painting.

"The ones we come to care for are our greatest weakness. Why did you win that ridiculous game? Because you had nothing to lose and everything to gain. The fear of loss is the stifling of power."

"Don't pretend like you don't care for anyone. Even if you don't give a damn about Jace, you wouldn't dare lose your precious Crown Prince."

The king tilted his head to look down at her.

"If destiny demanded it, Zia, there is nothing I would not give up."

The words echoed throughout the room, hanging there in a deadly silence. There was no reasoning with him. Not because he was pure evil, but because he had convinced himself that he was doing what was *right*. And the cause that he devoted his life to was bigger than any personal ties. Even that of his son. Aaliyah was right—he was the villain of their stories, but a savior in his own twisted little mind.

"Here is the deal. You and Leo are going to rewrite history. Together. Finish what Katya and I started. Him, the Atlantean bloodline. You, the Lemurian. Even though you are only half, the depth of your magic makes up for the rest."

The king began strolling toward the window again.

"I will not harm anyone you love. I will free your mother from servitude after the wedding. I will reinstate Jace as head of my armies. I'll let your dragon roam free. Your friends. I will even shelter your father down here, when the wave comes."

Her heart twisted.

"Is he alive?"

"For now," the king replied. "I am aware of how long finding and uniting the stones may take. It could take longer than the years that you have with your fragile, human life. I'm a patient man, Zia. Lemurian marriages are different, you see…"

Her head was pounding. She had never been inside of someone's mind for so long. Rho had warned her about becoming lost in another. It was time.

"When Lemurians marry, they are mated for life. It's not like humans with their empty promises and frilly divorces. The blood of the betrothed is joined together in a magical binding contract. Their lives share one tether. Which means, Zia, that you would become immortal should you marry Leo. It also means that you cannot harm one another no matter what, and since Leo is loyal to me…"

"I can't take a stand against you," she finished for him.

He looked over his shoulder at her.

"Yes."

"You're really that afraid of me?" She snorted.

The king smirked.

"You? No. It is what you *represent*. You are an unfathomable fairytale. A false hope to cover up their despair. Hope is dangerous, Zia. Too much freedom, and there is no security, you see. People don't actually want freedom. They want the illusion of freedom. Too many choices are paralyzing, after all."

He gave her a bitter smile, slowly shaking his head.

"Cells must collaborate and work together. If, say, a group of them decides to go against the greater good of the body, they become a cancer. I will not let you infect my people with your idealistic notions of a free world."

Run. That voice said. It was all the permission she needed. The walls began shaking. She backed away one step at a time, doing her best not to lose her balance.

The king pursed his lips.

"I don't think I need to explain to you what will happen should you refuse. I'll start with your mother. Perhaps I'll kill her before you can meet her. Perhaps I'll make you watch. Then I'll go for that Folder friend of yours. The golden faerie girl. And finally, my son."

Zia didn't wait for him to say anything else before bolting. She sprinted down the stairs, toward the pyramid entrance. She had never pulled herself from someone else's mind. All she could do was pray she would make it out before it collapsed.

She made it to the bottom of the staircase just as gravity turned over again, and she climbed the last few steps up to the library. The walls were caving in. The floors were collapsing. Books were falling everywhere. She craned her neck upwards. There were too many floors.

The throne room, the voice urged.

Zia raced up the levels, dodging the crumbling ruins everywhere. Bookshelves collapsed. Glass shattered from fallen oil lamps. Up and up she ran, without ever tiring. She had to make it back to her entry point before he snapped out of the trance.

Zia heaved her shoulder into the wall of the library. It opened. She leaped out without a second thought, and just as she shot a glance back, it collapsed entirely. The king was coming back into full consciousness, destroying this plane altogether. If she didn't make it in time, it wouldn't matter what room she was in. She would be trapped in his psyche forever.

By the time Zia climbed the crystal staircase up to the throne room, she saw faded outlines of Leo and the guards and could nearly hear their voices. The veil was thinning. She was almost there. Then Zia saw her own body, collapsed on the ground a few feet in front of the throne. Leo had her in his arms and was shaking her, shouting. His voice sounded like he was underwater. She raced toward herself and leaped with all she had just as the ceiling crumbled, reaching out for any aspect of herself.

The tether to her body snapped into place. She woke up, panting. Clawing at her own skin to make sure it was all real—that she had broken the link between her and the king. Leo's arms were tightly gripped around her. He hooked his arms beneath her armpits and hauled her up to her feet.

Her legs wobbled. She blinked several times, completely disoriented. It felt like she had crawled through muck and grime, having explored the depths of his twisted mind. She coughed several times.

The king's eyes were closed. He remained seated with guards on either side, ready to protect him. To kill her. Leo was the only thing that had stopped them from doing so. She had been right to bet on him.

"Are you *insane—*" he growled in her ear.

She shook out of his grip and turned to face him, her blood boiling.

"You know. You know what he's planning, and you're helping him *destroy* an entire species!" she shrieked.

His breath caught. He looked around the room, checking to see how many of the guards actually heard her. Then he opened his mouth to say something, to protest, but instantly shut it. The king had opened his eyes, fully returning to his body. They faced each other in real time. He looked at his son approvingly, ignoring Zia altogether.

"It seems I've underestimated her. You have found quite a prize, indeed."

For once, Leo had nothing to say. She could see him struggling to keep his composure.

"*Where* is my mother?" Zia snarled, baring her teeth.

"Until you either bring me the stones, or marry my son, guaranteeing your loyalty, I will hold true to my promise. Shall I demonstrate an example for you? It seems only fair, since you just violated my mind."

He snapped his fingers at the guards. Her stomach dropped. If he brought in her mother to torture her in front of her, she wouldn't be able to handle it. The double doors opened, and it took all of her strength to keep her eyes from closing.

It wasn't her mother that the king had dragged in chains into the throne room. It was Jace. They held him by his arms, one guard on each side, as his knees scraped across the tiles. He had several bruises on his right eye, which was swollen shut. His lip was split, and he had lacerations on his exposed back. The warrior she had come to know, and maybe even love, tortured into submission.

They dumped him on his knees in front of the king like a sack of grain. The chains clanked as he tumbled down. The king frowned, his white eyebrows knitting together.

"You got his blood on my carpet, you imbeciles."

The guards bowed their heads, murmuring an apology. Jace slowly turned to look at her. It seemed to take all of his strength just to lift his head. He immediately looked away.

"Leo." The king commanded.

Leo's face twisted in pain.

"Father, please. Don't make me do it again," he pleaded.

Icy fury burned in the king's gaze.

"Unless you wish to meet a fate similar to your brother's, *do it.*"

Leo turned to look at Zia, an apology written across his face. She didn't understand what was happening until he took one look at Jace and circled him in fire. Jace's eyes widened. He was reliving the trauma of his youth. His hands were already destroyed, and now the rest of his body was to follow.

"NO!" Zia ran toward him, but one of the guards grabbed her and tackled her to the ground. Her chin hit the stone floor, and she tasted blood in her mouth. He had a tight grip on her.

"Oh, come now, son. Those flames aren't nearly hot enough! You can do better than that."

Leo raised the heat, and Jace began to scream. It was a scream of true pain that broke her. She couldn't take it. She snapped.

Zia bit down hard on the guard's hands until she drew blood. He barked in pain and released his grip. She flipped over and took the knife from her boot, flinging it into the center of his chest. Blood sprayed and he immediately sank to the ground. She leaped up on her feet and yanked the knife from his chest, snarling at the king. Leo backed away in horror. There was nothing human on her face.

The other guard ran toward her, sword at the ready to bury in her stomach. She waited until he got close enough, and then flipped over him, landing on his shoulders. She wrapped her legs around his neck and choked out his airways until he sank to the ground and passed out. The tile was soaked in blood. None of the other guards moved on her—either they were completely terrified, or the king was *entertained.*

Zia took one look at Leo with a promise of death in her eyes. She could have sworn he shook a little. She whirled and raced straight into the burning fire and leaped on top of Jace, trying to cover him from the flames. Her skin singed in agony, but she knew the king wouldn't risk his precious Bridge. The flames immediately winked out. The floor was charred. When she inspected Jace's skin, and realized that he still had his hair and his blisters weren't bubbling, she realized Leo could have done much, much worse. They weren't even third-degree burns, but the smoke had gotten into his lungs.

"I'm so sorry," she whispered, the tears rolling down her cheeks. He could barely breathe. His head rested in her lap. He wheezed in pain, looking up at her. Those green eyes that had become a home. Her prince.

Her warrior. Her friend. She couldn't bear it. Not him. Not anyone she loved.

The decision wasn't really a decision at all. She would agree to his terms and surrender her freedom long enough for her loved ones to escape. They had sacrificed so much so she could keep going. When it came down to it, she had no fear of doing the same for them. If the king ever managed to find the stones, she would end her own life before he could force her to wield them and use the machine. Her heart was heavy, but there was a strange peace in her resignation, knowing that she would defy him until her last breath.

"None of them will come to any harm, and you will free them all?" she asked quietly.

"Of course," the king replied with a wide grin.

"I'll do it," her voice was empty.

Jace gasped for air, reaching his hand for her.

"Zia, *don't—*" and then his eyes rolled to the back of his head, and he passed out. She saw a single tear slide down his cheek. It would have shattered her, that moment, but her emotions felt far away, like she was on the ceiling watching them from below.

"Guards, escort him to a healer immediately. And give him his old uniform back, would you? He is a banished prince no longer," the king commanded.

The guards took him from her arms. She could feel the invisible wound in her heart rip open, ready to swallow her whole. If she broke now, he would win. She had made the wrong call, showing him her magic. She should have played along as Leo's pet and bought herself enough time to escape.

"You realize that if you break your promise..."

"You'll destroy everything I love," she finished for him.

The king nodded.

"Now you're getting it."

Zia settled her eyes on Leo. His face had turned ashen. She rose to her feet. Jace's blood was still warm and sticky on her palms. She turned toward the king.

"I may marry your son, but I will *never* bow to you."

The king's face tightened. He waved a hand in dismissal.

"Words you are unable to back up, I'm afraid. Son, escort her to her chambers. She has a wedding to prepare for, after all."

Leo was instantly by her side. He put a hand at her back, nudging her out of the throne room. She drew in slow, steady breaths, debating if she should run back there and try to kill the king right on his throne. The Crown Prince seemed to sense her silent debate. He gripped her elbow so tight her eyes watered and dragged her out of the room. A few extra guards followed them, keeping their distance this time.

Leo yanked her forward, walking so quickly that she nearly tumbled down the stairs. She ground her teeth together, still tasting blood in her mouth. It was highly possible a tooth was broken. Perhaps he wouldn't want to marry her if she was toothless and would just put her out of her misery.

"Keep moving," he said coldly in her ear. Every single guard and servant in the castle watched them as he dragged her from room to room. When they made it out into the gardens, she realized night had fallen with the cloudy sky. Even the stars were hiding from the king, it seemed.

They made it back to her chambers, and he barely opened the door before hurling her into the room. She tumbled onto the floor, her shins aching. There were too many bruises to count already.

Leo turned toward the guards and snapped, "That will be all."

Then he slammed the door behind him and leaned against it, cupping his face with his hands, slowing his breath. She remained on the floor where he tossed her, not bothering to stand. What was the point, when she had just sold her freedom?

"So—"

"You are the most *reckless, careless, daft* woman I have ever had the misfortune of meeting!" he shouted, running his fingers through his red hair.

She chuckled, leaning back on her elbows.

"Oh? Are we done with the, 'you're so beautiful, let me offer you the world' nonsense now? Am I finally meeting the real Crown Prince?"

Leo was instantly upon her, gripping her by the collar of her shirt and hauling her up to her feet. She could barely stand on her own. Her ears were ringing.

He sneered at her.

"I thought you were smarter than this. You just openly challenged the most dangerous man in the whole goddamn world! You don't have the stones. You don't have an army. You *barely* understand your magic. And you have no fucking plan!"

Zia's deep, blue eyes were swimming with pain.

"You burned him," she said, not caring that he was inches away from her throat.

Her face was close enough to feel his warm breath. Leo's chest rose and fell quickly.

"I didn't want to."

She cocked her head to the side, looking up at him. The last bit of rage that burned within her bubbled up, before she lost all feeling entirely. The exhaustion was alluring, singing to her like a siren.

"You're a coward who hides behind his flames. Without your magic, your title, you are nothing. And you will never come close to being a *fraction* of the man he is."

Leo wrapped a hand around her throat, tightening his grip. His eyes flashed into an empty darkness. It felt like there were two people inside of him, wrestling for control. She gasped for air, trying to bring her hands to her throat. Red spots clouded her vision.

"I really did want us to be friends. To have a true partner by my side, you know. But you have dug a hole far too deep to climb out of, Zia. Chosen to be little more than a prisoner when you could have been my wife. And now that wedding band will be little more than a shackle of your own making."

He dropped her to the ground. She pressed her forehead against the cold floor, gasping for air. Her hands were shaking. Zia could barely hear the door slam shut as he left, leaving her alone in the horrible silence of her room.

When she gathered enough energy to rise to her feet, she barely made it to her bed before collapsing. As all of her self-control slipped and her heart cracked, she broke into heavy sobs. It must have been hours of wailing, feeling the depths of her grief before her eyes swelled shut and sleep claimed her as she tumbled into sweet oblivion.

Her sleep was so deep she did not notice when Kali slipped through the door, took off her boots, wiped the blood from her body, the tears from her cheeks, and placed the blankets over her. Kali stood at Zia's side, looking at her. Studying her.

Kali had always been able to slip in and out of places undetected. It had been one of the many gifts that came with her extensive training. Even the king never learned her true identity. Leo had his suspicions, of course, but she made sure she was useful enough to him that he turned a blind eye. After all, to admit who she was would be to admit that she could kill him without half a thought, his flames snuffed out forever.

Kali walked out of Zia's room, passing the guards confidently like she had a very important job to do. Being so young had its advantages—people rarely suspected her. Especially with the way she presented herself like a child eager to please, in hopes of marrying some nobleman and rising in the castle ranks. She decorated her hair with flowers and braids, kept her expressions soft—people rarely noticed her at all.

They did not know that she was not of this place. That she had survived a far harsher environment than the vipers in this ostentatious court. Sometimes the artificial nature of the castle made her so sick she wanted nothing more than to reveal her true identity and burn it all to the ground. But there was a larger game going on, and she had a role to play in it. Just as Zia did.

Kali blended into the shadows as she ascended into the servant's tower, making her way up to the healer's quarters. She waited until one of the novice healers left the front desk before strolling right passed the entrance. The candles were burning low, dimming with the long night. The king didn't keep many healers on staff anymore—only the most gifted ones.

She heard a man's screams echo down the hallway and followed it. A familiar large, wooden door stood before her. Kali was always careful not to trigger any of the enchantments spelled over it. If she walked inside, she knew she wouldn't be able to walk back out again. It had been the king's way of ensuring his prisoner remained.

The girl knocked seven times. It had been their code from the beginning. Seven times would mean it was her.

"Come in," a woman's voice called.

The door swung open, and she saw prince Jace lying on the table, passed out. His whole body was covered in sweat. The stench of blood and piss hung in the air. Sahara Alexander was standing over him, placing a cold towel on his forehead. She looked so much like Zia, but her face was rounder. Softer. Where Zia was forged by grit and steel, Sahara was crafted from a gentle, healing force.

"I've been working on him for hours. They broke his bones, and his magic healed him while they weren't in the proper place. I've had to re-break them and heal the burns. It's going to take a while."

Kali remained standing in the doorway.

"Can you numb his pain?"

Sahara shook her head.

"The king forbade it. He had the guards wipe out my stock of herbs that would have helped, and if I use my magic to do it, he will know. He wanted Jace to feel every moment of this. I can only heal him in short increments. The pain is too much for his body to handle all at once..."

Sahara looked at Jace and shook her head, covering her face with her hands. She sniffled, then whispered.

"How is she?"

Kali weighed her words carefully, shifting on her feet. This was why she had come.

"They are breaking her."

Sahara's head snapped up.

"Torture?"

Kali shook her head.

"Not of a physical sort, but far worse. They are breaking her spirit. Stripping her of hope. She is to marry the Prince of Fire, in exchange for the protection of her loved ones. She is not like you. She is wilder. Unpredictable," Kali swallowed, "And she will not survive in a cage."

Sahara closed her eyes.

"It won't matter, you know. He will kill everyone she loves regardless."

"I know," Kali sighed.

Sahara remained unnaturally still, her empty eyes lost in thought.

"Then you know what you have to do, Kali."

Kali nodded.

"I will make sure everything is prepared."

The girl bowed at the waist and turned to leave.

"Wait!"

Kali froze, swiveling back toward Sahara. The woman's shoulders drooped. Her chin quivered.

"If they catch you, I can't help you."

"I knew the risk when I agreed to come here," Kali answered.

Sahara's throat bobbed.

"He'll kill you."

Kali's back stiffened.

"I am no stranger to death."

The girl bowed her head slightly before Sahara could say more, then turned to walk down the hall. The wooden door creaked shut. Kali blended back into the shadows and roamed the castle for several hours until dawn. The night had always been a source of comfort, a haven of invisibility for her. It allowed her to clear her mind in preparation for what needed to be done.

Kali would serve The Bridge as best she could. She would do everything in her power to make sure Zia Alexander had a true chance at stopping the king. After all, she had been training for this since she was born. It was her last chance to right the wrongs she had committed.

Kali walked and walked, strolling through the gardens and castle towers. She made her way over to the wide balcony that overlooked the sea. As she watched the waters churn and crash against the shore, something clicked for her—a missing piece to her plan she had not yet thought of.

The girl breathed in the salty breeze, enjoying the quiet before the storm that was to come. It was always this way, before a fight. There was a moment of mocking stillness. Time seemed to slow. The details of everything sharpened. Death was life's most clarifying force.

As dawn broke, and her eyes were blinded by the first light of the sun, Kali disappeared to set her plans in motion.

Even though it would cost them everything, she still wasn't sure it would be enough.

CHAPTER 20

> *It's easy to stand up against an injustice done by the hands of our enemies. Our brain can categorize it as good or bad, and file it away with ease. Yet to stand up to those whose approval we ache for most, to be willing to lose our own sense of belonging to deepen our sense of morality, that is when courage comes to the test.* —Kali

Three days passed of Zia going in and out of consciousness. Sometimes, she would wake up covered in sweat, screaming that she was drowning in a giant wave until one of the servants raced into her room to make sure she was alright. Other times, she would dream she was back with Jace and her friends at Aaliyah's. Safe. Happy. In love. Those were the hardest dreams—the ones where she'd wake up curled up in a ball, blinking back tears until she fell back asleep.

The only time she got out of bed was to use the bathroom. Never in her life had she felt so out of control of herself. It was like her light had gone out. Part of it was how demanding the magic had been—it drained her to exhaustion to be in the king's mind for so long.

She spoke to Kali once, when the girl forced her to take a few bites of soup, and Zia begged her to find out if Jace was alright. Kali had left without a word, arriving with news of him several hours later, only to find Zia snoring loudly, face-down on a pillow.

On the third morning, Kali was fed up. She came storming into Zia's room not even an hour after dawn, fuming.

She had taken those days to write letters to her friends to prepare them for what needed to be done. Kali had gone to the Zhulu bird pens in the middle of the night and strapped it to the back of the one bird she trusted. Just one of those letters could have gotten Kali locked up and tortured for the rest of her life, and the girl who was supposed to save them all was *hiding under the covers.*

"Get up," Kali said harshly.

Zia kept her eyes shut, not wanting to open them to her empty reality. If Hiro and the others were smart, they would stay as far away from the royal city as possible and live out their days while they still could.

Kali ripped the pillow out from under Zia's head, then snapped her fingers in her face.

"I said: *Get up.*"

"What's the point?" Zia grumbled.

"The point is that you are not the type of girl to stop participating in her own life. The point is that you are not going to ruin everything we have worked for to sulk about marrying a prince. The point is that you haven't lost. Not yet."

Zia cracked one eye open.

"Who's we?"

Kali froze.

"What?"

"You said 'everything we have worked for.'"

The girl's nostrils flared.

"Never mind that. I brought you breakfast. You're going to bathe and get dressed and get some fresh air."

"The healers told me to rest."

Kali began smacking her with a pillow.

"You have rested enough! Now GET UP!"

Zia tumbled off the side of the bed and onto the stone floor. Her limbs felt wobbly after sleeping for so long. Despite the heaviness in her chest, she felt her anger flare up.

"For a handmaiden, you have a horrible bedside manner, you know."

Kali scowled at her and then moved to pick up a large tray and place it on the dining table. It was enough to feed three people. Eggs and toast and jams and porridge. The plates were steaming. Zia brought a hand to her grumbling stomach—it had been days since she last had a proper meal.

She slid out of bed, wearing only an oversized men's button-down shirt. Kali had brought her an array of clothes that the male guards would wear. She found the shirts comfier than the itchy, lacey night-gowns they tried to stuff her in.

Zia plopped onto the wooden bench and immediately dug into her food. Her mouth watered at the taste—warm and comforting. It wasn't as flavorful as Laryx's cooking, but then again that had been his art, not his job.

Zia dropped her spoon for a moment.

"How do your parents allow you to be this bossy? Are they in the castle?"

Kali didn't look up at her.

"Dead."

Zia swallowed.

"Relatives? Friends?"

Kali's steely eyes narrowed.

"I'll be back in an hour to help you get ready. Try not to throw up everywhere after you've eaten yourself into oblivion."

She turned on her heel and left, slamming the door shut harder than usual. Zia supposed the girl's lack of an answer had been answer enough. She was alone, perhaps had always been alone, and somehow found her way into the castle.

After a few minutes, her thoughts of Kali dissolved as she ate her weight in food. The toast was her favorite. It was crispy and hot with melted butters and sweet jam. She was so entranced in eating that she didn't notice who had walked in.

"By the gods, what are you *doing?*" The Crown Prince stood by the door, his mouth gaping open like a fish.

She supposed it was a sight to behold. Her, not wearing pants, hair sticking in every direction, and fingers covered in jam as she stuffed her face. Not that it mattered—the king's whole doomsday speech had freed her of feeling any shame. What was the point, if the world was to end?

"What does it look like I'm doing? Eating."

"My dogs eat with more grace than you," his mouth twisted like he had tasted something sour.

"Then perhaps you should go bother them. I didn't invite you."

"I am the Crown Prince of Lemuria. I don't need an invitation."

Zia turned around to hurl a piece of toast at his head. It clocked him right in the forehead. She saw his fingertips spark with flames as he wiped his face.

Her laugh had an edge to it.

"And I thought I had a temper. What did you think was going to happen? You'd come in here after burning my—" She cleared her throat. "After burning Jace, nearly choking me to death, insulting me, and then what? I'd grovel on my knees for my future husband for gracing me with his holy presence?"

Leo closed his eyes and sucked in a sharp breath. She could feel him calming down, like a wildfire reducing itself to a candle flame. When he opened his eyes, they were clear. He looked frustratingly handsome.

His hair was down, little strands of red falling on his face. He wore a dark green coat with gold embroidery that was less showy than his recent attire. His dark brown pants were tucked into his boots, his shirt slightly unbuttoned, revealing the muscled chest beneath. The prince had style in the way that Ren did. She doubted his servants dressed him at all. It was obvious he cared.

The prince slowly approached her.

"May I sit?"

"You're a prince. I suppose you don't need an invitation," Zia glowered at him.

His mouth quirked to the side.

"Your wit is infuriating. You know that?"

He sat down on the other side of the table, eyeing her up and down. She suddenly felt vulnerable. The amusement in his eyes winked out.

"I came to...apologize." The word sounded forced, and she couldn't help but wonder if this was the first time in his life he had used it.

"I handled the situation poorly. Years ago, my father ordered me to burn Jace for going against him. I was eager to please him then. A boy that didn't think for himself—"

"Not much has changed, it seems," Zia interrupted him.

He rested his elbows on the table and leaned in.

"More has changed, my dear fiancé, than you realize."

She raised a brow, but remained silent so he would go on. Light spilled through the windows, and a beam of it hit his face, making his eyes look clear as they glowed a deep-sea blue.

"I earned my father's unfaltering loyalty that day, and it was easy to forget what I had done. Jace and I had competed with each other our entire lives. And he disappeared for years. My father didn't even send a scout to check on him, but I did. A faerie girl—"

"Meaghen," Zia countered, suddenly not hungry at all. The first girl that Jace had ever loved. Leo drew his head back.

"I'm surprised he told you. Yes, Meaghen. I wanted to know he was alright. I didn't realize how much I cared about him until he left. You don't understand the depth of your love until its absence, unfortunately."

"It was a disgrace to our bloodline for Jace to love a lower faerie. She didn't even have magic. I thought he deserved better. Eventually I told my father, and he ordered me to execute her. At first, I refused. And he..." Leo swallowed, staring at the floor. "Let's just say I haven't openly disobeyed him since."

"Openly?" Zia asked slowly.

Leo tapped his knuckles on the table.

"I am the Crown Prince. I have my own plans for this realm."

Zia stood up abruptly. The bench creaked as her legs pushed it backward.

"And what about your *father's* plans?"

Leo's eyes bulged.

"Be careful how you speak about him in this castle."

She pulled at her frizzy hair and stomped in circles.

"Who gives a damn what I say now? My *home,* the people I love are doomed."

Leo rose, and she could tell he was weighing his words carefully. He walked over to her, keeping a respectful distance.

"You are to be my wife soon, in a few short weeks. The king has ordered every servant in the kingdom to assist in planning. I told you before and I'll tell you again: I want a true partner by my side. You are nothing like a wife should be, but maybe..."

He smiled softly.

"Maybe you are what a queen should be."

It was tempting, she had to admit. The way his charm and presence felt like a magnet sucking her in. Yet Kali's warning echoed in her mind.

Be careful of powerful men who offer you the world when you were always meant to create your own.

Zia set her jaw in a hard line.

"I don't want to rule over anyone."

Leo blinked several times, debating before speaking. Every word, so careful and practiced to manipulate her in just the right way. Rho had been her training for this, she realized.

"Then work with me," he said in an exasperated tone.

"What?"

"Work with me. Don't resist the marriage. Be my friend. My partner. Lead by my side, and..."

"And you'll go against your father's plans?"

He rubbed at his neck.

"I didn't think so," she said coldly.

He stepped toward her.

"Look, Zia. It's complicated, and I can't discuss it with you right now. Just give me time. Let me show you our city. The people you could help."

He grabbed her hand between his two. They weren't callused like Jace's at all. They were soft and manicured. Too perfect.

"Where is Jace?" She asked. He dropped her hand instantly.

"His injuries were extensive. The healers will be spending a few more days on him before he can resume his post."

She glared at him, trying to sift through his words for the truth.

"I will take you to him as soon as he wakes, I give you my word. Just... please. Spend the day with me."

His blue eyes were pleading, glowing in the morning light that streamed in through the window. He turned her around to face the window, two hands at her shoulders. She looked down at the world below—the flying Zhulu's with their mighty golden wings, the tree highways, the siren rivers that ran throughout the quarters.

"All of this is about to be yours. Let me show you." His voice was like honey as he whispered at her neck. She shuddered.

It was a dangerous deck stacked against her, but Leo was perhaps the only card she had left to play. There was no other way the king would allow her to see the city. To learn and memorize its every exit, should she ever manage to escape. She was a terrible liar, but she had to try.

She turned around to face him, her enormous round eyes full of questions.

"Alright."

He brought her hand to his lips and kissed her knuckles. Her body went rigid, her cheeks heating. It was exactly how Jace had done it not even a week ago on what had been the best and worst night of her life.

In less than a minute, all that she held dear had been taken away once that spear hit Inka.

"I'll be back to escort you in a bit."

The Crown Prince was grinning from ear to ear as he left her room. When he opened the door, Kali was standing in the archway, and Zia knew without a doubt the girl had been listening.

Kali, despite being fully Lemurian, was no more than 5"3". The girl would probably grow to be at least six feet by the time she was Zia's age, but that didn't stop her from somehow staring everything above her down. Leo instantly squirmed out of her presence.

Zia slumped over to the bath. She washed her hair and her body, using the more fragrant soaps. Rose and frankincense. She avoided the sandalwood one again, not being able to bare smelling Jace on her own skin. When she finished, she walked over to the vanity and sat down without a word. Her hair dripped down her back. She stared blankly at the wooden desk.

Kali walked up quietly behind her and began brushing her hair. She was oddly perceptive of everyone's moods, for she was gentle with Zia now. Earlier, she needed to have someone snap her out of herself. Now she needed space to feel.

"How are we dressing today?" Kali squeezed the water out. Zia didn't bother to look up. She just kept staring blankly at the wooden table.

"Like a lady," Zia replied. She bit her lip, mulling over what she was about to do.

Kali stiffened, then resumed working on her hair and softly said, "Alright."

It was the longest she had ever taken to get ready. Ren had used faerie magic when she prepped Zia for her birthday, which saved hours. Kali had to hand trim her eyebrows and do her makeup and hair by hand. She braided Zia's hair into hundreds of little braids with bright orange gemstones woven and beaded in. She plumped her lips, adding a rosy color to them.

The dress Kali selected did not surprise Zia—the girl knew what she was doing. It was a beaded corset that faded into a deep orange hue with flowing skirts. She looked like a living flame. It was a nod to the prince's power. The color complimented her dark skin. Gold bangles adorned her ankles and her wrists. All of the jewelry was solid gold. Heavy. Ridiculous.

She barely recognized herself as she stared in the vanity mirror. It was the most feminine that she had ever looked. No one would question that this was The Crown Prince's fiancé.

"Where did you learn how to do this, Kali?" Zia asked, twirling one of the braids between her fingertips.

Kali stood a few feet behind her, assessing her work. It wasn't the way Ren had done, with admiration like she had just painted a masterpiece. Her eyes were fixated on every detail. Calculating. The same way a warrior might ensure they sharpened a knife properly.

"Beauty is armor."

It was strange hearing the words come out of the young girl's mouth. She always dressed very simply. Plain. Though that was probably intentional, too. Zia rubbed her hands along her skirts, feeling the smooth fabric. Her bracelets clinked together as she did.

"Someone once told me that beauty could be used to express more of who you are, but I feel like this buries who I am."

Kali walked toward her, eyeing her up and down in the vanity.

"They will always try to bury you, Zia. But they have forgotten something important."

"And what is that?" she asked. The light caught her face and the glitter on her eyelids sparkled.

"No matter the cage, wild women will always find a way."

It was the closest Kali had ever come to smiling, and it allowed Zia to feel a ray of hope in her heart. A knock sounded at the door, and the girl nodded at her. Zia heaved a deep breath and went to greet her future husband.

"Zia," Kali called before she opened it.

"Yes?"

"The prince is very…. convincing. Don't forget why you are really here."

Zia swallowed, averting her gaze. She opened the door to find him leaning against the frame. He backed up a step when he saw her, eyeing her up and down. It was the first time since they met that he had nothing to say. He opened and closed his mouth several times, searching for the right words. He smiled and shook his head, his cheeks reddening.

"You're perfect," he finally said, offering her his arm.

Kali helped her slip on her winter coat and gloves. It was likely to snow any day now. She looped her arms in the thick fabric, tying it around her waist. The girl seized the opportunity to display Zia in her dress before covering it with the coat to let Leo believe Zia was accepting her role as his princess, and one day queen. Again, everything was calculating.

Zia looped her arm through his and did her best to smile at him as they strolled out of the castle, and into the heart of the royal city.

CHAPTER 21

There comes a time in every girl's life when she is presented with a hall of mirrors. She has to guess which reflection is the true reflection. The mirrors can show any sort of temptation— a dazzling opportunity, a powerful prince. While it appears perfect, her gut will scream at her that this is not the truth. During this test, she has to trust the eyes of her intuition over what is being shown to her naked eyes. More often than not, she climbs into the mirror and becomes trapped within it. If the girl is able to survive, to shatter the false illusion, she will never silence her own instincts again. It is then that she emerges a woman. She learns to close her eyes and trust the reflection inside, over anything presented to her outside. Intuition is not a language learned easily, you see. —Sahara

They kept the Zhulu birds by the west castle walls facing the forest. All of them were perfectly groomed and brought out for training by the Shadow Warriors each day. One of them, the smaller one, stood out to Zia. She remained a few feet away from the pack, her shimmering gold wings were tucked in. She had a fire in her eyes that reminded Zia of Inka.

Prince Leo's was the largest of all the Zhulu's. He had an enormous lion's head with a gold collar around his neck adorned with siren tears, and a saddle mounted atop his back. Zia didn't want to know how they had come to acquire so many siren tear stones. Judging by the king's opinions on the sirens, it was probably through horrendous, endless torture.

"This is Tyberius," he stroked the neck of his Zhulu. Tyberius puffed out his chest and flapped his shimmering wings. She had to admit, Leo looked like he belonged in some chivalrous fairytale standing beside his noble steed.

He introduced her to a few other Zhulus that were not nearly as large as Tyberius. She let the birds sniff her out. They were more marvelous in person than she ever could have imagined. She walked over to a Zhulu that was slightly smaller than his. The bird was female, with more silvery wings. She didn't have the mane that Tyberius did, but there was a strength and wildness in her eyes that made Zia instantly like her.

"This is Azur. She is a bit headstrong, and doesn't let people ride her—"

He stopped himself as the bird locked eyes with her. Zia held out her hand, letting Azur smell her. Despite knowing that a Zhulu's teeth could tear her hand to shreds, there was something about Azur that she trusted.

The bird flapped its wings and screeched. Leo moved to get in front of her, but Zia stopped him.

"Don't. She won't hurt me," Zia whispered.

Azur puffed out her chest and screeched again. It was meant to scare Zia. A territorial display. Zia didn't move an inch. She held her ground and maintained eye contact with the Zhulu—not in a threatening way, but in a way that made it clear she wasn't afraid. Azur scraped her talons on the ground, her nostrils flaring. Zia ignored the way her heart raced, keeping her breath steady.

Finally, Azur bowed her head.

Zia grinned too widely, walking over to climb on her back.

Leo's breath hitched.

"Zia, no one has ever ridden her. She doesn't even have a saddle!" he said exasperated.

Zia swung her leg over Azur's neck and stroked her soft fur. The dress was certainly inconvenient for flying, but she made do.

"Relax, prince. We understand each other, don't we Azur?" She winked at the Zhulu. Azur's eyes lidded, and she huffed a loud breath in agreement. Leo ran a hand through his hair, shook his head and smiled, then made to put his foot in the stirrup before climbing onto Tyberius's back.

"Alright, Zia Alexander. Let's go see your new kingdom."

He made a loud whistle, and Tyberius launched into flight. The Zhulu's mighty wings kicked up dust in its wake. Zia leaned her head in close to Azur's ear.

Fly, my friend.

The Zhulu threw its head back slowly and let out a screeching roar, then leaped into the air after Tyberius. She pumped her mighty wings as hard as she could. Zia's hair was flying all over the place, Kali's careful work ruined. She clutched her coat tightly, trying to trap any semblance of warmth. Her nose felt numb in the frigid air.

They flew over the castle forest, circling the Black Salt Seas. Azur was catching up to Tyberius. After a few more huffs, they were neck and neck. Leo looked proper in his saddle, his spine straight and his hands on his reins in such a relaxed way.

Faster, Azur.

Azur roared and pressed on, leaving Leo behind. Zia threw her head back and howled, a laugh escaping her that she didn't know was possible given her circumstances. When she looked over, Leo was chasing her with his chest forward and an incredulous look on his face.

Though she still feared heights, she *loved* flying. It was a feeling of freedom unlike any other, where even the wind couldn't catch her. They flew over the Ghost Market, cloaked by darkness and fog. The Ace's Quarter, with its gambling markets and the major residence of the common people. Zia had always found it the loveliest in The Trials, with its enormous trees and wild gardens.

They flew over the tree highways—thick branches covered in moss that ran throughout the canopies. Red and orange flowers bloomed from them, as though the king even color-coded the flora to match his colors. Leo finally sailed ahead of her, landing in the Artist's Square. Zia had always wanted to spend more time there in The Trials, but it had never seemed useful in terms of leveling up.

She landed shortly after him in a wide stretch of grass that had a pen for the Zhulu's. They tied theirs up away from the other birds, though there weren't many—Zhulu's only belonged to the wealthiest of nobility. He slid off Tyberius, smoothing out his jacket and his hair. Then he offered Zia a hand. She would have refused it, but she was supposed to be getting along with Leo. Zia fluttered her lashes in a way she had seen Ren do a hundred times and delicately took his hand. She slid off Azur, and adjusted her dress on the landing, pulling her coat in close.

Leo tucked a few braids behind her ear and smiled.

"You didn't tell me you were a flyer."

Zia shook her head.

"I'm not. Or I didn't think I was. I'm actually afraid of heights."

Leo arched a brow.

"*Parodāi*," he said in the old language. His accent was far thicker than Jace's, having never left the royal city. She didn't recognize the word. He read the confusion on her face and smiled crookedly.

"It is Atlantean. In our language, beauty and paradox are the same word."

Zia frowned.

"How?"

Leo placed a hand on the small of her back, ushering them toward the markets.

"In our culture, we believe that the opposing forces within are what make us, us. My father tells me that Atlanteans were never just one thing. Here it is different. If you are a warrior, you will always be a warrior. If you are a healer, you will always be a healer. The magic makes it easier to categorize people."

He stopped walking, cocking his head to the side as he looked down at her forehead, staring at the tattoo there. Zia often forgot the three dots were even there unless she looked in the vanity. The prince had never commented on it before.

"You are a mortal human who can wield the greatest immortal power the world has ever known, and you are brave as hell, but act from fear for the people you love," he finished.

It took everything in Zia not to snort in response. Despite herself, she forced herself to smile at him.

"I didn't know you were a poet, Prince."

They started walking again.

"Ah. I leave that to my brother. And please, call me Leo."

Zia swallowed as he took her hand in his. She met his eyes.

"Alright, Leo. Show me your world."

They spent the entire day in the royal city. He ordered the guards to stay behind so they would have some privacy, confident in the safety within the walls of his own city. Zia quickly figured out that it was less that the city was safe, and more so that the subjects were completely terrified of him. Everywhere they walked, vendors and street performers froze. They either disappeared or their eyes went wide with fear. She wished they had ventured out in disguise.

He refused to take her to the Ghost Market, which was the *first* place she wanted to go. If there was a place to glean any real information, particularly on how to free Jace, Inka, and her mother, it was there. She claimed she wanted rare spices. He didn't buy it for a second. Apparently, the royals had a delicate agreement with Thanatos to leave the market untouched, so long as he supplied them with whatever they requested, of course.

The cobblestone streets of the Artist's Square were lit with rows of torches, warming them on the chilled day. They strolled through the market, passing by many vendors. Lemurian children ran through the streets with streamers. Bakers put out hot, fresh pastries with jelly fillings and powdered sugar. Jewelers displayed their finest, glittering pieces, especially when they saw the prince. He walked right up to the table, noticing a necklace of fine rubies with an enormous piece in the center. The vendor was an old faerie. His skin was turquoise, his wings tattered, and the whites of his eyes were yellow.

The faerie shook in his boots and he instantly bowed.

"Your majesty, it is an honor."

Leo dipped his chin approvingly.

"You are a fine craftsman. Your pieces are lovely. Especially this one," he gestured to the rubies. The faerie held it out to the prince instantly to feel, his hands uncontrollably shaking.

"It is one of my finest. Mined and brought all the way from the Redrock Mountains. Excellent taste, your majesty."

Leo held it up to Zia's neck and squinted.

"That will do nicely. We'll take it."

Zia put his hand down when he reached into his pocket.

"I don't need more jewelry."

Leo's close-lipped smile was cold. All the warmth and charm from earlier vanished in half a second, and she was reminded of the man who had nearly choked her to death in her room several nights before. She didn't want to admit how much it terrified her, how quickly he could flip.

He didn't like her challenging him in front of his subjects.

"Nonsense. You are the future queen. You need something far nicer to wear than that." He was staring at the necklace Ren had given her.

Though it didn't match her outfit, she never took it off. It was the only thing she had left of her friends. Her mother's swords were at Aaliyah's, so that necklace was her last piece of home.

Zia brought a hand to the sapphire at her throat.

"I...please. This means a lot to me."

Leo unfastened it from around her neck, placing it into his coat pocket.

"I am sure Kali will find a place for it. For now, I want you to wear this."

He fastened the rubies around her neck. They were heavier. Too heavy. Like a sparkling collar. Leo overpaid the vendor by quite a lot, who bowed several times with a million thanks. She was silent as they walked. Leo talked the entire day—he spoke of how he wanted to improve the lives of his people.

The first thing he would do was abolish the Ghost Market and banish the sirens from the river waters, keeping them back at sea. He wished to remove all danger in the city, so all his subjects had to do was simply go to work and be with their families. Zia didn't think that would go over well with the underwater realm, nor the creatures who profited from the market.

Everyone stared at her. She was feeling too much. Their envy of seeing a human with the Crown Prince. Their fear of what he might do. Their awe and blind worship. It made her want to crawl out of her own skin. She kept her head down as he talked, doing her best to convince herself that she could do this, that he wasn't so bad. He droned on about his palace duties, his pressures as a prince, his plans for when he was king. She didn't say a word in reply. The entire day, she overrode her intuition until it quieted altogether, and all that was left was a numb hollowness.

The sound of a piano broke the silence in her soul. It reminded her of the music on her birthday. She walked away from Leo, unaware that he had still been talking, and followed the pull she felt to the music. It was all that existed for her.

A crowd had gathered in the quarter square. Many of the vendors left their booths to listen, and Zia wondered if the performer was well-known in their city. Judging by the awe on their faces, it was their first time hearing the music. The pianist was an older man with silver hair hunched over the keys, his eyes completely closed.

The piece was a sad one. It started soft and slow, reminding her of a simpler time. Then it began to build further. Each key felt like a hand reaching out and drawing them closer in. No one took their eyes off the pianist. The music dusted off the cobwebs of her soul and slapped her awake.

A violin sounded, and the crowd whirled to see an older woman playing on the opposite side of the square. Her face was solemn as she drew the bow across the string like it was a thread connected directly to her heart. The two of them played, building up into a crescendo. It sounded like sorrow and joy joined hand in hand, dancing with one another across time. She heard sobs and sniffles in the audience.

When they ended. Applause broke out in the crowd. People were whistling and howling. Somehow, this piece of music had opened an entire group of strangers.

Zia blinked back tears. To have a gift like that, the gift to move people through art, was the most precious thing in the world. A part of her soul had been fed listening to their song. That is what had been missing in the human realm. People stopped valuing art, they stopped having a place to put their pain.

"That was a song for the fallen queen," the silver-haired man said, bowing at the waist. Judging by the deep wrinkle lines on his face, he had more than likely been here all those years ago when Mū was invaded.

The crowd fell silent. The man was looking directly at Prince Leo, his gray eyes piercing. The rest of the crowd turned toward the prince, holding their breath to see what punishment he'd bestow.

"May her spirit rest knowing that there are those of us who remember the true Lemuria."

The musician looked at Zia, standing next to Leo with the rubies around her neck, so clearly the prince's betrothed in her dress of flame. His gray eyebrows furrowed as he examined her with disgust. To him, she was The Bridge. Their last hope, now worn on the arm of the prince as little more than an accessory.

The king knew exactly what he was doing—destroying not just her, but what she represented.

Yet if she had learned anything from watching The Electi at Mei's, it was that behind every powerful man was often an even more powerful woman. She saw Leo's temper spike. His eyes darken. She knew that look. Had been on the receiving end of that look.

He took a step to walk toward the musician. His fingers sparked with flames.

She gently put a hand on his shoulder and brought her lips up to kiss his cheek. He went stiff, not expecting her affection.

"I know you wish to be loved by your people. Burning an elderly man alive in front of them will not win you their hearts," she whispered in his ear.

His head snapped toward her.

"If they think they can openly challenge the crown without consequence—"

"Only a fragile man kills everyone who challenges his views. You are not fragile, Leo."

A muscle feathered in his jaw. She felt like she was coaxing a lion to sleep. His breath shortened. She looped her arm through his, gently nudging him away from the quarter square.

"I'm starving, shall we get something to eat?" She asked as softly as she could, patting his hand.

He blinked several times, the darkness in his eyes lifting.

"Of course. I know the perfect place."

As they went to leave the square, Zia locked eyes with the violinist. The woman looked at her like she had known precisely what just happened. Her expression was pained, but she offered Zia a subtle nod of thanks. Zia looked away, not risking acknowledging their presence so as to set him off again.

The crowd cleared a path for them, whispering as they passed. She did her best not to shake, hiding the fact that she was riddled with nerves. Leo led her to the end of the vendor street and paused at a stand that was frying some sort of dish on a skillet. Her mouth watered as the scent of hot food wafted up her nose.

He gestured toward the woman who was rolling out fresh dough for the seared wraps.

"Zia, this is Talia. She makes the best food in the whole damn city."

The woman stopped rolling and wiped the powder off her hands on her apron. She had jet black, short-cropped hair, pale cream skin and enormous hazel eyes. The woman looked more alien than Lemurian, though there was something terrifyingly stunning about her. She wiped the sweat from her forehead and rolled her eyes at Leo.

"Enough with the flattery. We all know you just get bored of that ridiculous palace food."

"I wouldn't be eating that ridiculous palace food if you accepted my offer as head chef," Leo grinned.

Talia shook a finger at him.

"I am an artist. I want the freedom to make the kind of food that *I* want. Not cater to you royals and your terrible, over-the-top taste."

The two of them bantered back and forth. Zia instantly liked her. Hearing her snap at Leo eased her nerves somehow, although she was surprised he let her get away with it. The entire day, Zia had been acting as someone else, but as she watched them interact, she realized that wasn't what he needed. Not at all.

Leo was drawn toward people who put him in his place. Kali. Talia. Jace. Her. Which meant that there had to be a small part of him that didn't want to lose his temper. The man who stood before her was so at odds with the one who had been ready to burn an entire square to the ground moments ago.

She thought of what she would be like with his magic—if every time she felt rage, fire exploded out of her. Mei would have forced her to learn how to control it, but the king encouraged Leo's lack of control. He wanted Leo untamed and easily riled up. The prince was isolated. His people hated him, and those who didn't only wanted something from him. Isolation and loneliness made people desperate. It was the first time she had felt a true sense of pity for him.

He looked at Talia with nothing but admiration in his eyes. Even his smile was genuine. And it occurred to her that this small little interaction was perhaps the most intimacy the prince had in his life.

"You're a quiet one," Talia turned her attention toward Zia. The woman was sizing her up, and Zia knew exactly what she thought when she saw all of the finery.

"I'm not quiet. The two of you haven't shut up for twenty minutes." Zia joined in on their banter.

"Is that so? Well perhaps we should stop yapping and I'll make you a meal that will put you in a better mood."

"What's on the menu?" Zia replied.

"No one places an order here. I know what you need," the woman winked, strutting away toward the back of her tent. Her arms were cut and toned, like Zia's now were, probably from chopping and rolling all day. Yet the rest of her body was soft and curvy.

When Zia turned to face Leo, he put his palms up.

"Trust her. She really is the best."

Zia saw the way his eyes lit up. It was the way Jace's did when he looked at her. She felt his giddiness, but she said nothing. Several minutes later, Talia was back out offering them plates. When Leo tried to pay, she smacked his hand away. The moment she turned around, he tossed what sounded like a very, very heavy bag of coins on her table.

"There's a place I'd like to show you," he said, smiling down at her.

"Alright," Zia replied.

The two of them left Talia's and strolled toward the Zhulu pens. Leo carefully placed the food in the leather bag attached to his saddle. They each mounted their bird and took flight, riding on the wind toward the castle.

Zia used the few minutes of airtime to clear her head. She welcomed the cold wind that kissed her cheeks. She was to be his wife, bound to his castle, his family the rest of time. She shoved the thoughts away. She needed Leo to trust her, and that required connecting with him.

She flew straight through a cloud, her clothes damp as she emerged on the other side. She sniffled, staring at the castle forest below. It was different from the Red Grove's dry and gnarled trees by Aaliyah's. Or the faerie forest in Morganna's court that had been damp like a jungle. This one was lush yet dry. Everything in sight was covered in sprawling shades of green. The treetops were pointed like pines. The two of them landed in the Zhulu pens and dismounted.

Zia brought her forehead to Azur's.

"Thank you," she whispered to the bird. Azur huffed in response, then turned around to greet the other Zhulus. Leo held out his arm for her to take and jerked his chin toward the forest.

"This way."

Zia looped her arm through his, and they walked through the mist-cloaked forest.

As they walked, he asked her about her life in Periculum.

She did not spill the secrets of her heart, as she had to Jace. Instead, she told him about playing in The Trials. Her ruthlessness in the game, and of course her friendship with Hiro, and the way they became friends. Leo tipped his head back and howled with laughter when she spoke of the three kids she beat up with a lunchbox that had tried to bully him when they were younger.

"You had to have known that you were different. Special," Leo squeezed her arm.

Zia shook her head.

"It's not like that in Periculum. No one has magic, so it doesn't matter if you're 'special.' People are just surviving, trying to escape or get a leg up. It's all scheming to get even a sliver of power."

"That doesn't sound so different from my father's court," He chuckled.

Sunlight stubbornly tried to break through the cloud cover. She leaned into the warmth.

"Leo...why do you serve him?" She held her breath.

Leo's eyes darkened. He was silent for a moment, and she thought he may not answer.

"He wasn't always this way. Watching his home dry up into a barren desert, his kingdom starve to death...it broke something in him."

"But didn't all of that happen because of *him?*"

Leo laughed darkly.

"You've been spending too much time with my brother. There is a great deal that you do not yet understand. Thousands of years of tangled history..."

"Then tell me," She pleaded.

He smiled at her, but it did not reach his eyes.

"Another time, I promise. Now tell me, how did you wind up in Lemuria?"

Zia tried to hide the disappointment blooming in her chest, but she decided not to press him further.

"My birthday was coming up. When we come of age, we go into the system or wind up working some off-grid government job. All I wanted was to find the map...for me and Hiro to have a shot at freedom. I wanted to travel, to see the world..." she trailed off. A light drizzle dripped down the leaves of the forest trees. The sound coaxed her into a calm.

"And what would you have done? Had you not found the map and traveled to *this* world?" Leo asked, his eyes burning into hers. She knew what he was really asking.

Zia paused. She hadn't admitted this to anyone but herself yet. She brought her eyes to meet Leo's.

"I was different then. Harder. If they tried to take me, I would have killed them. And if I did not succeed, then I would have died before being held captive. Sometimes I think your father is right. That it would be better to wipe the board clean and start over. We've destroyed so much..." she whispered.

Zia paused when she almost stepped on a blue lotus flower. She didn't think they could grow this far from the mountains. Her heart twisted. Leo brought a comforting hand to her back.

"So why don't you let him? Bring the ones you care for here for protection and let him destroy everyone who wronged you. Everyone who did not see how extraordinary you are," Leo asked, turning her around to face him.

Zia cocked her head to the side.

"Because, Leo, people are not just one thing, like you said. We splinter off parts of each other, selecting which pieces are worthy of love and then wonder why the world is so gods- damned fragmented. We don't get to decide who is worthy of life. I may be The Bridge, but I'm not a hero. Your dad may be a conqueror, but there is still something in him *you* find worth fighting for, isn't there?"

Leo's red brows knit together. He ran a thumb over her palm gently.

"Sometimes, I forget how young you are. But I see that your human heart is full of ideals. You have not yet been jaded by history repeating itself on an endless loop. The old you had the right idea, Zia. She sounded ruthless, and like someone I would have enjoyed very much." Leo winked.

Zia stared down at the lotus. The speckles of mud on the petals.

She dropped her hand from his and locked into his gaze. He cupped her face in his hands, his eyes searching hers. All she could hear was the pit patter of the light rain dribbling down the leaves. She stopped breathing.

His lips crushed into hers. The kiss was urgent. Rough. He tangled his fingers in her hair and gripped tightly. That kiss she had with Jace—a feeling that stopped time and made her feel so alive she lost her fear of death—didn't occur. All she felt were lips pressed together. Her body was tense. It wanted to pull away, but she again lulled herself into submission, convincing herself this was right.

When he pulled away, his lips were swollen and a deep red color. His mouth curled into a smile of satisfaction. He held her face in a strong grip with both palms. He was undeniably handsome—the perfect picture of a prince.

"It is okay to feel the ache for power, Zia. It is okay to *want*. To not play the martyr and sacrifice yourself for what you think is a greater cause. Just stay with me, and we can accomplish all of your desires. Just stay with me, and you will be the most powerful queen the world has ever seen..."

He interlaced his hand in hers. Her throat locked up. She reached inside of herself to find any words that would counter his offer, any fire that might fight back. All she felt was empty dust and cobwebs. So, all she did was nod slightly and continue walking with him hand in hand.

The two of them climbed between two enormous Albizia trees that were blocking their lunch spot from view. Beyond the mighty trunks and wild leaves, there was a hidden flat stone ground with ruins crumbling around it that overlooked the ocean. It was enormous, and clearly abandoned.

"They used to train the Shadow Warriors here. Between the sound of the waves crashing, and the forest surrounding, no one could see or hear the training techniques."

Zia kicked a pile of pebbles over and watched the dust spray. Leo took her hand and brought her to the edge. The ocean was churning, and she could feel a slight sea mist on her skin. She thought of Ren, and the summer she spent falling in love with the siren.

Leo pulled Talia's food from his leather bag. They ate their seared wraps in silence, enjoying the curl of the ocean waves. She had to admit, Talia was an incredible cook. The food tasted *alive*. She could feel color flush her cheeks. It was difficult not to scarf the entire thing down, but she wanted to savor every bite. If she did wind up staying a while in this marriage, maybe Talia would be willing to teach her a thing or two.

When Zia was done, she put her plate to the side and crossed her ankles over the edge, letting her legs sway above the open sea. It made her toes tingle to be so high up, but she welcomed the sensation. Too many days spent in that suffocating room had been terrible for her mind.

"Leo, did you have friends growing up?" Zia asked, side-eyeing him.

Leo blinked slowly, like he didn't understand the question.

"We had hundreds of servants in the castle. I was never alone."

"That's not what I meant. I know you had Jace, but your relationship seemed to be based on competition. Did you have a friend? You know, someone you could talk to unfiltered."

Leo stared at the sun as it bounced off the rippling sea. He was quiet for a few moments, and when he spoke, Zia could tell it was the first time he was ever telling anyone this story.

"There was…a girl. A servant. She was my age. We would often escape to the forest and find solace amongst the trees, running away from our responsibilities. Her name was Sawyer," his voice grew heavy. "She was like me—a powerful Elymental. Her magic didn't show until she was thirteen, and she nearly drowned a few of the other young servants with a tidal wave when they chased her through the castle."

Zia swallowed.

"Where is Leila now?"

"Gone. She disappeared the next day. I never saw her again."

He averted her gaze, keeping his eyes fixed on the horizon. Zia let the conversation drop. She could feel the crippling loneliness that had followed him throughout his entire life. It must have felt really nice, to have a friend with the same burden and gift as him, even if it manifested as water. It was almost worse that he knew that kind of comfort before it was ripped away. Zia couldn't help but feel that the king had something to do with her disappearance. Leo would have been easier to control if he was isolated, after all.

He finally broke the silence.

"Your face, when you were watching that pianist..." Leo squinted. He was leaning back on his elbows with one knee up and looked like he'd be content to rest there forever. It was the most human she had ever seen him look. He was usually so rigid and proper, carrying himself with unnatural stillness.

"I've never seen anyone so moved by something before." It sounded like a question, but she didn't bite. He turned to face her. His nose was scrunched together, trying to see her through the harsh rays.

"You feel deeper than anyone I know, it's beautiful," he tried again.

Zia clasped her hands together and sighed.

"Yeah, I know. I'm a bit of a mess."

Leo shook his head and sat up, resting an arm on his knee.

"No, that's not what I said. I'm not sure if it is because you are mortal, and time forces you to feel everything so deeply and all at once, or if it is your magic...but you are the most alive person I have ever met."

She was saved from responding by the first snowfall of the season. They both looked up. Hundreds of little flurries fell from the sky in icy shapes. Zia breathed in the clean air, watching each snowflake land and melt in her palms. She smiled slightly. Snow would always be special to her, having gone her entire life without seeing it. Mount Shasta had been her very first experience. It felt like a lifetime ago.

Zia realized Leo had been staring at her the entire time. He slowly reached into his coat pocket and pulled out a velvet box. Her heart stopped dead.

"Lemurians don't normally exchange rings, because the blood bond is stronger than any jewel. But I have heard that this is the human custom."

Her head roared. She wanted to scream. It felt like she was at the bottom of a well, shouting for anyone to hear her. He opened the box, revealing an enormous oval ruby ring to match her necklace, with two mermaid teardrops on either side. It was no wonder he had purchased the necklace. This entire day had been planned—showing her his home, his special hiding place.

"I know that there is no part of you that desires this marriage, Zia. But despite our differences, I am happy we met. And I genuinely believe that one day, we could make each other happy. I promise I will give you the nicest life imaginable."

The ruby glittered, emphasizing his words. There was so much she wanted to say. That he would never make her happy, because she was struggling to make herself happy most days. That she did not care for a nice life. She did not care for any part of this at all.

Then she saw her mother's face. Her father's. Mei's. Hiro's. Ren's. Aaliyah's. Rho's. Inka's. Kali's. Jace's. The faces that she had come to care for fiercely. The people who had shaped her world. For them, she could do this. It was a very small price to pay, really. Her freedom in exchange for her people to have a fighting chance. Perhaps the royals were right, and this was her destiny. Even if everything in her screamed otherwise.

"Marry me, Zia Alexander."

Leo gave her a nervous smile, holding the box out. He looked very much the Prince of Fire as the snow fell around him. She took the ring out of the box and slowly slid it onto her left ring finger. A different kind of weight settled into her.

Leo smiled and hooked his fingers under her chin, pulling her in. Snow stuck to his eyelashes. She went rigid again. The guilt tore away at her gut. He could be right—perhaps there was a part of her that was drawn to his offer, to the way he unapologetically owned his desires and was willing to burn the whole world to the ground for it. There was something liberating about that sort of selfish honesty.

Their breath mingled. All she felt was a war waging on within herself.

"No," a voice interrupted them, saving her from choosing a side. The two of them turned to see Jace and the other Shadow Warriors standing behind him. He was dressed in the royal uniform of black. His knives were nowhere to be seen, and instead he was carrying the uniform sword that all the other warriors carried.

"Zia, step away from him." Jace's hand instantly went to his sword. The other warriors looked back and forth between the two princes, waiting for the call to throw Jace back in chains. Leo threw his head back and sighed.

"Apologies my love, this will only take a moment."

Bile rose up in Zia's throat. Her cheeks heated. She was betraying Jace to such a despicable level by marrying his brother, the man who burned him. Worse than that, perhaps, was that she was betraying her own heart.

Leo stood and pulled Zia up, then clasped her hand in his. Jace's eyes immediately flashed to the hefty gem on her finger. His jaw locked. She saw him examining her. The gold anklets. The dress. The jewels in her hair. The rubies at her throat. The ring. And she knew that he saw nothing of the woman he had fallen for. She suddenly wished she could disappear—slip out the back door and live out her days in the forest.

"She belongs to me now," Leo said, sneering.

Jace drew his sword.

"Zia belongs to no one but herself," he replied with a deadly calm.

Zia would have run away with him and damned them all to hell for that sentence alone. All of Leo's charm and power crumbled like a house of cards in Jace's presence. Everything in her body was aching to go to him. But she couldn't.

Leo's brows raised, and Zia wanted nothing more than to smack that smug expression from his face.

"The date has already been set, brother. In a few weeks' time, we will be blood bonded. It's not my fault you didn't have the strength to seize her when you had the chance. Just as you didn't have the strength to take the crown when we were boys. You never did learn that you cannot just sit on your ass and wait for destiny to deliver. If you want it, you have to *take* it."

Leo began circling Jace, flames sparking at his fingertips. The guards rushed forward, but he held up a hand for them to stay back. Jace grasped his sword until his knuckles turned white.

"If the way to the top requires that I climb on the backs of my people, then I have no right to wear a crown. To be a king is to serve. That's something you and father never understood."

Leo stared admiringly at the balls of flames in his hands, watching them bob up and down. The sea waves crashed against the castle walls, rumbling the ground beneath them. The two princes stood across from one another, fighting for what men had already fought for since the dawn of time. If only people bothered to learn from their history.

Leo whipped his hand and threw the ball of fire at Jace. Jace bent backward all the way to the ground, then flipped onto his feet and was instantly bringing his sword down upon Leo's head. He missed narrowly by a few inches, cutting off a few strands of red hair. The guards went to break up the fight, but Leo snarled.

"No. He's *mine.*"

The two of them forgot that there was a third warrior on that platform.

While they were fighting, Zia had rushed over to the guards, pretending that she needed protection. She let them bumble around like idiots for a few moments until she grew tired of watching them fight over their new favorite toy. Faster than anyone could register, she drew one of the guard's swords from its hilt and stepped into the ring.

Jace's eyes went wide as she disarmed him, knocking him to the ground and taking the sword right out of his hands. She held out the two swords with a feral look on her face. Leo's mouth thinned.

"Go to the guards. This is between us."

Zia snarled. It felt like she had been drowning, and just gasped for her first breath again. She was furious with herself for falling for any of it.

"If it's not the crown, then it's a woman. You two are pathetic."

"It's not proper for a future queen to—"

Zia was instantly upon him. She flipped over Leo's head and then jammed the pommel of the sword into his spine. He fell to the ground and she pinned his arms, then brought her mouth to his ears.

"You want to give me a 'nice' life? How much gold do you think my freedom costs?"

Leo was sweating, he growled into the floor and tried to shove her off him. She hit his jaw with her knee, burying the Crown Prince's face in the dirt. She lowered her voice so not even Lemurian ears could hear.

"What if you had to stand there and watch me try to kill Talia? I don't know how long you have been in love with her. I doubt anyone knows. I'm sure it's *improper* for a crown prince to love a street chef, after all."

Leo's eyes bulged.

"How did you—"

"I'm a woman. We always know. Don't worry, husband. Your secret's safe with me."

She released Leo and dropped the two swords, then dusted off her hands. One of the guards started clapping, until the princes both glared at him, and another guard whacked him on the back of the head.

Zia looked up at the sky and sighed, "I said I would marry Leo in exchange for the ones I love being safe. You, Jace, are messing with that."

She did not look at either of them. She knew that she would lose her nerve if she got lost in Jace.

"You have to leave me alone. Have them station you elsewhere," she said softly, staring at the ground blankly. They were the hardest words she had ever said. But she knew that there wasn't a fighting chance she would survive this marriage if he was always near. She wasn't strong enough. She would leave Leo in a heartbeat. There wasn't a spell in the world strong enough to make her forget the way she felt.

Zia swallowed, turning to face Leo whose face was covered in dirt. He spat blood on the ground. Everything in him wanted to reprimand her, but she knew he wouldn't. They both had mutually assured destruction now. If he harmed Jace, then she would harm Talia. She hated herself for it, but she had never minded getting her hands dirty. Not one bit.

Zia jutted her chin upwards, bowing to no one but her own heart.

"Not a wife, but a queen."

Zia watched Leo swallow his own words being thrown back at him. For the first time in his life, someone other than the king had something over him. She did not look at Jace as she picked up her skirts and walked away. The guards cleared a pathway for her, two of them trailing behind her as escorts back to her chambers. And though she could feel her heart cracking, Kali was right. She was not the type of girl who stopped participating in her own life. And they hadn't won yet.

This was her game now.

CHAPTER 22

She spent her whole life unable to control her rage. It was why she was drawn to the Prince of Fire, despite her best efforts. What she came to learn that he did not, was how to properly wield her rage. To not let it attack or consume, but to purify. To reclaim her joy, she would need to reclaim her pain—the grief that she had shoved deep, deep down. They sought to extinguish her fire, but I aimed to show her that rage could be sacred. Rage burns to the ground all houses of cards so we can see the open sky again. —Kali

The next few days were terribly boring. Leo was so infuriated by his own inability to control Zia that he didn't come see her for days. Jace stayed away, too. Though she sometimes spotted him from across the courtyard, watching her. He did not ask to be stationed elsewhere. After her wedding, she would have to demand it, even if it killed her to do so.

The lack of company left her with dress fittings. Picking place settings. Flowers. Music. A whole host of details that she cared absolutely nothing about. The distraction was nice, however. It kept her mind from wandering off into memories of far-away gardens, kissing his lips and getting lost in his emerald eyes.

By the second day, she asked Kali to handle it all— to throw the wedding the king wanted. She had a knack for knowing what the Crown Prince desired and dressing Zia accordingly.

When she told Kali about what happened, the girl called her an idiot in three different languages. When Zia asked her what *she* would have done in that situation, Kali replied that she would have shredded everyone into ribbons.

Kali was sharp. Too sharp for a normal fourteen-year-old. She was highly intelligent and ruthless. Her eyes were full of a wisdom that took most people a lifetime to earn. Or several. It made Zia wonder what Kali's life was like before the castle.

So, when she wasn't being stuffed into frilly gowns or tasting exotic juices and wines for the wedding, she would ask the girl questions. Most of them were met with, "None of your business, Zia," or, "I'm merely your servant." Yet there was always a twinkle of amusement in the girl's eyes, because they both knew she was lying.

One day, when they were working on different hairstyles for the wedding, and Kali had spent three hours sweeping Zia's hair up into a bun woven with crystal combs, Zia decided to try a different tactic. She took one of the knives and buttered a piece of hot, fresh bread. It melted in her mouth as she scarfed down the loaf.

Between bites she asked, "Who was the queen of Lemuria?"

"There is no queen," Kali snapped. They had spent so much time together within the past week that the girl's patience had worn thin.

"Yes I know, but...who is Jace and Leo's mother?"

The girl yanked harshly at a braid, and Zia howled in pain.

"This now makes me think the rumors are true, about humans having half the brain we do. You know very well that I don't have the answer to that question. Not even the princes know."

Zia scowled at Kali in the mirror.

"Don't deflect. You must know something. And you should be happy I have stopped interrogating you," she countered. Zia knew that would make the girl talk. Anything to get the attention off herself. Kali's eyebrows knit together in a deep frown.

"No one knows who sired the two princes. It was long after the king killed Katya. Whoever she was, he kept her hidden in the castle. We know it was a powerful magic wielder, because of Leo, and we know that she was Lemurian, but there are no records of her anywhere. The people never saw her. The king said that she was murdered long ago—killed by Lemurian rebels. Both princes spent years looking in secret for the truth, since the king forbade it. But no one knows, except for the faerie queen. That is probably her only true leverage against the king, and why he left her court untouched for so long. It is Lemuria's best-kept secret."

"Morganna? How would she know?"

Kali pursed her lips.

"Because *she* was there when both of the princes were born. I have heard whispers that she wiped everyone's memories after with her magic, including the boys."

Kali continued to work in silence, finishing up the last touches of her hair. Zia was lost in thought, mulling over exactly what Morganna's relationship with the king was. She wrinkled her nose when she saw herself in the mirror.

"I look like a gods-damned swan."

"A what?" Kali frowned.

"It's this ridiculous-looking bird in the human realm."

"So?"

"*So*, shouldn't the bride actually like her own hairstyle?"

"This is not about your preferences. We are putting on a show."

Zia grumbled something about being nothing more than a doll, and Kali smacked her on the back of the head.

"Don't you wallow in self-pity. Is that how you survived Periculum back in your world? Feeling sorry for yourself?"

Zia twisted in her chair to look at Kali. The girl had walked over to the table across the room, where sets of priceless crown jewels were laid out to choose from. Her back was facing Zia.

"And how did you survive where *you* are from?"

Kali's spine stiffened, but she did not turn around.

"I am merely a servant," she replied as always.

Zia tested her theory. It was a risk, but it was also the only way she'd extract the truth from the girl. In a flash, Zia snagged the butter knife and hurled it across the room. It sailed right toward Kali's shoulder.

Without even turning around, Kali caught it in her hand by the handle. She whirled it around between her fingers three times—a girl who was no stranger to weapons.

"And how does a servant know her way around knives?"

Kali turned around and threw the knife back toward Zia. It missed her by an inch, landing in the frame of the vanity, wobbling side to side. Zia threw her hands up.

"You could have hit me in the eyeball! At least I aimed for your shoulder—"

"I don't miss." The girl squared her jaw.

Her hair was in a low, tight bun. She wore her usual powder blue servant dress with flats. Her enormous, brown eyes were unblinking.

"Are you a spy?" Zia asked.

The girl snorted.

"A *spy?* I cannot believe that we are betting everything on you."

"Who is this 'we' you keep mentioning?"

Kali closed the distance between them, walking across the room. She placed both her hands on the arms of Zia's seat, their faces a few inches from each other.

"I am from a barren wasteland where only the strongest survive. From my very first breath, I have been training."

"For what?"

"For this. And the '*we*' I am referring to, is your mother."

Zia's breath shortened. She wasn't sure she was hearing those words correctly. A part of her hadn't believed that she was really alive. But Kali had seen her. Kali *knew* her.

"Take me to her," Zia begged.

"No."

She grabbed the girl's hands in her own.

"Kali, take me to her. *Please*," she pleaded.

Kali shook out of her grasp.

"No. You'll see her again, if you don't keep making a mess of things with your idiotic impulses. I'm telling you this so that you trust me, and maybe listen to me for once. There is a greater game being played here."

Zia's throat bobbed.

"I...is she—"

"She's alright. For now. He has her bound by a spell to the healer's quarters. She knows you are here, and she knows you are to marry the Crown Prince. I have kept her updated on everything my friends have… gathered on you since you walked through the entrance."

Zia's neck was covered in cold sweat, she brought her shaking hands to her face.

"We have to get her out—"

Kali squeezed her hand.

"The best way to get her out is to let me do your hair. And select your dress. And what dish you will eat. And the jewels you will wear. And for the love of the gods, can you *try* to at least not upset the Crown Prince further. Make a friend out of him, as best you can. You may need his friendship before all this is over."

Kali removed the combs from her hair, letting the braids fall to her shoulders. It was relieving, to not feel like her scalp was constantly being pulled and yanked at.

"Please trust me. The less you know, the better Zia. You're a horrible liar, you know."

Zia's mouth quirked to the side.

"I'll work on that."

Kali stepped back and smiled for the first time from ear to ear.

"I hope, for our world's sake, you never do."

Zia stood up and climbed out of her dress. This one had looked like a cake with its ridiculous puffy layers and long train that had been impossible to walk in. It was Atlantean fashion, apparently. Lemurians wore simple clothes- skirts and pants that were easy to move in. No fancy beading or frilly layering.

"I'll do as you say on one condition, Kali."

Kali fluttered her lips, gazing up at the ceiling.

"I cannot wait to hear what our world savior The Bridge of Lemuria wants now."

"Teach me."

"Teach you what?" Kali frowned.

Zia raised a brow, glaring at the girl.

"I know you've been keeping an eye on me since I got here, but I have been doing the same to you. I have never seen reflexes like yours, and I am willing to bet you are a better fighter than both princes combined. I want you to teach me."

Kali shook her head.

"No. If they catch me training you—"

"I know of a place they won't see or hear us."

The two girls stared at each other with eyes of steel, until Kali finally heaved a sigh of resignation.

"Alright. But from now on you do as I say without protest. We will train after moonrise, while everyone is asleep."

Zia grinned, folding her arms over her chest.

"Fine by me."

Zia and Kali spent the rest of the day preparing. Still no sign of Leo, mercifully. Kali finally selected a hairstyle that was less horrendous than the swan bun, along with a set of matching jewels. She finished all the remaining details for the wedding, except for the dress. Zia kept her promise—she didn't argue about any of the selections. It wasn't really her wedding, anyway.

They did their usual stroll through the garden, talking loud enough about the wedding for any spies to hear, and then ate dinner in her chambers by the window, gazing at the city of Mū. below. It had become their little tradition—to watch the lights of the glittering city and the gentle current of the bioluminescent rivers, to listen to the far-off music as it floated into her room, and to talk into the long night.

Kali pretended to leave her chambers for the evening. Zia cozied up in her bed with a book. It was a love story about sirens seeking a lost city in the trenches of the sea. She became so engrossed in the tale, that she nearly forgot she was meeting Kali. She looked around to see the moon rising over the spine of the mountain and threw back the covers.

Zia dressed in her preferred outfit of the guards. Black pants and a long-sleeve black top with a cloaked hood. She didn't have any weapons since they were thorough about making sure she had zero access to any after the incident in the throne room with the knife.

She braided her hair into a single, long frizzy braid down her back, and pressed her ear up to her door. Kali had promised the guards would be preoccupied at moonrise for exactly five minutes. That was plenty of time to slip out of the room. When she heard nothing, she slowly opened the wooden door. The torches were unlit. The guards were gone. She was completely covered by darkness.

Zia hurried, keeping her footsteps silent as she followed Kali's instructions for slipping out of the castle. She knew the exact guard rotations, and when there would be a sixty-second gap by the wall. It was nice to know the girl had an escape route, should Zia ever manage to free her mother. Zia knew the tree tunnels existed, thanks to the Mortemys, but she didn't know how to get to them without going through the heavily guarded Lost Library.

She scaled the wall of the castle and leaped off one of the stone ledges.

Zia landed on her haunches. The mossy forest floor felt like a sponge. The night was frigid. Though snow had yet to stick to the ground, it was certainly on its way. She could see her own breath in front of her. Zia was on high alert as she raced through the forest, doing her best to memorize every tree and opening.

When she made it to the twin Albizia trees and walked through to the platform, it was empty. Zia walked over to the edge, looking anywhere she could for Kali. She looked everywhere, but up.

Kali backflipped off one of the trees and landed right behind Zia without a single sound. Within a matter of seconds, Zia was face first on the ground, panting. It was the same exact maneuver Jace had done at Mount Shasta.

Zia quickly got to her feet. Her jaw dropped. The girl standing in front of her was not the same girl who had been doing her hair these past few weeks. Kali was dressed in a form-fitting, all black body suit. Her hands were gloved, and she had a cloak over her head that hid the majority of her face. She had dual blades in her hands, and more knives along her thighs than Jace, even.

If Death ever wore a skin, it was Kali's.

"Lesson number one: *always* remember to look up."

Zia was instantly upon her, but Kali dodged every blow with ease. Where Zia attacked, she melted into the shadows. After several minutes, when she was out of breath, Kali hadn't even broken a sweat.

"Lesson number two: don't attack unless necessary. Allow your opponent to make the first move and exhaust themselves, while you study the way they fight."

Zia snarled and lunged for the girl just as a wave crashed into the wall. The sea sprayed, landing on the platform in a *smack*. Kali pinched a place on Zia's neck, and she felt tingling move down her arm, rendering her body useless. Then Kali knocked her knees in as she fell to the wet ground.

"Lesson number three: know the body. It takes very little effort to render someone unconscious."

Kali released Zia's neck just as she began blacking out. Then the girl showed Zia exactly what parts of the body to hit on someone. It was invigorating, to be out in the open, covered in sweat and dirt as she reconnected with the parts of herself that had been shut down for nearly a month.

Kali strode over to the side of the crumbling wall farthest from the sea. She pulled out twin blades from behind a rock. They looked precisely like Zia's, only without the jewels— a replica made for this exact moment.

"Your mother told me you have something similar to these. I want to see how you use them."

Zia carefully took them from Kali's hands, examining the shining steel beneath the moonlight. Before she could look up, Kali had already unleashed blades of her own. She had not yet touched the many daggers that she wrapped around her legs.

Their weapons clashed together as they fought. Kali had said she didn't have a drop of magic running through her veins, but Zia had never seen anything like her in her life. There was no one in any realm that could even come close to her speed and stealth.

Zia could feel herself getting tired. Kali laughed.

"Are you going to give up the way you did after the throne room? Perhaps wallow in some more self-pity at how you never wanted to be The Bridge...how you are forced into an arranged marriage..."

Zia yelled so loud she strained her vocal cords as she brought down her sword on Kali. Kali was gone within an instant, and Zia's teeth rattled as the blade met the stone ground. When she looked up, the girl had rolled out of the way and disappeared behind the ruins.

Her voice echoed throughout the platform.

"Lesson number four: never, ever wield a sword with hatred in your heart. If you take a life, you don't take it lightly."

A blade was suddenly at Zia's throat. She dropped her sword instantly in surrender and sank to her knees.

It was then that Zia realized who her servant had been all along.

I am from a barren wasteland.

The pieces started to click in her mind as Zia realized all assassins came from the Ordos desert, but there was only one who was rumored to be able to fight like that. Jace had whispered stories of her throughout their travels, but everyone had assumed it was a grown man, not a fourteen-year-old girl.

"You're the Last Shadow."

Kali grinned wickedly.

It was a joke, really. That the king and the Crown Prince had no idea who was right under their noses.

Kali released the blade from her throat and went to sit next to her. Zia was truly stunned, and a wave of silence washed over them both. Zia looked up at the night sky and sighed, breathing in the cold air. Even the waves calmed. It was low tide, and the waters were sucked back. The waxing moon created a stream of silver light along the waters.

"We should go back. The waves aren't loud enough to cover the sound from prying ears anymore."

Zia nudged the girl's shoulders.

"Not yet. Let's just enjoy it for a bit."

"Enjoy what?" Kali asked, following her gaze.

Silver lined Zia's eyes. She did not realize how much her freedom meant until it had been taken away.

"All of it," she whispered, looking up.

Kali looked up with her, squinting at the constellations. It was a perfectly clear night. She couldn't remember the last time she did something spontaneous. Something without motivation or agenda. Just appreciating what was right in front of her.

Several more hours passed as the girls remained there, quietly looking at the world beyond with hope. It occurred to Zia that she had never found someone she could share silence with for as long as Kali. The silence that normally felt awkward, and needed to be covered up with empty conversation, suddenly felt full of answers.

They returned before dawn without anyone noticing. The guards outside her bedroom were snoring when they got back. Before Zia slipped through the door, she whispered to Kali.

"Thank you."

Kali took her weapons back for hiding. She was strapping them back in place beneath her cloak when she replied, "For what?"

Zia tapped her fingers on the wooden door.

"For helping me find my way again."

Kali nodded slightly.

"Get some sleep."

Zia went inside of her room and closed the door without saying anything else. She bathed and changed into pajamas.

By the time her head hit the pillow, the first sun rays peaked out above the horizon. She was snoring within seconds, drifting off into a dreamless sleep. There was only a week before the dreaded celebratory dinner, and little more than that before her wedding. She planned to train as much as she could, right up until the last moment when her life was bound to another's.

Zia spent the remainder of the week doing exactly as Kali said. During the day, she dressed as a lady who looked worthy of marrying the Crown Prince. She tended to the garden with the Tree People, helped in the kitchens, and met with many of the nobles. She and Leo had fallen into a tense truce. They only spoke when necessary, but she could have sworn she saw approval on his face as she charmed the whole court with him. She never saw the king, thankfully.

At night, she would shed her gown and slip into the darkness, training with Kali on the old Shadow Warrior platform. It had become a ritual for her—a place where the two of them could unwind from days of careful planning and boring conversations. They could get out of their heads and test the boundaries of their strong bodies.

Kali was by far the best teacher she had ever had. She pushed Zia beyond her normal limits, but also knew when the breaking point was and stopped. Ever since that first day, Zia no longer fought out of rage—that unsustainable fire that demanded all of her energy. Instead, she flowed like the gentle river waters by Aaliyah's garden. She was formless, taking the shape of what the moment demanded of her. She was nobody, slipping through Kali's fingertips. A silent, steady force. By the end of the week, Kali could no longer rile her.

Zia finally understood what Aaliyah had meant. There was no use attempting to master anything before she had mastered herself.

The night before the celebratory wedding dinner, neither of them noticed that they were not alone. Perched atop one of the forest trees, far enough away to go unheard and unnoticed, blending into the night sat Jace. He always guarded Zia's chambers from afar, protecting her as best he could on the night watch. The first night he saw her slip out, he followed her, then knocked the guards unconscious before her return.

The level she had improved since arriving in Lemuria was inhuman. She had gone from a decently trained young girl to a woman lethal enough to go toe to toe with the king himself. He couldn't take his eyes off her as she twirled and flipped with savage grace. It was a dance between her and Kali. Not even a fight.

"Do you think she is aware of who trains her?"

Jace nearly fell out of the tree. He hadn't noticed Leo sitting behind him. He leaned against the trunk like he owned the tree, his arms folded over his chest.

Jace ran his fingers through his hair, calming his heart.

"Did you have to sneak up on me you prick?"

Leo smirked.

"Riling you has been a favorite pastime of mine for centuries, brother."

Jace's nostrils flared, but he calmed himself. He had a great urge to leave his brother with a black eye on his wedding day, but he knew this time was sacred to Zia and Kali. If they discovered they were being watched, they wouldn't continue training.

"I think she suspects. How long have you known?" Jace asked.

Leo chuckled.

"I knew the day she applied as a servant. I had never been more terrified of anyone in my life."

Jace turned to face Leo and saw his blue eyes burning like silver fire in the moonlight.

"Then why didn't you tell father who the girl really is?"

Leo hopped off the tree gracefully, then looked up at Jace.

"Because, brother, despite what you think, I am not a monster."

Jace opened his mouth to speak, but Leo brought a finger to his own lips and jerked his chin toward the platform. The two of them turned around in time to see Zia tackle Kali to the ground, a blade at her throat. A wave crashed into the mountain, sea spray covering the platform as though in celebration. Zia had won.

Jace saw the pride sparkling in Leo's eyes. He didn't look away as he said, "I do care for her, you know."

Jace sighed.

"I know. Why do you think I haven't slit your throat in your sleep yet?"

Leo laughed and rolled out his shoulders, loosening his neck.

"She will be queen one day. With this marriage, I can give her a better life than you."

"Better doesn't mean happier. She hasn't chosen you," Jace replied coldly.

"And if she did?"

Jace watched Zia hold out a hand to help Kali up. She pulled the girl into an embrace and threw her head back to laugh loud enough to rattle the sky. He had never heard that laugh before. It was so free and unabashed.

"Then I would let her go," Jace answered, because that laugh was worth more than his own desires. That rare joy on her face was a work of art he would never capture, no matter how many times he drew her in his sketchbook.

It was why he hadn't told her the hidden truth he had known for some time now. He kept it tucked away in the back corner of his heart, hoping she might discover it. And he didn't want it to sway her decision—who she loved and shared her brief time on the planet with. She hadn't been given many choices in life. She deserved that.

Leo was gone not a moment later, disappearing into the night.

Jace watched all the way until dawn, as the legendary Last Shadow Assassin unleashed the force of nature that was Zia Alexander.

CHAPTER 23

They told me of love and all of its glory—sonnets written about battles bled to win a desired heart. Kingdoms that rose and fell, burned to the ground in the name of passion. My love for her was nothing like that. I loved her like the sun loves the earth. Never owning or taking what I thought to be mine, but instead providing enough warmth and light for her to become whoever she wished to be. I did not fall for her hoping I didn't get hurt. I just loved her and felt a great honor in the ways that love both challenged and changed me. —Jace

"Would you quit flinching? The bags under your eyes could carry the entirety of the royal riches!" Kali whined. She was jabbing Zia with concealer to cover up evidence of their long, sleepless nights.

It was the evening of the wedding celebration dinner. No expense would be spared as the castle was transformed into a party they hadn't seen the likes of for centuries. It had been a long while since Lemuria had something to celebrate. The union of Katya's descendant with the Atlantean Prince of Fire would bring peace and prosperity to their realm. Their magic combined would protect their world for the rest of time. Together, they would bring Lemuria out of middle earth and back to the surface, reclaiming their place in the world.

At least that was the story the blithering idiot of a royal secretary had spun when the people of Mū had gathered in the courtyard several days ago. He left out the part about genocide. According to him, the humans would willingly live in harmony with them, if Zia, one of their own, ruled beside Prince Leo. Apparently, the king hadn't let him in on his plans to mass murder her people—an insignificant detail the Lemurians didn't need to be aware of, of course.

Everyone was invited to the wedding in a few days. The commoners hadn't been allowed in the castle since the two princes were born to conceal the identity of their mother. It seemed that, despite hating the human world, the king had taken a page out of their government's book. Distraction. A sparkling story of peace and love that people would *want* to buy rather than the truth. Hypocrite.

Zia sighed. She had protested the entire thing to Kali many times, but Kali had assured her she just needed to be patient. To trust her plan. Zia kept suggesting different ways to break her mother out, but Kali kept snapping at her that only a powerful faerie could break the spell holding her captive.

"*You* don't look so great yourself, you know."

Kali's bushy eyebrows were sticking in different directions. Her hair wasn't braided but tossed into a careless bun. She gave Zia a rare smile, revealing her teeth that were too big for her mouth.

"I don't need to look great. I'm a handmaiden. You're their soon-to-be princess and future queen."

They both were exhausted. Their days were grueling planning and preparing for the wedding, and their nights, while liberating, had demanded everything from their bodies. Concealing the bruises and bloody marks was difficult. One of the days, Zia had forgotten to dress a wound on her shoulder, and it had bled on Leo's jacket when they sat next to each other and spoke to the nobles. When he looked at her in question, she had claimed she slipped and fell in the tub. He had just snorted in response.

"How long is this thing supposed to go for?" Zia groaned.

Kali finished applying the makeup to her face, brightening her eyes with powder crushed from calla lilies. By the time she was finished, Zia looked like a different person. A woman, glowing with happiness about her soon to be union.

Kali had spent hours undoing her braids, brushing through her thick hair.

"We've been over this. You'll go, you'll eat dinner with the royal court. The king will give a speech with his blessing. Then you'll dance with Leo. Then the rest of them join you in the dance. You smile and wave, say you're tired and want to be refreshed for the wedding. Go to bed. Done."

"I smile and wave, say I'm tired, and then we *train*, you mean."

Kali rubbed oil into her hair to calm the frizz.

"No. I have never seen anyone learn as quickly as you. You are as prepared as you will ever be. Rest will do you more good than brawling until you're bloody into the wee hours of the night."

Zia did her best not to show her disappointment. The training had become her lifeline. A tether back to herself. No matter how much she pretended to be the docile mouse, she could always turn into the wild, raging wolf come nightfall. But she had agreed to trust Kali and follow her instructions. It had been the first and only time she blindly followed someone else's plan.

Her outfit was in honor of Queen Katya and the Lemurians, meant to display the blessed union the king had droned on about. She wore a turquoise high-waisted silk skirt with two slits on either side. An off-shoulder, long-sleeve bandeau top of the same fabric showed off her collarbones. Her ankles and wrists were dressed in bangles. No jewels. The outfit was simple. It didn't shout for attention but rested in simple beauty.

Kali tied Ren's necklace around her neck, the blue sapphire matching perfectly with her outfit. An ode to Zia, and everything she had gone through to become who she was now. Her hair was gelled and tied back into a sleek ponytail braid, making her look fierce. Large gold hoops were on her ears. She looked like a warrior princess. Feminine. Lethal. Her eyes were lined with thick, black wings sweeping on either side. It made her bright blue eyes pop.

"Now *this*, I can get behind," Zia said as she turned to examine the full outfit in the vanity.

Kali chuckled.

"I thought so."

Zia stood and walked around the room, testing her comfort in the outfit. It was light and easy to move in.

"This is a difficult outfit to store weapons in."

Kali rolled her eyes.

"You won't be fighting with your fists tonight, my friend."

Zia slipped on her strappy sandals that tied around her ankles. She closed her eyes and sucked in a sharp breath.

"Let's go."

Kali walked with Zia into the gardens, where she had told Leo to meet her. He would have gone to her chambers, but she didn't want to give him the opportunity of having a private conversation with her. Out in the open with curious ears so close by, he wouldn't be able to question her.

Even the gardens had been transformed. String lights were hung around the perfectly shaved trees. Enormous candles were strewn all over the garden. Most of the flowers had been plucked and placed into bouquets lining the stone walls. The moon was nearly full, creating a starless sky.

Leo was pacing back and forth by the roses. He was dressed in his colors—a coat of burnished orange and red embroidery. He had an enormous gold chain around his neck with a Lemurian crystal at its center. No weapons visible. His hair was half up and half down, a bit more sleek than usual. The familiar smell of rose and cinder burned the inside of her nose.

When he saw her, too many emotions ran across his face at once—admiration and awe, rage and resentment. He had truly met a worthy opponent, and it made it difficult for him to decide whether he loved or hated her. Despite her disdain for him, she was also aware that they were two sides of the same coin. She had grown up with people who kept her temper in check and challenged her to be better, whereas he had spent a life in isolation, encouraged to lean into his own darkness in search for power.

Zia kept her face expressionless, her chin held high.

"Hello, Leo," she greeted him in Old Lemurian, standing before him in the firelight. He laughed coldly.

"That's all you have to say to me after all these weeks? 'Hello Leo?'"

Zia raised a brow.

"Of course. How else should I greet my future husband?"

A muscle feathered in Leo's jaw. He looked like he was about to explode. His eyes flickered to Kali, who stood behind her. He blew out a breath, and the fire in his eyes was gone. Leo offered her his arm.

"I would like to have an honest word with you in private, before we continue this ridiculous game."

Zia looped her arm through his.

"My dearest fiancé, this game was your idea. Don't be upset just because I have learned to play it better than you." She patted his hand gently.

He gripped her arm so tightly her eyes watered, but she refused to let up. Kali stepped in front of him. She looked slightly feral, baring her teeth under the moonlight.

"Your guests are waiting." The threat in her tone was blatant.

Zia understood in that moment that somehow, Leo knew who Kali was. The fear in the air was palpable, and he instantly backed down. He knew that by the time he even summoned his flames, she would spill his blood then and there in the garden.

What Zia did not understand was why he allowed Kali to remain in the castle. Why he had assigned her to be Zia's handmaiden in the first place. Games within games within games. It made her head hurt.

"Thank you, Kali, for bringing her to me," Leo said with tight lips.

He ushered Zia through the castle doors, where several guards were posted. She looked over her shoulder to gaze at her friend one last time. Kali winked at her, then disappeared into the night.

The guards all nodded at her in approval, admiring her as she walked. She could feel Leo's pride at having something other people desired on his arm. The halls were transformed. Their normally dim lighting was bright and full of warmth. Streamers were everywhere. Lights strung about. More paintings had been hung, mostly portraits of the royal family and their Zhulus. Fancy, finely threaded rugs rolled out. She could hear the sound of music flooding the hallway.

They walked through several archways framed with roses, until they approached the enormous double doors of the ballroom. They were made of crystal, perfectly polished and refined. It seemed as though every single royal guard in the castle was there, protecting the entrance. It made sense, since every "important" person in the city of Mū was through those double doors.

One man dressed in a fine, all white suit with tanned skin and long, blonde hair manned the doorway. He was tall and muscled. Gold earrings were pierced all along his ears. He reminded her a bit of Sam, the bouncer who guarded Mei's club—the humor in his eyes, the silent confidence he carried himself with, like he could cut down their enemies without a second thought.

The door guard nodded when he saw the two of them.

"Your Majesties."

The man looped his gloved hands through the door handles and opened them simultaneously. She was doing her best not to cringe at being called "majesty." If only Hiro could see her now, he would make fun of her until the end of time. She would give up all of her magic just to laugh with him right now.

Yet when Zia saw what lay beyond those crystal doors, she couldn't help but bring a hand to her heart. The dining table stretched the length of the room, with blue lotus flowers in the center. She hadn't mentioned to Leo what the flower meant to her. How did he know?

The silver haired musicians from the Artist's Square were there, playing the piano and the violin on the stage. She was surprised they had come, knowing how they felt about the royals. A ballerina in black point shoes and skirts twirled and danced to their music. No one paid any attention to them, but all Zia wanted to do was ignore the dinner and sit on the floor with her eyes closed, getting lost in their symphony.

The food even looked good. It wasn't the usual fancy food the royals ate. It reminded her of Aaliyah's, in fact. Similar bowls of flavorful rice and fish and veggies. A chocolate cake dripping as it had been on her birthday. Sparkling wines. Then she saw the enormous plate of Mac n Cheese and froze.

Jace. Jace had worked with Kali, to make sure that every detail was true to Zia. The music. The flowers. The food. It was his way of letting her know that while she may be stuck, she was loved, and that no matter how much she had to pretend, he still remembered. He *saw* her, every single inch, and he loved her without condition. Even now, when she was marrying his brother.

Her lips started wobbling, her body shaking. There was no way she was going to be able to do this.

Leo spoke softly in her ear.

"It is his wedding gift to you."

She nearly choked on her tears.

"You worked with him?" she whispered.

Leo squeezed her hand.

"Yes, Zia. I told you that I want you to be happy and would give you the nicest life possible."

She wanted to punch Leo's nose into his brain for taking any ounce of credit. Though she supposed that him allowing Jace to do all of this for her was likely the most selfless thing he had done in his life. She closed her eyes and let the music fill her soul for a moment. It felt like tasting spring water after wandering in the desert.

"Not here. Don't let them see how you feel," he growled, tightening his grip on her.

He was right. They weren't alone. The king was there, at the head of the table with that sparkling crown atop his head. It was the first time she had seen him since that day in the throne room, and he was every bit as awful as she remembered.

The worst of the court vipers sat on either side of him. In her time getting to know them all, she had been unimpressed to say the least. Zia wanted to know the people in the city, not the spineless court. But the king forbade her from wandering out on her own, and things had been awkward with Leo since she shoved his face into the dirt.

The only empty seats left were at the opposite end of the table. Leo would sit at the throne by the table head with Zia next to him. Across from her chair sat Jace. It was no doubt the king's way of entertaining himself by testing her like this. Jace had not looked up yet, but she could tell by the stiffness of his spine that he knew she was there. Her heart cracked at the sight of him. Kali said he had spent the past few weeks training the younger guards, disappearing at lunches and dinners. He hadn't talked to anyone unless absolutely necessary.

All she wanted to do was let every honest word pour out of her.

"Hold it together," Leo snapped, squeezing her hand so hard she thought the tiny bones might break. He escorted her across the shimmering room, and toward what would be her seat. He pulled out the chair for her and then pushed it in as she sat down. Their finest cutlery made of solid gold had been brought out.

Jace kept his gaze down, staring at the blank plate. She could have sworn his shoulders shook slightly. She could see his pulse was racing. The majority of his tattoos were concealed by his black jacket, but his shirt was mostly unbuttoned, revealing the ones across his chest. His dark hair had fallen over his face. He looked a bit disheveled, like he had spent the entire day running around.

Both of their self-control was hanging by a thread, it seemed. The clanking of glass sounded, and the chatter at the table died. The king's secretary, a stout man with his nose so high in the air Zia wondered how he could possibly see anything, was holding a glass.

"His Majesty would like to make the royal toast."

The king held the silence, basking in the table's attention. He looked back and forth between Jace, Leo, and Zia. She had no idea what Leo possibly saw in him, or how he could justify serving such a vile man.

"Congratulations, to our prized couple. The union Lemuria has waited on for thousands of years!"

The whole table erupted in applause. The king held up a hand and it immediately died. His voice boomed.

"I trust that our little get-together tonight is to the bride's liking. I am told that this food is the finest the human world has to offer," he chuckled darkly. The nobles laughed with him.

The king raised a glass.

"To The Bridge. The shining symbol of peace to our people. May she always remember her place."

Everyone but Jace and Zia raised a glass.

"And to my son, Leo. The Crown Prince, and future king wise enough to choose what is best for the realm, following in *my* footsteps."

Zia blinked slowly. The threat toward Leo was subtle. So subtle, perhaps no one noticed it. Yet she could see the fear in Leo's eyes as he gave a tight-lipped smile. Whatever agenda he had, the king was onto him.

"May their union flourish for an eternity!" the king shouted. The nobles cheered on with him, though many of them sneered at Zia.

Her eyes met Jace's for the first time. They burned into her like a brand on her soul. She opened her mouth to speak, but Leo stomped hard on her foot beneath the table. Her eyes watered, but she understood the warning.

If she failed the test and revealed her feelings for Jace, everything they had worked for would be pointless. Jace went back to pretending she didn't exist. The music started again. It wasn't the heart-wrenching piece they had played in the quarter square. It was light. Celebratory.

The rest of the dinner was torture. She could barely eat her food. Everything felt like a reminder of him. She didn't pay attention to the mindless conversations— the grand, overblown stories Leo told about the glories of being a fire-bending prince. She sat silent, with her head hung, doing everything to pretend like the situation was perfectly fine.

As the king was telling the story of how he conquered Lemuria, and dumped Katya's ungrateful body in the sea, Zia had to focus all of her energy on not flinging a golden fork into his majesty's eyeball.

She felt a boot lightly nudge her toes. She thought it was Leo at first, but when she looked up, she saw Jace staring at her. His eyes softened. He was doing the best he could to silently comfort her as they suffered together.

I'm right here with you. That's what that little nudge seemed to say. Even the slightest touch or look from him was full of more meaning than a lifetime of court conversations. She smiled slightly. Then heard a throat clear.

Leo was glaring at her. His expression cold. He clinked his glass, and the chatter of the table died down slowly again.

"I would like to ask my fiancé for a dance, if she would be so kind."

He stood and bowed at the waist, offering his hand.

She stared blankly at that hollow offering, then remembered where she was. Zia plastered a smile onto her face, making her eyes widen in awe like she couldn't possibly believe how lucky she was to be marrying her prince.

Only this wasn't her prince, and never would be.

She took his hand and strolled with him onto the empty dance floor. As she walked, she noticed the smirk on the king's face. He didn't believe her charade. Not one bit. Not that it mattered, if she was bound to Leo by blood in a few days.

Leo jerked his chin toward the musician, and the woman brought her bow onto the strings. The song was happy. Hopeful. A true celebration. The man hunched over the piano, following shortly after. The music filled every corner of the room, drowning out any and all boring conversations.

They all watched as Zia and Leo danced. She wasn't a dancer and barely knew the royal numbers. Leo was a master. He led her with such grace and ease that her lack of experience was almost unnoticed. He was the knight in shining fire, leading her out of the dark. Or so it appeared. Though she had to admit, she did enjoy dancing.

At the end of the song, he gently pulled her into an embrace and whispered in her ear.

"I know."

Her heart stopped.

"Know what?"

"About the training," he finished. Then pulled away and smiled, bowing at the waist. He turned toward the court, "Come celebrate with us! Your future king and queen wish for you to dance."

She was frozen on the dance floor. Chairs squeaked as everyone rose and stood, hurriedly making their way onto the ballroom floor. It had been a long time since they had a good party, and the court was ready to rejoice in every moment.

Leo offered a dance to a young woman whose lineage dated all the way back to Atlantis. She was from one of the wealthier families, and probably who Leo would have chosen had Zia not arrived. The woman had pale, cream skin and silky dark hair that fell below her waist. She looked at Leo the way he looked at Zia—the ultimate prize to be won.

A young boy with long gold hair who looked to be around Kali's age offered her his hand. The boy smiled smugly when she accepted and led her in a dance. He had nothing of Leo's grace, and she fumbled awkwardly to the song. Their height difference was laughable.

Zia was about to excuse herself after an hour of painful dances. She waltzed with nearly every nobleman of the court, save for the king himself, thank the gods. Leo relished in the attention from the women in the court. Many of them were several glasses of wine in, doing their best to whisk him away. Zia felt nothing when she saw him flirting with them. It merely gave her a break from his watchful eye. She went to walk off the floor, but the music changed.

It was the song from the Artist's Square. Katya's song—the music of remembering. She glanced around and saw Leo's face turn ashen, but he quickly masked it with perfect composure. It wasn't worth it to make a scene here about what the music meant. The piano was gentle at first. Every keystroke a wild motion. It wasn't flawless composure, but it was raw in a way few pieces of art ever were.

"May I have this dance, your majesty?"

His voice yanked at her heart strings. She turned around to see Jace standing only a foot away from her, looking more handsome than ever. He even shaved and was wearing the royal outfit of a prince. It wasn't Leo's flashy gold outfit, but his usual preference of black. Simple. Breathtaking.

She interlaced her hand in his, allowing herself the first real smile she had shown in weeks in front of anyone other than Kali.

"Always," she replied.

He pulled her in, and his sandalwood scent hit her like a freight train. The violin sounded just as they began their dance. They fit perfectly, knowing what move the other was going to make before they made it. He brought his cheek to her cheek as they waltzed, so gently brushing his lips over her skin that no one else noticed, but her whole body felt like it had been struck by lightning.

The piano built up into its crescendo, and she forgot anyone else was in the room.

"Thank you. For this. For everything," she said softly.

He shook his head and spun her outwards, twirling her around several times before pulling her in so close their breath mingled.

"I need to see you," he said roughly.

"No," she said, feeling the terror shoot through her.

"Why?" he asked, his face pained.

"Because he is waiting for us to slip up. For me to break my promise. Please," She begged him, though she wasn't sure exactly what she was asking. *Please forgive me? Please understand? Please leave me alone and stop being so wonderful so this can all be easy?*

"When did you get so scared? The Zia I know has triumphed over phantom panthers, dragons, and faerie queens. Surely sneaking out of her room at night should be easy."

"The Zia you knew had nothing to lose."

"Then you have something worth risking it all for now." He dipped her body low toward the floor, then pulled her upwards until their foreheads met.

"Meet me in my room at midnight. There are no guards. I'll get reassigned somewhere else if you want. Just give me this. Let me see you one last time..."

His voice became soft and pleading. All the bravado washed away. She blinked her tears away, hiding her face in his neck. The piano broke into its crescendo, and then the music silenced. The song ended as abruptly as before. She swallowed, looking up at him and nodded. It was as much for her as it was for him. He kissed her palm and bowed.

"Your Highness." He winked and walked back over to the dining table.

Zia excused herself back to her chambers, pecking Leo on the cheek as though they would do it a thousand more times throughout their lives. A few nobles wished her luck on her union, their smiles not touching their eyes. She did not bother saying goodbye to the king, though she could feel his gaze burning into her back as she left.

It took all the patience she could muster not to sprint out of the castle. Especially with the guards trailing her everywhere she went. She held it together all the way back to her chambers. She opened the door and slammed it shut, blowing out a breath as she sank to the floor. Her room was quiet. Too quiet.

She had been so relieved to no longer smile to the point of her face hurting that she had not noticed Kali lounging on her bed, munching on candy. Chocolate was smeared across her face.

"Since servants weren't invited to the celebration dinner, I took the liberty of snagging dessert from the kitchens. Hope you don't mind."

Zia groaned, pulling off her shoes and chucking them across the room.

"Only if you share."

Kali grinned.

"Well? Did you enjoy your surprise?"

Zia rubbed at her temples.

"You two may as well have carved my heart out and served it to the king for dinner. That *wrecked* me."

Kali snorted and plopped a chocolate into her mouth.

"Don't be so dramatic. You should feel lucky to be loved in the way Jace loves you. Most people never even get close to that. Even the Prince of Fire somehow gives a damn about you, and I don't think he's ever cared for anyone other than himself."

"That's not true," Zia barked back. She strode over to the bed and plopped onto it, stealing a sweet from Kali's plate. It had buttery caramel inside that melted on her tongue. Kali propped herself up on an elbow.

"You're talking about that street chef, Talia. Yes, Leo cares for her. But not enough to risk his crown. His title. I think that he likes the idea of her. It reminds him...that there is some goodness and normalcy left in the world. Left in himself."

"He hasn't risked those things for me, either, Kali."

"Yes, he has." Kali slid the whole plate of sweets over to her. Then she began to count on her fingers, rattling off.

"He lied about you knowing where the time stone is. Convinced the king to buy into this marriage instead of slaughter you. He didn't tell the king who I was, or that I am training you. He *let* me train you for god's sake..."

"That's not because he cares. He wants something. I just don't know what." Zia sighed and stared at the ceiling. She wanted nothing more than to get out of her too-tight outfit and into her pajamas.

"I suspect you'll find out soon enough."

Kali grinned, revealing candy stuck in her enormous teeth. Zia couldn't believe that this was Lemuria's most feared killer, and yet it was undoubtable when Kali allowed that beast inside of her off its leash. She had not spoken of who trained her, or what her life had been like growing up in the sand dunes. Zia didn't push her. Their friendship had become important to her, and she had learned from Hiro to give people the space and time they needed to share the burdens they bore.

"Kali, I need you to promise me something."

Kali's smile instantly disappeared.

"I want you to promise me that after this wedding, you will make sure my mom is freed. And Jace. You will make sure the others are safe. And once you do all of that..." Zia felt a knot in her throat. "If he somehow gets a hold of the stones...promise me you will end my life before he can use my blood to activate them and power the wave machine, Kali."

Kali sat up instantly, her light brown eyes turning dark.

"*No.*"

"Kali, you have to. An entire civilization can't be wiped off the face of the earth just so I can live. I can't go up against the royal family while I'm bound to Leo. You're the only one who can. The only one who has a chance at beating him."

Kali looked at Zia, unblinking.

"We need you. You are The Bridge. Katya's descendant."

Zia smiled softly.

"What you all needed was someone to believe in, and I think it's time you believe in yourselves."

Kali looked away from her out the window. Zia wasn't sure if she was fighting tears. The girl's shoulders drooped inwards and shook slightly.

"Swear to me, Kali. Swear to me that you'll do it. He won't stop at wiping out the humans. You know that. Men with something to prove will always take *more.*"

Kali was silent. Zia could see the girl sorting through all possible outcomes. She knew that she would never, ever break her word. If she agreed, she would hold true. Finally, Kali turned around to face her. Her eyes were red, but she brought her fist over her heart.

"I swear it."

Zia squeezed her hand.

"Thank you, my friend."

Kali wiped a tear from her cheek with the back of her palm.

"Ugh, don't make me cry!"

Zia chucked a piece of chocolate at Kali's head, and the girl's eyes widened. She lunged for Zia and chased her around the room until they both fell to the floor, laughing and rolling on the carpet. Kali snorted several times. It was the first time she actually looked her age.

The sound of thunder cracking shook the halls. When they looked up, they saw what looked to be fireworks sparkling over the city. The pigmented lights took different shapes- the king's insignia, outlines of faeries, sirens, dragons. And then, in a surprising amount of detail, a bright outline of Zia and Leo was drawn across the sky. She was in a wedding dress, Leo beside her. His crown was on fire. She wore a bright blue tiara. The powder exploded, turning into sparklers.

"It's called *illuminar*—a mixture of faerie dust and explosives. They haven't done it in years, but since there is a royal wedding that happens to be on winter solstice, it is a special occasion."

Zia's forehead was pressed against the glass. They were both leaning against the windowsill.

"I've seen it before. Ren used it in the caves that we entered through."

"Do you miss them?" Kali asked.

Zia sighed.

"Every day. I've never felt part of a family before. Mei was always so good to me, but my time with her always felt borrowed. Friends like these are different."

"Because they are the family that you have chosen."

Kali had her hand lightly pressed on the glass, watching the show below.

"I've never had friends before. Being the Last Shadow...I have always been on the move. The desert tribe I come from is brutal—it does not belong to any one court, and the assassins serve only Death. When we come of age, we are dumped in the middle of the dunes with no supplies, forced to fight each other until only one is standing. You'd be surprised how quickly those you thought were your friends would bury a knife in your spine for a drop of water. The need to survive changes people," she shook her head.

"The Test usually lasts several days. Mine lasted one hour. That was how long it took for me to kill them all and join the League of Ordos Assassins. I became the greatest asset to Ordos in a matter of months. Many of the elders in the tribe tried to kill me because I outranked them, and they felt I hadn't earned the respect of my title. They finally realized that for whatever reason, Death answered to me."

"Is Kali your real name?" Zia asked as casually as she could, not wanting her friend to stop sharing.

Kali pulled at a thread in her dress.

"We do not have names. Only titles. I chose this name when I came here, to the royal city. It means 'she who is death.'"

Her gaze slid toward Zia.

"I repeat the names of every life I have taken before I fall asleep. I did not want this, but Death has always been my closest companion. Until you."

Zia leaned forward and pulled her friend in for a hug.

"If I somehow manage to overthrow this moron of a king, then you will always have a place here—in the family that we have chosen."

"Don't get all mushy on me," Kali tried to escape the hug, but Zia squeezed her tighter.

"You may be spikey and hard on the outside, but I know you're a marshmallow on the inside."

"What's a marshmallow?"

Zia burst into laughter, releasing her from the embrace.

"Never mind. It's a human thing."

Kali's brows furrowed. She shifted her gaze toward the horizon. The moon was rising. It was nearly midnight. Zia was instantly on her feet, moving toward the sink to wash all the makeup off her face. She scrubbed the many layers caked on, watching as a stream of brown and black ran down the drainpipe. Then she unbound her hair, letting it fall in its wild messy waves. Zia shrugged on a comfortable t-shirt and sweater, along with cotton leggings and thick, wool socks. She walked over to the vanity and began unclasping her earrings and necklace.

"Why change? You looked perfect."

Zia shrugged.

"Because I don't need to be perfect with Jace. That's the whole point, Kali."

The girl just looked confused. A glimmer of joy shone in Zia's bright blue eyes.

"One day, you'll know what I'm talking about. I promise."

Kali yawned, rising from the bed.

"If you say so. I'll go distract the guards for you. Tonight's rotation is quite daft."

Zia smirked, shrugging on her warmest coat and boots. It was snowing heavily. By morning, it would be stuck to the ground. Winter solstice. Yet somehow, in less than 48 hours, she would be married. A wife. Immortal at 19 years old.

She hadn't contemplated that piece yet—that she would never die of natural causes. She supposed it wasn't the worst thing, since all of her friends were immortal too, but death had been the one certainty of her life—an inevitable end that forced her to contemplate what it is she wanted to do with her one and only precious life. Two days from now, things would be far less fragile. The thought of living so long terrified her. What if, in the suspension of time, she took for granted her moments?

Kali opened the door and motioned for Zia to hurry. Zia lifted the cloak above her head, securing it around her neck. She wore servant's clothes. If anyone saw her from a distance, they wouldn't find it strange that she was wandering the castle at night. There were always Lemurians working the night shift.

Zia hurried down the halls, tucking her arms in. The wind tunnel blew harshly, freezing her nose and her ears. She welcomed the fresh smell of snow—it was nothing short of magic to her. She watched the thick flurries fall heavily, coating the garden in a white blanket. Water droplets froze on the trees and roses. The candles had burned down, but the lights were still strung about everywhere, making it feel like a storybook. The moon was nowhere to be found, covered by the thick snowstorm.

Zia froze when she saw two people stumble out of the hallway. It was the raven-haired girl that had danced with Leo, on the arm of one of the shadow warriors that had been on the platform the day Leo and Jace sparred for her. She hadn't been allowed to get to know the warriors, which was unfortunate, considering she had the suspicion she would like them far better than the courtiers.

She tucked herself into a nook in the wall. They didn't even notice her as they stumbled passed, clearly drunk. The warrior whispered something in her ear, and she shrieked with laughter, like he had just told her a wildly inappropriate secret. Zia couldn't help but smile. The woman was bred for someone like Leo, yet she found herself drawn to a low-ranked warrior. Leo was bred for her, yet he was drawn to a street chef. She laughed silently at how she once thought she had any control over love at all. Ren was right: love shows the way, and the bravest act is to follow it against all logic.

Zia kept to the shadows, avoiding the glow of the faerie lights. She knew how to get to Jace's room—Kali had made her memorize a map of the castle, including the surrounding land and rivers. *Just in case*, she had told her. In case she somehow managed to escape one day.

Jace wasn't in the royal tower where the king and Leo slept. Ever since he was a teenager, he had chosen his chambers to be in the Shadow Warrior tower. He never wanted his soldiers to feel like there was a gap between him and them. He slept in the same type of quarters as them, ate the same food as them, and fought with them. They were his brothers and sisters.

Zia saw a flickering torch outside of one of the rooms and knew she had finally arrived. It was at the edge of the castle facing the forest. The tree branches were drooping from the weight of the fresh snow, sparkling beneath the moonlight.

Zia sucked in a breath and brought her fist to the door to knock. Before her knuckles hit the wood, she heard his rough voice say, "Come in." Zia looked up and silently prayed she wasn't about to turn her entire life upside down. Again.

She opened the door to find Jace nervously standing up from his leather chair by a crackling hearth. His room wasn't what she expected at all. She would have thought it to be barren and simple, as her father's apartment had been in Periculum.

Instead, there were piles and piles of leather books everywhere. An aisle with boxes of paints imported from all over the kingdom. Oil paintings he had done of different landscapes and faces all hung up over the walls. Sculptures. A writing desk with ink and pages strewn about. Piles of records all next to each other. Various instruments—a violin, a cello, a fiddle, and an enormous grand piano in the corner. It was a miracle he somehow fit it all in his room.

"Jace ..." she breathed, looking around and smiling in awe.

He scratched his head, his cheeks reddening as he grinned a bit sheepishly.

"Poetry, music, art.... being immortal, it is the only thing that has kept my finger on the pulse of life."

Zia whistled, turning to look at the paintings on the wall. There was a rendition of a siren with fangs and dark eyes. Another of an old mage. A Lemurian child playing with wildflowers. A detailed rendition of two withered hands interlaced.

"Who are they?" She asked.

"These are my people. Over the centuries, there are a few rare souls who come into your life and change you. I didn't want to forget them," he said, watching her reactions closely.

A particular painting snagged her attention from the opposite side of the room. She walked toward it slowly. There was a sheet covering most of it. She grasped the cloth with her fingertips and let it pool to the floor. He didn't stop her.

Judging by the amount of dust that swirled toward her, the painting had to have been at least a hundred years old.

An enormous pair of bright blue eyes filled the painting. They were fierce, unwavering, but with a glimmer of hope. Dark, chocolate skin contrasted them. A heart-shaped face and a full mouth with a slight smile begged the question:

"Is this—"

"Yes, it's you."

Zia brought a hand to her mouth, her eyes watering. She felt his breath suddenly at her neck, his warm presence lingering behind her, beckoning for her to turn around. And so, she did. When she faced him, all of the walls between them were gone.

"I dreamt of you, too," he said.

Jace held out his sketchbook to her—the one he had been so upset about her seeing in Mount Shasta. She opened it, and what she saw nearly broke her heart. The pages were filled with hand-drawn moments of her in Lemuria. Sitting on a rock reading on a summer day. Hunting. Swimming in the Black Salt Sea with sirens. Racing through the dunes of Ordos by his side. Different angles of her eyes. Her face. Her nose. Her lips. Her wild, untamed hair.

He drew the Zia that he dreamed of before he met her.

She kept turning the pages and saw the way the drawings changed. There was more weight and depth to them, the lines heavier and more layered. These were the real moments. There were sketches of her in Mei's library, wearing her mother's black cloak, standing on stage. Then her saying goodbye to her father, the twin swords in her hand and regret in her eyes. Then a closeup of Jace's scars from the first time she saw them. The two of them chasing each other through Mount Shasta's forest. The boat in the bioluminescent caves when they first talked alone. Nights spent at Aaliyah's going back and forth for hours. Her in that sparkling dress on her birthday. The two of them kissing. Inka's spine and mighty wings.

He had drawn everything. Every tiny, perfect moment had been captured by his rough shading and lines. It was their story without words. By the time she got to the end, there were still a few blank pages left.

"What goes here?" she pointed, looking up at him.

Jace stared intensely at the page, hoping if he focused hard enough, an answer might appear.

"Ideally, you *not* marrying my ass of a brother."

They both laughed uncomfortably. Zia walked up to him and cupped his face in her hands.

"I'm so, so sorry. I didn't see another way," she whispered.

Jace grabbed her hands in his. They felt warm and rough against her smooth skin.

"There is another way. We can leave—"

Zia shook her head.

"I won't leave without my mom."

"Zia, you can't marry him. You cannot be blood-bonded to him. There is no way to undo that. You'll *belong* to him, and he to you." His eyes were pleading.

She forgot how much bigger he was than her—a foot taller with broad, muscled shoulders and the quiet unshakeable presence of a mountain. Yet here was a warrior unafraid to bare his heart. What a rare, precious thing.

Her throat bobbed.

"I can't risk it."

He turned his back to her, as he walked toward the fire and threw his hands up.

"This isn't how this was supposed to go."

Zia remained where she stood, hugging her elbows.

"How was it supposed to go, then?"

He turned around to face her, his eyes watering. His cheeks red. His nostrils flared as he took in short breaths, then closed the gap between them. His lips were instantly on hers. His hands moving down her spine, toward her hips and pulling her close. Her mouth opened like a flower in full bloom. Everything in her body ached to be closer to him.

He lifted her by the hips and brought her against the wall. Her legs wrapped around him as the kiss became deeper. More urgent. Like this might be the last time their lips would ever meet. She shuddered, feeling the full weight of him pressed against her. He pulled off her cloak and her sweater until there was just one layer between them. She ran her hands under his shirt, digging her nails into his back. He moaned into her mouth, then brought his lips to her ear and nipped at the lobe. Her eyes rolled to the back of her head. She considered selfishly damning them all. For him.

He pulled back, gripping her chin tightly with his fingers. She stared into those blazing, sea-foam-colored eyes.

"Your eyes," She whispered, getting lost in them.

"They're staring only at you, love," He replied roughly. Her breath hitched as he brought his lips to the shell of her ear. "I have been in love with every hidden corner of your wild soul before our bodies met in this lifetime, and I will love you long after. Until this world is nothing but dust and dark matter."

Reality crashed into her all at once. She had never been more terrified in her life. Her heart raced. She froze. She couldn't do this. She couldn't risk his life or her friends. The silence stretched on for a horrible amount of time as she tried to find the words that would make him understand. He released his grip around her, hurt seeping into his eyes.

She stared at the ground, hot tears streaming down her cheeks.

"Jace, I am going to walk down that aisle tomorrow. And I need you to promise me that you'll let me go."

Her heart felt like there were a million glass shards stuck inside of it. Every beat was excruciating. She forgot how to breathe. This was too much. She didn't know if she could survive it. As she looked up to face him, to see the heartbreak and grief all over his face, she hated that this was what she had to do.

But it would be selfish to run away with him and shrug off all their responsibilities—to risk the lives of an entire world, just so they could be together. There was a part of her so tempted to do it, until the rest of Ren's words echoed in her mind as a steady anchor. *True love will never get in the way of your destiny.*

As much as she was asking him to let her go, *she* needed to let *him* go. To trust that if the gods were kind, then they would find their way back to each other. She had long since learned that whatever it was she clutched the tightest was what she needed to let go of first.

He cleared his throat, his voice low.

"That's what you really want?"

She went up on her tiptoes and softly brushed her mouth against his. It was bittersweet, as their story was. Her friend. Quite possibly the love of her life.

"Goodbye, Jace."

And Zia knew as she turned her back to walk away from him, there was nothing in her life that would require as much strength or courage as this—not any stones or kings or wicked faerie queens.

Nothing put one as in touch with the fragile beauty of life than the loss of a great love.

She opened the door, welcoming the frigid gust of wind and turned around to look at him one last time. He was staring at the painting of her eyes. He did not look back at her.

"One day, Zia, I hope you remember."

Zia shut the door before she could change her mind, his final words haunting her.

Zia sprinted back in the snowstorm, not caring who saw her. She ran and ran down the halls, back toward her room. She had to keep moving. If she stopped for a moment, she would fall apart.

Her breath heaved, choking on sobs. Her thighs burned. She raced on, forcing her legs to carry her. She could barely feel her body. Down and down the hallways she ran, the wind carrying her, pushing her forward.

Zia finally made it to her bedroom door, she flung it open and slammed it, she sank to her knees and let all the pieces of her heart shatter on the floor.

CHAPTER 24

I had to square with every ugly bit of myself that night. And you know what? In the hollow silence of that room, having lost the things I had given my life to, I felt a strange freedom. There was no one in the outside world that could change my experience inside. I finally understood what my mom tried to tell me in my dreams. It wasn't me versus the king or me versus Leo. It was me versus me. And no one could save me from me. It was ironically in my darkest hour that I found an uncoverable light. —Zia

Zia Alexander didn't get a wink of sleep. When the tears ran dry, she sat by the windowsill and watched the sunrise over the black sandy shores, rose-colored light pouring over the royal city. She felt a strange sense of peace. The winding river that ran through the various quarters looked like liquid gold. The city lights all winked out at once. It was still snowing heavily, coating Mū in a powdery blanket of sparkling snow. She could see the frost growing on her window.

She held a steaming cup of tea in her palms. She forced herself to take a sip, despite detesting tea. It tasted bitter, but it would give her the energy she needed. She would have sold her soul to Morganna for a cup of coffee from The Magic Bean café in Periculum. Still, the warmth was a small source of comfort.

The worst of it was over, she told herself. She had let Jace go and was walking through the valley of grief with her head bowed to her heart. There was a bittersweet serenity to the feeling. Making the decision wasn't the most difficult part—it was the in-between. Holding onto him through the engagement, not willing to let go of the hope for what they could have had if the gods blessed them with more time. Still, it was more than many got to experience in a lifetime, so she didn't mind the pain.

She could already hear the servants hustling and swirling about in the gardens. The ceremony would take place outside in the courtyard, where thousands of Lemurians would gather in just a few hours. The rest of them would watch the ceremony from beyond the walls. There were going to be enormous screens in every quarter, so that everyone was able to view the wedding. The entire castle had been preparing all week for it. It was the greatest show the realm had seen since Katya's death. Even the birth of the two princes hadn't inspired such interest. People wanted to believe in a love story.

Zia settled into that quiet place within herself that felt like being at the bottom of the ocean, beneath the chaos of her emotional tides. Kali called it the waiting room. Aaliyah had called it peace. Rho had called it nothingness. Zia didn't care what it was called, only that she would make it through the day.

It was around eight in the morning when Kali strolled into her chambers. Zia did a double take when she saw the girl—she was wearing the same outfit as last night, her hair tossed into the same messy bun. Her eyes were puffy. She had her normal no-nonsense look about her, but there was an impatience in the way she moved.

"Did you sleep at all, Kali?"

Kali waved a hand.

"No, I did not sleep. I was busy."

"Doing *what?* You look worse than after we brawl until dawn!"

"I don't see how that is your business," Kali snapped.

"No, but I care about how you're feeling," Zia replied softly. She didn't have it in her to bite back at Kali. There was something wrong. She could feel it. Zia stood from the windowsill and walked over to her friend.

"What happened?"

Kali rubbed her eyes and sighed, "I'm sorry. I didn't mean to snap. It was a long night. Today is…well let's just say if I don't pull this off, the cost will be all our heads."

Zia squinted, examining the girl.

"Kali, it's just a wedding. They won't execute you for one of the details going wrong."

There was an unreadable look on Kali's face. She evaded Zia's gaze.

"You should eat something," the edge to her voice dulled.

Zia debated sitting her down and forcing her to tell her the truth, but there was no point. Kali was a vault. She strode over to the breakfast table and glugged down one of the pink fruit juices. She ate sparingly, until Kali walked over and piled more onto her plate.

"Eat. You need strength."

"I'm not very hungry today. Besides, I'd rather not be so full they have to wheel me out of my own wedding."

"*Eat.*"

Zia conceded, sticking a fork in her eggs. She barely noticed the taste on her tongue. Her mind was in a million places.

Kali strode over to Zia's closet and pulled out the garment bag that held her wedding gown. When she removed the slip, she paused to look at Zia.

"What happened with Jace?" Kali asked, her eyes searching.

"I..." Zia swallowed, blinking back tears. "I let him go," she croaked.

Zia hugged her knees into her chest, waiting for Kali to say anything. She didn't.

"He hates me," Zia whispered.

Kali laid the dress out on the bed, then walked over to Zia and squeezed her hands reassuringly.

"He couldn't even if he wanted to."

Zia wiped her snot on her sleeve.

"You didn't see his face. He'll never trust me again."

Kali frowned.

"I'm not exactly an expert in this sort of thing. But when you are an assassin, you learn to read desire quite well. What people really care about. What they would kill for. What they would die for. And I think that the way he loves you is so rare, the whole universe would pause just to watch."

"Now the universe will watch me with his brother," Zia half laughed. Then she lowered her voice, "I can feel that I did the right thing. It was hard, but I feel strangely calm despite my whole life blowing up."

"Our fear of suffering is often worse than suffering itself."

"I guess you would know," Zia grumbled, resting her chin on her knees.

"Yes. I would," Kali smiled sadly.

Then the girl walked toward the rose gold tub to draw her a bath. Three other servants arrived to help Zia get ready, under Kali's supervision of course. They were older Lemurian women. One had brassy hair and a straight nose. The other was blonde and mousy-looking. The oldest one, who was clearly in charge of the other two, kept sneering as she was bossed around by a fourteen-year-old girl, lacking all awareness that Kali was The Last Shadow.

They scrubbed, plucked, and moisturized every inch of Zia's body. Then they started on her hair. The oldest woman, Maya, had such sharp nails she thought her scalp was bleeding. Kali redid most of her work, slapping her hands away and showing her how to do it properly.

The whole time, Zia focused on the breathing exercises that Mei had taught her. She barely noticed them poking and prodding at her. Her eyes remained closed as she climbed down the well within herself, every breath centered her.

She floated along within herself. Zia had never thought to explore her own subconscious. Everyone's looked different. Hers was an ocean. She let herself dissolve into the natural tides and rhythms of her psyche, until the space between her thoughts became the space she occupied. She forgot her own name. She forgot her story. She was nobody.

She heard a voice in the distance calling to her. It sounded like it was shouting at her above the surface. It took her a moment to puzzle together that the voice belonged to Kali. Then, the girl pinched her shoulder, and it was like Zia instantly shot back up to the surface. Her eyes flung open. The other handmaidens were gone.

"Where is everyone?" She asked.

"They'll be back. We're done, except for your eye makeup. You were sitting there for three hours." Kali said, hands on her hips.

Zia shook her head slowly.

"There's no way."

Kali held out the palette of gold eyeshadow that was in her hand and began patting it to the ducts of Zia's eyes. Zia did her best not to flinch. Having someone's finger in her eyeball wasn't a foreign feeling anymore, but it also wasn't a pleasant one. She missed Ren's magic terribly.

"What were you thinking about?"

Zia shrugged.

"For the first time in my life, I wasn't thinking at all."

Kali squinted as she examined her work, moving Zia's face to the right and left beneath the faerie lights.

Kali tightened her grip on her chin.

"Keep your wits about you. Pay attention to what you see and hear. And for the love of gods, please do what I tell you to."

She released Zia's chin, then brought over the wedding dress. Zia rose to step into it, then noticed that there was more than one outfit within the dress. She slowly raised her head to look at Kali.

"Kali."

"What?"

"You know I can't—"

Kali brought a finger to her lips.

"We can't risk talking about this. Not even in here. Swear to me, Zia, that you will do as I say. If I tell you to duck, you will. If I tell you to run, you will. If I tell you to do backflips and breathe fire for god's sake, you will."

Zia opened her mouth to protest, but then closed it when she saw Kali's chin was trembling. She nodded. For once in her life, she would blindly follow her friend into the dark, as Hiro had once done for her. Kali heaved a sigh of relief.

"Alright."

She opened the dress for Zia to step into. Zia's hair had been crimped in small, shiny waves. It was half up and half down, with little iridescent pins holding it in place.

The dress was not what she would have chosen for herself, but it could have been worse—a strapless, lacey corset with intricate beading that flowed into enormous, puffy skirts with a train that extended ten feet. The Tree People were to help carry it during the ceremony. The dress was a shimmering gold accented by the ruby necklace and ring Leo had bought for Zia. Ren would have fallen over backward if she had seen the outfit.

The guards knocked on the door, ready to escort her. Kali gripped her upper arm tightly when she went to answer. Her voice was so low it would have been impossible for any Lemurian ears to hear.

"Do you remember the maps I made you memorize? Every street and river?"

Zia's pulse quickened.

"Yes."

"Alright then. Best wishes for the bride. I'll be at the ceremony."

She pulled Zia into an abrupt hug and squeezed. Zia's eyes widened. Kali had never hugged her—only suffered through the times Zia forced her into it. When she pulled away, she winked, despite the silver that lined her eyes.

"Good luck, my friend."

"Thank you," Zia replied, and Kali knew that she meant for far more than just helping her get ready.

Zia kept counting her breaths as she walked toward the door. Inhale for four. Exhale for four. She grabbed the handle with her perfectly manicured hand and greeted two familiar guards. They had never spoken or looked at her directly, and always had their faces shadowed by enormous, thick hoods.

The same older servants were waiting next to the guards, there to assist with the dress as she traveled to the courtyard. They only spoke Old Lemurian, so they hadn't bothered introducing themselves to her, assuming she couldn't speak it. The oldest one, Maya, smiled tightly and bowed her head. The other two servants grabbed the train and gestured for Zia to walk.

It was early in the afternoon. The king's secretary had hired several performers from the royal city of Mū to entertain them all before the wedding. Everyone was invited, no matter where they hailed from in the realm. Except for the sirens. Despite strained peace with the faerie court, the royals had never gotten along with the siren court. The king called them uncivilized. Barbaric, even. Zia had just assumed that meant he couldn't control them.

As they walked, the servants whispered behind her.

"This seems like a lot of fuss for some ordinary human," the brassy-haired servant said in Old Lemurian.

"There's no way she's the one from the prophecy. Poor Prince Leo. She's not even pretty," the blonde one sneered.

"I heard she nearly destroyed his majesty's throne room and held a blade to Prince Jace's throat. She threatened the king saying she'd kill him if he wouldn't let her marry the Crown Prince," Maya exclaimed.

Zia snorted. The lengths to which the truth got twisted were comical.

"That can't be true. How could a human threaten the longest reigning king in history?" The brassy haired one whispered.

Maya lowered her voice further, "Maybe she's got magic of her own. If she's really The Bridge—"

Maya was interrupted as the three of them slammed face-first into Zia's back. They didn't notice that she had abruptly stopped walking. She shot a look over her shoulder and spoke in Old Lemurian.

"You know, it's not very polite to bash your princess on her wedding day," she said, examining her freshly manicured nails.

Maya's eyes bulged out of her head. The others gasped and put hands to their mouths. They instantly bowed.

"Your Majesty, I'm so sorry, we never would have said anything unless—"

"Unless you thought I couldn't understand you," Zia scowled at them.

She brought a hand to the female guard's shoulder.

"Can you please see to it that these three are removed and never assigned to me again?"

The guard's hood fell, revealing a familiar face. Zia blinked slowly when she found herself staring at none other than Alita, the blacksmith from The Trials. Her eyes were full of anger as she looked at the ladies. She had a shaved head, piercing eyes, and wore several daggers along her body. Alita jerked her chin toward the other guard, an enormous man that never spoke, and he began dragging the ladies away. Maya yanked out of his grasp.

"P-please...don't tell the prince." Her hands were shaking.

What was the punishment when a servant stepped out of line? How bad had the king or Leo disciplined them in the past? Zia squared her shoulders at the woman.

"Unlike you three, I deal with my problems directly. Now get out of my sight before I personally drag you out. I am not as nice as our friend here," she snapped, gesturing to the male guard, who didn't look nice at all.

He dragged them all away. Zia bunched up her silk train in her hands, then turned to Alita, who had an amused look on her face. She had bright gold eyes and light brown skin with a sprinkle of freckles all along her nose.

"This dress is odious," Zia grunted, doing her best to walk without help.

"This court is odious." The guard replied under her breath.

The two women grinned at each other.

"Is your name Alita by any chance?" Zia asked as casually as she could.

"Yes. How did you know?" Alita frowned.

"Oh, no reason. I heard one of the other guards say your name," she replied quickly.

Alita grabbed her silk train, and Zia yanked it away.

"You really don't have to do that."

Alita smiled at Zia with her full lips.

"For the princess and future queen, it is an honor."

They walked slower than necessary. Alita seemed to sense that Zia was savoring every last second of her mortal life. It felt like she was walking toward her own execution, except everything was far more sparkly than the gallows.

"Alita…you don't happen to make weapons, do you?"

Alita smiled from ear to ear, revealing her sharp, perfectly white teeth.

"Yes, majesty. I am Lemuria's finest blacksmith. They brought me on as a guard not too long ago, since I make all the Shadow Warriors' weapons."

Zia felt chills bloom on the back of her neck, turning toward Alita.

"Did you ever make twin blades with two sapphires on the hilt? For my mother? Sahara Alexander. She's a healer—"

Alita grabbed Zia by the elbow, her eyes narrowing.

"Keep your voice down, majesty."

"Call me Zia before I vomit all over my wedding dress, please."

Amusement danced in Alita's eyes. She dipped her chin.

"Alright, Zia. Yes. I made those blades for her. She is why I accepted my post here two months ago. Sahara is the kind of woman you don't say no to, you see. A quality, it appears, that she passed on to you."

Music sounded in the distance. The performances were starting.

"Why did she want you in the castle?"

Alita's eyes darted, searching every corner and castle wall for anyone listening.

"For you, Zia. She said it was a matter of life or death."

Zia's head was pounding. The whole world had played in The Trials for nearly two decades, and yet, the entire time, the game had been a blueprint for her. Because of her mother's and Rho's invention, she knew the city like the back of her hand. She knew who to trust, and who not to. Alita hadn't been in her guard rotation before, which meant there had to be a reason she was there on her wedding day of all days.

Alita ushered her quickly toward the courtyard. They passed the gardens and crossed a crystal bridge that was built over the mouth of the river that flowed through the city and into the sea. It was high up enough that the fall would be deadly. Even for a Lemurian. Zia did her best not to trip and conceded to allowing Alita to help carry her train.

On the other side of the bridge, there was a pyramid-shaped archway with roses dangling from the top point and several faerie lights glittering along the sides. Zia was doing her best not to shiver. The king had asked Leo to use some of his magic to seal the courtyard in a cocoon of warmth.

They cleared the archway, and warmth instantly enveloped Zia. It was the afternoon, but they only had a few hours of sun left, since it had been setting earlier and earlier.

A thousand heads turned to look toward Zia at once. They were all packed into the courtyard, standing shoulder to shoulder—thieves and gamblers from the Ghost Market, artists dressed in their finest, Lemurian families, and faeries.

The courtyard smelled sweet. Too sweet. Flowers, incense and flavored wax candles all permeated the air, as though they could cover up the stench of the lie they were telling. The crowd cleared a path for her, revealing her soon-to-be husband. He was sitting next to the king and his inner circle, sipping a glass of wine as he made the rest of the table laugh.

He looked immaculate as always. His dark red hair was slicked back into a tight bun. He had his finest crimson coat with gold embroidery and the king's pyramid insignia. His leather boots looked brand new, and one of the Tree People sat on their knees polishing them.

She steadied her breath, walking faster, grateful for the grounding presence of Alita behind her. She prayed Kali would arrive soon. She could use another familiar face.

As Zia walked, she passed some faces she recognized from her day in the city with Leo, including Talia who gave her a small smile. Many of them whispered in Lemurian, staring at her with curious eyes. Zia did her best to tune out the conversations. Either they thought she was their perfect savior, or a harlot stealing their prince's heart. Praise or blame—it was all the same to her, at this point. None of it was real.

There was a small row of chairs for the royal family and the closest courtiers beneath the stage. A thick line of guards separated them from the people of the city. She took a seat in a red velvet chair with gold lining next to Leo. He smiled approvingly when he saw her. The king didn't so much as turn his head to look at her, though his sneering, sniveling advisors certainly did a good, long examination. She crumpled in her seat, thankful to be facing away from the prying eyes of the crowd.

Alita stood next to her, guarding her for the day. The best of the Shadow Warriors had been selected to protect the royal family. Except Jace. There was no sign of him anywhere. Zia didn't blame him, nor did she expect him to appear at all.

The stage was crafted of flower and stone, with a floral archway in the center for them to marry under. The archway had images of Zia and Leo carved into it, along with the King's insignia and Leo's fire. It was a gift from the Tree People. There was no carving that acknowledged where she had come from, or any semblance of who she was before being his wife.

An enormous, single flaming lotus flower floated in the center of the archway—a symbol to honor their love. She wished she could throw it on the stage and burn all of it to the ground.

"Happy wedding day," Leo whispered into her ear.

She didn't smile or say anything in return. After the hell she had been through last night, there was simply no point in faking anything. They would be blood-bonded within the hour, after all. But before the ceremony, the performers would put on a show. She closed her eyes, listening to the distant sound of the river when she heard a familiar voice.

"Happiest of wedding days to our Crown Prince, Leo, and his soon-to-be wife!"

She didn't have a name. Just "wife." That was how they would think of her from now on.

Zia looked up from her seat to see none other than Stefan and Dex on stage, the two mages she had fought in The Trials. She straightened. All the characters from The Trials, appearing on her wedding day. Her mother had somehow prepared for her this moment. She thought of her locked away in the healer's quarters.

The first thing she would demand as princess was that her mother was freed.

Stefan and Dex looked identical to how they had in The Trials. Stefan had white hair, pale skin, and two different colored eyes. He had a horrible grin that would have sent children running, and spindly limbs that made him appear like he was on stilts. Dex was a stout, meaty man with muscles on top of his muscles, who clearly acted as Stefan's bodyguard. They were both mages, masters of voodoo and the dark arts. They were also the most connected people in the Ghost Market—they had their hands in nearly every dealing.

"Long may they reign!" Stefan chuckled darkly. He held out a long, black staff with a flame burning on the end. He blew on it harshly. The fire exploded on the stage, then took the shape of an enormous dragon. The dragon sailed above the crowd, doing circles and opening its enormous jaw. Zia could feel the heat burn her cheeks. It made her think of Inka, locked in the castle dungeons. She had freed the mighty creature from one tyrant only to give her to another.

Leo was watching the dragon in awe and erupted into loud applause. The crowd followed seconds later. Stefan did many different fire tricks, in honor of the prince. He showed a rendition of Leo slaying a siren. Of Zia and him, married. Many different burning depictions, all meant to blow up his ego, as if he needed more of that.

Still, Zia paid close attention. There was clearly something her mother wanted her to see, if she thought Stefan and Dex important enough to have Rho help her build characters for them. Stefan bowed at the waist for the applause, then held up a hand for them all to fall silent.

"My magic pales in comparison to our magnificent Crown Prince. Would his Majesty come onto the stage and give us a demonstration?"

The crowd yelped and hollered. Leo shook his head, feigning being shy. Zia knew it would take all of ten seconds for him to race onto the stage. She was right. The prince rose from his seat and climbed onto the platform, standing next to Stefan. He was wearing his crown of wildfire. He held up both hands for the audience to quiet.

Then his eyes turned into burning flames. His hair. It erupted all around the stage. A wildfire, beautiful yet destructive. He picked up the flaming lotus in the center of their wedding archway and placed it on his head, in the center of his crown. Then he blew a breath toward Stefan, encircling him in fire.

"Should I burn him?" Leo laughed. The royals laughed with him, delighting in the demonstration of his power. Zia twisted in her seat to see several members of the city crowd shifting nervously. They were used to the prince burning people alive.

The flames grew hotter.

"Your majesty, if you could please not roast me alive that would be marvelous," Stefan called.

But Leo was looking at his father, who was nodding in approval. He didn't stop.

Stefan muttered beneath his breath, then took out a familiar powder from his pocket. It was the black, explosive powder that blinded everyone in The Trials when Zia had rescued the siren. He slammed it on the floor just as the fire around him exploded, and the powder exploded with it.

When the blinding smoke and flames cleared, Stefan and Dex were gone.

Everyone clapped, thinking it had all been a show, but Zia saw the frustrated look in Leo's eyes, and the disappointment on the king's face.

Zia fought a smile, for she now knew exactly where to find that disappearing powder, or any other unsolicited items she might need. Since the real-life versions of them wouldn't know her, or remember how she had thoroughly pummeled them, she could convince them to do business with her. She would need to pay through the teeth for their discretion, though.

The following hour flew by faster than she would have liked. Circus performers from Morganna's court took the stage, doing back flips off the castle walls and bending their bodies into shapes that made it seem like their bones were made of taffy. The kingdom's favorite singer, a faerie with bright pink hair and rose-gold eyes, sang all of the old Atlantean songs. Each performance was met with the level of applause that the royals gave.

The silver-haired musicians, whose names she desperately needed to learn, came onto the stage. They were to play throughout the whole ceremony. Several of the guards moved a grand piano for the older man. It was nicer than the one he usually played on. His wife was ready with her violin. Both of them wore white suits and bowed to Zia. Not any of the royals...just her. She was surprised Leo didn't incinerate them on the spot, let alone allowed them to come at all.

The Lemurian man didn't touch his piano, but the moment the violin sounded, Leo stood to face her, offering his hand.

"It's time."

She felt the hundreds of eyes burning into her back and accepted. There was a tug at her skirt, and she whirled around to see two of the Tree People already grabbing her silk train. One of them was the same one who had been there in the tent when she was captured. They walked up onto the stage. She felt like her legs were made of jelly. Still, she kept her chin held high.

It was nothing like a human wedding, save for the archway and the audience. First, one of the Lemurian priests was to say a list of prayers in their honor. There were no vows, because their blood was the vow. Then, the king would give a speech, offering a blessing. And finally, they would fill each other's cups with their blood and drink. Zia would become immortal, bound to Leo forever. She wasn't sure how it worked with the magic—if they would share each other's powers, somehow.

Everything about the ceremony felt wrong. Snow was falling harshly, but it melted on the invisible dome. Leo stood across from her with the flaming lotus on his head. One of the Tree People brought a silk cushion with a tiara on top. They had it specially made for her to match her ring—a giant blood ruby in the center, with crushed mermaid tears all surrounding.

Zia bent down, allowing them to place it on top of her head. She couldn't help but notice the way their branched hands shook as they did it. When she rose, she noticed the musician still hadn't touched his piano, despite his wife playing her violin.

A Lemurian priest was making his way through the crowd. He was an older, wrinkled man who was bald. His body trembled as he walked, his eyes nearly white, like the king's. He wore a tall pyramid-shaped hat and red silk robes. A giant crystal hung from his neck.

The whole crowd seemed to be holding their breath as he made his way up the stage, under the archway. His robes covered his feet, making him appear to be floating toward them. The way he held his chest out and his chin high certainly made him seem like he was above such a thing as a wedding.

He nodded slightly to Zia, and then to Leo. Lemurian priests never bowed. Since they were the mouthpiece of the gods, they technically weren't under the king's reign, though they relished in his luxuries.

He held up both hands and smiled, speaking in Lemurian.

"My blessed children, thank you for gathering here today. Every union is a symbol of our final union—the one with us and the gods. Today we unite two mighty bloodlines to create peace and prosperity for all of the gods' children."

He gestured toward Zia. She thought he smelled like rot.

"There is nothing in existence that is not held within the gods' arms! Even the human species, with whom we share this great planet. From this moment forward, we shall accept them as part of our people! When we rise to the surface again, there shall be a place for them, and we will show them the ways of our people."

The priest sneered slightly, and Zia could hear the nobility chuckle. The place they had in mind for humans was at the bottom of the ocean.

"Today, our Crown Prince of Fire, Leo, shall be joined with our long-awaited Bridge, Zia. Their blood shared is an unwavering commitment to serve not only each other, but all of Lemuria!"

He raised his hands up and the whole crowd cheered. The priest then closed his eyes and placed a hand on both their shoulders. He began praying quickly. There were ten different prayers. For their loyalty. Their health. Their prosperity. Their power. Their love. It went on and on, and with each prayer Zia felt like the walls were closing in. She wasn't sure she was breathing. His hand on her shoulder felt slimy. She wanted to hurl her guts up all over his pristine robes that clearly had known nothing of the suffering of his people.

When he was finished, his eyes opened, looking colder than ever.

"And now, a word from our mighty king!"

Zia forced her face into neutrality as the king rose from his chair, walking onto the stage. The guards followed him, and with each footstep, she felt her blood boil. All she could think of was the day in his throne room, and her promise that he would never own her. She didn't feel that way now as she stared at the empty crystal goblets.

The king stood in front of the archway and prattled off a boring speech similar to the one he had given at dinner. Zia could barely hear it. Her head was roaring. This was a worse fate than death, she realized. Binding her life to a man like this, to a family like this, terrified her, and was becoming real all at once.

Her eyes darted around the unfamiliar crowd. There was a sea of people, yet she had never felt more alone in her life. She did her best not to fidget and pull at her dress.

Zia looked toward Leo, who was watching his father with pride. Though he may have a war waging within on what was right, in the end he would always choose the king.

The panic started to claim her. Her breath shortened as she looked for any sort of exit, when she saw two cloaked figures moving through the crowd, toward the front. Zia noticed them because of the way they were dressed. Two figures in black, keeping their heads down. No one noticed them but her.

Zia saw two familiar blades with glittering blue jewels at one of the woman's sides. Dark skin and a full mouth. Zia's heart raced. She thought she was hallucinating, until she saw a familiar flash of golden hair peeking out of the other woman's cloak. Once they arrived at the front of the crowd, the golden-haired woman lifted her chin. It took everything in Zia not to pass out.

Zia was staring straight at Ren—her amber-colored eyes, that familiar confidence and smirk. She winked, then ran a hand over her face as she turned pale, her hair now a dark brown and her lips thin. She looked like any other person in the crowd.

Which meant that holding the blades next to her was her mother.

When Sahara looked up, Zia beheld the blue eyes that mirrored her own. Sahara put a finger to her lips, and then pulled her hood back over her face. Kali had said it would take a powerful faerie to break the holding spell, and Ren was one of the only faeries left with undiluted magic. Somehow, she had found them. She had come back for her friend.

"Zia," Leo muttered harshly.

Zia snapped her head back to face Leo. He was holding a blade out to her. She hadn't noticed the king finished his speech and was now seated in his chair again. The priest held the two cups underneath them. Zia slowly took the shimmering blade, her hands somehow remaining steady.

Leo stared into her face, searching. He could see the panic in her eyes. He smiled softly and brushed her hand in comfort, chalking it all up to wedding jitters, not that she had just seen her long-lost mother whom she thought was dead for eighteen years.

"For my princess!" he said loudly, his voice booming. He sliced his palm, turning it over to fill the crystal goblet with his blood.

She tipped the blade into her palm, watching her blood slowly fill the other goblet. They handed each other their cups. She could smell the stench of iron rising from it. His blood was darker than hers. She held the cup in her hand, lifting her eyes to meet his.

As Leo was about to toast, she understood why the musician never touched his piano. The top of it lifted, and a small cloaked figure in a black body suit crawled out of it so fast, no one even noticed. Save for her. Zia interrupted him, shouting, "For Lemuria!"

The whole crowd cheered. They raised their goblets. She was about to bring the cup to her lips when the violin stopped. The rest of it happened too quickly, as though time sped up, racing against itself.

The Last Shadow assassin drew a blade across the priest's throat, and he dropped to the ground like a pile of bricks. Her face was covered in black fabric, but those fierce brown eyes were unmistakable. They were the color of the sand dunes in the setting sun.

She cut down the rest of the guards within seconds and knocked the goblets to the ground. Blood and crystal shards shattered, flying across the stage. Twenty men were upon her, and more piling in through the crowd.

Alita was instantly at Zia's side, ushering her away.

"Protect the royals!" she shouted to the other guards, pulling Zia off the stage.

Yet as Zia looked at Leo's face, at the fury and betrayal in his eyes, she knew that he knew this would be the last time he'd see her. He should have incinerated her on the spot, but she noticed the flicker of hesitation in his eyes.

"Now would be the time, Zia, to wear your *real* wedding outfit," Alita said as she pulled her through the crowd.

Zia ditched her ridiculous shoes and unzipped the dress as they ran, revealing the second outfit Kali had beneath it. Thick, armored pants with blades and knives all along the pockets. Zia slipped her arms into the long sleeves, shrugging them over her shoulders. She threw the tiara on the ground and ripped out the combs in her hair.

They were never going to let her marry Leo.

They were only buying time to free her mother—they knew Zia wouldn't leave without her. What better day than a royal wedding, when every guard in the kingdom would be occupied?

Alita grinned at her as they raced toward the exit.

"Welcome back, Zia."

"She's escaping!" Leo shouted across the courtyard. Every guard and member of the crowd turned to face her. They all hesitated, seeing their almost princess dressed like a killer.

"Bring back my wife, dead or alive!" he yelled.

The crowd raced toward her. All the guards that had been fighting Kali abandoned the brawl to chase Zia. Alita's eyes widened.

"Hurry!" she said.

"No shit," Zia snapped back as they sprinted through the stone archway.

They ran over the crystal bridge, careful not to slip on the ice. Arrows were flying over their heads. Alita turned around to throw daggers and knives. Zia was out of breath, trying to figure out the best exit.

They were nearly across the bridge when Alita grunted as an arrow hit her in the shoulder. Then in her thigh. She hit the ground. Zia turned around to race back for her.

"GO! Hiro will find you at Kali's place."

"Alita—"

"LEAVE before all of this was for nothing!"

Zia hesitated for half a second. She saw the crowd of people all shoving each other to squeeze across the bridge. Whoever seized her would surely win a steep reward. Zia threw several daggers to hold off the guards, hitting a few of them in the chest. It was all she could do for Alita.

Alita stood up, clutching her shoulder as Zia raced toward her.

"Go," Alita shouted.

But Zia would not turn around. She continued hurling daggers toward the guards, until there were no more weapons to spare. Just as the last dagger took flight, and she was about to reach her, Alita leaped off the bridge.

There was no way she could survive the fall. Zia screamed her name, seeing her body hit the water. The river current turned red with her blood. She stood there paralyzed for a moment, until an arrow sailed past her ear and the guards flooded the bridge.

Her heart twisted as she pivoted back, clearing the other side of the bridge as tears ran down her face. Alita had known Zia would never leave her. Yet another person who had died for her.

Zia kept running, doing her best to move in a random pattern to avoid the arrows. She raced through the tunnels, trying to make it to the exit she and Kali always used to clear the castle.

Torches lined the corridors as she sprinted through them. She supposed one perk of the wedding was that the castle was void of guards, all of them currently pursuing her from the courtyard. She quickly approached the wall she and Kali always used and dug her nails into the stone, heaving herself up and over it. Voices shouted in the distance. They were fast, but she was faster.

She fell over the stone wall, landing on her feet. Her ankles rang out in pain, but she ignored it as she raced through the snowy forest and onto the crumbling Shadow Warrior platform. Zia panted as she looked around for Hiro. Shouting his name would be useless. This was the worst place they could have chosen to meet—the only way out was the forest path, unless she chose to brave the sharp rocks and the tumbling sea waves below.

"I should have known you would betray me."

Zia whirled to find Leo leaning against a tree with his arms folded over his chest.

"Leo, please—"

"Please? I gave you more than you deserved. I would have given you everything," he snarled as he walked toward her.

She could hear a stampede of footsteps in the distance. The crowd would find them soon.

"You had to have known that I would never serve your family."

Leo chuckled.

"Of course, my family is monstrous. And you are the righteous savior of Lemuria and protector of humanity. Tell me, Zia, what has humanity honestly done for the planet? My father was right. You're all the same. Selfish. Numb. A virus to the earth."

Zia pulled out one last hidden dagger that had been sewn into her suit. His eyes roamed up and down, noticing the change.

"I watched you train every night, you know. So did Jace."

She nearly choked hearing his name, Leo threw out his hands, and flames danced at his fingertips as he circled her.

"What is it about you, Zia? Why are you special? Is it a spell you put on us, to make us love you?"

Soldiers yelled, barreling through the forest along with members of the crowd. Right as they cleared the two Albizia trees, Leo encircled the whole platform in fire.

Zia shook her head.

"You don't love me, Leo. I don't think you even know what love is."

Her face heated as his flames sailed toward her. She flipped out of the way in time, skidding to her knees on the platform. He bared his teeth.

"I offered you the world."

"I was always meant to create my own world," she said coldly.

Zia raced to leap over the edge, taking her chances with the rocks, but the flame shot up like wildfire. She jumped back, feeling it singe her arms. When she turned around, he was a few feet from her.

"Why, Leo? Why did you lie to the king about your suspicions that I knew where the time stone was? Why did you keep me alive?"

Leo whispered as low as possible.

"Because, Zia, after we were married, I was going to imprison my father. I was going to have you, a Psukhē, go through his mind and discover the identity of my mother. I was going to make you see if she was still alive. It's why I didn't let him kill Sahara—because I *understand*. I am merciful. And then, I was going to kill him. You would have been my queen, ruling at my side for an eternity."

All this time, Leo had waited for her, because The Bridge was meant to return with Katya's powers. It had always been in the prophecy. It was why he hadn't killed his father for the throne yet, because within his mind was the truth about his mom, who he had spent centuries looking for.

Leo brought a hand to her throat. She could feel her skin blistering and boiling in his tight grip.

"But I have no use for those who betray me." He dropped her to the ground. Her knees slammed onto the concrete, but she barely felt the pain. As she coughed up smoke in her lungs, all she could see was his boots walking away from her.

"Goodbye, Zia," he said coldly.

She gasped for air, crawling toward the edge. The whole platform was encircled. There was barely any oxygen left.

Zia heard a loud *thump* on the ground. She opened her eyes to see Leo, gripping at his shoulder which was gushing blood.

Because buried in his collarbone was a silver arrow.

"Hiro..." she called weakly, collapsing onto the ground.

A great roar rattled the sky, followed by the sound of flapping wings. She looked up to see the great shadow of a dragon hovering above her. Ice shot out of its mouth, turning the flames into a glacier wall. The temperature went from boiling to freezing.

Inka.

Zia stumbled to her feet, barely able to hold herself upright.

The dragon sailed in a circle, preparing to land. Zia dug her feet into the ground, doing her best to steady herself as gusts of wind shook the platform.

And sitting on her back, top hat and all, was Hiro.

He grinned.

"Come on, Z! You don't even invite your best friend to your wedding?"

She burst into tears and laughter, her whole body shaking as she wheezed from the smoke in her lungs. She couldn't believe that this was real. Her best friend had come back for her.

"We don't have time for all that! Get on, before that prick of a prince decides to turn us into ash."

Zia didn't have any strength left. She tried to stand, but her legs wobbled. She nearly hacked up her lungs coughing. Hiro Folded right off Inka's back, appearing beside her. He bore her weight.

Inka blinked her large yellow eyes at Zia as if in hello. Hiro scooped her into his arms and carried her. Getting her onto Inka's back proved difficult, but she used her last remaining energy to haul herself up.

Several soldiers attempted to climb the wall of ice. Inka roared, shooting icy spears their way, imprisoning them in their own frozen tombs. Leo was already gone from the platform. Zia couldn't see him anywhere.

"Inka, we're on a tight schedule here!" Hiro shouted. He squeezed Zia tight as the dragon snarled in response, then flapped her wings, preparing to launch them into the sky. Within seconds, they were airborne, sailing above the forest.

As they flew higher and higher up, Zia saw shining red hair below. Leo was staring up at her from the forest floor, his face twisted in fury. He had a clear shot at them and could easily burn Inka's wings, forcing them to fall out of the sky again. Only a few more seconds until they were concealed by the cloud cover.

Instead, he simply nodded at Zia, making it clear that those few seconds he was giving her were a gift.

"How the hell did you—"

"I'll explain later, Z! Your mom and Ren are meeting us at the ship," Hiro shouted.

"What ship?" she yelled.

"There is a pirate who goes by Ash. He's the only one crazy enough to get us out of here. Rho is at the Ghost Market negotiating with him, and that's where I'll be dropping you off, and picking up Kali. We all have to split up. They'll expect you to be with me."

"Won't they see that I'm not with you?" She asked.

"No. That's why Kali is wearing the same suit as you. From this high up, they won't be able to tell the difference."

Inka began to fly lower and lower toward the edge of the Black Salt Sea. The Ghost Market rested next to the shores, and the waves were loud enough to drown out the flapping of a dragon's wings. The darkness and fog that covered the market was thicker than usual as it mixed with the solstice snow. The sun was finally down. She could already feel the temperature dropping.

Zia stroked Inka's neck.

"It's good to see you, old friend," she said.

Inka huffed in response, circling over the black sands.

"Why can't Inka just take us? Why do we need a ship?"

Hiro snorted.

"Traveling on a dragon isn't very inconspicuous. Ren's magic isn't strong enough to cloak us the whole way. Besides, Inka needs to seek out her kin."

The last remaining dragons, all slumbering in secret across the realm, finally ready to wake.

"Where are we going, Hiro?"

He squeezed her tight. She winced, feeling the burns on her skin.

"To Katya's body, where the second stone is. In the heart of the siren court. It's why we need Ash. He is the only one who has traveled there and survived. It is also the only place safe for us now," he added.

She could trust the sirens. Her mother had made sure that she would know that by hiding the answers in The Trial with one. They braced for impact as Inka slowed, landing on the shore-break. Her claws dug into the black sand.

Hiro unfastened a pouch from around his neck and placed it around Zia's. She knew what it was before even checking.

"From Aaliyah. Protect the stone at all costs, Z."

Zia clutched it tightly at her chest.

"I will."

He winked at her.

"I'll see you on the ship. We're going to wait in the water for Kali. You need to get to the Ghost Market. Look for Rho."

Zia threw her arms around Hiro, gripping him tightly.

"I missed you," she said through a half sob.

He squeezed her tight, and she ignored the pain that sang through her body.

"Together?" he asked. The question they had always known the answer to since they were kids.

She wiped the tears from her cheeks and nodded.

"Together."

"I'll see you soon," He grinned from ear to ear. Then he handed her his hooded cloak, so at the very least she could hide her face. She bunched it in a ball so that it wouldn't get wet with the rest of her suit.

"Oh, and this..." he tossed her the Mortemys's talisman—a black bone with a thousand hairs wrapped around it from his endless trove of victims. It was no longer wrapped in the cocoon Ren had placed around it to conceal its magic.

Zia had almost forgotten the rules of the Ghost Market. To enter the market of death, she needed to bring an offering of life to Thanatos, the ruler of the market. Depending on the value of the bone, certain levels of the quarter would be available.

Hiro pulled his top hat over his eyes.

"The Mortemys is one of the most feared creatures in Lemuria. The bone should be worth more than enough to give you access to the highest level where Rho and Ash should be."

Zia fought the urge to toss the slimy bone in the seawater. Her stomach dropped at the sight. For a moment, she could almost smell the Mortemys—death and rotting flesh.

She slid off Inka's wing, landing in waist-deep water, the salt burning her blistering arms. The waves threatened to suck her back. She raced onto the sandy shore, avoiding the magnetic pull of the tides, but she could barely catch her breath. Her lungs still burned from the smoke.

Zia stepped onto the sand, toward the Ghost Market above, wearing the most sought-after stone in history around her neck, to find the pirate that would lead her to freedom.

CHAPTER 25

> *I'd rather be ruled by honest thieves and outlaws than a king robbing his own people of freedom, disguised as a savior.* —**Stefan**

Entering the Ghost Market had been easier than she thought. The ghoul's that guarded the entrance made her skin crawl—some were missing eyeballs, others were decaying with exposed bones. Still, they hadn't even asked for her name when she tossed the Mortemys's talisman of bone at their feet. One of them simply examined it, nodded to the other, and then unlocked an entrance that was hidden next to the main one.

There were five different doors for the five different levels, and she was going straight into the highest. She was surprised when they gave the talisman back to her. Apparently, Thanatos had orders for objects of dark magic to be brought to him directly. She was to cross the ghoul river and give the bone directly to him immediately upon arrival. Zia hoped the wolf was easier to deal with in real life than in The Trials, but she doubted it.

The small underground tunnel led directly to the highest level of the Ghost Market. That was the level that was reserved for only the most powerful of mages, thieves, smugglers, and assassins. It took years for dealers to even get to the third level, so those at the highest were usually either old as dust or managed to collect particularly nasty artifacts. She wondered what bone Rho had given the ghouls to get there.

The tunnel was wet and humid. It reminded her of the entrance of Lemuria. Zia kept Hiro's cloak on, despite the fabric rubbing up against her burns.

All along the walls were carvings in Old Lemurian. She read enough to realize they were confessions of people's horrible deeds and suffering. It made her quicken her pace. The mouth of the tunnel opened up to reveal a marketplace. Fog wrapped around the different tents. Magic concealing the quarter left the Ghost Market in a permanent night. There were a few low-lit faerie lights bobbing up and down. Enough so that she could see. As she swiftly moved toward the ghoul river to find Thanatos, she did her best not to draw attention to herself.

Lining her path was every type of black-market vendor: valuable jewels, weapons, hover ships, and potions. There was a man selling rare animals—river serpents that could carry up to one hundred thousand pounds, useful for smuggling. There were yellow leeches that could cure any poison, sucking out the venom even if it had spread to the heart, and purebred Zhulu babies worth enough to feed a village. Zia wanted to bust open the cages. She could feel the fear and pain of the animals. Yet she knew by looking at their master and the seven ghouls that guarded his tent, there was no way she would walk out of that alive in her current state. One thing at a time.

She continued walking past more vendors. Assassins for hire. Oracles. Until she heard a familiar voice grab her attention.

"Ah, yes. I see it in your future! You will marry a prince…" he sneered, reading to a young Lemurian woman.

She whirled around to see a violet-colored tent with tonics all lined up next to each other. Little powders were exploding over an enormous pot, and in front was none other than Stefan shuffling cards.

"Are you sure?" the girl whispered back.

"Oh, yes. The human won't live long enough to see her twentieth birthday. Not to worry," he chuckled, shuffling the cards behind his back.

The young Lemurian woman thanked him and tossed him a few gold coins, then walked away. Zia realized that it had been the raven-haired girl from the court. Perhaps she didn't care for that Shadow Warrior after all. Zia slid behind a lamp post as the girl passed.

"You must be in true trouble if you're hiding in the most lawless place in the realm," the mage chuckled darkly.

She looked out from around the lamppost to see him staring directly at her. He had his ankles crossed on a table and was smoking a cigar. He puffed little rings into the air, then continued shuffling his cards. He curled a finger, motioning for her to come forward.

Zia strutted over to Stefan, keeping her cloak over her head. As she approached the table, she couldn't help but stifle a wheezing, guttural cough.

"You certainly need a tonic. Black lung is unbecoming for a young woman. Luckily I have just the thing."

Stefan stopped shuffling his cards. He paused and took a long drag of his cigar. She needed to give the bone to Thanatos, but she was growing weaker with each passing moment. His help was hard to refuse.

"Fine. Give me your best healing tonic."

"And who might I be brewing said tonic for?"

"Isn't the whole point of a Ghost Market discretion?"

Stefan chuckled. Dex walked up and placed a small glass vile in his hand, then disappeared back into the tent. Stefan twirled it between his fingertips.

"Of course. Except, the payment owed for *this...*" he shook the bottle in his hand, "...is far less than I would make handing over a runaway bride. After all, no one gets burn marks in Mū unless it is by the Crown Prince's hand."

Zia grit her teeth, then removed the cloak from her head.

"What do you want?" she snapped.

Stefan gave her an oily grin, then leaned back in his chair.

Zia squared her shoulders at Stefan.

"Since the young prince tried to burn me alive today, I am less than inclined to return his *almost* wife. Though I do love a good reward..." he rubbed his fingers together.

Zia wanted to wipe that smarmy look off his face, but she calmed herself. Sahara had put him in The Trials for a reason. Zia couldn't trust him, but he could certainly be useful.

"What do you want?" she asked again.

Stefan sighed, tapping his fingers on the vile.

"I wouldn't complain if you gave me one of those stones everyone is losing their mind over."

Zia scoffed.

"Even if I had it, I would rather be burned alive than hand it over to you."

"Perhaps that shall be your fate, when I hand you over to his majesty," Stefan snapped his fingers, and the whole market fell silent. All of the vendors and buyers began walking toward them slowly. There was an unspoken law amongst Ghost Market vendors. If one of them needed help, the rest banded together. Honor amongst thieves, she supposed.

Zia smirked.

"It wouldn't be in your interest to hand me over to the Prince of Fire. Especially when I have an object that would be of far more use to you..."

Stefan's eyes flashed in hunger.

"Oh? I'm listening."

The crowd was closing in on her. An idea began to form in her mind. It was reckless, but she didn't have time to debate. She opened her robes, displaying the Mortemys's talisman of black bone hanging from her neck. Stefan's eyes widened.

"How in gods did you get *that*?"

He snapped his fingers, calling off the attack. The crowd froze, then returned to their booths. A faerie in the tent next door chugged a glass of blue liquid then smashed it on the floor. The shards went everywhere.

Stefan licked his lips and leaned in.

"Do you even know what a mage could *do* with this? We have hunted The Mortemys for years, but no one has ever come back."

"Well, now there is nothing to hunt," Zia snapped.

Stefan pursed his lips and folded his arms over his chest, examining her.

"You've earned my respect."

"Oh, thanks. My life is complete." Zia placed a hand over her heart.

Stefan chuckled darkly and stood, returning to the back of his store. He pulled several vials and tonics, placing them into a purple velvet pouch. Then he walked back over to her, dumping it on the table.

"I'm going to give you several gifts, human. Each one will save your life on multiple occasions." He pulled out the tonics one by one. "This vial can heal any wound or poison. It is made of a healer's blood mixed with a yellow leech. There is only enough for one use, so spend it wisely. Even if the victim is on their last breath, they can be saved by this." It was a tiny, circular glass vial with black liquid in it.

"This vial is for your lungs. And this..." He took out a thin, long vile with orange liquid.

"This is the bottled magic of a Folder. It is how I escaped your darling fiancé today. Use it once, and you can go anywhere. Though my little eyes tell me that you already have a friend who can do so..." he wriggled his brows. "And, I believe you know what this is. My entire supply of explosive powder, capable of wiping out our entire beloved city within minutes." He put the enormous jar into the velvet bag, then brought his two different colored eyes to meet hers.

"You really want this talisman, don't you?"

"Of course, but an old mage has to appreciate that a human took out one of the most feared monsters in the realm. Especially when *we* have failed to do so for thousands of years."

She was beginning to understand why Sahara had put his character in The Trials. He was clever like Rho, except without a conscience. There was no way to be sure that he wouldn't betray her, or that she was making the right choice by slighting Thanatos his bone. But she needed his help.

Zia pulled the Talisman off her neck and dangled it in front of him.

"I'm supposed to give this to Thanatos, but I am choosing to give it to you. What I would like in return is value far beyond what is in this bag."

Stefan frowned.

"This is the best I have to offer."

"No. *You* are the best you have to offer. I don't trust you, but you are the most connected man in Mū. And I am sure a man as smart as you would bet on the winning side."

Stefan cocked his head to the side, his fingertips pressed together.

"Who's to say you're the winning side?"

Zia winked.

"That's a gamble you'll just have to be willing to make. I'm getting on a ship captained by a pirate named Ash..."

Stefan froze and blinked. Zia raised a brow. "Ah. You know him."

"Yes. He is not a fellow worth crossing. You'd be better off swimming to the siren court."

Zia shook her head.

"I will take my chances. I want you to report to me while I'm gone with any inside information on the royals' movements. I want you to gather your friends—the smugglers and thieves and any other vicious creatures you can find that don't like the king's rule. I want you to help me build a rebellion large enough to take out the Atlantean royals. And when all of that is done, and I give Lemuria back to the people, I will make sure that you are the High Mage of the realm."

Stefan tied the velvet pouch delicately.

"There is no High Mage. You're asking me to risk a great deal for something that doesn't exist, human."

Zia placed the Mortemys Talisman in his hands, his chipped black nail polish showing in the dim light as he grasped it.

"There is if The Bridge says there is. Besides, what's life without a little risk?"

Stefan shuffled cards and pulled one out of the deck. He smiled at the card.

"Thanatos will try to kill you when he realizes you slighted him, you know."

"Everyone is trying to kill me these days."

Stefan gave a low, dark laugh, then slapped the card on the table.

"Be careful, Zia. Only a fool cheats death."

"Do we have a deal or not?"

He grinned, placing the necklace around his neck, and offered her his hand.

"Agreed, Your Majesty."

"I'm not a majesty."

Stefan held up a finger, his eyes darting down to the tarot card.

"Is that so?"

Zia did her best to ignore the sinking feeling in her gut as she stared at the tattered Queen of Hearts card that rested on his wooden table. She ripped off the cork of the healing vile with her teeth and chugged it. The burning pain in her lungs eased within a minute. Mages certainly were experts in their potions.

"Excellent. Now, where can I find Ash?"

Stefan jerked his chin toward the tavern by the gushing river that separated Thanatos's level from theirs.

"Getting roaring drunk at the end of the road."

She nodded, shrugging her cloak back over her face, then shouldered the velvet bag.

"One more thing," he called.

She looked over her shoulder.

"History has a way of repeating itself, Queen of Hearts. It would benefit you to remember yours before it's too late..."

Zia rolled her eyes, knowing that Stefan thrived off of messing with people's minds. She clutched the velvet bag close, feeling uneasy about the explosive powders clanking around in there.

She could feel everyone staring at her as she walked. Thanks to Stefan drawing attention to her, she now had the eyes of the whole market, though they mercifully didn't know who she was.

The gushing river drowned out much of the chatter in the market. Zia could smell the stench of sour ale and wine from the street as she approached a bar. It reminded her of a scrappy version of Mei's library. Faeries gambled. Lemurians drowned themselves in liquor. The owner, who was also the bartender, was a woman with three snakes growing from behind her head who bit anyone who couldn't pay their tab.

Zia cleared her throat as she walked in. The tavern was low-lit with open walls that overlooked the raging river. It was said that the dead swam in those waters. Plenty of brawls resulted in certain death when someone was tossed over the edge. There was a strange cheerfulness in the air—it was a place where people could be and do anything they wanted. The Ghost Market, despite its lack of complete morals, also lacked judgment. No one asked where you came from or where you were going—they simply got roaring drunk.

"What can I do for you, sweetheart?" The woman greeted her at the door, her snakes hissing around her head. She had green skin and a sparkling black gown with a plunging neckline that left very little to the imagination.

"I'm looking for a pirate," she kept her voice low.

The woman examined her, the three heads circling around her, eyeing Zia up and down.

"A pretty thing like you, looking for a pirate. How tragic," her voice was silky.

Zia cleared her throat.

"He goes by the name of Ash."

The middle snake revealed its fangs, venom dripping from its mouth.

"You sure you want to find him? I don't think you know what you're asking for."

"Hey, Meds! Quit your yapping and get me a refill!" an old smuggler called from the bar. She had seen him in the tent with rare animals.

"Would you excuse me for a moment?" Meds said politely. She turned around and walked toward the bar, then refilled the smuggler's drink. Right when he lifted the mug to take a sip, the middle head lunged and sank its fangs into his wrist. He screamed out in pain, staring at the gaping holes in his arm. No one in the tavern reacted at all, quite used to such behavior.

"Say 'please,' next time," she said as she walked away, strutting back over to Zia.

Zia, who had seen a lot in her short lifetime, still found herself shocked.

"You were saying, sweetheart?"

"Um, Meds, is it?"

All three snakeheads smiled.

"That's right, baby. Short for Medusa. All my customers call me Meds."

"Right. Meds, if you could please take me to him that would be great. You'd be saving my life, really."

The snakes hissed in pleasure, nodding slightly.

"He's in the back, gambling with some obnoxious faerie. I swore to stop letting those damn faeries in. You can't trust a clever creature."

Zia couldn't help but smile ear to ear. Even the thought of seeing Rho gave her a feeling of comfort.

"Come on, I'll take you to him."

She followed Meds through the tavern, hugging her cloak tighter. No one batted an eyelash at her. It helped that the majority of the room was belligerent. They walked past the bar and through thick black curtains to a private room.

The room overlooked the river. One of the Tree People was playing the saxophone in the back with a giant mug of ale next to her. Zia immediately locked eyes with Rho, who sat at a giant round gambling table in the center of the room.

The pirate, Ash, sat across from Rho. He had his back toward her, though she could understand within seconds why people warned her of him. His energy took up the whole room. His presence was intoxicating. He had dark tanned skin, chestnut-colored hair that fell to his shoulders, and a bandana around his head. Gold rings covered every finger. His deep red, thick leather boots were perched on the table, and his hands were clasped behind his head.

Rho saw her and smirked.

"Who are you?" he asked.

"Nobody," she grinned. The golden-eyed faerie smiled back.

"You gonna be alright, sweetheart?" Meds asked, all eight of her eyeballs glaring at the two men at the table.

"If you knew this girl, Meds, you would be asking *us* that question," Rho chuckled.

Meds hissed at him. Zia held up a hand.

"I'll be fine. Thank you," she said softly.

Meds handed her a glass with blue, sparkling liquid in it.

"First round is on me," she winked, and then disappeared behind the curtains.

"So, you're The Bridge," Ash said flatly. He didn't bother to turn around and face her. She knew, right then and there, that he would be a raging pain in her ass. Zia strutted around the table and parked herself on one of the red stools that overlooked the river.

He was undeniably handsome. Not in a conventional sort of way. His life seemed to be dangling by a thread, and there was a permanent streak of humor painted in his hazel eyes. An enormous scar ran down the left side of the pirate's face. He was tattooed everywhere. All along his arms were different symbols and pictures—fire birds, the sea, the face of a siren. His skin was the journal he inked his life story on.

"*So,* you're the pirate," Zia raised a brow.

Ash waved a hand in the air, his gold jewelry catching the light.

"At your service. Maybe."

Zia twirled the glass of blue liquid. Rho took it away from her.

"I wouldn't drink that. You'll wake up in a few days with a horrible headache."

"Sounds like a fun time," Ash winked. He had a dark mustache and a stubbled beard. There was a confident laziness to the way he carried himself, like nothing could rile him.

She turned her attention to Rho.

"Hiro sent me to find you. What do you need?" Zia frowned.

Rho tapped his knuckles on the table.

"I need you to convince our pirate friend here to join our cause."

Zia frowned.

"What? I thought he was already convinced. Hiro is riding a dragon to his ship!"

Ash took a drag of his cigar. He tilted his head up and blew the smoke toward the ceiling.

"Yes, I directed the Folder where to find my ship, but told him I refused to captain it without meeting you. I only even considered meeting you as a favor for Rho here, who is an old friend."

"'Friend' is a generous term," Rho grumbled. He tucked his wings in slightly.

Ash shrugged, putting out his cigar.

"Oh, don't be so dramatic. We've had some great times."

"Yes, like when you slept with my girlfriend," Rho snarled.

Ash held his hands up.

"And now I hear you've got a pretty boyfriend! What's the harm, mate?"

Rho lunged for Ash, leaping onto the table. Within seconds, the pirate took his bottle of whiskey and smashed it over Rho's head. Any human would have been knocked out by that, but being an immortal faerie had its perks. He was up a few seconds later, fists up to fight. Ash responded by twirling a dagger between his fingers and grinning.

"Maybe I won't help you after all, Rhoedlyn. Maybe I'll just collect the bounty on *her* instead," Ash flung the dagger toward Zia, and she caught the handle of it.

Zia looked up at the ceiling and sighed.

"It's a shame," Zia took a step off the wall, pulling her hood back from her face.

"What is, darling?" Ash offered a crooked smile.

"That such a legendary pirate is going to die in such a boring way," Faster than the two of them could register, she leaped onto the table and went to knock the pirate's teeth in. He was quicker than she expected—she barely evaded his dagger as he lunged toward her, skidding on top of the table.

She swiftly rolled under the table and plunged her blade up through the surface, narrowly missing his face by a few inches. He flipped the table over, sending Rho flying, and dove for her. She jumped onto his back and pinned him to the ground, twisting his arms until his eyes watered, then threatened to gut him. He yelled, "ALRIGHT, ALRIGHT! Woman, please leave my insides on the inside."

Zia Alexander released him, then went to lean against the wall, readjusting her cloak over her head. She folded her arms over her chest. The saxophone never lulled for even a moment.

"Now that that's settled, where were we? Ah yes, you agreeing to captain us before I make you swallow your own teeth."

Rho nearly choked on his laughter.

"The Last Shadow is a fine teacher, it seems."

Ash started to laugh uncontrollably, gasping for air, then took a sloppy swig directly from Rho's wine bottle. Wine dribbled down his chin and onto his shirt. He smirked.

"The Last Shadow? For the love of gods, Rho! What have you gotten yourself into?"

Rho didn't answer. He was still struggling to control his temper. Zia saved him a response by strutting right up to Ash until she inches from his face. He wasn't much taller than her, but his presence made him seem like a giant.

"I'll keep this short, Ash. I don't have the patience to sit here and blow up your already overblown ego to try to convince you that keeping the stones out of the king's hands is the right play. So, you have two choices: you can agree to captain us to the siren court, or I can toss you into the river with the ghouls. Up to you."

Ash grinned crookedly.

"Do you think I made it this far from agreeing to petty threats?"

Zia pulled out the jar of explosive powder from her purple bag.

"Perhaps not, but I doubt you'll make it much farther if I blow this whole place to hell."

Ash narrowed his gaze, eyeing her.

"Nice try, but our beloved hero wouldn't kill so many innocents."

"That's the thing, pirate. I'm not a hero, and no one in this market is innocent." Zia held his gaze. All the color leached from Rho's face, as he realized that she was not the same young girl he had trained in the meadows.

Ash sighed and stepped away to sit back down in his chair, readjusting his bandanna. He rolled another cigar.

"The thing is, Zia, you cannot scare an already dying man with the threat of death."

Zia frowned and looked at Rho, who just shrugged.

Ash rolled up his sleeve all the way, revealing dark black glittering veins spidering everywhere. Poison.

"My last trip to the siren court didn't go so well. They have a venomous bite, you see. I had one of the mages slow the spreading, but I'll only have a few months at best. So, you can understand why I would prefer to spend them enjoying life's pleasures, rather than traveling back to underwater hell."

He looked down at his own arm, then shook his head as he loosened a breathy laugh.

"It's all just part of the love story, I suppose. Death by an underwater goddess—a fair enough way for a pirate to go out."

"Don't you want your life to mean more than that?" Zia said coldly.

Ash snorted, running his hand over his beard.

"My life has meant a great deal, sweetheart. I've lived more than anyone I know."

Rho slammed his fist on the table.

"You promised."

Ash raised his brows to his hairline.

"I promised nothing, Rhoedlyn, other than to consider it. This is my answer: *no*. I care about you, old friend, but the truth is, I simply care about myself more."

Zia took the vial out of her pouch that could cure any poison. It was the one made from yellow leeches. She dangled it in front of Ash.

"Would this sway your decision?"

Ash snapped up from his chair, his mouth parted as he narrowed in on the vile in her hand. He blinked slowly.

"*Where* did you get that?" He asked. His chest rose and fell in short breaths.

"Let's just say it pays to have a mage on your side," She wriggled the vile.

He swallowed, and she could see the crack in that swaggering exterior. His eyes were misty. "*Liquid life*," he said in Old Lemurian. It sounded lovely rolling off his tongue. "I have searched everywhere, pillaged and bled for enough gold to buy it. Even a drop could extend my life by years. What mage could possibly be powerful enough to brew this much?"

Zia smirked, crossing her arms.

"I'll give your compliments to the chef."

He closed his eyes and breathed sharply through his nose. "Alright, Bridge. Seems the tides have changed. You've got yourself a captain."

Ash held out his scarred, tattooed hand toward her. They shook on it, and she did not miss the look of awe on his face. "You, my dear, are something else," he said in a way that didn't sound like a compliment.

Suddenly they heard shouting, and Meds immediately burst through the curtains. She took one look at the hole in the table from Zia's dagger and all three snakeheads looked murderous.

"Which one of you *morons* lead the royal guards into my gods-damned tavern?"

Through a crack in the curtain, Zia could see guards flipping over every table. They were tearing the place apart. For her. Ash poked his head out, then turned around to face Meds.

"Ah, that's unfortunate. Meds, honey, what's a few guards?" he said in his most charming voice.

Meds gave him a look that would have sent any man running.

"*Nothing*, except for the fact that Thanatos is here. Not once since the city was first built has the royal family stuck their noses in Ghost Market business. He wants what they seek as ransom—a human girl, who slighted him his bone, and is apparently the runaway bride of the Crown Prince himself."

She turned to face Zia, walking toward her. The snake heads were lunging and hissing.

"Sorry, sweetheart. Business is business."

Zia backed toward the edge of the platform. Her heels scraped the crumbling edge, and she nearly fell into the river.

"Keep your word Ash, and *then* you'll get what you want," Zia said harshly.

Ash saluted her, then slipped out the curtain door. She had no doubt he would survive.

Zia took out the orange vile of tonic that encapsulated a Folder's magic.

"Tell Thanatos sorry about the talisman," she said with a hellish grin across her face.

Then she tossed the velvet bag to Rho and smashed the vile of Folder tonic on the ground, thinking of the forest by the castle. It was her closest route to the ship. She wasn't sure how Folder magic worked, but she focused on the scene with every emotion and sense she had.

Just as she did it, she saw Rho shrink with the bag into an ant. He would be impossible to catch in the bar as a shifter. The mage's explosive powder and tonic would be safer with Rho.

Within seconds, Zia was flying through time and space. She smelled the scent of evergreen that hung in the air, and then landed on the muddy ground. The cold wind bit into her skin.

She clutched the pouch around her neck, checking to make sure the time stone was still there, and sighed in relief. Her head was spinning and her stomach churning. She decided then and there that she despised Folding.

The voices of guards sounded in the distance. Zia whirled around to see the west stone walls of the crystal castle. She had Folded too close. They knew she was there.

Zia grunted, hauling herself to her feet, and then ran faster than she ever had in her life.

CHAPTER 26

If you want stillness, learn your chaos. If you want bravery, learn your fear. If you want strength, learn your weakness. If you want freedom, learn discipline. —Kali

Zia Alexander was sprinting through the forest. Her heart was pounding like a bone drum. Its unsteady rhythm roared in her ears despite the months of careful training. Her legs barked in pain as she silently commanded her body to move *faster, faster, faster.*

Understanding crashed into her as she realized she had stumbled directly into one of her dreams. The forest was a blur of green around her. She moved swiftly between every tree and rock. The mossy earth felt like a spongy springboard beneath her callused feet. Mud squished between her toes. The wind blew harshly in her direction, offering her its speed.

They were close, and she knew he would be with them this time.

Cold sweat trickled down her brow and burned her eyes. She blinked harshly as her vision blurred. Zia was filled with dread as she approached the edge of the mountain, knowing the leap she would need to make. She skidded to a halt just in time to see the roar of rushing water. Whitewash tumbled into an abyss, landing amongst sharp black rocks.

She heard laughter in the distance—the kind of horrific, triumphant laughter that turned her blood to ice. They were almost to her now. There was no way out. She would be hunted until her final breath.

Zia clutched the pouch around her neck, truly understanding what she carried now. She wouldn't waste time delaying the inevitable.

Zia laughed as she prepared to make the jump. At least her end wouldn't be a boring one.

"*Zia!*" a familiar voice shouted.

It was too late. He had found her through dreams and reality. Her heart twisted in pain. Zia dared a glance over her shoulder, looking at his face one last time. He took a step toward her.

"Zia," Jace pleaded again.

There was so much she wanted to tell him, but none of it mattered now.

"I'll see you again..." she whispered softly, swallowing the lump in her throat.

Zia sprinted toward the edge without hesitation. Her final step came too quickly as she was suddenly airborne. She vaguely heard him shouting in the distance.

Time seemed to halt as she was suspended in the air. Zia's breath caught as she gazed below. The drop was even farther than it had been in her dream. Much farther. The jagged rocks looked like the mouth of Death grinning at her. She grinned back in challenge.

Any sense of control dissolved as gravity took over, bringing her closer to the ground.

The few seconds of the fall seemed to stretch on for an eternity. She crossed her arms over her chest and kept her body straight as she finally met the bottom. Water smacked into her bones like concrete. She had triumphantly evaded the rocks.

The current held her under, and she couldn't tell up from down as her body tumbled. She kept fighting, trying to reach the surface, but the strong rapids were disorienting. Her lungs were on fire. She needed oxygen. Soon.

Zia opened her eyes in the murky water, and when she began to swim, a sharp pain shot through her collarbone. She knew it was broken.

Zia slammed into a thick branch and barely grasped onto the end. Her palm stung as the bark cut into her skin. She managed to get her head above the surface and gasped for air. The current was too strong to stay above water for long. Her muscles desperately ached, but she tightened her grip on the branch.

A woman's scream shook her. Zia whipped her head around, to the other side of the river to see a familiar figure standing there with her hand outstretched. This time, it was undeniable who stood there.

For the first time, Zia came face to face with her mother.

Then the branch began to break.

She fumbled for another handhold but there was nothing.

"MOM!" Zia shouted hopelessly. Terror ripped through her vocal cords with a scream until no more sound came out. She didn't fear for her own life, she feared that everything she worked for and fought to protect was about to be erased.

The branch broke free, and a wave of whitewash pulled her under.

And then the world went black.

CHAPTER 27

I never figured out how to belong in the normal world. I felt quite disconnected from it all. Yet out in the ocean, I was connected to everything the water touched. We are not so different, really. Ebbs and flows. Destructive storms and days of glassy, peaceful waters. The Sea kept my heart stolen away, and I spent a lifetime returning to Her unpredictable tides again and again, knowing one day I would carry nothing but the stories of my life. One thing they'll say about me is that I damn well enjoyed every blasted minute of it. —Ash

"In the trenches of the Sea
where the fish are lifetimes old,
you'll find the realm's greatest treasure,
seek it if you're bold...."

A woman's voice floated through Zia's dreams like a long since forgotten lullaby. She was singing in Lemurian. Zia could smell the sea breeze and hear waves tumbling in the distance. Soft hands brushed her hair away from her face. She felt a gentle rocking, as though she were in a cradle.

"The sirens know what She holds,
is worth more than glittering gold,
keepers of our past,
until we remember at last…"

The voice was soothing, coaxing her into a kind of peace she had never felt in her life. It was a lovely dream—one that she would be content never to wake from. But the rocking became more intense, and she felt a harsh warmth on her skin. Light blinded her eyes.

"Zia, honey, it's time to wake up."

Zia opened her eyes to find Sahara Alexander looking down at her. She looked exactly as she had in the photo by her bedside table—dark skin, a sprinkle of freckles on her nose, big blue eyes, and a warm smile. Her wild curls fell over her face like a curtain as her gaze softened on Zia.

"Am I dead?" she croaked.

Sahara chuckled softly and shook her head.

Zia scrambled to sit up, not believing that this was real. She turned to her mother to take in every detail of the face she had dreamt of her whole life. Her mouth wobbled, her heart completely cracking open.

"M-mom?" she asked, half choking on a sob.

"It's me, honey. It's really me," Sahara responded.

Tears gently fell down Sahara's cheeks. She nodded and smiled wide enough for Zia to see she had dimples. Her eyes were glistening, and it reminded Zia of the clear ocean after a heavy storm.

The sobs poured out of Zia as she threw her arms around her mother. Sahara held her tightly, rocking her gently and stroking her hair. They weren't the sobs of grief that overcame her when she left Jace. They were tears of bittersweet joy. She had come *home*. In this woman's arms, who smelled like sage and a hundred different herbs, Zia finally felt safe enough to fall apart.

Somehow, they had found each other again. From a video game, all the way to crossing worlds. Zia's whole body shook. Finding her mom was the only reason she agreed to follow Jace to Lemuria in the first place. It had been her driving force, carrying her through her fears and her defeats.

"I know baby, I know," Sahara said softly. Zia clutched her like a life raft, afraid that if she let go, she might disappear again. Sahara held her for what could have been a minute or a lifetime. There were some moments that meant too much to cover with words. And so, the two women sat there, sailing toward the horizon in silence, content to just be able to hold one another.

When the tears subsided, Zia finally pulled back to look at Sahara. She was in her blue healer's robes and had ditched the black cloak Ren had her wearing at the ceremony. Her hair was wild, sticking in every direction just like Zia's.

Zia looked around to survey the ship. Not just any ship. A pirate's ship. The sails were black, the dark wooden deck sleek and freshly washed.

It was high noon. The breeze was blowing, carrying salt spray. It made a whistling noise.

"Hiro and Ren are both in the deck below. They helped me get you to Ace's ship. I kept you sedated while I healed your collarbone," Sahara said gently.

Zia blinked several times, bringing her hand to her collarbone. Not even an ounce of pain. She felt the time stone resting in the pouch at her neck and sighed in relief.

"Tell me everything," Zia said, through the snot and swollen eyes. Despite it being the woman who had given her life, she barely knew anything about her. They were half family and half strangers. They sat knee to knee. Zia was no longer in her battle suit—they had changed her to a pair of baggy pants and a white ribbed tank.

Sahara brushed a thumb over Zia's cheek.

"My tale is a long one, and not nearly as exciting as yours. You first. What was your life like growing up? Is—" Sahara stopped herself, sucking in a full breath to prepare herself. "Is your father alive?" she asked, her eyes searching.

Zia looked away for a moment, hugging her knees into her chest. She closed her eyes, bringing up the words she had carried with her all the way from Periculum. Zia wanted to make sure that she got every word right.

As she spoke, it felt like a tight knot slowly loosened from around her heart. Her voice was barely above a whisper.

"I honestly don't know, but he gave me a message for you. He said, 'tell her that I never stopped loving her. Not for a single moment. That she was the north star that always guided me back home, and I will see her again someday. In this world or the next.'" Zia barely finished before bawling her eyes out all over again.

Even if the king had taunted her that he was alive, he could have easily been lying to get her to agree. Her dad had a target on his back from the government and the royal family. If he wasn't on the run, then he was in the ground. Because of her. The guilt slowly ate her alive.

Sahara seemed to understand all of this and more. She closed her eyes and breathed in the ocean air. Then she grabbed both of Zia's hands.

"Thank you."

Zia's face crumpled.

"I'm sorry. They came for us, and he—"

"He did exactly what a father should have done." Sahara leaned in, cupping Zia's face in both her palms. "Sweetheart, it's not your fault."

Sahara grabbed her face with a surprisingly strong grip, forcing Zia to meet her eyes.

"Listen to me: *It's not your fault.* You have done wonderfully. When you turned twenty, your father was meant to tell you everything. To give you a choice: you could remain in the human world and live a normal life, or you could come here. Lemuria is the other half of your birthright, but we knew you would always be hunted by the king."

Zia hung her head. She couldn't help it.

"Hey," Sahara lifted her chin with two fingers. "We made a choice, honey. Everyone gets to choose, especially humans, what it is they wish to do with their precious time. He chose to be with me. To have and protect you."

Zia felt her face heat. She wanted to tell her mom the truth—that her dad resented her for Sahara leaving, that he could barely look at her most days, that the grief had hardened and changed his heart.

Yet as she watched her mom look out at the sea, tucking a strand of curls behind her ear, she saw in her eyes that she was looking beyond the horizon. As though she may see the man she loved, just beyond those sparkling waters. Zia decided then and there that she would not tell her. If he was alive, then she would square with that when she saw him. If he wasn't, then the best of him would live on through Sahara's memory.

"Mom, how did you know I was The Bridge?"

Sahara turned back to face her with a knowing smile on her face.

"It was written. In the *Book of Lemuria*, a child from our bloodline was meant to not just unite the stones but create peace between Lemuria and the humans once more. We needed each other, you see. I suspected it would be my child. Then I had a dream, and I saw your face. I saw you holding the stones before I even left Lemuria. I woke up sobbing, knowing you wouldn't make it past your first year if he knew you existed."

She smoothed out a piece of her robe.

"So, I went to Rhoedlyn. No one trusted him in the castle. We never knew what side he was on, but if you were going to have a chance, then I knew I would need his mind. There is no one smarter in the realm."

Zia couldn't help but smirk, knowing how much Rho would have loved to hear that last bit.

"Rhoedlyn had studied humans for centuries. He said the best way to tell the truth was disguised in a story. So, we created *Legends of Lemuria*, and built out each level of The Trials, hiding our world in plain sight. The king eventually figured out that I was The Architect and imprisoned me, but the game so openly exposing the realm scared him enough to back off from the humans."

Zia chewed on the inside of her cheek, nervous to ask the question she had been wondering since she first saw her dad's safe.

"What would have happened? If I had chosen to stay. To live out my days living a normal human life."

Sahara shook her head.

"We would have remained under the king's reign, possibly forever."

Zia wiped her snot with her sleeve.

"So, it's all on me then."

Sahara frowned, "No. We all have a puzzle piece to the greater cosmic picture. This is simply yours."

"You better be mopping up my deck after! We don't need to slip on your tears, and you cry more than the damn ocean goddess herself!" Ash interrupted from one of the sails that he was adjusting. He landed on the ground, his boots clanking on the wood.

Zia glared at him, and he held his hands up, backing away slowly.

"Right, I'll just go drown myself in the sea, then. I'm only the captain!"

She couldn't help but crack a smile. Ash's loyalties were subject to change based on the value of an offer. However, as far as pirates went, his presence wasn't the worst. Zia noticed around his neck he had some sort of an instrument dangling from a thick leather strap. It looked like a mini flute.

Sahara interrupted her thoughts.

"Let's get you something hot to eat, honey. You were out for a full day. You need your strength."

Sahara rose to her feet, offering Zia a hand. Zia's whole body was so tight it felt like a car without oil. She shook out her legs and rolled out her neck, doing her best to wake up her limbs. They walked slowly toward the deck, where a buffet was waiting. Luckily, Ash already had the ship stocked since he was planning to embark on a voyage.

They walked down the steps into a dilapidated dining hall with several rusting stools. Ren was lounging in a skirt and a silk black button-down top, her wings poking out on either side. She was applying lipstick when she saw Zia in her compact vanity mirror.

The faerie was instantly on her feet, racing to pull Sahara and Zia into a hug so tight it nearly crushed their lungs.

"We really just pulled that whole thing off!" Ren cackled.

Sahara smiled warmly.

"Thank you, for risking your life to free me."

Ren shrugged.

"It's kind of just what we do for each other out here. Besides, we would have missed seeing Zia in that *hideous* gown—"

"Watch it," Zia barked.

Ren arched a brow, her pointed ears twitching slightly.

"All I'm saying is, that damn assassin could learn a thing or two about aesthetics."

Zia's eyes darted around the room.

"Kali. Where is she?"

Ren piled food onto her plate.

"Relax. She's riding Inka ahead of us to scout our destination."

Zia sighed in relief. Sahara put a comforting hand on her back, leading her to the wooden table so that she could eat. They sat side by side on the wooden bench, with Ren across from them. Port holes lined the walls, revealing the surface of the sea. The water was electric blue, transparent all the way to the bottom.

Ren squinted, looking back and forth between Zia and Sahara.

"You really are the spitting image of her. Nice gene pool," she winked.

Sahara shifted in her seat, clearly uncomfortable at her physical appearance being commented on. Zia shook her head, all too used to Ren's antics.

"Where's Hiro?" she asked.

Ren snorted, examining her long pointy nails.

"Where do you *think?*"

As though in answer, Zia heard clanking in the kitchen. It sounded like several pots crashing together. Then Hiro stumbled out through the double steel doors, holding three different plates on his arms with everything sweet— fruits, toasts, juices, and then Zia saw the stack.

"Are those—"

"Pancakes! Damn straight, Z. Found some of the ingredients in the city before we broke you out. I carried them in my pack all the way to the ship. Priorities, you know? I figured my best friend would appreciate it after almost getting married to that flaming lunatic."

Zia couldn't help but smile and shake her head in awe as he put down plates in front of all three women. They were almost exactly as they had been in Periculum—a fat stack with berry sauce dribbling all over the plate.

She noticed Sahara watching Hiro closely, the ghost of a smile on her lips. He sat down at the head of the bench, taking his top hat off to reveal his hair stuck to his face. He wiped the sweat from his forehead and whistled.

Sahara squared her shoulders to face him.

"Thank you, Hiro."

Hiro had a mouthful of pancake already, but said between bites, "No sweat, Sahara. Breakfast is the best meal there is!"

Sahara's mouth twitched up at the sides.

"No, I meant thank you. For looking after my daughter. For being a home for her when I…. could not. I owe a great deal to you and Mei."

The words were heavy, and Zia could tell they were uncomfortable for her to say. Sahara leaned in and put a hand on his shoulder.

"Where is she? Did she come with you?"

Hiro put his fork down, suddenly less ravenous. His hands were fidgeting.

"No, she didn't. When we found the map in the Boneyard, it ended the game. Clever, by the way. Hiding the translation with the siren."

Sahara shrugged.

"It was Rhoedlyn's idea. We didn't want you to believe the propaganda the king spewed about them when you arrived. We wanted you to know you can trust them."

Hiro grinned with pride.

"Of course, it was. Anyway, all the pods shut down. Mei got us out, knowing that every government assassin would be looking for us. She always had a plan with Z's dad, you know, in case they came looking. He had the book and the blades in a safe. Anyway, she…. fell behind."

His eyes became empty, like he was somewhere else all of a sudden. Zia hadn't seen him cry about it once. He hadn't brought up Mei since they left. She knew that he had shoved the thought of her possible death down into such a deep place inside himself. Sahara opened her mouth to say something, but he interrupted her, holding up a finger.

"Speaking of which! Z, I believe these belong to you."

Hiro scrambled toward the other side of the room where a tall bag was propped up against the corner. Zia made eye contact with Sahara and shook her head, letting her know that she shouldn't press him on it. If Hiro was deflecting his feelings, it was best to let him sort it out on his own. He would talk about Mei when he was ready.

He pulled out Zia's twin blades and brought them over to her. She didn't reprimand him for potentially getting his sticky, berry sauce hands on the handles. Zia held the familiar blades, running her fingers over the glittering sapphire jewel, and smiled. It felt like another limb that was part of her body. She hadn't felt them since Aaliyah's. She turned toward Sahara, who was grinning ear to ear.

"Alita made those for me when I was about your age. I barely used them as a healer, but I carried them with me to the human realm when Rhoedlyn and I were building out The Trials. It felt like they were waiting for their rightful owner."

"*She* has certainly used them," Ren smirked. She had already devoured her pancakes.

Zia laughed and turned toward Ren.

"So…. what happened after we got captured?"

Hiro slammed his fork down.

"You missed it, Z! It was epic. Aaliyah is a badass. She was so furious she brought winter, creating a snowstorm in the sky. She came up with the whole plan of getting you out. We were going to just barge right in and get you, but she told us to wait until the wedding. She knew exactly how to get Inka out, and Sahara. I mean, the woman knows the castle like the back of her hand. She should lead the Shadow Warriors," he chuckled.

"Where is she?"

Hiro stood up and began collecting plates.

"Well, she said she can't leave her property yet. That she will face the king when it's time. You know how she is, ominous riddles and all that."

Zia did know exactly how she was. Her gut was screaming at her that something was missing. If Aaliyah had risked giving Hiro the time stone, it was for a reason. It would have been far safer to leave it with her while they hunted for the other two.

"Why did she give you the stone, Hiro?"

He nearly dropped the plates at the question and set them on the table. There was a heavy, awkward pause. He scratched the back of his head.

"Well...that's the thing, Z. She said that once we were safe on the ship, you needed to use it. Before we got to the siren court."

Zia's eyes widened. She looked at Ren for confirmation. The faerie nodded, her thick lashes blinking slowly. Zia shoved her plate away, losing her appetite.

"No."

"Z, it didn't sound like a suggestion..."

Zia rested her head in her hands, rubbing her temples.

"Each stone holds a drop of the gods' power. Katya didn't use them for a *reason*."

Hiro snagged his top hat and placed it back on his head, then picked up the remainder of the plates.

"Apparently, she did Z. Before the king arrived. It was how she knew that he was coming, and why she split them apart in the first place. The time stone shows us the past, and all potential outcomes of the future. Besides, I'm sure the time stone is probably easiest to wield. Love and death just sound.... well, like a lot."

Zia balled her hand in a fist, her knuckles turning white.

"Did she say *why* she wanted me to use it?"

Hiro shook his head.

"She just said to tell you that this was the only way you'd remember."

"Remember *what?*"

"I don't know, I'm just the messenger and pancake provider! You're supposed to wield it before we get there. That's all."

Zia blew out a breath.

"It will take weeks to get there."

Hiro bit his lip.

"Well.... you should do it sooner than later, Z. If you wield the stone too close to the court, the sirens will sense its magic and try to take it. We can trust them, but not to that extent. Their queen will want the stone for herself. Especially since they already guard one." He swallowed slowly, "Aaliyah said to do it before the seventh sundown. We will be far enough from Mū that they won't be able to track us, and far enough from the underwater court."

Perfect. She wanted to flip the table over, her ears turning red. Every time she so much as got a tiny bit of rest, there was some other magical object to wield or riddle to solve. Sahara stroked her back lovingly.

"Just rest, honey. You have a few days. Let your body recover."

Zia nodded. She didn't have a choice, anyway. Not with the king having his machine at the ready.

Ren stood up and disappeared into the kitchen, her hips swishing as she walked. When she returned, she was holding sparkling faerie wine and several glasses.

"Enough with the gods and magic and all that nonsense. We need to take a page out of the pirate's book and celebrate our wins when we have them."

Ren filled each glass to the brim, giving it to each of them. They drank until sundown, Zia filling them in on her side of things. Hiro laughed until he fell on the floor when she told him of her days in the castle, dressing up and parading around on Leo's arm. They fell silent when she spoke of leaving Jace. That it was the hardest choice she ever had to make. The wine was like truth serum—the words tumbled out without permission.

Ren filled her glass up again and clanked it against Zia's.

"Cheers to being courageous enough to love and brave enough to lose."

Not long after, Ash came down the stairs and was shocked to find them all lying on the floor. There were several empty wine bottles all strewn about. He hooked his thumbs through his belt and whistled, "I've made men walk the plank for draining my liquor supplies, you know."

Ren hiccupped, swirling her empty glass around.

"I'd like to see you try. Come join us, pirate."

Ash didn't need any further invitation. He drained the last of the bottle. Then he began to tell stories of his piracy. He spent much time in the siren court. At first, they intended to drown him, but he offered to smuggle them goods from the city—spices, foods, weapons, potions, whatever they desired. He quickly became the only Lemurian allowed in and out of the court.

Zia supposed that he had been comfortable enough with the idea of death because he had seized nearly every moment of his life. He had more stories than anyone she had ever met. Great loves. Terrible losses. Adventures at sea, sailing wherever the tides took him.

They spent the remainder of the week doing exactly as Ren had instructed: enjoying themselves. Every night when the stars came out to greet them, they would dance on the bow of the boat. Zia and Sahara would talk all day, filling each other in on the gaps of their lives. Sahara had been confined to the castle when she returned from the human realm, but the king hadn't locked her in the quarters until Zia entered Lemuria.

She had worked on all sorts of wounds and illnesses, quickly becoming the most powerful healer in the realm. She traveled all over the continent, discovering new herbs and creating healing potions that had never been made before. She explained how her magic worked, like it had its own consciousness. Sahara said it was more like being the paintbrush, rather than the painter—the magic used her as a tool for healing her patients. Zia found it fascinating, since hers was nothing like that.

Hiro became the resident chef on the boat. He got along swimmingly with Ash, since both of their currency was cheap humor. Toward the end of the week, they were both a deep tan color with salt crusted skin. Hiro often helped him with the sails, asking for more of his stories. It kept him occupied from thinking about Rho or Mei, and Ash could talk for hours.

Ren spent the majority of her days with Zia and Sahara. The three women would nap in the sun together or spend hours laughing about their many escapades. It made Ash uncomfortable, to have such women on board whispering at every hour of the day. He often would flirt with Ren, doing his best to charm her. She couldn't have cared less, and dismissed him so harshly that he would go sulk at the opposite end of the ship.

On the final sunset of the week, Ren walked over to Zia. Zia was leaning over the edge of the ship, looking at the horizon. Sahara was next to her. They were both silently appreciating the sky's colorful performance.

Ren grabbed Zia's palm and dropped a familiar object in her hands. Zia looked down to find the necklace that she had gifted her on her birthday.

"How?" Zia asked, holding it up.

"Kali saved it. She said you never took it off, until he made you."

Zia nodded. Ren smirked.

"Besides, it's way prettier than those ridiculous rubies he made you wear. I mean, they just *shout* that the man is compensating."

Sahara chuckled behind them, her eyes twinkling with amusement.

"She's right." She walked up and unfastened the necklace, putting it around Zia's neck. Sahara turned to face her, examining her.

"You've become a phenomenal woman," she said with great pride.

Zia sighed.

"I have no idea what I'm doing, Mom."

Ren interrupted both of them.

"Who the hell does? That's the most fun part! We're all just making this up as we go. Might as well be bold with it!" Ren threw her head backward, watching the sunset upside down.

Sahara shook her head, smiling softly.

"Again, she's right."

The last of the rays sank behind the ocean. The sky turned a sapphire and lilac color with dusk. They all ate dinner on the bow of the boat, wanting to spend their last night beneath the stars. No one knew what would happen when Zia used the stone tomorrow.

When they were stuffed and had drained the last of the pirate's liquor supply, they all laid on their backs and gazed into infinity. They were quiet for a few hours, appreciating the gentle waves and the warm air. Every part of Mū had its own seasons, from the sand dunes to the royal city. It had been winter solstice when they left, yet a week out into the open sea, and it was as warm as the Caribbean in the human world.

They were all permanently covered in salt, their hair messy from the changing winds. There was a freedom that seemed to permeate each one of them—the kind of freedom that could only be felt in open, endless waters. Not confined by any mass of land. No need to watch their backs from the king. They were safe as they rode with the tides.

Ash stood up and disappeared to the deck below, then returned with an instrument. It looked like a fiddle. He propped himself up on a stool he brought from the kitchen and began to play a cheerful tune.

"Who knows this one?"

None of them answered, though Zia could hear Ren humming along. Ash stared at her until she met his gaze.

"Come on, Renny."

"Call me that again and I'll drown you," Ren cut him a glare, her amber eyes looking like laser beams.

Ash brought a hand over his heart.

"I solemnly swear to never call you said unspeakable name again, if you sing this one song for me."

Ren rolled her eyes, but Zia could see the glimmer of joy there. The truth was, she loved singing, and didn't get to very often. Ren began tapping her foot to the rhythm of the fiddle and sang toward the empty sky.

"There once was a sailor
who fell in love with the sea,
he spent his life

trying to win her heart..."

Her voice sounded like a siren's song. It had a magnetism to it. Ash played harder on the fiddle; his brow furrowed. Sweat began to drip from his chin.

"He knew there was no woman
as lovely as she
and couldn't stand to be on land
for even a moment apart..."

Zia had to admit, Ash was as good at the fiddle as Ren was singing. She supposed he had a lot of time at sea to practice.

"One day he leaped
from his treasured ship
to offer her his love,
and on that night,
a storm came 'round,
drowning his body
where it would never be found..."

The song ended, and Hiro immediately sat up.

"That is the most depressing song I have ever heard!"

Ash grinned crookedly, his eyes never leaving Ren.

"I think it's actually quite accurate. What better way to go out than for love?" he winked at her.

Ren scoffed, shifting uncomfortably under the weight of his gaze. Zia smiled slightly. It reminded her of how she had been when she first met Jace all those months ago. Hiro clapped his hands together.

"This is potentially our last night together, in case Z destroys the fabric of time."

"Thanks, Hiro," Zia groaned. She was still lying on her back looking at the stars.

Hiro grinned sheepishly.

"*Anyway.* I would like to dance! Give me something upbeat, would you?"

Ash bowed slightly.

"Of course. I live to acquiesce to all your requests," he said in a mocking tone.

He began playing a jig, and Hiro was instantly on his feet, swirling under the stars. After a few minutes, he grabbed Sahara's hands and hauled her up, spinning her around and around. Sahara was jarred at first, but then she turned out to be quite the dancer. She knew all of the Lemurian dances and swirled and kicked like the world could end at any moment.

The two of them came over and each grabbed one of Zia's hands. She protested, but then was hauled to her feet. Hiro was right—it may very well be her last chance to dance with the people she loved.

No matter what happened tomorrow, the past few days with Sahara had been some of the best of her life. Her only regret was the last time she saw Jace. She wanted to take back her goodbye and tell him to come with her.

Hiro led the two of them around the boat, and they all stumbled with the rocking of the tides. They laughed and laughed, dancing for hours. Zia stole his top hat and placed it on her head. Then Sahara took it.

Ash never stopped playing. Zia didn't fail to notice that he inched closer to Ren at the end of every tune, nor did she fail to see that Ren didn't inch away.

Sahara finally sat down, out of breath and covered in sweat. She seemed so much lighter than before. She threw her head back and cackled, "I haven't had this much fun in my entire life, I think…"

Hiro twirled several times, then bowed at the waste at the end of the song.

"That's a true tragedy."

Ash quieted the music, changing the tune to be calming. They all sat shoulder to shoulder, looking up in wonder. Sahara and Hiro chatted for a while. She asked him about Rho, avoiding any questions of Mei. Hiro cheerfully told her of their love story—how Rho was the smartest person he knew and seemed to *see* him immediately. Sahara, knowing Rho quite well, said that he was incredibly lucky to have found Hiro. It was the first honest relationship the cunning faerie had ever found.

Zia was out snoring, their conversation background noise as she floated in and out of dreams. By the time dawn came, Ash was curled up next to Ren. He had placed his jacket over her. Hiro was face down on the floor, drool sliding down his chin. Sahara was curled up in a ball next to Zia.

They all slept as the ship carried them onward, toward the heart of the ocean.

When Zia opened her eyes the next day, the stone around her neck felt like dead weight.

It was time.

CHAPTER 28

As a parent, I wanted to protect her from pain and suffering, but as a woman, I just knew better. She was not mine to shield from life, because that makes for an unseasoned spirit. I was there to encourage her to experience as much as possible and trust herself to navigate the world in all of its unpredictable challenges. —Sahara

Zia woke Hiro up first before the others. He yawned loudly, about to protest, until he saw the look in her eye. He was instantly on his feet, with a blanket wrapped around his shoulders. They walked down to the deck below. Zia brought him into the old kitchen, since it offered the thickest walls to conceal sound.

She sat on the counter while he boiled hot water for the tea and adjusted the bandana around her forehead. The pirate fashion was actually quite functional, given how much the wind messed with her hair. Not to mention it covered the three dots on her forehead.

Hiro's eyes were slightly puffy, his hair in complete disarray. He certainly looked like he had danced all night. The boat creaked as it gently rocked, and there was something peaceful about watching the sun wake up in the middle of the sea.

"Alright, Z. What's up?" he yawned again, pulling down different spice jars.

Zia gripped the tile counter, her feet swinging nervously.

"You're a folder. You know more about bending time and space than anyone."

Hiro took a pinch of several different herbs, compiling them all into a bowl to mash up.

"I can fold across space, Z. Not time. I can't go to the past, or peer into the future."

Zia rolled her shoulders out and loosened her neck.

"That's a shame. We probably wouldn't have gone through half of the nonsense we did."

Hiro began mashing the herbs and smiled.

"True, but then we wouldn't have half of the stories that we do."

He poured the hot water on the herbs and let it steep, then turned to face her. It smelled heavenly, despite it being tea.

"Z, time is complicated. It's not linear like in the human realm. In my experience as a folder, when I'm in that in-between realm, the past feels *alive*. As though everything that has ever happened or ever will happen is occurring at once."

Zia tilted her head to the side.

"How?"

Hiro shrugged.

"I don't know. I also don't know what you'll see when you use that stone, but my intuition tells me that you need to be careful. It can be tempting to want to change things—stop certain events from happening."

Zia raised a brow.

"What events?"

Hiro placed a sifter over two large mugs and then poured the tea with as much grace as Kali had fighting. He held it out to her, and she took it in both palms, feeling the steam rise up to her face. He didn't take his eyes off her when he spoke.

"Events like the king conquering Lemuria, or Katya's death. Events like your dad or Mei..." he swallowed, unable to finish the sentence.

Zia gripped the mug tightly.

"Why shouldn't I prevent him from conquering Lemuria? That would save us all a lot of time, don't you think?"

Hiro shook his head.

"The god of time works in a mysteriously intelligent way. If the king hadn't conquered Lemuria, Jace wouldn't have been born, your mother never would have been sent to the human world, and you wouldn't exist.

We wouldn't be best friends, and Rho..." he rubbed the back of his neck. Then spoke low, "I understand, the urge to want to save us all from suffering. Your dad tried to do that for you. Do you remember what you told him?"

Zia blinked, remembering.

"Pain is a part of life, and by trying to protect me from it, he only caused more of it."

Hiro smiled.

"Exactly, Z. Don't you see? Everything that we thought would break us, *made* us. So, I am begging you..."

He walked toward her and gripped her shoulders tightly.

"*Please*, for the love of the gods, no matter what you see, you have to let it unfold. We don't understand the repercussions."

"Then why use it at all?" she asked, taking a sip of her tea. She immediately spat it out on the ground. Hiro cackled slightly.

"The tea is not for taste, you goon. It's meant to strengthen your magic, sharpen your senses. And as far as your question, I don't know," he shook his head. "Aaliyah said that you needed to remember, so that's the only clue I can give you. The answers to our future are in the past. Start with going backward."

Zia bit her lip, debating her next words. She knew it may be her only chance.

"Hiro, I saw your father."

Hiro became unnaturally still. She kept talking.

"When Inka and I got shot out of the sky, I woke up in a tent. He was the one who folded me to the castle."

"How did he seem?" His voice was hoarse.

Zia wanted to soften the blow, but after the conversation they had just had, she couldn't.

"He felt...cold. Hardened. He loyally serves the king. I tried to escape, but—" she blew out a breath. "He's nothing like you, Hiro. Maybe things would be different if he saw you."

Hiro stared at the floor for a few seconds, then forced a smile across his own face.

"Maybe."

"Hiro, are you okay?"

"I'm fine."

"'*Fine is not a feeling*," she threw the words he had once spoken to her back at him.

Hiro's smile became genuine.

"Clever. I'm honestly just glad that he's alive. Mei was always so worried..."

He looked back at the ground and kicked up dirt on the wooden floor.

"I am sure he did what he needed to in order to survive."

Hiro grabbed his tea and began sipping on it. The look on his face made it clear the conversation was over. She could practically see him locking the information behind a backdoor in his heart. Probably near the same door he kept Mei behind.

Zia threw her head back and chugged the tea all in one fell swoop. Her whole body shuddered. The herbs tasted like ear wax. She slammed the mug on the counter.

Hiro smirked.

"Well, that's one way to—"

"We go now."

"What?"

Zia slid off the counter.

"We don't know what will happen, and I can't do goodbyes. Especially not to her."

Hiro's brows furrowed.

"Z, I seriously think you will regret that."

Zia took a sharp breath into her chest.

"I just...can't. I already said one goodbye to Jace. If I give myself that moment with her, I don't think I'll be able to do it."

Hiro's features softened. He looked like he was debating pushing her or not, but their friendship had always embraced whatever the other chose to do or be at any given moment.

"Okay, Z. Let's go."

Hiro led her above the deck, and under the sails to the stern of the boat. The rest of them were still dead asleep. The wind had a bite to it in the morning— Zia hadn't expected the chill. She wrapped her cloak in tight, carrying her blades by her sides. The possibility of death had a strange way of crystallizing life. She became hyperaware of every detail around her—the squeaky wooden floorboards beneath her feet, the different currents in the water, the way the morning light hit the sails, making them appear iridescent.

She had only felt the fragility of her life one other time—in the café in Mount Shasta when an assassin held a gun to her face. If she was to die anywhere, she was glad it was in Lemuria, and that she had at least gotten to see her mom again. To know her. To laugh with her. Cry with her. Dance with her. Tell stories with her. It was more than she had hoped for.

They sat on the ground, knee to knee as she unfastened the pouch and took out the time stone. It was so small, so light she wondered how it could possibly hold so much magic in it. Yet she could feel it, pulsing in her hands. The flesh of a god.

"Aaliyah said you needed to pour a few drops of your blood on it, and then you simply *link* with it the same way you link with people. She said each stone has its own consciousness."

Zia moved to take out one of her blades, but Hiro pulled out a small silver knife. He rolled his eyes at her blades.

"We're not amputating your hand, jeez. I said a few drops."

Zia grinned sheepishly. She offered her hand. He took it in his own and hesitated. The whole world slowed.

"When you got captured, I didn't know if I would see you again," his lips shook as he forced a smile. She could see silver line his eyes.

"Hiro, don't—"

"And I wanted you to know, Z, that you are a once-in-a-lifetime friend. Watching you these past few months, seeing you feel at home in Lemuria, seeing you get so strong and brave, seeing your heart open again..." A single tear fell down his cheek. It was the first time she had seen him cry since they were kids. "It is an honor to call you my family. And no matter what happens, I will follow you anywhere, Z."

It was too late. She was crying now.

"Together?" she whispered.

Hiro nodded, "Together."

He sliced her palm and turned it over to drip onto the stone. As Zia watched the blood meet the stone, she could feel it rumble—like the power had been slumbering, and now it was waking up.

"Give 'em hell, Z," he grinned at her, then released her hand.

Her eyes rolled to the back of her head as her magic rose up from the deepest place inside her. Like lightning striking, she linked with the stone and gave herself fully over to time.

CHAPTER 29

The pressure of time is the fear of death. —**Aaliyah**

Zia was falling, and there was nothing she could do to slow down. Her body flipped over several times. Down and down, she went, gravity tugging her under. The sky was dark and stormy. She didn't even scream. It was oddly silent as she free-fell through the void.

She squeezed her eyes shut, trying not to get nauseous. Within seconds, she slammed into the ground. It felt spongey. When she opened her eyes and moved her palms, she realized that she was on top of a sand dune. Each grain was so soft, so fine that it was nearly invisible. She clutched some of it in her hand, watching the sand waterfall back to the ground. She patted her body down and sighed in relief. She still had her blades.

Zia hauled herself onto her feet and looked around. She began walking through the dunes and grunted, sweat immediately coating her body. Kali didn't get enough credit for growing up in a place like this. It was difficult enough just to walk. One step tired her like a thousand.

Her mouth was parched, but she kept going. One foot in front of the other, hauling her knees up. Her thighs burned and her calves cramped. She focused only on her breath, not allowing her thoughts to wander.

There was nothing around her but empty desert that longed for the day it was once the sea.

She felt like she was trudging through the sand for hours. Her head was pounding as she walked. Silence was its own sound in the desert. The sand seemed to suck up any noise. Even the shuffling of her feet immediately got drowned out.

Though Zia could see lightning in the sky, and dark threatening clouds, she couldn't hear it. Could not feel the wind, or the storm. It was like she was in some sort of strange capsule. She wanted to find the edge. It appeared close, yet for every mountain of sand she climbed, a hundred more stretched on in front of her. The edge was an unattainable mirage.

She pressed on, but without any water, her body was giving up. Zia fell to the ground on her back, resting for a few moments. She closed her eyes and immediately began coughing up sand. It had gotten into her lungs. She groaned. This was not what she had expected.

"They should have picked a camel to be the chosen one," she grumbled to herself. The sand was strangely comfortable. It formed to fit her body and felt like a warm hug. Perhaps she would stay there and just rest her eyes for a while...

Get up! A voice shouted.

Get your ass UP. The voice rang out over the dunes.

The ground beneath her began to rumble like an earthquake. She immediately shot up and turned her head up to see the dunes were shaking and changing shape. Zia sprinted toward the edge. However far it may be, it was her only hope.

She squinted her eyes and saw a sandstorm in the distance—an enormous, furious cloud of brown swirled toward her. Zia didn't care. She just needed to make it to the edge. The edge was her only hope.

Zia roared and barreled toward it, keeping her eye on the lightning that shone through even the wall of sand. On closer approach, she realized the sand was not shifting toward her horizontally, as wind normally would. It was falling from above, like a waterfall.

"It's an hourglass," she whispered. Of course. The psyche of the time stone was an hourglass.

If she stayed in the hourglass for too long, she could become frozen in linear time, trapped forever. No wonder no one was insane enough to try to wield a stone. Even if they somehow could link with it, the landscapes were deadly enough. Yet Katya had done it, which meant Zia could.

Zia pulled her bandana down to cover her nose and mouth from the oncoming sand. She had to get around the waterfall of sand. Kali had said that the assassins mapped their way by the stars in the dunes, but she didn't have that luxury. So, all she could do was haul ass toward the lightning and hope it was the right direction.

The ground was shifting from underneath her, bringing her closer to the sky. If she ended up under the waterfall of sand, she would be buried. But if she stayed on the outskirts, just above the surface, the rising mountain of sand would eventually press her toward the edge.

Zia remained light on her feet, continually moving so she wouldn't sink. Every step had her knee deep in sand, but she kept going as Kali had taught her. It was a dance.

Down and down the sand poured, filling up the hourglass. She could see the narrow opening the sand was pouring through, but anytime she looked up, her eyes were blinded by flying grains.

There it was. The edge. The mountain of sand filled the space, pressing her toward the glass. Her body slammed into the edge, her cheek pressed against it. She reached to grab her blades, but the sand was too heavy. It felt like hundreds of pounds burying her.

With her last remaining strength, she freed her right arm. She took the hilt of her blade and began slamming it against the glass. The lightning on the other side flashed brighter. It was the only way she could see.

She banged the hilt of the blade against the glass again and again and again. The sand had covered her whole body, all the way up to her shoulders. It was creeping up her neck, threatening to devour her whole.

Keep going, that voice said.

She slammed the wall a few more times and gulped her last breath down before the sand covered her face entirely. She was buried by the dunes, trapped in time.

And then, there was a small *crack* noise.

The break in the glass spider-webbed up and up the walls.

Until the hourglass exploded into a million shards and she was free falling through the void once more. Zia gasped for air, no longer entombed by sand.

Zia landed midair, like gravity had suspended itself. She would never grow accustomed to nearly dying every five minutes. Aaliyah had never said what would happen if she died in the mind landscape of another, but Zia had a feeling it wouldn't be pleasant.

She looked around to realize that she was in a library.

In the center of the library was a wooden table with a single, dark object on it. Zia floated toward the table, propelling herself forward with her arms and legs. She had never considered what a luxury gravity was—it was surprisingly difficult to move midair.

When she approached the table, grabbing its edges, she realized it was a pocket watch. She removed the cover, to find a compass on the inside.

This was it. This was how she would sail through time.

Zia clutched the watch in her palm, then moved her arms the way a swimmer would, hauling her body toward one of the shelves. As she approached, she realized each book had a name on it. She was in the A section, and immediately searched for her mother's name. There it was. In the middle of the shelf.

Alexander, Sahara.

Yet when she went to open the book, she felt that tugging sensation pulling her toward the end of the A's. She knew before she saw it, what book she was meant to read.

Atwater, Aaliyah.

Zia pulled the book from the shelf and opened it. Only instead of words, the blank pages changed into memories. Every single memory Aaliyah had. Every thought, every action, was recorded within time.

Zia thumbed through the pages, trying to figure out what she was supposed to know. It felt like a violation, but everything in her body was screaming to look. Zia stopped when she saw the king's face. He was far younger, his normally white hair a deep red, like Leo's. Aaliyah's hair was black as night.

She felt a horrible sense of dread as she looked at the page, but it didn't matter. She gripped tightly onto the pocket watch, knowing that was her only way out, and tumbled into Aaliyah's memories.

Zia landed in the king's chambers.

She remained hidden behind one of his curtains by the window. She figured being seen by her future mentor and her future enemy was not the wisest move, so she pressed her body against the wall, watching through the crack.

The room was cold in every sense. Priceless gems were everywhere, along with various weapons. There was an enormous tapestry with his insignia, but no books or art of any kind.

Aaliyah still had her long, raven hair that fell to the floor, and her staff that had an orb resting on the top. The king was pacing around the room. He was far easier to read, his rage perfectly on display.

"I was supposed to be with the queen! My child was meant to be The Bridge, not some useless Lemurian without magic," he snapped.

Aaliyah brought a hand to her belly, where there was a swollen bump.

"I am the realm's most powerful Elymental. My blood is rich with magic."

The king whirled on his heel.

"And yet, our child has *no magic.* We had a deal. I would make you queen if you provided me with a proper heir."

Hurt flashed across Aaliyah's eyes.

"Power comes in other forms than magic. You of all people should know that. I betrayed my best friend, the realm she built, to give you a son."

The king sneered, "No, you betrayed her so you could rule."

Aaliyah jutted her chin upwards.

"And I will pay for that mistake for the rest of my life."

The king smiled horrifically.

"Yes. You will."

Aaliyah backed away as he walked toward her. She held up her staff and the torches in the room exploded like wildfire. The king was unafraid, though. He towered over her as he stood, looking down at her.

"If you betrayed her, then you will betray me someday. And I have no use for a son without magic."

"GUARDS!" he shouted.

The Shadow Warriors instantly barged through the door. She was surrounded. Aaliyah brought both hands to her belly. She could try to fight her way out, but she was horribly outnumbered, and threatened by their magic. Zia could see it. She was terrified for that baby in her belly.

That baby, who would grow up to be Jace one day.

"Wait!" she shouted. "I will birth you another son. I have seen him in my dreams..."

The king waved a hand.

"Lies. Make sure she suffers, would you?" he snarled at the warriors. They nodded and began closing in on her.

Zia could see it on her face. Aaliyah had known then and there that she made the worst mistake of her life.

Zia's palms twitched at her side. Hiro had told her not to intervene, but she had to do something. He was going to murder Aaliyah. The man she would one day love. The guards were closing in on her.

"Call upon your oracle. The one who told you of Lemuria. If she does not see the vision I see, then you can kill us," Aaliyah said, her voice shaking.

Zia had never seen her look so vulnerable before. It broke her heart.

The king held up a hand, and his warriors stood in place. He snapped his fingers.

"Bring her to me."

Two warriors disappeared out the door. The others remained in place, weapons at the ready. The king clasped his hands behind his back, like he was deciding what to eat later in the day. Such a casual decision, really.

When Zia turned to look at Aaliyah, she saw the Elymental staring back at her with those silver eyes. Zia's heart raced, but the woman nodded so slightly it was nearly imperceptible.

It was a nod of recognition.

The past is alive. As though everything that has ever happened or ever will happen is occurring at once.

Which meant that this moment had already happened, and Aaliyah had known Zia would exist long before Sahara was even born. Zia was going to step out from the curtain, but Aaliyah held up a hand, looking away from her.

If Zia tried to help her, then it would change the past. She and Jace could die. Leo may never be born.

An enormous spider slowly crawled through the crowd. Her eyes were milky white. Aaliyah had said the spiders were oracles, but Zia had never witnessed one of them make a prediction. The guards retained a healthy distance as they led the spider to the center of the room, doing their best to conceal their disgust and fear.

"I was traveling the cosmos, my king, when one of your dogs interrupted me. What is it?" The spider asked in a raspy voice.

The king chuckled.

"Yenna, I am trying to discern whether or not to kill this woman. She claims she is still of use to me and will birth me a proper heir with magic one day. I'm disinclined to believe her. Tell me the future."

Yenna's pinchers clicked together.

"The future is a dangerous place to travel, my king. It is subject to change, and no more reliable than a dream."

The king waved a hand.

"Yes, yes. Enough with all the warnings. Just tell me what happens."

Yenna closed her eyes. Zia could see them moving beneath the lids. After a few seconds, the spider collapsed on the floor. The guards didn't dare move in to help her.

The spider leaped back gasping for air. Her wide eyes looked like two full moons.

"The original queen will once again rise, and unite with the true king, a union of the bloodlines…"

It felt as though all the air had been sucked out of the room. Even the king had the decency to look terrified. Is this what Zia needed to know? Katya would rise from the dead, somehow? If all stones were united, and Zia had the power of the gods at her disposal, perhaps she would be able to bring her back.

"Far from now, a girl will be born. She is not of our world. Katya's blood will run through her veins, but she is human."

The king's face twisted in fury, his face turning purple.

"A human?" he seethed.

Yenna ignored him.

"There will be two princes, born and bred to fight, one born of fire, the other born of night…"

"A Prince of Fire?" the king smiled triumphantly.

"The Elymental's power will transfer to your second son. He will burn brighter than the kingdom has ever seen, but if he is not trained, the fire will consume him one day, and we will all be left in an endless night."

The king glowered at the oracle.

"That's enough."

The oracle gasped for air.

"The girl is our salvation. She will right the wrongs of the past by mating with your son. She is the True Bridge—"

The king drove a blade through the spider. She crumpled on the ground, belly up with her eyes closed. He placed the sword back in its hilt and wiped his hands.

"That one will drone on forever if I don't stop her. Such boring talk."

He moved toward Aaliyah, who was pressed against the wall.

"I find myself in a predicament," the king said as he paced, enjoying the audience of his warriors. Aaliyah said nothing. She just stared at him with cold hatred.

"You see, I have known for some time about your rebel forces. As soon as you realized you weren't going to be queen, you planned to take what I treasure most: my crown."

Aaliyah's eyes widened. She opened her mouth to protest, but he held up a hand.

"I was going to kill you and the babe, but seeing as I need you to birth my second son, who will be a worthy heir with his magic, it appears I can't wash my hands of you yet."

He smiled, looking out the window.

"So, I have made a little deal with a dear friend of mine."

Right as he said that, a familiar figure floated through the doorway. Zia would never forget that face for the rest of her life. Morganna walked in, her golden hair shimmering, her horrible black wings fluttering behind her. She had an empty vial around her neck.

"Ah, Morganna. Queen of the Faeries."

Morganna flashed her teeth, her red lip curling back.

"You said you had a bargain I couldn't resist."

The king nodded toward her.

"Yes, as a matter of fact. I want you to place a spell on Aaliyah. She will give birth to my second son. After she does, I want you to forbid her from seeking either of them out. I want you to cloak her existence from them. Erase any memories my first son will have. She will not be able to so much as speak a word of who her children are to anyone. She will be banished, and live out her days alone, forced to think of her betrayals. She will be unable to so much as sleep. And I want you to blind her, so she will never see their faces. She will never know her sons. And...you will wipe everyone in the castle's memories of who their mother is. They will not remember her. Everyone, except for me."

Morganna twirled the empty glass vile between her fingertips.

"That's quite a large ask, majesty. What is your end of the bargain?"

The king's eyes slid to her.

"In return, Morganna, I will leave the faerie court untouched. You will rule over it, uninterrupted."

Morganna scoffed, "That's hardly a fair price. The rebels in your court are a growing force. Your kingdom is rotting from the inside out. You are weak, and the faeries could easily overtake you right now."

The king nodded.

"Ah, but then you would never get your hands on the stones."

Morganna pursed her lips. Her black eyes turned red with hunger.

"I'm listening."

"Do this for me, Morganna, and you will not just be Queen of the Faeries. You will be Queen of Lemuria. For when The Bridge is born, and unites with my son, we will be in control of them. We will have them find the stones, and we will take them for ourselves."

Morganna placed a hand on her hip.

"You do realize that a faerie bargain is bound by blood? If you try to break it, you will die."

The king took Morganna's hand in his own.

"The gods chose the wrong queen when they had you craft the stones for Katya."

Zia had to give him credit. His magic lay in his ability to perceive the desires of others. He played Morganna like an instrument. She took the necklace off her neck and opened the empty vile.

The king sliced his palm, dropping his blood into it, filling it to the brim. Morganna closed her eyes, uttering a spell, until a spark of magic flared through the room. She placed the cap on the vile and hung it back around her neck, then smiled at him.

"We have a deal."

Aaliyah began shaking as Morganna walked toward her. She hardly had a chance earlier, fighting the Shadow Warriors, but the ancient Faerie Queen was more powerful than all of them combined.

Morganna began chanting, waving her hand over Aaliyah's mind.

"No, *p-please!*"

Zia had seen enough. She clutched the pocket watch tightly, thinking of the library, filling her body with how it felt to be there, and flung herself back through time. She opened her eyes, coughing up dust as she found herself exactly where she started.

She was suspended by the A section of the shelves, holding Aaliyah's book in one hand and the pocket watch in another. At least her theory had worked. Zia slowed her breath, calming her heart rate. She then placed Aaliyah Atwater's records back on the shelf. It was why Leo had been so desperate to have her rummage through the king's mind. It was why the king had agreed to the wedding in the first place. The oracle had predicted it already.

Aaliyah was Jace and Leo's mother.

CHAPTER 30

A life of absolute certainty is a life that's contrived. We crave the answers, but the questions are what make us keep going. There are no failures, really. It's just life unfolding. —Hiro

Zia could barely process what she had just seen. Jace had spent his whole life wondering who his mother was, and they had just unknowingly spent months together. Aaliyah was bound by magic, unable to say anything. It must have been excruciating for her to know that he was her son, yet still bear the burden of that secret. It made sense why she had taken such interest in him and asked him about his life at every dinner. She had gotten to know her son as best she could. It was one of the reasons Zia had to wield the time stone—she had to make it out alive, if only so the truth didn't die with her. So that the secret that Aaliyah was forced to bury within herself would be freed.

Zia looked around the library and saw endless shelves of records—Lemurians, Sirens, Tree People, Faeries, but not just those who were of the realm. There were records of humans too. The life of every single creature, dating all the way back to The Beginning. Her whole life she had craved answers, but when they appeared before her, she found herself feeling uncertain.

She could look up anyone—Hiro, Jace, any ruler...it was all there. She could spend an eternity in this room, drunk on knowledge, and never return to her human life, which was filled with nothing but mystery.

As she debated what path to take, a series of memories flooded her mind in absolute clarity.

History has a way of repeating itself, Queen of Hearts. It would benefit you to remember yours before it's too late... The mage had warned her.

*She said that this was the only way you would remember...*Hiro told her when she asked why she needed to use the stone.

One day, Zia, I hope you remember... Jace had said when she left him.

The only history she needed to learn was her own.

She sailed back toward A, to find her own name, but the pocket watch burned in her palm like a brand. When she opened it, she saw the compass was pointing away from A. Zia floated through the library, following the big and little hand. All she could hear was the ticking of a clock, echoing across the walls.

Zia knew what record she would find before she landed at the shelf—a part of her had always known.

It was a thick black book with scripted gold writing.

Queen Katya of Lemuria.

Zia opened the book and stared into a pool of the queen's memories. Before diving in, she clutched the pocket watch and whispered, "Show me the truth."

CHAPTER 31

I tried to tell him that time isn't linear, and neither was our love. Every heartbeat felt like the ticking of a clock when I saw our fate. I had nothing left to hold onto but trust. —Katya

Zia opened her heavily lidded eyes and looked around. When she stared down at her own body, she was shocked to find that it wasn't hers. She was viewing the memory through the eyes of another. The eyes of Queen Katya. Despite seeing through Katya's eyes, Zia still remained conscious—like she was watching through a window.

Only, Queen Katya of Lemuria was not yet a queen. She was eight years old, racing through the forest. She was looking for a dragon. The elders had warned her not to go near them, but the dragons had always been her friends—she had been able to talk to them ever since she could remember.

The wildflowers were in full bloom. It was the height of spring, and the land was flourishing. She laughed as she wandered through the trees, gently touching them as she passed to say hello.

It had always been that way. She could talk to any living thing—climb inside of it and understand how it felt, what it needed. Whether it be the smallest ant or the largest dragon, Katya listened to all the realm's creatures.

Her ecstatic joy vanished when she heard a screeching sound in the distance.

Katya sprinted through the forest to the Redrock Mountain ridge. She panted as she ran, feeling fear for the first time. Even from miles away, she knew her friend was in trouble.

When Katya made it to the ridge of the mountain, she saw Storm, the lightning dragon. Dragons were the original Elymentals, each one belonging to a different form—wind, lightning, thunder, water, fire, ice, earth. Storm had black scales with white-tipped wings. He could summon lightning at will, and shoot it out of his mouth.

Standing in front of the dragon was a young boy. He had dark hair, green eyes and bushy eyebrows. He was holding up a spear, threatening the dragon.

"What are you doing?" she shouted.

The boy turned around, surprised to see her. They had never met before. It was rare to find Lemurians her age.

"Getting rid of this beast, what does it look like I'm doing?" he shouted back.

She could feel the fear in his heart.

Katya walked up to him and ripped the spear from his hands, tossing it over the edge. His eyes bulged out of his head.

"*Have you lost your mind?*" he yelled, backing away from Storm.

The boy braced himself as he watched Katya march straight up to the screeching dragon. She locked eyes with it, and the dragon stilled. Even though she didn't speak, he could tell that she was communicating with it.

Not a moment later, the dragon bowed.

Goosebumps grew all over the boy's skin. He watched as she stroked the dragon's forehead, whispering softly to it, "He didn't mean it, Storm. He just doesn't understand you, so he got scared."

The boy frowned, taking a step toward her. The dragon huffed, its nostrils flaring. He stepped back again. She coaxed the dragon into a calm, then turned to face the boy.

"You may apologize now," she said haughtily.

The boy gave her an exasperated look.

"You can't be *serious.*"

"Apologize. You scared him."

"*I* scared *him?* I was exploring the mountains when he just dropped from the sky!"

Katya glared at him.

"Lemuria is Storm's home."

The formidable look she gave him immediately made him resign his protests. She had a stubbornness to her that would not yield to anything, least of all him. The boy took a step forward, holding his palms up.

"I'm sorry," he said a bit flatly.

The dragon's eyes widened as it snarled. The boy's hands began shaking.

"I really am sorry. She's right. I was afraid." He cleared his throat, "Your lightning is extraordinary, by the way."

The dragon's eyes lidded, like it was pleased by the compliment. Katya grinned, turning to face him.

"I'm Katya."

The boy clasped her hand in his own.

"I'm Zhu."

"Like the Zhulu birds?" she asked.

His cheeks reddened slightly.

"Yeah. I was the first to ever ride one this time last year. Everyone in Ordos nicknamed them after me, and I guess it spread through the continent."

Katya grinned ear to ear.

"So, you're from the sand dunes. I've never met anyone from that side."

All Zhulu nests were in the sand dunes. They preferred the harsh, hot climate for birthing their younglings. Their eggs needed extreme heat to be brought to hatching.

Zhu nodded, his green eyes widening.

"I think I saw you flying the fire dragon one day during my travels from Ordos. That was you, right?"

Katya dipped her chin.

"Yes, it was me. And her name is Nagendra."

Zhu rubbed his neck, his green eyes glittering.

"Do you think you could maybe teach me how to fly? I can ride a Zhulu all day, but a dragon is a different story."

Katya squinted, eyeing him up and down.

"One day."

"When?" he asked.

She shrugged, looking at Storm.

"When they think you're ready."

Zhu watched as Katya climbed on top of Storm's head, her small body looking like a speck in comparison to the dragon's mighty size. She held onto Storm's spine, looking like a force of nature.

"I'll see you around, Zhu!" she called, grinning wickedly at him.

Storm flapped his wings and tilted his head up to the sky to release a mighty roar. Lightning shot out of his throat and hit the sky, making it look bruised in shades of purple and blue. He launched off the mountain ridge and sailed toward the horizon.

Zhu knew, even then, as he saw her hair flying freely in the wind and heard her musical laugh echo across the realm, that she was the love of his life.

The moment froze, and even while in Katya's body, Zia was aware of the sound of the clock ticking loudly again. The world around her became a blur, as she watched years' worth of seasons change before her very eyes as memories unfolded quickly before her.

She and Zhu spent the majority of their years together. Katya showed him Lemuria, since he hadn't seen much outside of Ordos. He quickly learned of her magic—that she could communicate with the land itself and all creatures who existed within it. He taught her how to hunt and defend herself, in the way only people from Ordos knew how, and she taught him how to connect with the world around him.

Zhu never returned to Ordos, choosing to settle with Katya by the Black Salt Seas. She loved to be near the sirens. They were her dear friends.

By the time they were teenagers, he planned to ask her to mate with him. He was certain that she was his match, as his parents had found before him. On her seventeenth birthday, they climbed back to the mountain ridge where they met.

They sat on the edge of the ridge, their feet dangling over the cliff.

Zhu cleared his throat, "Katya, I got you something."

She had been humming one of the Lemurian songs, absentmindedly. "Hmmm?"

He took out a necklace from his pocket—a black, glittering stone with a pyramid shape of gold around it.

"It's a memory necklace. I had the faeries make it. You can place the most important ones in here. I know you're always saying how precious every second is, so I thought I'd give you a way to revisit them." His smile was hopeful as he handed it to her.

She beamed at him so brightly it filled his heart with a bittersweet joy—like watching the most beautiful flower in the world bloom, knowing one day it would wilt. She tucked her dark hair behind her ears.

"How does it work?"

He placed her palms around the necklace, and the stone glowed as a small picture of the two of them sitting shoulder to shoulder was encapsulated in the gem. He cupped his hands around hers and squeezed warmly.

"This will be my very first memory, then," she smiled softly.

He was about to work up the courage to tell her how he felt, when she interrupted him.

"I have something for you too."

She whistled loudly, and within a few minutes, he saw the silhouette of a dragon sailing toward them. Storm was flapping his wings through the clear skies, bringing clouds with him as he flew. He landed on the ridge; his silver eyes bright.

"Go to him," she whispered.

Zhu had never been comfortable with dragons, no matter how much Katya tried to convince him they were gentle at heart. Still, though, he carefully walked toward Storm and sank to his knee.

"Hello, old friend," he said softly.

Much to his surprise, Storm bowed his head.

Seeing Zhu happy was the only birthday wish Katya had.

Zhu half-laughed in disbelief, bringing a hand to his heart.

"Are you sure?" He asked the dragon quietly.

Katya playfully whacked him on the shoulder.

"What do you mean is he sure? You're wasting time!"

And so, Zhu and Katya climbed on top of the dragon. He wrapped his arms around her waist, and Storm sailed into the sky. They flew, circling all over Lemuria as the sun set over the rolling hills. Zhu let out a howl, his joy echoing to the ends of the earth. When they finally landed, Storm dropped them at the shores where the Ghost Market would one day be.

Waiting for them there was every creature on the continent. They slowly climbed off Storm's back, Zhu offering Katya a hand. She landed on the black sand, dusting off her bare legs.

"What is this?" Katya asked.

The Queen of the Faeries, Morganna stepped forward, along with Aaliyah, the first Lemurian who could wield any element. A splashing noise sounded, and Katya turned around to see the Siren Queen's head bobbing up and down in the ocean.

It was Morganna who spoke.

"There needs to be a Queen of Lemuria. The gods have chosen you."

Katya froze, then shook her head. She didn't miss the bitterness in Morganna's voice.

"I do not want to rule over anyone."

Those exact words had come out of Zia's mouth, once.

Aaliyah stepped forward.

"Katya, it is not just the gods who have chosen you." She gestured toward the forest, where every creature from the realm was sitting, watching—from the Lemurians, to the dragons, to the Zhulus, to the fire birds, to the serpents in the sea.

"Why?" she asked.

"Because you can give voice to the voiceless. We have never seen magic like yours before. You can hear the desires of every creature in the realm—of the land itself. You can meet their needs. We believe the person with the most power should be of greatest service," the Siren Queen answered, her coral tail splashing in the calm tides.

Morganna stepped toward her clutching something in her palm. She took Katya's hand and placed it in her own. Three small stones were pressed together, stacked vertically. One a red color, one indigo, and one a glittering emerald.

"What is this?" Katya asked.

"A way to control the most uncontrollable forces in life: Love, Death, and Time." Morganna looked less than pleased to be handing her the stones.

Katya shook her head. Morganna tilted her head to the side.

"Protect them with your life, Katya. They will allow our magic to flourish until the sun has burned through its last flame."

The Tree People approached her next, holding a crown crafted of Lemurian crystals. She bent down for them to place it atop her head.

"To Queen Katya of Lemuria!" Aaliyah called.

"*To Queen Katya of Lemuria*," echoed back the crowd.

No one noticed the disappointment written all across Zhu's face. If she was a queen, then he could never be with her. He had nothing to offer her—no wealth or stature. Only his heart.

By the time she turned to face him, he had replaced his sorrow with an encouraging smile, and pledged to support her for the rest of time.

The moment froze again. The ticking of the clock sounded, and Zia watched as her surroundings became a blur yet again.

When time slowed down, Katya was a full-grown woman. She was in a snow-covered forest with Zhu.

"Katya, you don't know that he'll come here. It could have just been a dream."

Katya folded her arms across her chest.

"Zhu, I do know. It will be years from now, but I know. I used the time stone. I saw into the future. I saw his dark heart. He will destroy everything that is good about our world. I am begging you, *go*. Take Storm and travel as far away from here as you can."

Zhu held his ground as he stood inches away from her face, his expression stony.

"If you think for one second, I would ever leave you—"

"Why should we both die?" she shouted.

"Because I love you! I've been in love with you since I first saw you flying on Storm's back all those years ago!" Zhu shouted back.

Katya blinked back tears. She brought a hand to cup his cheek. "Zhu—"

"It doesn't matter. I don't need you to say anything. I just need you to know that people care about you. Lemuria needs you, Katya."

Katya's mouth wobbled, the tears falling uncontrollably.

"I love you too, Zhu. Always."

His breath shortened, his green eyes glittering with hope. Their foreheads pressed together, and he breathed in her scent. He brushed his mouth over hers softly, embracing their first kiss. It was urgent, but tender. Something he had wanted to do for far too long. It felt righter than anything she had ever known.

"Kat, even if we only have a few years together, it will be worth it. Whether I have a minute or a lifetime with you, it will be a gift from the gods."

She sniffled.

"Zhu, it just feels selfish. You should go."

Zhu's jaw locked.

"I would rather die with my people than live a coward. Do not ask me to flee again."

It was the first order anyone had ever given her as a queen, and the only one she would follow. She nodded, kissing him again, stealing every bit of happiness for herself that she could.

The clock sounded again, and Zia watched as memories flashed across her eyes. Katya's eyes.

Katya and Zhu celebrated their love in a Lemurian ceremony, their lives now sharing a tether. Time continued to unfold quickly. Katya was pregnant, her belly swelling. Then came the birth. Zhu wept tears of joy as he pulled his baby girl into the world. She saw the girl grow up, the girl who would be Zia's great-grandmother, and watched as Katya raised her in the forest.

Zhu taught the girl, whom they named Kehlani, how to hunt. He taught her how to track animals. How to fight. Katya showed her the ways of their people. She introduced her to every creature, making sure Kehlani understood all the different cultures and traditions.

And then one night, Katya had another dream—she saw a wave so tall it would wipe out Lemuria forever, and the King of Atlantis grinning as it drowned her people.

She knew time had run out.

Katya took the stones and brought them to Aaliyah, begging her to separate them so the king could never have the power of a god at his disposal. Aaliyah hid the time stone in the orb in her staff, told Katya to keep the love stone, and gave the stone of death to Kehlani, to pass down through future generations.

Queen Katya of Lemuria had seen her own time run out and knew death was coming for her. She made Aaliyah promise to look after Kehlani, passing her off as her own daughter. Katya gave her memory necklace to Kehlani to keep, so she could see the happiest moments of her mother's life were raising her.

On the eve that the king arrived, Zhu and Katya went to the mountain ridge where they first met to spend their last moments together. It was from there that they saw a fleet of hover ships coming in the distance. They had never seen technology like it.

"This isn't fair. I need more time with you," Zhu said, his voice croaking.

Katya turned to face him, her blue eyes swimming with truth.

"Our souls are bonded, Zhu. Even in death, we will find each other again."

Zhu shook his head, clasping her hands in his own.

"How do you know, Kat?"

She cupped his cheek, the way she always had.

"I've seen it, Zhu. In time. We will come back, once more, in different bodies many years from now. You will remember me. This life will come back in bits and pieces in your dreams." A tear slid down her cheek. "But I will not remember you, my love," she whispered.

He heaved a sob. She held his head up, forcing him to look at her.

"You will know me by my eyes. They will be the same. You'll see them in your dreams."

From somewhere inside Katya, a memory came to Zia. Jace had painted her eyes. He had traveled to the human world to find her again, but he didn't tell her what he remembered. He had been on the verge so many times, but he chose not to.

Jace had wanted it to be her choice to love him again—not because of their past or some prophetic future. Despite everything in him burning to be with her, he never told her who they both had been.

Katya brushed her lips softly against his.

"I love you, Zhu."

The kiss was long and deep. Zhu clasped his fingers in her hair, tasting her for the last time, breathing in her scent. Then he pulled away to face her.

"I will always find you," he promised.

And he had.

Come nightfall, Queen Katya of Lemuria stood face to face with the King of Atlantis on the edge of the Black Salt Sea shores. He offered her an alliance through marriage, to share the power of the stones together and rule over the realm. She refused, holding her chin high. Before she could take her last breath, he drove a sword through her heart. Blood bubbled in her mouth, and before death claimed her, she saw the image of Zhu bleeding from the same wound—their tethered lives both meeting an end.

The king dumped Katya's body in the sea, unaware that she had been blessed by the gods, Ra and Rhea. The earth immediately began to rumble and shake. The sea began to retreat into itself until the water couldn't be seen for miles.

"It's the Great Wave from the queen's vision!" he heard someone shout.

More shouts began to rise. He ran toward the castle to take cover.

Several Elymentals and magic wielders rushed to the shore and stood in a circle. They attempted to combine their magic and create a protective shield that would seal Lemuria in another realm. Aaliyah was leading them all, doing her best to protect the entire continent, but their magic could only stretch so far. Her ears rang, her nose bled, and she had to fight to use every last drop.

Not everyone would make it to safety in time. Anyone outside of the edges of the Ordos Desert, the Faerie Court, and the royal city would perish, as the magic couldn't reach beyond those lands. Many Atlanteans and Lemurians would die that day. Particularly the king's entire fleet.

The Great Wave came, wiping out a third of their beloved continent, as the rest was doomed to sink beneath the surface, confining them to middle earth.

Until the long-awaited Bridge returned to right their past wrongs.

CHAPTER 32

Keep going, despite there being nowhere to arrive. —Zia

Zia snapped back into her own body. She was floating aimlessly in a dark void. She clutched the pocket watch, trying to picture the library and find her way back. Instead, she felt a harsh pull yanking her forward like a rip current. She saw a small speck of light, and as the current tugged her toward it, the light became blinding and enveloped her.

Zia slammed into the ground. Only it wasn't the library she had landed in. She was on a grassy knoll, with endless stars above her. The land was empty, except for rows and rows of hourglasses. It wasn't anywhere she had seen on either Lemuria or earth.

She realized that she was in a garden of time. The hourglasses stretched on as a vineyard would. Then she heard singing in the distance and began walking through the rows to find the voice.

She saw a shimmering man who was missing a tooth, humming into the night. He didn't have a body, it was more of an outline. He looked Lemurian—tall, dark skin, and long silver hair. Zia walked over to him.

"Um, excuse me?" she asked.

The man kept humming, dusting off the old hour glasses.

"Sir?" she asked again.

He turned to face her, then threw a rag at her.

"Help me dust these off, would you?"

She gave him an exasperated look, but took the rag and started dusting off the glasses. One by one, they dusted off each time piece. After completing a row she tried again.

"Where am I?"

The man shrugged.

"In the universe, of course."

She frowned.

"Uh huh. And who are you?"

He chuckled and threw the rag on the ground.

"Ah, I thought you knew! I appear in many forms, but I believe the humans call me Father Time. This is just the form your own mind decided to meet me as. I could take another form if you'd like!"

Zia blinked, unable to tell if he was serious. Yet after everything she had just seen, there was no point in questioning it.

"Why am I here?"

Father Time shrugged, picking up the rag again.

"Well, I suspect it is because you used the stone. A delicate thing to tamper with, but you did wonderfully."

Zia grabbed Father Time's wrist, pulling it away from the glass gently.

"Can you please tell me what I'm supposed to do?" her voice cracked.

Father Time looked at her, his eyes full of sympathy.

"Walk with me," he said. She strolled next to him, focusing on the galaxy above. It was comforting to look at.

"Each one of these, Zia Alexander, is a world." He pointed to the rows of hourglasses. "From The Beginning to The End, I flip the glass and watch the sands of Time unfold. Even I don't interfere, you see. Each person is a grain of sand, making up the greater whole. They don't remember how many times they've done this dance. Forgetting is a blessing, as I'm sure you now realize. Best not to carry anything into death."

Zia looked at each hourglass, marveling at how many worlds there were.

"Why do so many worlds exist?" she asked.

"That is the ultimate question, isn't it?" Father Time winked at her.

He paused as they turned a corner.

"You have a choice, you know."

Zia eyed him.

"Do I? I mean, it seems like two worlds rest on my shoulders."

Father Time interlaced his hands.

"Even so, destiny and fate are married. One is always willing to die for the other. If you create your own destiny, you can escape your fate. Follow your fate, and your destiny will change! They are like two rivers running toward the same sea of eternity. It is your choice, what to do with your time."

Zia looked at the endless rows of hourglasses—all the lives that were happening at once. It seemed so insignificant, and yet each grain of sand was infinitely precious. She understood why people would go mad if they knew all of this. The truth was difficult to swallow.

Zia turned toward Father Time.

"I...don't think I can go on. It's too much—the stones, the king, Morganna. I can't do this alone," she whispered, feeling a lump in her throat. Ever since she had walked through the cave entrance, her life had been one exhausting whirlwind after another. Not to mention the entire other life she had just relived. Her soul had never felt more tired.

Father Time gave her a comforting smile, then looked up at the stars.

"Child, you have never been alone. Not for a single moment."

As he said that, she felt hands clasp her shoulders. Chills ran down her spine. She turned around to see her mother, Sahara. Her father. His grandparents. Great grandparents. Dating all the way back to the first humans. Their hands rested on each other's shoulders, connecting one life to the next.

Toward the end of the line, she saw her great-grandmother, Kehlani. And finally, at the very end, stood Queen Katya of Lemuria, smiling at her.

"Beneath your feet, Zia, are the shoulders of your ancestors, carrying you forward," Father Time said.

She realized the gravity of how many lives had to be lived for her to even be born. Each ancestor full of their own trials and triumphs, loves and losses. Every decision they had ever made influenced who she'd become.

She felt them like they were a part of her.

"Keep going, Zia," Katya said.

"Keep going," Kehlani nodded.

They all sounded, one by one.

Keep going. Keep going. Keep going.

The words left their lips like wisdom being tattooed on her soul. Until finally, her dad spoke.

"Keep going." Those stubborn brown eyes met hers.

Then Sahara.

"Keep going, honey," she said softly.

Zia closed her eyes, feeling their power run through her—their strength, their wisdom, every experience they had lived, now flowing through her veins. Zia took one last look at each of them, her eyes lingering on her father.

"I will," she vowed.

Zia turned to Father Time and smiled through her tears. She took a deep breath, then clutched the pocket watch in her hands.

"Take me home," she said.

The tick-tock of a clock sounded, and one by one her ancestors faded into nothing. The last thing she saw was Father Time smile at her, saluting her in farewell.

Zia was moving through the void again—a holy bandit on a ship without sails, learning to embrace the mysterious tides of a human life. She floated along until she saw another light.

As she approached it, she realized it was Ash's ship. Her body was lying there, with her friends all surrounding, her mother's hands cradling her head.

Zia slammed back into her body and woke up clutching her chest, gasping. Sahara, Hiro, Ren, and Ash were all there, ready to help. Zia felt her mother's soothing magic. She sat up and looked around.

"I'm okay," she said, smiling at them. Their faces were full of concern.

She rose to her feet, silently walking over to the edge of the bow. She was vaguely aware that they were talking to her but couldn't register their words. She leaned over the edge, resting on her elbows.

As she looked out at the glassy waters, at the setting sun and the clouded horizon, she saw the shadow of wings emerge in the distance. It was the silhouette of a dragon. Inka.

The ghost of a smile played on her lips, until she truly realized what she was looking at. Zia gripped her hands on the railing, squinting.

Another dragon broke through the rosy cloud cover. Then another. Until an entire fleet was soaring toward their ship, roaring in the sky.

The dragons will rise again with the true queen.

She tipped her head to the sky and roared back as the dragons sailed over the ship, circling above them.

Footsteps sounded behind her. Hiro. He had his usual toothy grin spread across his face.

They stood next to each other, shoulder to shoulder, watching the mighty beasts above.

"What now, Z?"

Zia Alexander, long lost Queen of Lemuria, smiled with a hope in her heart that she hadn't felt for lifetimes.

"We keep going."

END.

The Trials: The levels a player must pass in the virtual reality world, *Legends of Lemuria*. Players level up through sparring and acquiring artifacts. The ultimate prize is a map that leads to three priceless stones.

The Electi: The wealthier class within the country. They live in gated, sectioned off neighborhoods guarded by the military.

Somnium: The most popular cryptocurrency coin exchanged within The Trials. The value shoots up and down in vast extremes, creating a clashing of classes.

Elymentals: Magic-wielders capable of manipulating the earth's elements. Most of them only have enough of the gift in their blood to wield one—fire, water, earth or air.

Folders: Lemurians who can teleport. Usually short distances, but a full-powered one could hop between worlds.

Healers: They are capable of healing wounds on a cellular level, manipulating genes even. Yet, with the weakening of magic, most are only able to cure surface illnesses and shallow wounds.

Shifters: Shifters are always faeries. Most of them can only change mundane things—hair or eye color. There is only one bloodline left capable of taking any form they can dream.

Psukhē: Psukhēs can link with another's psyche and feel their emotions, even explore the locked doors of their subconscious. Yet, if not careful, they become trapped within another's minds forever, their bodies nothing but a shell. A full powered Psukhē would be able to completely absorb the magic of another temporarily, but there is a cost: using that much magic takes years from their lives.

Assassins and Shadow Warriors: Though technically not magic-wielders, the god of Death whispers in their ear and they have a talent for killing.

Oracles: Only the spiders were gifted with oracular sight, with one exception. The past, present, and future all blur together for them.

Ghouls: A ghoul is a soul that was stuck in the realm after death, unable to peacefully pass on. They are only found in bone yards and the Ghost Market.

Mages: Lemurians gifted with the ability to manipulate magic through spell work and ritual. It is said that mages are able to speak the language of fate through tarot. Considered dark magic.

Faeries: Gifted with long life and great beauty. Each faerie possesses magic in their own way—mainly the ability to wield blood bargains. A deal with a faerie is said to be more dangerous than death.

Sirens: Half demon, half fish. Most sirens have the ability to affect the tides in some small way, though they are unparalleled to the magic of their queen. They devour the souls of those who cross them.

Lemurians: Tall humanoids gifted with eternal life. Not all are blessed with magic, but those who are have substantial powers. They are protectors of the realm, entrusted with keeping peace and balance in the land. Ever since stones were separated, their power has weakened.

Atlanteans: Their only magic is immortality, but they are gifted with great knowledge of the sciences. Their technology is unparalleled. Ever since the Great Wave, most have died, and now Atlanteans and Lemurians alike all live together in the royal city of Mu.

Fire Birds: Enormous red-feathered birds with flame tipped tales. Their sole purpose is to guard—entrances to forbidden places, treasures, royalty, contraband, etc.

Hantu: A phantom panther that can turn invisible. Strictly found in mountains. They have ruby-colored eyes and a venomous bite. They prefer cold climates, namely snow. By the time you see one, you're marked for death.

River serpents: capable of pulling up to 100 tons. Small, emerald water snakes mainly used by smugglers. They can cut a voyage's time in half. Very rare. Very expensive.

Zhulu: Great, regal white birds the size of a large horse. They have the head of a lion. Sharp talons that can cut deeper than any blade. Only reserved for royalty and the wealthiest of nobility.

Dragons: The first Elymentals. There are five dragons that control the elements: lightning, wind, water/ice, fire, and earth.

Sprites: Deadly, small faeries guarding the faerie court border. They speak their own language and carry venomous small arrows. Often mistaken for bees or butterflies, sprites draw people in with their unassuming nature.

Antiqua: Butterfly fish. Revered as sacred in Lemuria. It is said a soul's final life returns as a butterfly fish, and they take their final swim through the great river.

Helius flower: When boiled and drank, it is a bridge to the underworld, but can often cause those who drink it to go mad.

Corellia flower: When boiled and drank, it is a bridge to the heavens, the gods' world. These flowers allow for communication with the gods, but they were mostly destroyed by the king and haven't been seen in thousands of years.

Blue lotus: Causes a high, dream-like state that expands one's consciousness and enhances magical ability. Mostly smoked by faeries.

Willow bark: Acts as a pain relief, used by healers.

Vasalisa: The river goddess, whose lover was killed in battle. She wept for 700 years and her tears became the rapids that run through Lemuria.

Rhea and Ra: The goddess and god of creation. They danced for several days and worlds unraveled beneath their feet.

The god of Death: Watches over the Ordos assassins.

ACKNOWLEDGMENTS

Though this book has my name as the author, countless caring hands left their fingerprint on the story. So many times, I thought the book wouldn't come out, and through the support of loved ones, I kept going.

Dad, this book is for you. Thank you for introducing me to fairytales. I can only imagine what it was like for you to be at work all day, having to come up with a new story every night. Who knew the adventures of the crystal caves would lead to this?

Mom, thank you for always being my first reader and listening to me for countless hours as I puzzled this world together. I hope to have half as much courage and wisdom as you one day.

Jordyn Denning, I cannot express the amount of gratitude I feel for your guidance with this book. One of the best seasons of my life was sitting at random coffee shops and spending eight hours with you, pouring over these chapters. Thank you for being my best friend, for your honest edits, and for challenging me to make this a better story. You believed in the book before I found the courage to and helped it go from a blob of clay to a sculpture.

Dakota Adan, thank you for being my Hiro and for your words of encouragement as I struggled to get this story published. I hope you understand how much your friendship has impacted me now. No matter what life throws our way, we always find a way as a family. Together.

Alexis Ren, I hope this book gives you a little glimpse into how much you mean to me and the world and how huge and fierce your heart is. You are my whole heart. If you ever need a reminder, you can borrow my eyes through this book now.

Ricki Bodner, thank you for being the alien who lost a bet and had to come to Earth to deal with all of us. I don't know where I'd be without all the random businesses you build for us, your loyalty, and your sense of humor.

Dariusz Wegrzynowsky, where would I be without those home-cooked meals and giant bear hugs? Thank you for breeding the real-life Inka and for all your support.

Sammy Shawi, without you, Jace and Zia's story would have been more of a trope than a relationship—thank you for showing me that to love someone is to be their best friend, for building me a real desk, and for Seven. This book wouldn't be half as good without him curling up at my feet and lending me his magic.

Kayra Satya, you are Mother Earth in a person. So much of the inspiration for the realm of Lemuria came from our time in Hawaii together. Thank you for your unwavering kindness.

Nadia Damaso, I appreciate your advice for the meals in this book. Zia's passion for cooking was largely sparked by watching you create art in the kitchen.

Brittany Louks, thank you for being my oldest friend and showing me what it looks like when a woman decides she can will her dreams into existence.

Chelsea Kauai, thank you for braving the unpolished draft of this book. I don't know many people who would have suffered through reading a 500-page PDF on an airplane. This story was published mainly due to your generosity and support.

Alex Carson, I pictured your daughter reading this as I wrote it. Thank you for letting me be the auntie to such a special child and for your uplifting voice notes. I hope you and Leila enjoy this.

Alex and Mimi Ikkon, thank you for helping me find the right home for this story. You two are impacting the world in such a positive way.

My We Are Warriors girls, I love you all so dearly. Our community is like a comforting fire endlessly burning every Friday, keeping us all warm through any storm that comes.

Noelle Beams, Kristina Parish, and the Thought Catalog team thank you for believing in this book. From the cover art to the illustration to your edits—you made this book the best version of itself. I appreciate you saying yes to a poet who dreamed of dragons.

And finally, to you, my reader. May you always keep going despite there being nowhere to arrive.

ALLIE MICHELLE is a 3x bestselling author and viral spoken word artist who believes the best place to hide the truth is in fiction, and our stories are the fingerprint we leave on the world. She has performed as a poet all across the globe, and is the co-founder of the women's wellness community We Are Warriors, where she has supported thousands of women in telling their stories. She can usually be found with a bowl of coffee and her nose in a book.

INSTAGRAM.COM/ALLIEMICHELLEL
TIKTOK.COM/@ALLIEMICHELLEAUTHOR

The Guilty Twin
Holly Riordan

Hot Tea and Mercy
Rae Lashea

The Poet's Girl, A Novel of
Emily Hale & T.S. Eliot
Sara Fitzgerald

Through The Veils of Mystery:
Into The Depths, An Exploration
Of Invisible Inner Realms
Kristina Bazan

Available Now at ShopCatalog.com

THOUGHT
CATALOG
Books
THOUGHTCATALOG.COM